I0612043

Glass House Books

Flight

Anne Vines' first novel, *The Ship Wife*, was published in 2023 by Glass House Books. A feminist historical account, *The Ship Wife* is based on a true story and a real woman from Australia's colonial past.

Anne's short fiction is published in *Word U Up* (2014), *Award Winning Australian Writing 2015*, *Wasafiri Online Magazine* (2016), *Ring of Words* (2018) and *Boroondara Literary Awards Anthology 2020*.

Anne won the Boroondara Prize in 2014 and the Keith Carroll Award in 2020 for short stories. She was shortlisted for the Alan Marshall Short Story Award, *The Age* Short Story Award and the international *Wasafiri* New Writing Prize. She was commended in the Varuna Harper-Collins Award in 2007 and in the Victorian Premier's Literary Award for an Unpublished Manuscript, 2008.

Anne has worked on her novels with writers Toni Jordan, Lee Kofman, Sydney Smith and Janey Runci, and with Peter Bishop and Helen Barnes Bulley at Varuna Writers' Centre.

Anne completed a Bachelor of Arts at the University of Melbourne, concentrating on Literature and History. She taught at secondary schools in Ballarat, Melbourne and London and at the Council for Adult Education, Melbourne. She co-wrote the VCE English and English Literature courses and was a State assessor in those subjects.

Anne has lived in England and Germany, and travelled extensively in Ireland, Spain, Italy and France. In the UK, Ireland, Europe, USA, South America and Asia, she carried out research in libraries, archives and communities for her novels.

Anne's second novel, *Flight*, takes a new look at World War II in Australia. It focuses on Melbourne society in 1942.

Glass House Books
Brisbane

Flight

Anne Vines

Flight

Glass House Books
an imprint of IP (Interactive Publications Pty Ltd)
Treetop Studio • 9 Kuhler Court
Carindale, Queensland, Australia 4152
sales@ipoz.biz
http://ipoz.biz/shop
First published by IP in 2025
© 2025 Anne Vines (text); IP (design)

This book was written on the traditional land of the Wurundjeri people of the Kulin nation. The author acknowledges and pays her respects to their elders, past and present.

Printed in 14 pt Avenir Book on Caslon Pro 12 pt.

ISBN: 9781923435049 (PB) 9781923435056 (eBook)

 A catalogue record for this book is available from the National Library of Australia

Contents

1. At the Windsor

Peter:

Melbourne, Australia, February 1942

In the mid-afternoon, downtown Melbourne was so sleepy and quiet, I could have driven a herd of horses down its straight, wide streets.

Places out of reach of the war made me mad. Folks strolled about as if blitzes and bombed-out streets were things of the past. They didn't know how lucky they were. Aussies had joined up fast in great numbers, but the slow pace here at home, and the comfort downtown got my goat. I couldn't help it. Weren't these folks scared that Japanese planes might zoom down one day soon? Or were they just good at hiding their fear?

My shirt stuck to my back as I walked up the Collins Street hill. A hot wind blew along the sidewalk, dry heat like Texas. I loved Melbourne's blue cloudless skies, strong sun and clear, piercing light.

People stared at my uniform and wings, maybe the first American ones they had seen. A kid selling newspapers on the street stood ramrod straight and saluted me. Older folks looked past me in that British way I knew from my time in England. It was fun exploring a new city again; I liked hunting solo. I walked fast to race the clanking streetcar as it came up alongside.

Two tall churches overshadowed the sidewalk and shut out the sun. Their mumbo-jumbo signs about scripture and sin gave me the shivers. I walked on, back into the sun. The heat dried out my nose and mouth and drenched my armpits. At the top of the hill, the land flattened out, and big trees shaded the sidewalk. Brass plates beside doorways announced rich men's clubs and expensive medical rooms. At the wide junction with Spring Street, there were tall buildings every way you looked, and vast green parks beyond.

Along Spring Street stood the Windsor Hotel, a square, stone joint, not tall like New York hotels. Australian officers at my billet said it had the best English afternoon tea – just what I needed after a hot walk. The old-time dress of the doormen and porters aped the big London hotels, but inside there was nothing of London's exclusive dazzle, either in décor or customers. The downstairs lounge was full of women dressed like English ladies, yet the mood was noisier and more relaxed than London. Was it because so few men were there, or because these dames mostly knew each other?

Once through the glass-panelled doors, I made my way between the tables. I'm not the type to blush, but the women's stares burnt my skin. These dames had probably forgotten the English newsreels in '40 when my Spitfire and I scored close-ups, but maybe they had seen my photo in their newspapers the day I arrived. Now they all had a damned good look.

I was used to the hunger in women's eyes and the invitation of their leaning bodies. With most young men away, heaps of girls didn't hide their loneliness or their yearning for someone new.

I settled down near the entrance in an alcove by a tall window, with plenty of light to read the newspapers. I liked a spot where I could see everyone and get out fast.

The huge room with its high ceilings and silent fans cooled me down. When I scanned the papers I'd grabbed at the entrance, I wished I'd looked harder for *The Times*. These local papers had less detail about my RAF pals.

The last thing I had expected was to end up in a different theatre of war from them, across the world. But after Pearl

Harbor, I couldn't stay in the RAF. I had to fight alongside my countrymen. I went straight into the American air force, even though the great US of A hadn't done much for me.

The news wasn't cheering. Hitler had been overstretching his forces, and now that the Americans were gearing up, his back was up against the wall. It still stunned me that the Japs were such a powerhouse from a base of puny islands, but I knew better than most guys that what counts in the end is not the size of an outfit, but its toughness.

In between reading reports of bomb damage and mass death, I spotted a tall redhead giving me looks from under her lashes. Her blonde friend was giving me the come-on, too, with warm smiles. I loved the flirting game; it made you feel like you mattered. You were either a natural at it or not, though you improved if you practised. And like flying or fighting, the risk was half the fun.

A waitress in an English-style black dress and white apron hovered at my side. Probably twice my age, she blushed and batted her eyelashes while I told her it was coffee I wanted, not tea, and I preferred it strong. She walked off, still smiling. Older women usually liked me, and I liked them, even if they mixed motherly softness with a flirty come-on. To be honest, I couldn't always tell which it was, and I sort of understood it could be a bit of both.

There was a sudden murmuring in the room, and a turning of heads towards the entrance. Two fine-looking girls were arriving.

The second one was a knock-out. She made a beeline for the big windows and looked rather put out, as my English pals would say, to find me hogging the brightest one. Her mouth was even sweeter when she was startled. She had those liquid dark eyes that glow and burn. I had noticed that most Australian girls looked healthier than the pasty skinned ones in England.

She was slim but not skinny, with the sheen and colour of a sun-filled life. Her long glossy curls were a bright brown that women's magazines would have a special name for. Most good-looking girls know they're pretty, but she had no preening airs. No false cold manners either; she didn't bother to hide how much the sight of me stirred her up. What struck me most was how happy she looked. I had to date this girl.

I glanced at her left hand. Sure enough, a sparkler big enough to buy a house. Just my luck! A ring might slow things down.

I stood and smiled. I wanted to offer her the alcove, but there was something so classy about the way she held her head, that I was scared she'd cold-shoulder me. If I took it slow, maybe I'd make her melt.

It was enough to begin with when she smiled back. It was a smile to spark a lifetime of daydreams. But then she looked away like a duchess. Well-bred, probably trained by a dragon of a mother. She sat down. Her companion smiled too – she recognised me, but my gal hadn't a clue who I was.

She met my eyes again as I sat back down. I stared fixedly at her, possibly the wrong move, but I couldn't miss a moment. I sent my warmest smile and watched her thaw – and fight it. Oh, honey, let's just get to know each other, cut out this ping-pong game of glances. We kept playing it. The fresher I got, the more she flushed.

All at once, she stood up and marched to the magazine shelf. For a second, I considered joining her. But maybe she'd feel cornered. She chose *Punch*, not *Country Life*, thank the Lord. Walking back, she shot me another glance. Maybe she wasn't as shy as I'd thought. I smiled back full force.

She sat like a statue, the magazine forgotten on her lap. It slid off. I lunged to the floor and held it up to her. I could have kissed her I was so close. Her eyes burned into me. Why not, I wanted to say, though I knew damned well why not. It made me blue, gazing at her, with my bad luck and all her class. Once she'd learned the first thing about me, she'd know I was the last guy for her.

"Thank you." Her voice was gorgeous, like her – silky, golden and soft.

"My pleasure, ma'am. I'm Peter."

I wanted her to repeat my name, or just say hello in her satin voice, but she kept gazing silently as if I was the one person she wanted to see. I waited a long time and gave her a look of half reproach before I uncoiled myself and stepped back, still breathing in the zing of her perfume, lost in imagining how her skin would feel. She looked like the kid left out of the game, though I bet she never had been.

The waitress brought my coffee and fussed about before giving the girls their tea.

"Miss Beauregard," she called each of them in turn.

So they were regulars. Sisters. Probably classier than I'd feared. I overheard their names: Faye and Edith. Faye was my girl.

Usually, I wanted to throw a girl over my shoulder, not sink to my knees and worship her. She was too much of a lady for me to gauge how out of control she felt, but she hardly responded to her sister's soft-spoken remarks, so maybe she was as far gone as I was. I tried to concentrate on what the hell to say.

Blow me down if a guy didn't suddenly break in on the game and speak to me. In French. I forced myself out of my trance to face him. The Chef, Henri something or other. I shook his hand and told him to speak slower. He was thanking me for what I had done against the Nazis, for Britain and for France.

"De rien, Monsieur," I said. "C'est mon plaisir et c'est mon honneur. Vive La France."

My French was not much better than a Creole kid's in New Orleans, but you couldn't miss what he was saying if you knew a few words of the lingo.

I stole another look at Faye. She was flushed, eyes shining, eavesdropping. I grinned at the chef, said I loved his coffee and nodded madly when he told me he had given me a precious brew of the real stuff. There was a buzz of chatter as he left.

She smiled at me, like she'd made up her mind. The room was golden with sun, and fragrant with her deep French perfume. My spine heated up. She was waiting for me.

Ordinary pick-up lines wouldn't do for her. I had my opener almost figured out, but, for once, I was too slow. She looked away, across the room. Her face froze: everyone was staring at her, frowning, smirking, sneering – with not a speck of sympathy for her or me. She went near as white as the little gloves she pulled on fast. She glanced at me for a second, her face tense and sad. She said something to her sister that I couldn't catch, then switched on her poise like donning a mask. With her sister in tow, she swept out in full duchess mode. I turned to the window and stared out at strangers. Story of my life.

2. Looking for Her

Peter:

Melbourne, February–March 1942

I walked up to the Windsor every afternoon that week, but she didn't show. I drank a lot of Henri's coffee while umpteen society dames gave me the eye.

That Saturday night, I found someone better than them at the Tivoli, a burlesque and variety theatre in Bourke Street. Lots of the girls onstage were pretty, but I chose Iris Kelly from her first dance number, when she high kicked in the front row. She was a stunner: red-gold hair, fine long legs, lively face. It had been a while since I had turned up at a stage door, but I grabbed some roses and talked my way in. From the moment I held out the flowers, she was crazy for me.

We made a date for her first night off and went dancing at the Flinders Street Station Ballroom where a good orchestra was playing. It gave me a kick to feel her energy and the way she could move. I loved dancing with showgirls. She told me heaps about herself and seemed okay with me not telling her much. She was good-hearted, a great talker, and fun. Yet I kept thinking about Faye. Looking into Iris's blue eyes, I was remembering those dark ones.

A week later, I couldn't face it sober, so we went to the Trocadero, a dance place on Princes Bridge where you could get drinks if you paid through the nose. Melbourne stopped selling liquor at six o'clock, of all times, but, like anywhere, the rules could be bent. That night, we took a room at the Federal, a hotel up the other end of town. Iris was keen, but I made sure she really wanted to spend the night. I can't stand guys who put the hard word on dames. She told me she'd been with a few guys, but nothing longstanding. I treated her nice, and we had a good time even if I did lie awake afterwards thinking about that gal at the Windsor. I'd never lost sleep over a girl before. It felt dumb, holding Iris and seeing someone else in my head. Why was I making myself blue about Faye Beauregard, when I didn't even know her and when Iris was beautiful and crazy about me?

Beauregard didn't sound like an ordinary name. At my billet, a mansion as grand as those in the South, I decided to get some answers. There were few American officers there yet, and I had gotten friendly with some of the Aussie airmen. Like lots of their countrymen, they would talk to you about nearly anything straight away. When I mentioned her name, they told me that the Beauregards were well-known. There was Major General Maurice Beauregard, who was now back from Europe and at Army headquarters in Melbourne, and Sir Henry Beauregard, a judge who had two daughters, Edith and Faye. A couple of pilots who seemed to come from richer backgrounds had met them at university – another strike against me, though she might take for granted that I had been to college, because almost all pilots had.

The girls' dad was nothing short of the Chief Justice, which in Melbourne meant the Governor's deputy. What a joke. I had spent half my life keeping out of the way of guys heaps less powerful.

The day after my second night with Iris, the Allied Supreme Commander, General Maddox roared into town on a special train, and most of Melbourne turned up to cheer. I was ushered right up front to meet him. He stuck me next to him for some photos and most of the newsreel. Maddox was mad for publicity. So there I was on the screen at the movies before the feature. Iris was thrilled.

When I heard about the reception for Maddox at Government House a couple of days later, I guessed I might get a bit of special attention there, what with my RAF connection. Faye's father would likely turn up, as well as her uncle, the General, so I hoped she might, too. Melbourne seemed so British that I figured there would be well-dressed ladies scattered on the lawns to keep types like me sober and behaving themselves.

From my billet in Canterbury, we drove to the reception and soon were winding along the Yarra River, a brown, slow-moving waterway that snaked downtown from the outer suburbs and the hills beyond. The roads were ludicrously empty.

Government House was a white mansion overlooking a lake in the middle of vast gardens, lawns and woods. It was slap bang next to the Botanic Gardens, where I had wandered a few times, appreciating the shade. I hadn't realised there was as much park next door for the Governor.

I scanned everyone in a skirt, but she wasn't there. I stopped downing champagne and chatted to my air force Colonel. He said that they needed my experience, and other stuff that I could only nod at. I drummed up a few questions, but I was still on the look-out for Faye.

A group of folks appeared out of the house. A couple of old guys, two older women, but not her. I summoned a waiter and got a glass of water. If I was going to meet her, or her mother, I didn't want to look red in the face.

Then Maddox waved us over. He threw me impossible questions about air strategy. He probably knew I hadn't seen the terrain, let alone worked with any personnel there yet. Neither had my new Air boss. I guessed the Aussies could have filled us in on a lot of things, but the American generals assumed the upper hand from the start.

After Maddox finished with me, I was presented to the Governor and a few minutes later to the Chief Justice, Sir Henry Beauregard. He was damned impressive, I had to admit, with a lively manner like Faye's, quick talking and moving. His mouth was sterner, of course, and his posture more pompous, though his English reserve was almost humble compared with Maddox's swagger. Sir Henry's wife was pretty, but not in Faye's vivid way. She was fair, with fine features and an irresistible, soft voice. Her manner was warm. She might have been more of a flirt in her day than her daughters were. I gave her my best smile. I didn't have a hope in hell with Faye, save for a lucky fluke, but I had learnt in England how important it was to get in good with the mother.

Sir Henry introduced me to his brother the Major General – his rank was like our One Star Generals. He had a rougher appearance than Sir Henry, probably from years in the army and heaps of hard drinking to dull the stench of death.

"I'll never forget the news of you Fighter boys in '40," he said, with a quick grin. "Marvellous flying and shooting. No British or Allied fighting man will ever forget it."

I doubted that, but I appreciated him saying so. It was enough that a few guys like him would remember. He seemed one of those regular officers, decent, iron hard, with the melancholic, restless eyes of a leader who had to carry mass casualties.

Once the big shots let me go, I found myself drinking with Chris, a pilot from my billet. He didn't stare down his nose at me the way some of the officers did. Damned cheek, given my kills, but fancy talk and college education were all that counted with them. When they talked of New York, they didn't mention the parts I knew best.

Later, Chris and I walked down St Kilda Road, a tree-lined boulevard as wide as any in Paris.

He said, "Guess you heard that Maddox is gonna run for President after the war. He wants success fast. Let's hope he's got pull in Washington and can get us the planes we need."

Before Maddox was to meet Prime Minister Curtin in Canberra, the Governor would be hosting a ball in his honour. That was okay by me. Faye would be there for sure.

3. The Match

Faye:

Melbourne, June 1940

When Clive Wilson proposed, I nearly laughed. Not just at the idea, though it was ridiculous, but because he didn't actually *ask* me.

"You and I should get married, Faye."

His flat tone irritated me from the first syllable.

"Oh, Clive," I said, "what a surprise."

I had come over to play tennis – that was all.

We were at his parents' place in Toorak. His proposal popped out as we took a break in his mother's conservatory. Behind the glass, we sat in bright sunlight, protected from the winter wind, but the moist air felt fetid and too hot. Face to face with dripping ferns and breathing in smelly plant fertiliser, I struggled to hold back laughter. I hadn't given him the least encouragement. I had made sure that he hadn't even kissed me.

"I don't see why it's a surprise, Faye." He didn't even look at me!

His grey eyes darkened as he stared ahead across the wide lawn. The males in his family rarely showed emotion. Had I upset him? How much? His chin was jutting out, as usual. I had an urge to grab his head and push that chin back a bit. Both he and his father looked like farmers in newspaper cartoons.

I took a deep breath. "Clive, I don't believe I've given you the slightest sign that I think of you as anything but a friend."

I meant to speak gently yet firmly, but it came out sounding like my father: formal, precise and cold.

He grunted and ran a hand through his dark, straight hair. Thin strands of it fell on his damp forehead and stuck there. He seemed unaware of how unattractive that looked. He made no attempt to push the stray hairs back.

"We've been spending a lot of time together. And you know I've always liked you."

"Well, yes, but *marriage*, Clive? For heaven's sake."

My skin felt clammy. He had never asked me out before the war, only after most of the other boys had gone overseas to fight. So, naturally, I had presumed that his interest in me was not serious. Of course, I hadn't hinted that I only accepted his invitations because the other boys were gone. How could he have presumed that I was keen on him, was pursuing him, was waiting for him to make a move?

What a mess. Yet it was rather fun, too – a boy loved me. What would he do or say to show me how much?

He kept staring straight ahead at the rose garden. How astonishing his lack of enthusiasm was! And how irritating. But, as the silence went on, I felt a bit unnerved. He wasn't confident or articulate. He did nothing with finesse. He would never forgive humiliation. His face dripped with perspiration, perhaps not only because of the humidity. How could I help feeling sorry for him? For a boy so reticent, a proposal must be terrifying. But had he rehearsed? Alas, not enough.

Finally, he said, "It's perfectly natural that you and I should end up together." He sounded matter-of-fact, as if he were recommending a place for lunch. "We've known each other all our lives. The Wilsons and the Beauregards have always been friends."

Not our fathers, I felt like retorting. It was difficult to imagine them ever being mates, even at Grammar. Later, they lived in different worlds; my father shone at Cambridge and at the Bar back in Melbourne, while Clive's father stayed on his cattle stations. Admittedly, Clive's mother and mine got on well, though mostly because mine made such an effort.

I took a quick look sideways at Clive's stolid face as we sat next to each other on the low, wooden bench. How could he say, "end up," as if our haphazard meetings added up to a romance, as if I'd had any sort of decent social life this year since the war whisked off all the boys? He was the only one of the old crowd still in Melbourne for my twenty-first last month. Of course, I had danced with him a bit. Whatever had he, and our mothers, imagined on the strength of a few dances?

He sat calmly, as if I hadn't poured cold water over him, as if I had said "yes." I might have known that nothing I said would topple his certainty. His whole family had an unshakeable faith in their views, an unquestioned confidence that their wishes were bound to hold sway. Had he ever had a moment's doubt?

"Just because we've known each other for ages doesn't mean it would work," I said quietly. We hardly knew each other, really. I wished I dared say just that. I tried to catch his eye, unsuccessfully. "There's a lot more to marriage than to friendship."

"Of course. But we'd make a go of it. I've always thought you were the best girl around, Faye."

I waited. Here was his moment to enthuse. It wasn't much of a surprise when he didn't. Like his father, he was a man of few words, the sort who only spoke about himself or his land or sport. He frowned, seemed to be waiting. I almost laughed again – he was expecting me to declare my feelings! He presumed they were positive. But then, I had assumed that tennis meant just tennis and hadn't bothered to check if anyone else was playing with us today. I kept my mouth shut and stared straight ahead at an odd-looking tropical flower.

He grinned and grabbed my hand. "I said I'd marry you when we were ten, remember?"

I wanted to pull my hand away, but that would have been too rude. I stopped feeling sorry for him. For years, I had been dying to fall in love, to have a man fall in love with me, and this was what I had won? A *fait accompli* proposal from childish, unromantic Clive. My blouse was starting to stick to me – I needed some water, or a cup of tea. "Oh, Clive, that was just when we were children."

"Well." His chin jutted out further in triumph. "I meant it. And I still do."

He gave me a calculating, snaky sort of look. It would have given me the shivers if I hadn't been so hot and if I hadn't always known that he was pretty harmless. What on earth did he really feel?

I hadn't thought of it for years, how he had brayed at a children's party at my grandmother's country property to a garden full of kids, "I'm going to marry you, Faye Beauregard," and everyone laughed like mad. It should have felt romantic now, his attraction to me for so long. But I couldn't detect the slightest scent of romance; he didn't show a speck of excitement or affection as he sat there, so solid and jowly. His hand was heavy and still around mine. My head started pounding. The stuffiness in the conservatory was making me feel sick.

I looked across at the terrace, where his mother was surely about to offer afternoon tea. Mrs Wilson was sitting inside at the table, staring at us. Did she know? How *could* he have told her first? The insult put steel back into my backbone.

"I need a drink of water, Clive. And some fresh air. Thanks for the compliment, but I'm afraid I can't think about anything serious right now."

I stood up.

Slowly, he unbent his large frame. With a quickly covered scowl of anger, he said, "Time for another set," in a commanding tone he'd never used to me before, then strode to the court.

I grabbed a palm-full of water from the garden tap and

followed. Glancing back at the terrace, I saw his mother stand and then disappear.

Clive served a faster ball than usual. My arm felt shaky as I returned it. Then he sent a speedier ball. Straight at my head. I ducked.

"Sorry," he called, sounding pleased.

I waved nonchalantly.

When he came to change ends, I said quickly, "The sun's getting low, isn't it? I'd better be going, Clive." I surprised myself, sounding suddenly and disappointingly like my mother, over-polite, self-deprecating and deferential. "Say goodbye to your mother for me."

He must have been dreading the moment when his mother saw how unexcited I was by his offer.

"Jackson can run you home," he said, sounding relieved.

At least he had the sense not to suggest driving me himself.

"No, thanks. I'll walk. I told Peg I'd drop in this afternoon."

A convenient lie, but what a relief it would be to tell Peggy. Of all my friends, she would see the funny side of the afternoon.

But, as soon as I began, I saw my mistake. Peg's face lit up with elation – and a hint of envy.

"Oh, Faye, he's the best catch! I knew he'd ask you. He's proposed before he goes overseas. How marvellous, you lucky thing!"

I felt half like shaking her and half like hearing her present the case for Clive. What could she argue, except that he was rich? Though Peg had to be careful about money, she wasn't blinded by wealth, surely? Clive barely acknowledged Peg, and the two never talked together, but even so, she had to see how different he and I were. She couldn't possibly think our similar backgrounds made it fine, however unromantic she always insisted she was. I began to feel downcast, as well as annoyed. An unwanted proposal was more unwelcome when it wasn't your first. This was my third, and the most depressing. No-one had blamed me for refusing the others.

"Why on earth do you think I said yes?"

That shut Peggy up. Wide-eyed, she stared for a long moment. "Even you couldn't refuse Clive *Wilson,* Faye. Your mother would want you to accept him."

I felt a flash of dread and resentment. Mummy would indeed. I gripped my cup of tea and looked defiantly at Peg. "Well, I haven't actually given an answer."

"Why not?" Peggy blurted out. "Faye, I know you think love should be like in the great novels, but *really.*"

I laughed. "Literature doesn't lie. In any case, I must feel love for the man I marry."

"It depends on what you mean by love, doesn't it?" Peg grinned. "I'm looking for good character, considerate manners and shared interests. No agony or adoration for me, thank you very much. Not that I'm in any danger of that sort of thing. Men don't look at me the way they do at you. Just as well. I have no intention of losing my head over some stupid fellow, or of pining for him and getting all upset."

Usually, I didn't mind Peg's barbs. She consumed the great romantic novels and films as mere entertainments or jigsaw puzzles or, occasionally, works of art, whereas to me, they were old friends, cherished memories, and crucial guides to my life.

Peg leaned forward. "Faye, Clive can give you everything, even more luxury than you've grown up with." She broke off at my critical glare. "You get along well together. You'll come to feel fonder of him when you're married." She slumped back and looked a little impatient. "Faye, you know I think your ideas about love are daft."

"When one of us falls in love, we'll see who is right!"

We laughed. We could always disagree quite happily. It was why we got on so well, in addition to our love of literature – and

Gary Cooper.

Peggy smiled. "Anyway, it's good that you haven't said no outright."

I shrugged. "I was too stunned."

"Just as well, Faye." Peggy gave up and reached for a fruit scone.

I was hungry, but Peg's mother cooked the sort of food I couldn't bear – *English Woman's Weekly* stodge, worlds away from the sponge cakes and silky éclairs Mrs Wilson's cook turned out, war or no war.

When I arrived home, my mother was waiting with an unusually impatient air. *She* knew too. I pictured her and Mrs Wilson with their heads close together over morning tea, their eyes gleaming in anticipation. For a second, I seethed. Then I had fun watching Mummy beat around the bush.

Her smile was excited. "How is Clive, dear?"

"Fighting fit as ever, Mummy."

My mother gave a laugh usually kept for acquaintances. "Oh, yes, he's certainly a fit young man. Is he talking of when he will be joining up? Will he be going overseas?"

"He didn't mention it." As I sprawled on the sofa, Mummy didn't even frown.

"Oh, I thought he'd be making plans for his future now that his poor granny is after passing away."

I shrugged and hid a smile: Mummy's English was turning Irish, which only happened when she was distracted or upset.

Her eyes darted about. "And does he think he might be buying a place of his own, at all?"

I couldn't keep a straight face. At my first words, my mother hugged me in delight, but at the full disclosure, she crumpled in disappointment.

"Oh. So, you haven't given him an answer?" She gripped my shoulders. "That's all right, my dear. You're a sensible girl. A lady should take her time to consider a proposal."

I had to smile. Sometimes, Mummy could be quainter than the nuns at my old school.

She took my hands. "He's such an excellent prospect, Faye. You don't dismiss a proposal from a family like that in a hurry."

"I'd be marrying him, not his family."

The smile my mother suddenly trained on me was unfamiliar, almost cynical. "Oh, my dear, a girl does marry the family, too. But it won't be a problem, in your case."

I was only too aware of Mummy's case. Melbourne's leading families condescended to tolerate her for her husband's sake, so long as she toed the line, but some kept rubbing it in that she could never be one of them or get close to their standards.

I said, "Wouldn't it be a bit of a problem for *me*?"

"No, dear, that's what is so wonderful about the Wilsons: they don't give a fig about religion. Clive likes you, so that's that. To them, church is a small part of life, not a badge of honour or a battleground. They won't mind having the wedding at St Patrick's. They understand that you'll want to be married as a Catholic. It's the reception they care about, and of course we'll have that at the Windsor, so everyone will come. The Wilsons have always admired your father's family. They won't freeze you out because you're a Catholic. Nor will anyone else. It won't be like it was for me. You are a Beauregard, not an Irish nobody like I was."

I smiled. "There's not as much bitterness in Melbourne now between Protestants and Catholics, is there?"

My mother shrugged and then nodded.

I didn't like to add that, even so, my parents' marriage – or any mixed marriage, as the Church called it – looked rather daunting. I didn't want to choose a man because of his faith; I had merely assumed that a Catholic husband would be the easier choice. Mummy had never actually told me and Edith to marry Catholics; she certainly hadn't made it plain how relieved she would be if we didn't.

What a shock: Mummy wanting me to marry a Protestant for security and position. Some people said that was what *she* had done, but of course, Mummy was mad about Dad. For the first time, I wondered which motive she had felt first, love or security, and which had been the stronger.

Of course, as ever, Mummy wanted the best for me. In her eyes, a Beauregard who married a Wilson had double social insurance, wherever she chose to pray. Mummy had ironed out any potential wrinkles with Mrs Wilson. But how could she fail to see how annoying that was? I would have liked – I expected – my mother and the Wilsons to wait for my decision. Yet the real worry was what my mother seemed to be taking for granted.

"Mummy, I'm not in love with Clive. How can I marry someone I don't love?"

"Romance is not the most important thing in marriage, or in life."

But Mummy was a romantic, like me – wasn't she? I hesitated and then said, "I suppose some people can live without romance." More easily than they could live without a family, a home, or a country. Or food or money or good health. Given Granny's and Mummy's stories of how the Irish had suffered through invasion, famine and war, it wasn't so strange that for Mummy, security and prosperity were paramount. But I had grown up in *Melbourne*. I said firmly, "I'm lucky enough to have a choice. I don't want to live without love."

My mother released my hands and smoothed her skirt. She spoke softly, but her insistent tone was one she rarely used with me. "He loves you, my darling, I'm convinced of that."

Surprised, I met her confident gaze. "I'm not sure how he feels about me."

"You're very young, my dear. Clive is shy and not one to say a great deal. I think he feels a lot more than those slick fellows who speak so grandly. Talk doesn't mean a thing."

She moved closer and folded me into her arms.

Just then, her hug felt cloying.

It had never occurred to me that we might be at odds about anything important, let alone love and marriage. My head throbbed. I should have known that Mummy thought Vera's son was a great prospect. His dullness was nothing: he would inherit vast lands adjoining the Beauregard station. As soon as I seemed to notice Clive, her hopes had zoomed to the skies. I gave her the benefit of the doubt – she knew me, she valued my intelligence, and my artiness: she wanted and expected an educated, cultured man for me, one I would choose. If I hadn't spent time with Clive, she wouldn't have pushed me towards him, would she?

She smiled. "I would be so delighted if you married Vera's boy. He's a strong, steady man from a very successful family. You have so much in common. Faye, you say you don't know how he feels. Darling, do you really know how *you* feel?"

Somehow, I wasn't sure anymore. During the past few years, at university and on holiday in Europe, I had instinctively kept to the safety of the group. No-one had tempted me to leave it. Certainly not the wolves that panted after debutantes, nor the stuffy or political types at university. The boys from Church and from the country near my grandmother's station were all merely friends. So far, painting a portrait gave me more delight than any man. I hadn't felt any of those feelings I kept reading about with avid yearning. Was I going to feel them now? Surely not about Clive!

4. The Wrong Signals

Faye:

Melbourne and Portsea, June 1940

Upstairs in my bedroom that night, I sat in my armchair in front of the fire and felt a fool. If only I hadn't danced so often with Clive at my twenty-first. Why hadn't I realised that Mummy would leap to conclusions – and negotiations? The party had been a tame, disappointing night, with so few boys and with war shortages. I had simply tried to make the best of it. How the war turned things upside down. How foolish was I, assuming it wouldn't affect *me*.

Of course I was looking for love, but I was in no hurry. I didn't need a proposal. I certainly didn't have to accept a man I didn't love. I had years yet, well, several anyway. Someone would appear one day – someone not at all like Clive – and I would *know*, wouldn't I?

*

After his proposal, Clive didn't telephone or come to call. Then his mother invited my family to dinner the next week. I refused to feign illness. Why should I hide?

The instant I arrived, he loomed at my elbow. He sat next to me at the table. He was as monosyllabic as ever, so I did not have to look at him much. My father led the talk as usual, analysing the war and the changes it was making in Melbourne. My mother and Edith and I joined in, with supportive remarks from Mrs Wilson.

After dinner, Mrs Wilson prevailed upon me to sing and play the piano. Usually, I enjoyed entertaining friends and family, but, for once, I resented this duty of the young female. To refuse wasn't done. I chose some pieces that Clive would find highbrow, and which couldn't be construed as coquettish. He stood close to the piano and fixed me with an admiring, if placid, gaze. Afterwards, sitting over coffee, I felt glad of Edith at my side as he talked to us about football and horse racing.

*

In a fortnight, my mother invited his family back. He told Edith and me some news about the boys overseas, and things seemed easier and more interesting.

After that, it seemed that everywhere I went, there he was. For several weeks, I managed to avoid being alone with him despite his surprising efficiency at shadowing me, but one afternoon, he appeared at my house, and my mother contrived to have urgent telephone calls to make in her sitting room. I felt like inventing an appointment and sweeping out of the house. Of course, I couldn't. I sat opposite him in the front parlour under the bay window. Sunlight streamed onto Dad's little Corot and Degas paintings on the far wall. I fixed my eyes on their calm beauty.

As he proposed again, I silently awarded him marks. Better tone, Clive. Better facial expressions. Nicer smile. Marginally better words. But still not romantic. Was I expected to take him seriously just because he was trying harder? I wondered who had helped him. Would he ask anyone? His father? I nearly exploded with laughter. Wooden old Mr Wilson! How he had won pleasant, pretty Vera was a puzzle, except that she loved animals, and he owned the best horses and dogs in the State.

Clive slowly finished; no question, merely a statement expecting endorsement. Annoyed though I was, I would be polite.

"Clive, I appreciate the honour, and the effort you've made. It can't be easy returning to this topic."

Actually, he showed less stress than at his first proposal, presumably because he couldn't imagine a second refusal. He sat stolidly. His face did not change.

I said, "I'm not sure that you and I expect the same things from marriage."

With a slight frown, he shook his head. "Of course we do. You worry too much, Faye."

I took a breath. "Clive, I don't know what this means to you, what you feel about me."

"Faye, you're the best girl in Melbourne. You're so far above all the others, I'd be mad if I didn't want to marry you. You're such a lady, you don't even have to think about the right way to behave. And you're beautiful. And kind. You'd never hurt a fly. Some girls are real cats. We'll have the best life, Faye. You're a talker, I'm not. That works in a marriage. We won't fight. I won't mind if you go to the ballet and keep up your painting. I'll build you a studio. I'll need to go up to the stations sometimes, of course, but not for long, unless you want to go, too. We both love riding and swimming and traveling. We can go to London if you like and have holidays in France. After the war, we can have a honeymoon there. You'll know where to go to in Europe and what paintings and furniture to buy. We'll have a marvellous life, Faye. I'll give you everything you've ever wanted. Just say yes, Faye."

He paused, but not for long; I was taking a deep breath and formulating the least insulting answer I could think of when he blurted out, "Well, if you can't yet, I'll wait for as long as it takes."

He stared at me, looking pleased rather than loving. It was the longest speech I had ever heard from him. It was not much of a surprise that he didn't talk about his own heart. He would show me how he felt. I couldn't help feeling rather cheered by his picture of how I compared to other Melbourne girls. It did seem harder to discourage him, perhaps foolish, perhaps unfair?

There was warmth and admiration in his smile.

I had to break the silence. "I don't – I can't just say yes, I'm sorry, Clive."

He looked down for a moment, but no frown appeared. When he looked up, there was almost an appeal in his eyes that started to make me feel uncomfortable and almost guilty. "All right, Faye. I know you're no meek little filly. You can't be hurried. That's another reason I like you so much."

Were some men constitutionally incapable of saying the word, love?

I studied his face.

He took my hand and smiled, and that appeal was there again. "Let's give it a go, Faye. Come riding with me this week. I'll bring my horses around whichever day suits you."

So, I had to agree. It was sensible; I owed it to him, or even to myself. Like most men, he expected females to agree with him. Like most girls, I was used to that. It took a lot of effort to convince a man you meant what you said. With most of them, you hadn't a hope of winning an argument. Even to try, you had to be awfully sure of yourself – and, though I considered myself confident in general, I found that on this matter, I wasn't.

One fresh, cool morning, Clive brought two marvellous horses to my door. We set off along the tan, the path around the Botanic Gardens. When he helped me down, quite unnecessarily of course, I liked the firm bulk of him straining against me, his big hands hot around me. He flushed and held me for a long moment. There was a hint of fire in his eyes. At last. What would it feel like – what would he be like if I showed him I wasn't really a restrained convent girl or a proper Toorak lady but someone who could love him so strongly, so intensely, that he'd never want anyone else?

I hoped we might lie on the grass near the tan or sit at least, and he would show me – let me show him. But he didn't suggest it. I didn't either. I was afraid he would guess what I was leading up to and think I was common. We rode back to my place and had tea. My mother again made apologies and flitted off somewhere upstairs, and Clive sat demurely and drank his tea. When he said goodbye, he leaned down and when our eyes met, I looked for that fire. Instead, he seemed guarded, but there was a slight hint of heat as he kissed me gently, and the warmth of his arms around my shoulders gave me a sense that he did love me.

We went riding two or three times a week after that. I felt I had no grounds to break it off and he seemed to be happy to do whatever I wanted. I found I enjoyed that, curiously, even though the men I admired in stories were not docile. But naturally, he only consulted me in matters of leisure or style.

One morning, we left the horses at his place and walked back to mine.

He said, "We could build a new house if you like. Or if you see a house you want, we'll buy it."

We happened to be walking past a mansion twice the size of my house and slightly bigger than his.

"How about this one?" I joked.

"Sure."

I presumed he was joking or boasting. It was hard to read his impassive face.

That afternoon, I asked my mother how wealthy the Wilsons were. I expected a vague answer, but she was exact. No wonder Peg had drooled. No wonder girls played up to him. No wonder he assumed I was after him. But that showed how little he knew about me.

So, he could buy me the art collection of my fantasies or as many frocks as I liked from Paris couturiers. Unimportant, but rather fun to imagine.

He let me organise our outings. I thought that was sweet. He wasn't very bright, of course, none of his family was, but, unlike some men, he always listened when I spoke. I didn't expect much talk from him. It didn't seem to bother him that I was attending the university.

"Did you ever think of going yourself, Clive?" I asked one day. "Studying economics or doing an agricultural course at college?"

He looked surprised. "Why would I do that? It would be a complete waste of time."

"It wouldn't interest you?"

He shook his head disdainfully. "Why would it?"

"Well, I thought it might be useful to see the latest research into animal husbandry or crops or soil or water usage. Or trade trends in meat and wool, I don't know." I trailed off.

"Our managers learn all that. I like to supervise and have a say in the decisions. I learn more from that, and more from Dad than I'd ever learn from teachers or reading." His tone was certain, with a touch of contempt. "It was bad enough at Grammar. I couldn't wait to leave. So much of education is completely useless."

I laughed. "I won't use much of what I study, but I can't imagine not having read the great books or learning French and Latin or appreciating the art of different times."

"Girls like you enjoy reading and looking at art. Your girls' school offered you subjects that are suitable for ladies."

I looked sideways at him. "Useless ladies' subjects, I see. Teachers need to know them. I'm lucky not to have to use my studies in classroom drudgery."

"For you, they are ladylike pastimes. Quite right too, they give you the info you need to choose art for your home and to help your kids."

I hid my amusement. Ladylike pastimes! How annoyed my Classics professor would be if he heard that.

"You'll be finished with university soon, won't you?"

"Yes, unless I do a post-graduate degree. A Master's." I gave him a mischievous look, but he did not glance in my direction.

He shrugged. "If you like. Do you want to?"

"Probably not. I'd rather paint."

Clive nodded. He saw painting as a suitably feminine hobby. He probably thought I painted flowers or fruit. He never met me at the Gallery school, where I concentrated on life drawing and portraits; nor did he meet my fellow students, mostly male and unconventional, and not from my sort of background. They would have put him off entirely and perhaps changed his view of me. Most of my family and friends took no notice of my dabbling and daubing. My mother discouraged me from socialising with classmates or artists. I could hardly imagine seeing them socially; it would surely be embarrassing. Unlike most of the students, I hadn't the slightest wish to become a real artist or to sell anything.

Like his parents, and like most people in our circles, Clive held old-fashioned ideas about ladies and wouldn't countenance them working for a living. Actually, the women in my family didn't work, except for charities and so on. Some younger women I knew, especially at the university, talked of having a career or profession, but only until they married. A few of my school friends taught for a time, or like Peggy, took up clerical positions out of financial need. What a bore. How could a job be better than doing what you pleased?

When I had children, I would spend lots of time with them, as Mummy had with Edith and me. Clive seemed eager for children too. He took them for granted. It occurred to me that some people couldn't have them, but no-one in our families seemed to have that problem. His father, so choosy about his cattle, sheep, horses and even dogs, probably thought I came from good stock. I hoped he included Mummy's side in that; they were the real survivors.

It wasn't Mummy's excitement or Clive's certainty, but rather his consistent attention and the increasing pressure I felt in his embraces that kept me imagining what it might be like. Newlyweds. Parents. On the country stations. In town, in a new house and eventually in his parents' lovely old one. At Portsea. Over in London. In a French Chateau. Picturing it gave it a sort of romance, like a story.

I was having such fun I started to wonder if I *had* fallen in love with him, in a gradual, gentle way. Sometimes it happened like that in films and books. It always annoyed me when people said you would just *know* when you were in love. Did everyone? Clive was so proper and reserved. Of course, he was shy. But I kept expecting and waiting for a real kiss, like the ones so vivid in novels and films. The passion and ecstasy I imagined so fervently, mine as much as his, couldn't creep up on me gradually – it must flame, all of a sudden. I hoped for it all the time.

1941, Portsea, Victoria

At the start of '41, my family held our usual New Year's Eve party at our seaside house at Portsea. Clive and his family were there, and I suspected that our parents, or our mothers at least, hoped we would make an announcement. Clive didn't push me, and I had no answer to give him. There were few other boys, only my cousin, Nigel, the three Clifton boys, who were in reserved occupations essential for the war effort, and the youngest McNamara boy, Patrick, who intended to enter the priesthood at the end of summer.

After supper, at the party, Patrick gave me a teasing look. "You haven't danced with me the whole night, Faye. How can I go home without a dance with you?"

He had an Irish way about him, with his touch of blarney and his twinkling green eyes, so I danced with him for a while. Clive wasn't much of a dancer and had gravitated to the older men who sat smoking and listening to my father.

"Faye, you could be a torment to a man, don't you know?" Patrick said softly as we whirled to a halt. I looked up to catch his teasing twinkle, but his eyes were sharp and mocking. I hid my shock – and annoyance. Why should I feel ashamed? I found Peggy and Edith and forgot all about him.

At midnight, everyone sang 'Auld Lang Syne' and thronged around, kissing and wishing each other "Happy New Year."

As I got to the end of the terrace, Patrick swept me up, kissed me full on the lips, and clasped me to his body. He turned away from the lights and took a step under the overhanging tree, where it was dark. His mouth was soft. His hands were gentle on my neck and arms. A new, delicious ache tingled frantically through me. It was too lovely to be embarrassing. I forgot to wonder if anyone was looking at us. Then he squeezed my hand and slipped away. I walked into the light. Clive came over and gave me a public sort of kiss, but he held me more firmly, and I wondered if he'd seen Patrick kissing me.

At the end of the party, Patrick farewelled me formally. Three weeks later, he entered the priesthood. Whenever girls muttered "what a waste," as Catholic girls did about a nice-looking boy entering the seminary, I wondered if he'd kissed them.

*

The Portsea summer seemed longer with the young men gone. Edith and I swam every day, unless a hot north wind sprang up. Before the war, Clive had stayed at Portsea all summer, like all the boys. Now, he and his father were indispensable at their cattle stations. He went up to the country straight after New Year's Eve and only visited his mother again in her big house on the cliff once more that summer. He went swimming with me, together with Edith and his sister. Before he arrived, I imagined long walks on the beach and our first real kiss. Alas, Clive didn't walk; he ran, and not at my pace.

But the night before he left, he said he loved me.

5. Anti-Climax

Faye:
Melbourne, May 1941

When I finally said yes, Clive smiled and kissed me with more affection, and my heart rose. Now he would be less guarded. And I could be too. Had he ever held serious doubts about my answer? However much I was dying to know, I couldn't ask him yet.

Mummy shrieked and kissed me and practically danced around the parlour after I told her. What fun we would have, planning and shopping.

When I told my father, we were in his library, and the bright window behind him cast his face into shadow.

"Congratulations, Faye." He spoke more softly than usual. "I hope you will be very happy. You deserve a marriage to a husband who knows what a prize he has won. I suppose Clive loves you very much. I can hardly imagine a young man who wouldn't. And you love him, too?"

I rushed up and embraced him, and he hugged me back hard as I said, "yes, of course." I wished I could have blurted out, "But how do you know if you're really in love?" When I saw a hint of worry in his eyes, I was touched and a little alarmed.

How would he feel about being related to the Wilsons, to Clive's father? He never seemed close to his old schoolmate. But it couldn't have bothered him, really, because after that one telling question, "And you love him, too?" he asked nothing else, though he was famous in court for interrogating people until their stories evaporated, and the habit crept into family life often enough. What a relief to have his approval.

Edith didn't have a word to say against it, now that I had made up my mind. But I was hurt to see that she wasn't enthusiastic. She and I had never disapproved of each other's close friends, let alone boyfriends. How would I bear watching my sister trying to put up with Clive?

Because of the war, there was a stronger taboo about speaking against a girl's choice of spouse – within limits, of course, because Melbourne, as Uncle Eddie joked, was a town where social class, suburb, religion, occupation, income, house size and marriage partners were prescribed for everyone, and perhaps most of all for those who thought they were at the top. In most people's eyes, Clive and I were a perfect match.

What had Mummy said to Edith? The three of us weren't used to keeping secrets from each other. I felt a new loneliness. I hadn't talked much to Edith about Clive in the last few months; I had kept my developing romance safely away from her comments. Yet couldn't she see that it was going to be a good marriage, not merely a good match?

After the announcement appeared in *The Argus*, cards and letters of congratulation clogged the mailbox. You'd think I had really done something. To a lot of people, I had just become someone. It gave me an inkling of what my mother had faced.

The press pounced. Posing became my new occupation, one that Clive seemed to know. The press seemed keener to snap the Wilsons than the Beauregards, despite my father's and my uncles' achievements. Mrs Wilson commissioned an artist to paint me. Unfortunately, he wasn't one I admired, but he was well known.

Apart from my mother and Peggy, no-one seemed to have noticed how unsure I had felt about the marriage for months. It was almost flattering to find that my air of self-possession was so convincing.

Everyone's air of knowing it already must have been why I felt a bit let down – though of course, I was excited, too.

June 1941

Our engagement party was held at Clive's house. I wished my parents still had Belmont, our old house, but, like many families, we had been forced to sell and move to a smaller place several years ago because of the Depression. The Wilsons' house was determinedly grand and boringly decorated, but it had a ballroom with a balcony and a large terrace.

Clive had finally enlisted with the Army. His parents made a fuss about it at the party. Older male relatives and friends of Mr Wilson came up to congratulate Clive and his parents on his enlistment. That announcement seemed to make more of an impression on some guests than my appearance as his fiancée.

Everyone came to the party. Even the Governor and his wife, whom I knew a little because of Dad's position as Chief Justice. The Vice-Regal presence delighted Mrs Wilson and her family, who didn't move much in those circles. All the young girls sighed over the Aide-de-Camp, but I found him willowy and pompous, the sort of condescending Englishman who'd driven me batty on holidays in London, even, or especially, when proposing to me.

When I wafted past Dad, he was talking about the war. Aunt Lillian, his sister-in-law moved away: her husband and sons were overseas fighting. Aunt Isobel, Dad's sister, took her arm and distracted her with lively talk. I joined them for a while. Isobel might have been considered the one in need of comfort, for her husband had recently died quite suddenly, though at home, not at war. She missed him terribly; tonight, I was thrilled to see that her joie-de-vivre was back.

Mrs Wilson had hired a good band. I found that I had to coax Clive a bit, especially when the fast numbers took over. While we bobbed sedately around, and I toned down my dancing to fit in with his, my uncle Eddie appeared to whisk me off. Clive looked thankful to get off the floor and a little embarrassed because he wasn't used to Eddie's jokes.

Eddie whizzed me about so fast I was almost breathless when the bracket finished. We escaped to the fresh air on the balcony.

"Shall I get you a drink, Faye?"

"No, let's catch our breath. I'm glad I was with you for those songs."

"Thank you, it was a stroke of luck for me to dance them with you! Whatever made you choose such a flat-footed fiancé?"

As usual, his delivery made me laugh. He gave me one of his looks. Sometimes, he made me feel unsure, in a way no-one else did. He smiled and then caught me off-balance again. "No doubt he avoided dancing lessons and preferred to shoot native animals."

"He dances when he has to."

"But you love it, my dear. And he may not feel he has to dance, once your courting is over."

"Oh, Eddie, he'll dance when I want him to."

"Hmm. Not a dancing family, is it?"

I giggled. "Well, I'm sure Mr Wilson used to dance."

"Not in living memory, Faye, possibly not in dead memory, either."

"Well, Mrs Wilson isn't keen on dancing."

"No, but you are, my dear. Are you sure he's such a biddable boy? He doesn't look it."

We stared across the empty dance floor to where Clive was standing next to his father, their chins jutting out at the same angle.

"By the way, what does your father think of your engagement? I didn't think the Wilsons were quite up to his standards."

I felt chilled. What criticisms did Eddie expect that Dad would have about Clive's family? Dad had approved, of course, but it didn't surprise me that Eddie hadn't discussed it with him. Apart from their age gap, they were the sort of brothers who were poles apart and seemed obscurely opposed to each other. I wished I could have talked to Dad the way I could to Eddie or Mummy, but none of my friends could really talk to their fathers.

I lifted my chin and said firmly, "Dad knows we're in love, and that's what matters to him."

"Love conquers all? Ah, the confidence of youth. Cynics like me should shut up. Let's get a drink."

All the way home, as Clive and I walked along the dimly lit street under the wintry trees, I wondered how he would begin, how it would feel. Now that we were engaged, less restraint was expected. What that actually meant, I hadn't a clue. I wished I had listened more to schoolyard tales of the facts of life as experienced by the faster girls, instead of retreating in embarrassment with friends like Peggy. All I knew was that I wasn't supposed to initiate anything. Most boys I'd gone out with thought like that. Clive looked surprised if I even took his hand.

We walked all the way down Domain Road and reached my corner. The Botanic Gardens stretched darkly into the distance. On the corner was a grassy patch with an empty bench. If only it would occur to him what a perfect spot it was. I paused my chatter – as usual, I was doing most of the talking – but to no avail. We turned the corner. In another few minutes, we would reach my house. I looked up at him, with my eyes as sparkly as I could make them. I slowed right down so that he would, too.

I leant down to adjust the strap of my shoe, unnecessarily, and looked up again.

At last, he fired up. But instead of a manoeuvre like Patrick McNamara's, he shoved his mouth onto mine, gripped me with hands like pincers, and pushed his big head and shoulders down into me till I feared my neck would break. The smell of tobacco and the taste of beer on his breath were slightly less revolting than the overall drowning wetness.

I tried to push him away, but he only leant in harder. How long would he persist? Panicking, I felt a depressing sense of failure. Was this what people meant by not hitting it off? How much worse it would be if he were on top of all of me, squashing and twisting tender parts of me that had never been touched? Oh, my heavens, if this was physical intercourse, as the Church called it, I'd have to become a nun!

Just when I thought I couldn't bear it another second, he unstuck himself and moved back awkwardly. My lips felt bruised. My ribs were sore.

"Better stop now, eh, or we'll be at it all night," he laughed.

I felt sickened. He hadn't even looked for my reaction, or sensed it. Without meeting my eyes, he started walking and then, as an afterthought, took my arm and held it under the elbow, a schoolboy dancing-class grip I loathed. Thank heavens we were only two minutes from my house. Conversation was beyond me. I was incensed with him, with myself, and with God. Why had He made men so clumsy? Or women so sensitive? Why was love so uncomfortable?

At the door, Clive took my key, turned it in the lock, returned it to me, and pecked my cheek. "Well, goodnight, old girl. Great party, eh? Sorry about that back there. Won't happen again. Bit carried away."

"That's all right, Clive," I heard my voice sound flat and tiny. "I hope we'll have some time together, before you go overseas."

God knows what he made of that. How could I tell him we

must get over this, and touch like lovers, sweetly, gracefully? I had to believe it was possible.

I went up to my room, feeling sad, sore and stupid. I heard Edith moving about next door.

I ran into her room and sobbed and laughed. "Oh Goodness, Edith, I don't think I'm cut out for marriage. I just had the most – oh, I couldn't stand it. It was vile! Even at Deb parties, it was never so horrible."

Thousands would have just laughed, but dear Edith looked sympathetic. "Faye, you must be exhausted. Perhaps Clive was nervous."

"And a bit drunk," I said angrily, thinking of that taste and smell.

"Oh, dear, that *is* a worry." Edith had adopted our mother's horror of drunkenness.

I laughed wildly. "I'll have to be a nun. Me! Can you believe it! Dad will be aghast."

Edith smiled. "Faye, I don't think receiving an unpleasant kiss is a reason to embark on a religious life."

No, apparently giving a pleasant one was. I laughed, recalling Patrick Mc Namara and that extraordinary tingling he sparked in seconds.

September 1941

I stood with my parents and Clive's on the wharf, in the shadow of the troop ship. All around us, shivering in the cold spring wind, families with flags in their hands strained to see their boy as he climbed the gangway and then leaned over the rail. Clive walked steadily up, looking ahead or at his feet. At the top, he turned and looked down at us, grinning glumly. Mrs Wilson was holding back tears. Mr Wilson had his usual impassive face, but his hands were clenched. Mummy grasped my hand and tucked it under her arm. Dad gave me and Mrs Wilson a kind look.

"He'll have a relatively comfortable journey," he said.

Mrs Wilson nodded frantically, then dabbed her face with a handkerchief. I looked down and turned away. When I glanced back, the four of them were watching me. Mummy patted my hand.

"I knew you'd be strong, Faye dear," she said.

Mrs Wilson smiled at me and patted my shoulder. "Yes, dear, good for you. We can count on you to be sensible. Clive likes that, too."

Next to me, a girl was convulsed with sobs, leaning heavily on an older woman.

"He'll come back all right, love," the woman was saying.

But the girl kept shaking. Her sobs turned to a wail. Around me, other women looked strained and bereft.

It was so different from last summer when I had farewelled the first troop ship. Then everyone had smiled brightly in feverish excitement. We shouted, waved and jumped up and down. I kissed a dozen boys, as if it were a party. It felt like Empire Day, Show Day and a Royal Tour rolled into one. The sun sparkled off the water; girls screamed out boys' names; bands played, and streamers whizzed in the wind. No-one cried.

My family had come to farewell their own. Wan and stoic amid the frenzy, Aunt Lillian waved off both her sons. She would be alone in Australia; her husband, Uncle Maurice, was already serving overseas, and her own relatives were in England. Gran hadn't come to see two of her three grandsons mount the gangway; she said that last time was enough, farewelling her sons, Henry and Maurice in the last war. Aunt Isobel, whose son Nigel had not enlisted, refusing to leave her alone in her widowhood, had come to say goodbye to her nephews, and to support Lillian. My parents had done the same. But to me and my girlfriends from school and church, the occasion was another event in our social calendar. We breezily assumed that the war wouldn't take long. Our parents didn't tell us how foolish that idea was.

I held a sort of wake at my place that night – dinner and drinks for deserted girls. We sat on my balcony looking at the trees in the Botanic Gardens, intoning a litany of the boys we would miss. There was something morbid and hysterical about it. Edith left us early for bed. But even Peggy got caught up in it, pointing out that we were like our aunts now; some of us would end up old maids. A few of us tittered. But we had assumed, before the war erupted, that most of our crowd would get married in the next year or two.

"It's unlikely this war will be shorter than the last one," Peg said, ignoring our groans. "The nicest boys have enlisted first. Who will be left when it ends?"

Thinking of that night again now, I felt angry and unnerved. Of course, I wanted our boys to beat the Nazis, but it was horrid to be losing hold of my life. It was grim to see bustling Melbourne turn into a ghost town, full of old people and bored girls, to hear rumours spread about certain girls and married older men, and to watch my friends go out with boys they wouldn't have considered before the war.

My father glanced at me and smiled, the way parents did at overexcited children, lest they burst into tears. "He'll get your letters fairly quickly," he said gently. "And his letters should arrive regularly, too."

I smiled at his unusually tense face and felt myself blush. For the first time in my life, I felt horribly close to a fraud. I wasn't anywhere near distraught. Not like the poor, loving girl nearby.

I stared up at Clive's distant face, so hard to see clearly against the sun. His blank, stolid posture showed no sign of distress. His farewell kiss, admittedly in public, had been no more than affectionate. He had nothing much to say except goodbye. I couldn't imagine what he'd find to write.

I needed to get used to the fact that he couldn't show emotion. But there was a knot in my stomach. I felt more shocked at myself than at him. It was awful that he was heading into danger but how much would I miss him? As the ship tooted and slid away, what I felt most was free – to paint, read or go to films and lunches without having to worry about whether he was happy about it. He had been taking up a great deal of my time; he had expected to be consulted about everything I did. The streamer in my hand strained and then snapped. My shallowness staggered me. I had always thought of myself as passionate and loving. Mummy whispered to me how proud she was of my self-control. My insides ached. How revolted my parents would be if they knew I was just heartless.

6. En Plein Air

Faye:

Melbourne, September 1941

The week after Clive shipped out, Eddie invited my mother and me to morning tea. He hardly needed to invite us; my mother often just dropped in, with or without me, and Eddie had recently told me that he hoped I would do the same, on my own, if I liked. Eddie was quite the eccentric: he kept no servants, and he liked to cook. His efforts were inspired by his travels in Europe and by his boyhood on the Beauregard country station.

That morning, he had made a poppy-seed cake and some cheese biscuits that I liked.

"I think I've got them right this time, sharp and peppery enough, but not too much?" He laughed. "Moira, when are you going to hand over your soda bread recipe? Would you rather dictate it? You know, I took my attempt at your stained-glass window cake over to Meredith's. She was impressed."

My mother looked scornful for a moment. She didn't have much time for Eddie's artistic friends, especially those who abandoned good houses in town.

She said, "Oh, Meredith! Doesn't she have a cook these days?"

Eddie smiled. "No, she cooks rather well herself now and takes afternoon tea quite seriously. She's building a pretty garden, Moira. You would like it. You should come and visit with me some time – you and Faye both."

Mummy laughed and shook her head.

I said, "I'd like to go there one day. To see their art collection most of all, and to see what the artists there are painting at the moment."

My mother said, "Eddie, that painter chap she has living with them, the one she thinks is so brilliant, is his work good, do you think?"

Eddie said, "I think he will get a lot of notice when he finishes a body of work. I intend to buy several of his pictures. I'll probably have to fight Meredith for some of them! Right now, he's in the army, of course, though his leave seems to bring him back to Meredith or send her up to where he is stationed."

Mummy rolled her eyes. "And this new husband of hers still says nothing, I suppose. The cheek of her." She had an amused, excited look that I didn't often see.

Eddie said quietly, "You remember how worried Hal and I were about her. She has chosen a better man this time. He's patient, he loves her and he's what she needs, I believe. Anyway, they get along. They live in a world of their own, and you understand that, darling, don't you?"

He smiled, and Mummy did, too. I wished I could have seen them when they were young. They often reminisced about how they met on the train from the country, and then Eddie introduced Mummy to his brother. Mummy often recounted with laughter how Eddie had announced to Henry and to her, very early in the piece, that they were a good match. Mummy was always saying what a dear, kind man Eddie was.

Though I hadn't the faintest idea what he meant about Meredith, it didn't feel right to ask. She must have had a tragic love affair. Mummy apparently knew and didn't seem to want to tell me. How old did you have to be to share in Eddie and Mummy's gossip?

After our tea, we walked in the garden. Mummy advised Eddie on the choice and arrangement of his annual planting and regularly gave him cuttings from home. I enjoyed the sun and the fragrant air while my mother and Eddie talked about plants.

When we were about to leave, Eddie said, "Would you both like to come with me to visit Norbert Swenson? His house is lovely, and the wildflowers and blossom trees will be pretty at the moment."

My mother looked doubtful. "I don't think so, Eddie dear. It's an interesting house, but I have so many commitments for the war effort."

"How about you, Faye? The chaps there are doing some work that might interest you."

"Thanks, Eddie," I said. "I'd like to. My teachers at the gallery school speak quite positively about Swenson and the painters at his place."

Eddie said, "Moira, it might be good for Faye to have a distraction now that she is a lady in waiting."

I laughed.

Mummy's face softened. "Faye dear, you do deserve an outing. Not that I imagine the artists there are our sort of people."

"Not at all, darling," Eddie grinned. "You would hate them. So bohemian. Faye, you may find them amusing, or tiresome. Who knows?"

Mummy looked a little uncertain. "Eddie, I would worry if I were not utterly sure that you will look after her every moment."

"Don't worry, Moira. There are no handsome young blades there. To Faye, they will look like old tramps!"

Mummy laughed and gave him a hug as we left.

The following Friday, Eddie and I drove out to the Swenson artists' colony. I was eager to meet these artists, who were independent of the gallery school and the city galleries. I had been thinking that, if Clive were killed, I would not want to join the growing group of young widows gadding about; instead, I might establish a gallery.

Even in Eddie's big car, the corrugated dirt road felt bumpy as we drove into the hills on the outskirts of Melbourne. High grey-green gum trees towered on either side of us. It was a bright, blue-skied spring day, warm enough for me to wind down my window, breathe in the cool air fragrant with eucalypts and wildflowers, and listen to the high-pitched, icy pings of the bellbirds that sounded like the top notes of tin pipes in tall, empty churches.

The turn-off was a sharp, muddy corner, and we climbed up steeply to the open gate. Eddie swirled around the dirt driveway to a stop. The buildings of honey-coloured stone and wood were European in style; they stood quaintly but gracefully defined, their gables and towers incongruous against the background of blue-green eucalypts. An unruly vegetable garden and high, waving flower bushes surrounded a brown waterhole and a slimy green swimming hole. Ducks and geese strutted about.

Norbert, the founder of the place, was better known to Melburnians for his eccentric life than for his paintings. A thin, bearded man in shabby, old-fashioned clothes, he took us on a tour. The cleared paddocks looked rather like green European fields, but the hills nearby were blue-grey with forests of gums.

Inside the main building, we sat in a huge, long room with high wooden beams, tracery windows and a vast log fire.

Several artists in old, dirty clothes came to join us for lunch. Three women in badly cut trousers and baggy cardigans brought out soup, German bread and sausage. One was about my age, and the others looked about ten years older. Most of the men were middle-aged. The women waited on everyone and sat down at the end of the table, barely contributing to the conversation. From the kitchen came sounds of children and a quiet female voice. I wondered if I should help carry and clear away, as I would in some of my school friends' houses but decided against it.

Norbert, at the head of the table, led the discussion of art and philosophy. The absence of war-talk was delightful, but disappointingly, I found myself excluded from the conversation, except when Eddie turned to ask my opinion. He did so often, and I spoke at length, to the obvious surprise of the other women sitting mutely. Norbert, and all the men apart from one sculptor, took no interest in my remarks and continued to address Eddie and each other.

"Do your children go to school, Mr Swenson, or do they learn at home?" I asked Norbert, intrigued to picture his household's relations with the locals.

"My wife teaches them here. They learn much more."

His claim hung unanswerably in the air. I wondered when his wife would emerge, and why the children were kept out of sight.

A young woman who had disappeared with the dirty dishes reappeared with a baby and, to my astonishment, began to breastfeed it by the fire, in front of us all. The infant's sucking and gurgling would have seemed sweet to me had I been observing it in a nursery or a lady's bedroom, where I had watched women in my mother's family feeding babies often enough. Here, I felt embarrassed; one of the painters gave me an amused, sneering glance. When the feeding finished, the woman detached the baby's mouth, and her breasts were in full view. I was mortified at my own conventionality, yet the whole thing felt like a performance for a voyeuristic audience.

Later, Eddie led me out to watch the artists working. One was finishing a bright, elegant leadlight window and another was painting a beautiful landscape watercolour. As we returned via a wide sweep of the paddocks, we saw two people on a blanket in the sun. The pair seemed to have another source of heat as well; the man was only in a shirt and the woman was naked. She was one of those at lunch who had said nothing.

Even at this distance, I could see that she looked better without her ugly clothes. The man was lying half across her, and she leant her head back, abandoned, excited and free. People said Norbert had fathered several of the women's children. I flushed, doubly embarrassed because I was next to my uncle. Eddie laughed for a second and steered us in the opposite direction.

I was glad when it was dusk, and we were speeding back to town. "Eddie, who's married to whom? I couldn't work the group out."

"I think it's a somewhat fluid situation there, Faye. They make their own choices. Why should it concern anyone else?" He glanced over at me. "Not everyone is cut out for marriage, you know."

It always puzzled me that he wasn't married. "But most of those artists have children. You can't just chop and change after you have a family."

He lit a cigarette with his elegant gold lighter. "Does life have to stop when you have a child?"

"Well, no, but a child is the most important consideration," I said. "People should behave responsibly when they are parents, not follow their whims."

"But people fall out of love, drive each other mad, come to hate each other. Surely you don't think they should stay together then, even if that *is* what your medieval church says?"

I swallowed. "I believe love is the most important thing in life."

He smiled. "Bravo, Faye. And that's what everyone we had lunch with believes, too." He laughed. "Except for Norbert. He only believes in his art."

The memory of Norbert's pompous face and skeletal figure angered me. I hadn't met his wife; the woman had been as ignored as a nineteenth-century governess.

I frowned. "But just to move from woman to woman

whenever you feel attracted: what kind of love is that?"

He sighed and said quietly, "There's the intensity, the passion, the truth of it. It can be honest."

I thought of the array of attractive ladies Eddie was photographed with in the society pages. He never brought any of them to family parties.

He glanced at me. "Don't you read about love like that in Classics and English and, above all, in French?"

I smiled. "Books are more convincing than people, sometimes. When I'm reading a good book, I can feel quite sure that passionate, romantic love – even *l'amour fou* – is real."

"It certainly is." He grinned. "It's most alarming when I meet it in my travels."

I laughed. "But in novels, passionate men are such monsters. They have no responsibility or kindness."

He sighed a little wearily. "Kindness is important, and, alas, it can be overlooked in passionate affairs. But perhaps one day you will have to ignore your father's attempts to censor your reading, don't you think? And reject the ridiculous restrictions of the Pope?"

I felt foolish and juvenile. Eddie's bookshelves were full of recent French novels as well as the latest English and American ones. I had a yen to browse through them. What would they show me? Suddenly, it seemed absurd that my father assumed he could forbid me from looking – rather Garden of Eden, really!

Eddie said, "There must be some men you like in books, Faye?"

"Oh, Mr Darcy and Mr Knightley, of course."

He snorted. "The princes from *Cinderella* and *Sleeping Beauty* – Austen just trots them out again, you know."

I felt irritated for a moment. These were the books I loved most. But he had a point. My head had started to ache.

Eddie glanced over. "I'll admit that happy wedded couples do exist. Your parents have shown me that. But not even their bliss can turn me into a fan of marriage. It seems to lead most couples into reinforcing each other's faults. But look here, I'm sorry, Faye. This isn't the time to be saying such things when you've just farewelled Clive, and especially when you believe in love and marriage ever after, as I suppose you do."

"Yes. One love for life: it's what I believe. Not just because the Church says so. I think that's how people are made."

"Perhaps some are. But some of us find that falling in love happens over and over and not where and when we expect it or plan it."

"Can one plan to fall in love?" I felt a lurch inside.

He shook his head, turned on the radio and found some good swing.

For once, I couldn't pay attention to music and had nothing I wanted to say. How I would hate to fall in love over and over. It would be so unromantic. I wasn't a flighty sort of person; I had made my choice, and it was a good one. Clive's awkwardness had decreased a bit, and didn't it show that he hadn't been fooling around with other women, the wrong sort. He still made me more uncomfortable than excited, but we would learn about love together.

The vision of the couple on the grass flitted back into my mind and stayed there, like a vulgar version of a Manet painting. I couldn't stop seeing it. I loathed that pair, so common – but their joy left me feeling unsettled, scared and strangely unsure of myself.

The darkness grew denser until all we could see was in the twin circles of the headlights. How disappointed was Eddie in my choice of Clive, and in me generally, especially this afternoon? My cheeks burned; how childish I must seem to him. My elation over the past few months seemed immature now, and perhaps a terrible mistake. I might have been chosen – by Clive, I hoped, rather than his parents – but I didn't feel loved. Clive would never be ardent like that man in the paddock. From the time I could understand stories, I had trusted in love and believed it would be the greatest experience of my life; now I feared I would never lean back in ecstasy while my lover saw nothing in the world but me.

7. Beyond the Pale

Faye:

Melbourne, February–March 1942

O ne hot afternoon that summer, I went into town with Edith
to see *Joy of Living*, an American film the newspapers said
was funny. For the first time, in the cinema foyer, we had to
run the gauntlet of a small group of American servicemen, who
tried to speak to us.

"Hi, baby."

"How 'bout you join us, honey?"

"Hey, good lookin,' where ya been all my life?"

I wriggled impatiently and Edith frowned stonily. Without a
falter in our pace, we strode past the grinning faces that pushed
in far too close.

Inside the auditorium, thankfully, the group of Yanks sat up
the back, where a few females seemed willing to sit next to them.
Afterwards, out in the street, the same fellows stood lounging
around; a couple of them had nice faces, but they chewed their
repulsive gum and bellowed in harsh, twangy voices. There were
only a few Americans in Melbourne so far, but everyone from
the Governor down said they would pour in soon.

None of my crowd would be seen dead with a Yank.

The film disappointed us: a shallow Hollywood story about
a rich girl who made a mess of her life till 'a real man' appeared.
We left the theatre and walked up Collins Street on the shady
side, looking forward to a good tea at the Windsor. One could
depend on it being free of Yanks. Yet this time, surprisingly, here
was a Yank, sitting in state in front of a bay window.

Though I was still recoiling from the oafish grins and over-familiar stares of those Yanks at the cinema, the gaze of this one had a different effect: I don't usually blush, but, straight away, I felt heat rising up to my face. My lips felt thick – was I gaping like a schoolgirl? The sun streamed over his hair. His eyes twinkled, like a boy's in a picture book, but his gaze was forceful, almost fierce, wanting my attention, yet expecting me to cut him. The strangest mixture of confidence and awkward humility. A hint of anguish just below the surface. The loneliest face I had ever seen.

For a second, I thought of Clive's face at our engagement party, and at the wharf – his arrogance was different, not tinged with self-doubt or the slightest need for anyone, least of all me.

I forced myself to sit down and tear my eyes away from the American. Edith was smiling at him, with a silly, stunned look I hadn't seen on her face before. I had to look at him again. He put a cigarette to his lips; they were finely shaped, and at their edges were sad, wry lines; his mouth, his whole face made me think of Gary Cooper. He stared through the smoke; his smile seemed sweet at first, then like Coop's in rare moments, it smouldered, grew flirty and intimate. What cheek! Yet I felt a surge of joy. A floating feeling whooshed all over me. It made the Patrick McNamara tingle seem mild – that tingle was back and the ache, too; I recognised them though it had been so long. They grew stronger moment by moment. Could Edith tell? Could *he*?

When he picked up the magazine I dropped, he told me his name. Peter. His voice was like warm water.

The chef appeared suddenly in the lounge. That rarely happened. He was new to the Windsor, a French refugee. Isobel had considered hiring him. He stopped at the American's elbow and greeted him. To my surprise, the American answered in French. His accent was not bad for a Yank. Whoever *was* he?

He looked across at me when the chef had gone, as if we were alone. We would never meet, yet he was someone I could love; that was as clear as the shaking of my fingers. I had never thought I was the kind of girl to be swept off her feet. How hilarious, how reassuring, but how terrifying that it only took a smile. What a waste that he was a Yank!

As he stared, I felt a sadness in him, starker than loneliness. It made me want to cup his face in my hands.

What if I spoke to him, or let him speak? How Eddie would sneer or sigh if he could see me, I who claimed that love was the most important thing in life, no matter what my mother said.

I gave him a look, willed him to speak, to flout the rules, to break the spell.

In the agonising wait, I glanced around the room. The whole crowd was staring at me, condemning me. How I hated them all, and this beastly room. Blast the Windsor! Why did I have to see him here? Would we meet again? Could either of us forget this moment?

As I stood to go, I felt his disappointment right through me. Yet there was something infuriating about his proud bearing, as though he knew he'd conquered me.

*

It bothered me that Edith might mention the American at home. She didn't immediately. It popped out, apparently by accident, the next evening after dinner, when we were all listening to Mozart on the gramophone in the parlour. Entranced as ever by the music, I was staring out the front window across at the tall dark trees of the Botanic Gardens.

My mother and sister were talking about the ability of an acquaintance of Mummy's to dress as though there wasn't a war on.

"When I saw her at Bridge at Vera's, I just couldn't believe it," Mummy said. "Another silk frock from Paris. I suppose she brought trunks of things home just before the war."

"She was wearing a wonderful suit yesterday at the Windsor," Edith said. "Wasn't she, Faye?"

"I didn't notice," I said.

My mother gave me a look of surprise.

Edith said, "I almost didn't either. It was rather hard to notice anything except that American pilot."

"An American? At the Windsor?" Our mother spoke sharply.

I tried to keep my face blank.

Dad looked amused. "Moira, if some Yanks have the sense to find the Windsor, it's rather mean to complain. We're their hosts, just as Londoners were ours in the last war."

"He was quite handsome and seemed rather at home," Edith told our parents. "It was Captain Stephens, the Battle of Britain Ace."

I stopped myself gaping and snapping crossly at Edith. Had he been in the newspapers? I couldn't bear the war news, which was why I skipped the papers these days. Why hadn't Edith told me who he was – if not that afternoon, then afterwards?

Edith avoided my eyes. "Monsieur Henri came out to speak to him."

"Oh? That is strange," said our mother. "I hear the Yanks are shameless flirts. I hope he didn't talk to you."

"Of course not," I said at once, in a panic, astonished to find myself lying. Would Edith contradict me?

Edith glanced at me. "He hardly took his eyes off Faye," she teased.

I stared at her. Why did she want Mummy to know? Had she forgotten that she had reacted to him herself?

"Oh, my goodness!" Mummy panicked. "Did people notice? Who was there?"

Dad laughed as he usually did at Mummy's social anxieties; people didn't sneer at her in front of him.

He smiled at Edith. "Remarkable record, that Stephens chap." He turned to Mummy. "Moira, we can't worry about the way lonely servicemen look at the girls."

I almost laughed; usually he was abrasively critical of any boy who noticed his daughters, especially boys not of our class. And how odd to see Mummy, of all people, judging a whole nationality as though they were beyond the pale.

"Lonely servicemen can cause havoc with all sorts of girls," Mummy said crisply. "Not only the sort of girls you might expect. You know how it happens, Henry, when people meet in these circumstances; it seems so desperately romantic." She smiled at him.

"Indeed, I do," his face turned younger and cheekier, making Edith and me smile. "Would you have been as intrigued by me if we hadn't met during the war?"

"Oh, Hal, I would have fallen in love with you whenever we met – as well you know." Mummy smiled in the special way she kept for Dad. A moment later she said, "Faye, you didn't take any notice of this man, did you? You always have such good sense."

"Mummy, everyone stared at him. It's not as if I'll ever see him again." I tried to sound nonchalant while my heart was beating fast. I felt Edith staring at me.

"It'll be too bad if we have to give up going to the Windsor." Mummy frowned.

Dad gave his short laugh. "You and your friends are so attached to your little stamping grounds. You sometimes seem less aware of the tragedies overwhelming half the world. You need not fear that American airmen will overrun the Windsor. That captain will probably disappear within a month once he is on active service. Pilots have a shocking casualty rate, you know. Even if the poor devil survives, he'll end up in the islands somewhere."

I held my breath. If that boy were shot out of the sky – I could barely stop myself shaking at the thought of his perfect face burnt and shrivelled, his bright eyes blank and still.

I felt ashamed: so many deaths, Paris taken, England attacked, and yet what moved me was the possible death of a pilot I didn't even know.

I turned away from my parents and my sister and stared out of the bay window again. Would he spiral down in a burning plane, plunge into earth or ocean, bullets tearing his flesh and destroying that unforgettable face?

Two weeks later, I saw his face looming above me, on the big screen, in a newsreel, next to the American Supreme Commander, General Maddox. I turned to Peggy to see her reaction. Peg rolled her eyes the way she did about film stars. I shook with silent laughter. It was more exciting than when I saw Gary Cooper in a close-up for the first time. The screen filled next with footage of the Battle of Britain; it made me catch my breath, more so than eighteen months ago when I had first seen it, because *he* was in it, and I knew him now. I saw him leap down from a Spitfire and flash that smile I knew by heart; he looked as unflurried as if he'd been for a joy ride.

My palms were sweaty. Afterwards, over supper with Peggy, I didn't admit I had really seen him up close.

Later that night, alone on my balcony, I leant over the rail and looked across the tops of the trees, beyond the river, to the near lights of the city. When he leant close, it had felt – surely that couldn't be what people meant by 'you just know'? I twisted the diamond on my finger around and around. What if I weren't engaged? The way he made me feel – as if we could race into some sort of love – I had never felt that before, but perhaps he had, perhaps often? I would never forget those few minutes. Would I feel that again, for someone else?

Flight

The temperature finally dropped, and the breeze cooled my cheeks and bare arms. I couldn't stop seeing his eyes, that exciting, alarming gaze, and his face, that look he had, a strange, remote sadness, a frightening fierceness, as he silently made me an offer, a declaration – a challenge? – how brave he was to show me that he desired me and hated to see me go. I stood there for a long time, remembering.

8. In the Spotlight

Faye:

Melbourne, March 1942

I stepped down from the car, let go the chauffeur's hand and tried not to blink at the camera flashlights as I walked up the stone steps and then the inner staircase of the Town Hall. If you blinked, there you would be in the society pages of *The Argus* and *The Women's Weekly* looking like a stunned rabbit in the headlights. I lifted the skirt of my long ballgown and leaned on Eddie's arm as we negotiated the long flight of steep, red-carpeted steps. It was annoying not to have a proper partner, but, with Clive overseas fighting, I could hardly ask another young man. Eddie was great company, but how boring to be with one's uncle at the biggest ball of the season.

My dress was elegant and expensive – but for whom? The orchestra was good, but who was there to dance with? Apart from Eddie's expert dancing, I had little to look forward to, a few sedate dances with Uncle Mo, my cousin Nigel, and my father.

Inside the foyer and the hall, the atmosphere was just as I expected: too many American uniforms. Thank goodness I was on the Governor's table on the balcony, with Edith and everyone, though of course the obligatory American general would be there, too. At least he was the top one, Maddox, whom everyone was talking about. He had brought along his wife; it was rather admirable of them to stay together while he was running a large part of the war. She seemed quite self-satisfied, or was it just her American way of holding her head back and constantly smiling? When she spoke, her accent grated. I sighed. It would be a long night. I wondered how well Maddox knew Captain Stephens. How high-level or perfunctory was the captain's role? He would be sitting somewhere below the balcony, thankfully. Unfortunately.

I was glad of the champagne's distracting fizz and of Eddie's entertaining chatter. Then Mrs Maddox expressed an interest in Australian art and monopolised Eddie with questions. When my parents went downstairs to dance, and Edith and Nigel followed, I escaped to the Ladies' Lounge. I didn't need the lavatory or the mirrors, but it was a relief to sink into a soft chair. For a short while, I found some girls from university to chat with. When they drifted back to their tables or to dance, I put on fresh lipstick. What a boring night it was going to be.

I tipped the woman at the entrance to the lounge and walked out. When I looked ahead at my table, straight along the corridor, my back quivered: Captain Stephens was standing there. My face felt hot, but I took a breath, raised my chin and tried to glide more slowly. My hands felt too warm in my soft gloves. It *was* satisfying that he was seeing me in my new dress; its draping gave me a very good line. He looked sophisticated in dress uniform, his hair gleaming and his skin glowing.

As I slipped into my chair, the governor was making the introductions.

Eddie relaxed everyone with his enthusiasm. "Call me Edward, Captain. I'm the youngest brother with no title or any importance whatsoever. I'm absolutely thrilled to meet a live Ace. Well, sorry, not meaning to remind anyone of dead Aces, but I'm so impressed by you fighter chaps. Such skill and bravery."

Captain Stephens smiled with warmth but also a touch of wariness. What cheek to be cautious about dear old Eddie, probably more of a gentleman than this captain had ever met. "Thank you, Edward; it gets easier with practice."

Eddie grinned. "For some fellows, perhaps."

The captain shot him a surprised, appreciative glance, his face relaxing into a wry smile.

When the governor introduced him to me, I had to stop myself from extending my hand as Eddie had. I kept my smile under control.

He leapt into a compliment. "Miss Beauregard, Melbourne has many beautiful ladies here tonight, but you outshine them all."

Southern gallantry, presumably. How clichéd. How ridiculous. And presumptuous. I refused to give him the expected grateful simper. I thanked him quietly. How disappointing to discover that he was so gauche.

The governor stepped into the silence that followed. "Captain Stephens, how right you are. We are all accustomed to seeing Faye and Edith eclipse the room."

He swiftly introduced Edith, and the captain paid her a compliment.

Then he turned back to me. "Miss Beauregard, may I have the honour of a dance with you? Maybe now, or maybe you could fit me in later?"

I could hardly breathe. How dare he leave me no option. "Thank you, Captain. Alas, I'm afraid I am engaged for as much dancing as I can manage tonight." I thought my tone held a laugh that softened my words. In any case, they wiped the arrogant smile right off his face.

I glanced around the table: my mother was surprised, my father disapproving, the governor's wife alarmed, the governor masking annoyance, Mrs Maddox scornful, General Maddox uncomprehending, Edith and Nigel embarrassed, and Eddie absolutely upset. He was frowning at me. Oh Lord, should I back down? Had I been rude? Was I obliged to dance with Yanks? I opened my mouth, but the captain was quicker.

"I understand, ma'am. I wish you an enjoyable evening." He turned to farewell the table.

As he half bowed, I saw that hunted look that had struck me at the Windsor. The smiling, clichéd flirt had vanished.

How could I have been so cutting?

"Captain, please excuse my weariness. Now that I've had a moment to think, I remember that I do have some dances free."

He turned back to me, his cheeks hollow, his eyes haunted and dark.

I said quickly, "In fact, I'm free in the next bracket, after the band takes its break." The current bracket had just started, and I wanted time for us to recover our composure.

Eddie was wriggling in embarrassment, but Mummy gave a relieved, amused smile.

"Excellent, Faye my dear," my father said smoothly. "And, Captain, after your dance, do please join us here for a drink and a longer chat. We have so many questions about London. I look forward to it." His enthusiasm evoked a murmur of agreement around the table.

The captain farewelled me with a bow, his face still grim. His boyish confidence had turned into a closed politeness that could not cover a hint of panic. I found myself smiling at him and feeling more foolish than before. He summoned a faint smile and strode off fast.

I looked imploringly at Eddie, and he rose to take me to the dance floor. Conversation in front of the Americans was impossible. The whole table would avoid commenting on my behaviour, thankfully; they had the war and Melbourne to discuss.

Safely dancing, I said softly, "Oh, Eddie, don't you understand?"

"Not really, dear. Rather baffling how hard you are to please."

"But the Yanks are so… embarrassing."

"He was being sincere. He was giving you a compliment. Faye, I wouldn't have expected you to exclude a person because of his nationality, especially now, considering what's happening to innocent people under the Nazis."

Eddie could be so exasperating. "For Heaven's sake, Eddie. I don't have to be nice to a man just because he's a Yank."

"You don't have to be rude to him, either. You wouldn't have left an Englishman standing there like that."

"I didn't mean to be rude." It felt strange lying, especially to Eddie, but he had upset me. "I didn't refuse him only because he's a Yank. He seems to think I should be bowled over by him. It's annoying. He was at the Windsor the other day, and he kept staring at me."

Eddie grinned, then sighed. "He looks as if he really likes you. Why did you refuse to dance with him at first? Surely not because of some nonsense about it being cheap to be seen with Americans?"

If Eddie only knew how it felt to be judged the way girls like me were, by everyone. It was fine for him to be a rebel. I admired his views about the Spanish Civil War and the Fascists and Nazis in Europe; he had condemned Hitler's party from the first, before most people saw how bad it was. But how deflating he could be. He frightened me for a second, but, as Mummy said, he was often too extreme.

He said softly, "I saw how he looked at you just now. We all want a look like that, and few of us get it."

His words kept beating though the music. "A look like that."

The orchestra stopped. Eddie led the way to an outside balcony. I leant over the cool stone rail and breathed in the warm air.

"You think I'm being silly and conventional, a silly convent girl, don't you?" I laughed.

"Well, the question is, do you like him, Faye?" He smiled disarmingly and lit a cigarette. "Sorry, I'm being mischievous. It's the champagne! I'm an old scallywag. But it always disappoints me when people go in for self-sacrifice. Not a fan of that."

I didn't know what to say, or what I wanted to say. He leant over the balcony and smoked. I stared out over Collins Street. He hadn't mentioned my engagement. I didn't want to think about it.

After a while, I said, "It's just so irritating. I feel as if he is playing me on a long line, and I'm flopping about, gaping and breathless."

Eddie stared ahead. "I sympathise, but how do you think you made *him* feel? You pulled him right out of the water, hook in mouth, and then threw him back in for another chance."

I laughed.

Eddie said more gently, "He did seem to suffer a bit, don't you think, which suggests that he's not a tough lady-killer after all, however much he might look like one. And he does have the taste to like you, my dear. We can hardly blame him for that."

I looked away. "He did look terrible. I felt awful about it."

"Well, these boys live on their nerves. They have been through stages of hell that we can't imagine."

I took in a breath.

"You do like him." Eddie glanced at me, then faced the street. "Who wouldn't?" he said softly.

Having him admit it aloud for me was frightening, yet a relief. What was happening to me? What was going to happen? Well, nothing much. I was engaged, for heaven's sake. I couldn't disgrace my parents. I wasn't in love.

Eddie took a long pull on his cigarette and checked his watch. He grinned. "I say, it's nearly time for your dance with him. I'd better escort you back to the table or to the Ladies' to primp and pace about. Which is it?"

I put a hand to my hair. "Heavens, I probably look a fright."

"Never, Faye. But you might feel more composed if you go and stare at yourself in the mirror for a moment."

I laughed and walked swiftly to the Ladies'. Thank goodness there were no girls I knew in there, only a couple of older women. I sat on a velvet seat in front of a large mirror and stretched my back. I tugged off my gloves. I might have known that Eddie would come out with something outlandish. He probably welcomed passionate affairs. I wasn't that sort, even though I adored films and books about such people; even though from childhood the stories that fascinated me most were of Lancelot, Guinevere and Elaine. Now that I was grown up, I only half-expected love to happen to me. I had never understood how love made some people lose their senses and become powerless, as if swept away by a tidal wave.

It was a mystery I had expected to solve in adulthood, but somehow it stayed inside the pages of books. Perhaps just as well, as Peg would say. It was fun to giggle over the rules with Eddie, as even my mother did sometimes, but, in the end, what was the point of breaking them?

The room was empty now. I smoothed my hair, put my gloves back on, and stood to check the fall of my dress. Along the wall were a series of long mirrors on the dressing tables. As I moved, the mirrors rippled. I felt a little dizzy. As I turned to leave, a row of my reflections paused. An infinity of Fayes. Like a girl in a film. In moments, his hand would be on my bare back. I would grasp his shoulder. As I walked out, the red velvet walls seemed to pulse. I turned and stared one last time at my many faces.

At my table, I watched Peter approaching. Was he starting to hate me? I took a sip of water and pressed my lips together. How ridiculous to feel so nervous. He was in front of me and met my gaze. His twinkle was challenging. His poise was impressive;

was this show of generosity genuine? He held out his hand, clasped mine for the first time. Bother gloves. I could feel Eddie and everyone watching as we walked away.

9. Pas de Deux

Peter:

Melbourne, March 1942

I got to the ball early and hung about the foyer. You couldn't miss Faye as she came up the red-carpet staircase on an older guy's arm. Her long dress in creamy satin clung to her, shoulder to knee, like Jean Harlow; Faye matched Harlow's figure and spirit, but looked classier, like Loretta Young or Hedy Lamarr. Press photographers kept snapping her and the guy. They handled it like they did it every day. I would scan the papers at my billet and the magazines at the Windsor next week. I had never carried a photo of a girl when I flew, or anytime, but maybe I'd make an exception.

Iris had waited for me to invite her to this ball she'd never got within a mile of before. She had a show on at the Tivoli, but she would have wangled the night off. She even suggested coming after the show. I talked like I would be tied to Maddox all night. She looked as if she didn't buy that line, but she didn't challenge me.

My breathing was fast already but my heart practically skipped when, as I hoped, Faye sat down at Maddox's table. Her parents and sister were there already, hobnobbing with the Governor and being polite to Maddox and his wife. Faye's partner had the family eyes and the quick talk, like her and her father. Ridiculous of me to be cheered at that because what difference did it make, I wasn't in the race, but I couldn't help feeling elated that he was a relative instead of a lover. Not that a girl like her would have a lover, not yet anyway. Her innocent flirting at the Windsor made that plain. He seemed casual and modern, without the general's ramrod, ready-to-die-for-our-king air, or the old-world, English I'm-in-charge-here manner of Faye's father.

Maddox would show me off. He and his publicity guy knew how much the Battle of Britain meant to these Melbourne types. I kept off the drinks for when he would call me over and get me to speak, or more likely, make me stand there like Exhibit A, while he did all the talking. I didn't want to dance, except with her. After a little polite chat with Maddox's staff on my table, I went to sit with some Aussie pilots from my billet, and refused drinks, to their consternation. I laughed even more than usual at their talk to make up for it. I was getting to like their stories, which they called yarns. Most of them were set in the country, "the bush" they called it, and every yarn had a punch line that made the speaker look dumb, ignorant or unlucky. Mighty different from the average Yank tall tale where the hero never took the pratfall. In England, I had come to enjoy the art of understatement and to appreciate the genuine modesty of guys in my squadron. Aussies used a similar understatement, exaggerated to a degree where you had to read between the lines. It was like a code. Sometimes it was defensive, like Irish gangsters I used to know in New York, and sometimes one guy would aim to belittle another, like men of any breed, but often it was honest and humorous, and made you feel one of them. It was a damned good way to get through hard times.

When Maddox sent for me, she wasn't there. As we began the introductions, I hardly paid attention, apart from the judge, I was so jumpy that she mightn't appear. Thank the Lord, Maddox was holding forth when she did. I watched her all the way along the passage. I could watch her walk all day. She had her hair piled up, soft not severe, with white flowers in it. If someone had told you she was famous, you would have believed it. She was wearing lipstick, and it made more impact than on practically anyone I'd ever seen; it was dark red, the only sharp colour on her. The flush deepened in her cheeks as she reached us.

She sat down next to her escort, and he gave me a look of sympathy which cheered but horrified me – what the hell was my face revealing? The others didn't seem to have noticed, so maybe he was quick that way.

He rose and held out his hand, unlike everyone else. When he praised me and Fighter Command, I waved it off, like I often did.

But some guys were made for it. From the start, I knew that I was born to fly fighters. Some guys wanted a co-pilot and a crew, like in the bombers; guys like me were better off with no-one to slow them down.

Edward was beaming back at me. I had one friend in the family. And maybe two, for Faye's mother was asking me questions with a coquettish, thrilled look I received a lot from older women. I remembered just in time to call her Lady Beauregard.

The governor introduced me to Faye. She flushed a little. I felt like a statue I was so tense. I watched for my moment to ask her to dance. She might not want to, with any Yank, or with me. I tried to say it in such a way that she could knock me back without it looking personal. I wasn't too sure I had gotten the wording right. I felt like a cardboard cut-out from a Southern musical, but so what.

Her face didn't give me hope. I stood there like the cartoon mutt who doesn't see the stone falling towards his head. It felt like ten minutes. I realised too late she might have taken my words as pinning her down rather than giving her an out. Her silence was so long I couldn't keep staring at her. I glimpsed Edward practically squirming in discomfort, probably embarrassed at my clumsiness, or maybe what he saw as my arrogance.

When she gave me the brush-off, it was all I could do to stand my ground. I tried to get myself together to take my leave. But I was stunned when she suddenly did an about-face and told me to come back later.

I hightailed it back to the Aussie pilots and gasped for a scotch. A beer would have done less damage, but the Aussie stuff was strong, and she mightn't like the smell. The pilot next to me started commiserating about Melbourne girls' snobbery. Then I saw Faye and Edward walking down to the dance floor. She looked upset.

I thought about the instant impression Edward had given. Honest. Friendly. Likeable. Probably queer. Not in uniform, though perhaps he was young enough. He seemed out of line with the rest of the family, much friendlier, so I figured they must look down on Americans. Or just hate my low-class kind. But she seemed to take a lot of notice of him.

She vanished into a bathroom after their dance. I waited till she reappeared. I didn't want to miss the start of our bracket, but I wasn't eager to get there too soon and be forced to make small talk with the top brass when I was keyed up to high heaven.

Walking up to their table was easier this time, though my chest felt tight, almost like at scramble call. The look she gave as I took her hand eased my muscles but sent my mind racing. Walking down to the dancefloor with her on my arm, I felt like I'd bought up Australia.

"Glad you said yes," I said. "I guess you don't come to public dances, I mean balls, very often." My clumsiest opener ever, I swear.

She looked a little cagey, though unsure too. "Not really, no. I used to go to dances at friends' places before the war." She threw me a look as if she expected I wouldn't believe her.

I smiled. "I had a flyer friend with a ballroom at his place in England. Great for parties."

It was better once we were on the floor, and I had hold of her. She felt more nervous than I was. She was breathless before we got started. The band was playing 'Please'. The lyrics were so right I almost laughed. At 'Fascinating Rhythm', I moved up a gear. She kept up well, but I could tell she hadn't danced like this in a while. Her face changed from startled to excited. There wasn't much time for talk, and she had little breath and attention left over. As 'Puttin' on the Ritz' struck up, I swung her out at arm's length.

"Okay, Miss B, let's strut a little."

I would have pulled her back in again if she had shown the least embarrassment, but she sashayed like a showgirl. It made me smile. We swung into some up-town jive and some two-step and fox trot. As we sped around the floor, I saw Edward leaning over the banister, cigarette in hand, watching us with a smile. I asked her if I could lift her for turns. She was so light it was a breeze. She grinned like a kid and her cheeks glowed. Maybe no-one had taken her flying like that.

There was bound to be a slow one soon, and, to my joy, it was 'Night and Day'. We whirled slower and slower almost to a stop, and I caught her gaze. And kept it. I hitched a ride on the throbbing rhythm and the crescendos. I drew her closer and put my cheek down next to hers. It was harder to do than you'd think; she was so tiny, despite her high heels. I had always loved the tune of 'Night and Day'. For the first time, the words *you are the one* didn't sound like such a dumb line.

I spoke soft and low. "Miss B, I know it's fresh, but I've gotta say this: you're the most beautiful girl I ever met."

Her eyes were dazed and bright. I hugged her as much as I dared and felt a returning pressure.

"Can't you give me a chance, Faye? I wish you would."

She seemed unable to speak, and looked almost like she might cry. But then she smiled.

I bent and lifted her till our cheeks met for an instant. When I set her down on her feet, our eyes locked again. Hers were serious, longing, and to my surprise, lonely. Was that how I looked, too? As the song ended, I felt a kind of ache as we moved apart. Her hands slid out of mine. I slipped a hand gently around her waist and guided her through the crowd to the stairs.

"That was too short," I said. "Can we dance again?"

She nodded and, after a pause, said, "I'd like that."

As we walked upstairs past an outside balcony, I said, "I wish we could go out there, just the two of us, and talk. I'm gonna have to answer the usual battle questions back at your table, and you're gonna be bored to death."

She murmured a polite objection and then laughed in agreement.

The governor had a chair all ready for me around near him and Maddox, away from her. I had to stop myself staring at her. The conversation went as expected, and her eyes glazed. A couple of times, she caught my eye, and her face came to life for a moment.

Edward delivered me from the scores and tallies. "Captain, the story I find fascinating is how you brought some three-quarters-dead chap back from France – in a single-seater, ladies, may I remind you."

Maddox flexed his shoulders and took over the tale, which was almost a relief. He had heard it from my superior officers. It sounded like a story about someone else.

At the end, Edward said, "And is your friend all right? Flying again?"

"Sure," I said. "He's going great guns. I knew if I could just fit him into the plane, he'd make it."

"Sounds like a heck of a flight," Edward grinned. "He must have bled all over you. Sorry, ladies, to be so ghoulish, but isn't it amazing? Captain, I can't imagine how on earth you controlled the plane with a comatose man squeezed in behind you. It was a brave decision."

"It wasn't like I had a choice."

He nodded.

"I couldn't have left any good flyer there, let alone Hube."

The thought of the ones I might have left behind registered on Faye's horrified face. I looked away. She was still getting acquainted with war.

But it was one of my best memories ever, that moment when Hube came to, as we landed, and he said, "Great Scott! Pirate, have you brought us home?"

Faye's father leaned forward. "Hubert Dennison, wasn't it? Lord Frederick's son?" He had a lightning delivery and a steely glare that must have shaken men with quiet lives.

"That's right, sir," I said, and then worried that I'd called him the wrong thing. I had another try. "We often flew in a pair in England, Sir Henry, and in flights over France."

When I led her to the dancefloor again, it felt like a date. She had taken off her gloves, and you wouldn't believe the difference that makes when you dance. 'In the Mood' struck up, and we laughed and went like crazy. The next song was 'Begin the Beguine'. It was one of those melodramatic songs I used to yawn through, but dancing with her made it beat through my pulse. It seemed to affect her, too. She shivered when the singer sang *the dead desire I only remember.*

I grabbed my chance. "I never felt like this before, Faye. I'm crazy about you."

Desire was in her eyes now, but I couldn't kid myself she'd act on it. Ever. She wasn't the type. Maybe she didn't know she'd be fireworks; I knew that for us it would be like diving, like floating, like flying. If she ever let me near her, it would be hell to leave. I'd never been the heartbroken type, but she could be the one I'd miss. And I wouldn't even have to go. When her real guy came home, she'd drop me flat. Or if, beyond all bets, I won out over the fiancé, how long was I going to last? I'd used up my chances in this war, made a joke of the statistics already. And I never stayed with anyone; nothing lasted with me. The word I kept trying to shove out of my head was 'doomed.' Because we were, whether the war killed both, one, or neither of us.

A cornet rang out. Shrieked up high. Drums throbbed and boomed. 'The Golden Wedding' – dumb name that I never understood, but the horn sure sounded gold. This guy could blow. He whined and yelped so you felt it head to toe. Dancers were stopping to watch him, but I wasn't falling for that. We threw ourselves into quickstep, jive, lifts, you name it. At the end, the horn player was popping his eyes out till the final note stretched up our spines and out our heads. I twirled her in a lift for the whole finale. People were standing back, watching us. When we stopped, she leant on me, dizzy. We stayed near the band, close together, till the crowd thinned.

Then I saw Iris. I should have known. Smart girl like her figured she could walk in at this stage of the night, and she had the looks to get away with gate-crashing most places. Like the showstopper she was, she picked the prime position, at the end of the second step. You couldn't miss her, dolled up like a star, smiling straight at me. Then she called my name. Held out her hand, like a lover. Faye turned to me. Coldly. I shrugged, then nodded at Iris, and we walked past her. They say it never hurts to show a woman her rival, but with Faye, I didn't feel so sure. Our formal farewell at the table was more strained than it might have been. All my elation fell away. I walked back to Iris, dog-tired. Would I meet Faye again? I'd always wonder, what if? But would she?

10. Up in the Air

Peter:

Melbourne, March 1942

Maddox's publicity office had lined me up to do some flying for the public in Melbourne the next week – to rev up support and admiration for us Americans, and to make people put their hands in their pockets for the war.

"It will be combined with an event for charity, for a Church of England boys' school and an orphanage," Major Rogers said. "The orphanage is run by the Catholic Church, but you're a Mick, so that won't worry you."

My body went rigid. I hadn't been called a Mick since I was sixteen, and then it had been a joke. But, of course, my papers said I was Catholic. Rogers' tone made me wonder how many other US officers were. The Catholics I knew would never aim high, and, down South, the rich guys and gals had a rule: no Jews, Blacks or Catholics.

He glanced at me and said, "The orphanage is a pet charity of the Deputy Governor's wife. She's a real live wire. Mrs Maddox likes her."

My pulse was racing. If Lady B was involved, maybe her daughter was, too. Faye would see me fly.

*

The day after the ball, I went to the airfield to take a closer look and to schedule some flying. Not that I needed the practice – I grabbed any excuse to get back in the cockpit.

The orphanage I was to fly for, Lady B's charity, happened to be in a suburb near my billet. Maddox's office told me it would be a good idea to make an appearance there sometime, nothing official, a polite visit. There were to be speeches from some top brass at the boys' school, but nothing for the orphans. Typical, so I would damned well go there. It was more than a good walk away, but long walks calmed me down and kept me in shape. So, the next afternoon, I walked over and found myself at the gate of the orphanage. It was dumb, but until I saw the brick building and the statue of a man and child, I hadn't expected that it would make me shove back memories I had denied for years. My face must have been a sight. I skulked away beside the high wall till I could get my expression close to normal. I had to knock on the front door, and act like an officer and an ambassador. No doubt, they had spotted me. Prisoners always have their eyes glued to the outside.

I marched in and swallowed down my panic. Thank the Lord, they were nuns, not priests. The nun in charge seemed genuine and not off her rocker, unlike many of the priests and nuns I had seen. She offered me tea in what she called the parlour, but I baulked at sitting on an uncomfortable chair and thinking of things to say. Instead, I accepted a glass of water in the kitchen. The kids were boys; right now, they were at the local church school. There were a few babies, too. Mother Agatha didn't explain where they came from, and I didn't need to ask.

When the boys came in from school, they thronged around, and the older ones asked about my flying. Unsurprisingly, they didn't get to see the newsreels. The little kids looked lost and uncomprehending, so I asked if we could play ball. They found a couple of worn basketballs, and we went outside to an asphalt area with a basketball ring. I had way too much of an advantage, so I was glad when an older kid brought out some cricket gear and they could teach the rookie. When they took a break, I swung one of the little kids up on my shoulders, and we pretended I was a plane. Then the other small kids had to have a turn. Mother Agatha smiled and watched till the kids had all been flying. She gave me a look, and I said so long.

"I'll come play again," I said to the older kids, "and when you come to the airfield, you'll see some real flying."

*

I caught sight of General Beauregard that same night at the Tiv when I arrived after interval to watch Iris and take her to the Fed. Aussies shortened most names, and I was catching the habit. Beauregard roared at the Jewish comic and smiled benignly through the tap act by Iris and a few others, all with hardly a stitch on. I was standing smoking in the foyer when he passed me on his way out. With a smile, he put me at my ease.

"Glad you've found one of Melbourne's real gems, Stephens." I figured he meant the Tiv, not Iris. "I hear you also found the Windsor."

I grinned back hesitantly, wondering if Faye, or her parents, had told him about her seeing me there. "Yes sir, I met your niece there. Well, I didn't exactly *meet* her, of course, till the dance – I mean the ball. She's a wonderful girl."

"The best. The best." He gave me a stern stare, as if to let me know I had him to answer to, as well as her father. "I don't have a daughter, but I'm the luckiest uncle this side of the black stump."

I'd heard that weird Aussie saying before, something to do with wildfires I presumed, so I didn't do a double take. "Yes, sir. She's the best."

He nodded and gave me another of his stares, rather like those of his brother the judge, but less uppity and irritating. Then he said, "Good to find the less stuffy part of town, too."

I noticed he was with a couple of officers and no females. I guessed the place wasn't on his wife's social map. After they headed off, I bounced on my heels and thanked my lucky stars he hadn't spotted me with Iris.

11. Up and Down

Faye:

Melbourne, March 1942

I couldn't admit to anyone that I could hardly wait for the flying demonstration, or that, much as I was looking forward to seeing Captain Stephens in the air, I was far keener to see him on the ground.

When the day came, I dressed with care; I would have done so anyway, but, as I chose, I was thinking of his gaze.

The speeches were forgettable, but then a pair of planes did a short fly over and loop.

At the end of the runway, a small plane was waiting. It looked tiny.

I guessed it was him before the announcer said, "The moment we have all been waiting for: Battle of Britain Ace, Captain Peter Stephens, will take off in a few minutes and show us what makes RAF and US flyers the masters of the sky."

"As if they are all of Captain Stephens's standard," Edith murmured to me, but I could hardly answer I was so preoccupied by the sight of the plane, and by imagining him inside. I had looked up a newspaper and magazine article about him. I couldn't ask anyone about his record, but I took note when Dad happened to comment about his astounding number of kills.

The flimsy plane taxied along, looking alarmingly unsteady, as if it might tip over at any second. My chest tightened and my hands clenched. Fighter planes looked more solid on the cinema screen.

And then, so fast, the plane soared up.

It was amazing to see the small light craft lift, and swoop, and skim the trees. It climbed till it was hard to see. Oh, for binoculars, but, like everyone's, mine had been commandeered by the government for the war effort. I wished I had thought to bring opera glasses. If only I could see Peter inside. When he did a roll, my throat tightened, and my stomach lurched. The loops and heart-stopping descents were equally alarming. I pictured him moving like that with a German or a Japanese plane shooting at him. How did he keep at it, time after time? How did any of these boys? What nerve they had.

When he flew quite low around the edge of the airfield and waved, he was waving to everyone, but I felt it was just to me. Then he flew up at a crazy, nearly vertical angle, and my heart was thumping. More fast rolls. The crowd was shouting and applauding now. This was more than you saw in war films or newsreels – this was astounding. Mummy was laughing excitedly, and Edith was gasping.

Then he landed, the little plane bobbing and bumping to a stop. As he jumped out, it was like a film, except for the people shouting and the children screaming.

I could barely see him behind the surging crowd of kids and, I was annoyed to see, girls running to him. One dared to plant a kiss. As he strode through the crowd, I realised with anger that she was the one from the ball, and she was clinging on tight. Other girls were crowding in, and one or two managed hugs, while the kids were yelling at him for autographs. It was all a bit much, really.

As the kids thinned out, he came closer. He was holding the girl by the arm as she leant on him, her arm around his waist. Would he just walk by? I moved my head and smiled.

He saw me. He smiled back, but not that full strength one I remembered. He dodged through the kids to face me. He was only feet away.

I said, "That was marvellous, Captain. Astounding. I was terrified when you did those loops – ridiculous of me, I know. It mustn't seem dangerous at all to you, especially when you're the only one in the sky. I had never noticed before how graceful planes are, and how precise, like instruments in geometry. And how they hop like birds when you land."

"Glad you enjoyed it, Miss Beauregard."

As my mother congratulated him, I glanced at the girl, still with her arm around him, though he had dropped his from her. She was striking and skilfully made up; she was more beautiful than I had noticed at the ball. She was almost glaring at me. Peter made no introductions.

When Mummy finished her speech of praise, I said, "We mustn't keep you. The governor and officers will want to thank you."

The girl was looking me up and down like a cashier. I met Peter's anxious, warm gaze and then turned away. As he left, I felt his disappointment and the girl's relief.

On the drive home, Mummy laughed, "He'll be fighting off a bevy of girls like that one."

I took off my hat and tossed my head. I couldn't wait to reach our cool veranda and have an iced lemonade. I stared angrily at my shoes. There was a deep scratch on one. I should never have worn them. I'd never get another Italian pair till this dratted war was over.

12. Putting on a Show

Peter:

Melbourne, Sydney, Queensland, New Guinea, March 1942

Doing the flying demo was fine. Inviting Iris wasn't. But I owed it to her. And she would have turned up anyway. She was as excited as I'd ever seen her and went on and on about what she would wear.

The day was warm but not windy, with barely a cloud. Perfect for the audience. Fun for me. Good to be flying again.

Walking out to the plane, I felt completely relaxed, nothing like at RAF scrambles when I was tense as wire, ready to scan the sky for the likeliest kills, every instant poised to shoot, always on the look-out for the one sneaking up behind.

I sat in the cockpit and looked around. Piece of cake. I taxied, took off and roared over the crowd.

My body tensed as the Gs kicked in, and then I felt my lungs fill and my mind clear. The plane behaved like a perfectly-trained horse. I did all the tricks twice. When I climbed out, a crowd ran out to meet me, most of them girls tottering in high heels. Iris outran the pack and reached me twenty yards from the fence. She put her arms around me and kissed me right on the mouth, the last thing I wanted just then.

The kids from the orphanage broke out of their lines, yelling and rushing at me. They were like a jumble of pups. Close behind them came hordes of boys in British-style school uniforms. I grinned at their excited faces. Flying for this crowd wasn't just entertainment or a way of getting them to put their hands in their pockets. I was inspiring kids to sign up and fight if the war stretched out long enough, and that seemed likely. The enthusiasm they were feeling would kill lots of them.

I signed my name for kid after kid in school blazers and tried to smile at their shining eyes. How did their parents stand it? They paid for the war with their taxes, and then with their kids. Proud to make the sacrifice – full of hope. The whole set up made me shudder. Yet what choice did any of us have? We couldn't just roll over and take it.

You didn't have a second to think about flyers dying while you were in the air, you were so intent on surviving and getting hits. Only when you saw a comrade go down, or you heard one screaming as he burnt did you give your losses a thought. After you touched down, and turned off the tense watchfulness of combat, you had to take in who hadn't returned. As your tours mounted up, so did the numbers of faces of the lost ones, getting fainter in your mind.

I'd been in London when the bombs set things alight, with the air raid sirens sounding at night. Next morning you saw whole streets burnt out.

I walked off the field with Iris hanging on tight. When I got to the fence, there were the Miss Beauregards, probably writing me off as a fast Yank who bought the tart on his arm. I felt a heel for being ashamed of Iris, but I dropped my arm from her straight away, though she kept her grip on me.

Thank the Lord, my smile seemed to melt Miss B. I grinned like a half-wit and flushed like a kid at a party when her mother and sister praised me, too. When I turned back to Faye after thanking her sister, I saw she had got Iris's number and wasn't happy. Neither was Iris. They eyed each other like cats, still and stiff. Iris's fingers pressed into my waist. It hadn't bothered me before how much face paint she wore. To tell the truth, I didn't often see her in full sunlight. She looked beautiful like always, yet out of place, like she'd strayed off a movie set. Funny thing was, we actually were on a movie set because Movietone had been filming my flying for a newsreel and for other fund-raising events. They would have had the cameras still rolling when I landed and jumped out. Maybe Iris would be on screen for a moment and would look normal, not overly made-up. Though I appreciated women dolled up, I loved how Faye's lashes and brows weren't coated in paint. I saw she had lipstick on, but it wasn't dark and thick like Iris's. She went into her duchess act, so I propelled Iris on fast. As we left, I saw Iris checking everything Faye had on, right down to the fancy shoes. I couldn't blame her.

Iris was rattled by Faye, but she didn't say a word about her. She invited me home for what they called tea, their evening meal.

When the speeches were over, we drove to Iris's side of town where the streets were narrow and full of potholes. Some houses had broken windows and trash in the front yard, and others were painted or washed down with their brass-plated doorsteps polished shiny. Almost all of them were small and poky, and there were few driveways, and no cars outside. I hadn't passed one on the road, either.

Her house was a narrow wooden place painted to within an inch of its life. There was a low white wooden fence and a pocket-handkerchief garden bursting with flowers. She led me down the shared driveway to the back door. We entered through a lean-to made of flimsy stuff and then went up a step into a room where a crowd stood drinking and talking, with swing music booming out of a gramophone.

An old guy with a weather-beaten face loomed up, a bottle of beer and glasses in his hands. "Welcome, Captain. Would you like a beer, mate?"

Another old guy came up with lemonade and half-filled Iris's glass without asking.

She rolled her eyes at me. "My uncles think I still drink

shandies."

"Well, so you should," said the old guy, with a fond grin.

Iris introduced me around till I lost count of aunts and uncles, let alone cousins, plus spouses or sweethearts. Kids of all ages ran about. Once or twice, a toddler grabbed my legs, steadying himself or taking a rest. The noise grew and the room got hotter, and someone turned up the music.

Iris pulled me towards the kitchen.

"Mum, stop for a sec and meet Peter."

A plump woman with a soft, lined face looked up with a smile. "Peter, I've been looking forward to meeting you. My word, you're even more handsome in real life. I saw you on the newsreel with General Maddox. It's nice of you to come to our little party. Make yourself at home." She bent to the wood fire stove and pulled out a tray of pies and then one of baked potatoes. "Have another drink and try one of my pies."

I helped her carry laden plates into the room across the hall where a large table was already stacked with sandwiches, little sausages and high cakes.

"You've gotta try Mum's sponge cakes later, too," Iris said.

"Sure. That one with strawberries looks swell."

"Yeah, and the passionfruit one's a beauty."

Her mother said, "Have you seen our girl dance, Pete? Isn't she good?"

After the hot food ran out, someone moved the kids to the sidelines and started to dance in the wide hall between the kitchen and food room. I took Iris's hand, and we started to fox-trot. Folks moved to give us space.

Iris's eyes sparkled. "Want to give a bit of a show?"

I swung her out, and we strutted and tapped, me faking it and her stepping perfectly. I did some lifts, and the women went "ooh", and the guys whistled. Kids were poking their heads between the adults' legs to get a view.

After a couple of songs, Iris shouted, "All right, show's over. Get on the floor, lazybones!"

The floor got crowded, and we danced closer. Iris put her cheek on mine.

Later, someone put on a Sinatra slow one, and we took a break for drinks. In the tiny bathroom next door, Mr Kelly took bottles of beer out of a small metal bath full of ice. I half shuddered, imagining Iris's smooth skin in there, but then I saw there was a porcelain bath, too, next to the wall. Mr Kelly offered us more beer and Iris tipped the bottle up to get herself a full glass.

I said to him, "Iris tells me your sons are in New Guinea. That's where I'm bound. How are your sons finding it?"

"Bloody hot, jungle too thick to walk through, but Jackie and Ted are tough lads. They don't mind. They're keen as mustard to get close to the Japs."

"That's great, sir."

"None of that sir stuff with me, son. Jack or Pa is what I'm called in me own house."

I offered him a cigarette, which he took with a smile. "Thanks, Captain. Quality."

"Call me Pete," I told him.

He asked me if I had been to Iris's show. "You should have seen her in *Forty-Second Street*. She brought the house down. They'll revive it soon, don't you think, love?" He beamed at his daughter and then turned back to me, "Dancing like Shirley Temple from the time she could move, and now like Ginger Rogers, eh?"

"She's wonderful," I grinned. "Best partner I ever had."

Iris flushed.

"We knew she'd be on the stage, make a bob or two. And behave herself in that fast show crowd." He glanced at me, and I felt a bit rattled till he grinned at her and added, "But you can have a bit of fun too, love, eh? You're a smart girl; you can look after yourself." He turned back to me. "You know she's working at the munitions factory, too? Had a promotion already."

"You must be proud of her, Jack."

Her mother popped up beside us, her hands full of dirty plates for the washing up. "Yeah, we laugh about which job is doing more for the war effort. The Tiv cheers up you servicemen, doesn't it?"

"Sure does, Mrs Kelly."

We moved to a room up the narrow passageway and found some soft chairs. Iris pushed me into one and draped herself over the arm, leaning on my shoulder. I put my arm around her. She looked as graceful and pretty as a movie star. I passed around my cigarettes and started on another pack. Iris and most of the gals lit up, too.

An older lady served us cake, and I made a fuss over the sponges and the stewed peaches and cream. I didn't have to pretend; they were as delicious as the Windsor's. I would have said so, but I wasn't sure this crowd went there too often.

I offered more cigarettes. Whiskey and sherry were passed around. Guys asked about my flying and the progress of the war. They were careful not to go near losses and deaths of my colleagues, but they were keen to hear about the Spitfire. Women oohed and aahed and asked about London. The way they talked of it was strange and nostalgic; it sounded as though none of them had been there, but they knew the landmarks well from older relatives or movies or songs. Kind of like the way Momma Johnson and other folks in the South talked of New York. They knew they'd never get there, but they sure enjoyed hearing about it from Buzz and me, the one time we managed to go back to Momma's.

I breathed easy and stretched out my legs like everyone else. They treated me like I was one rung below Churchill. They topped up my glass and listened to my every word with shining eyes.

Iris was looking at me like she owned me, like she was saying, *her* family wouldn't give you the time of day. Damn right.

Late in the night, we sang songs like the ones I had heard folks sing in England, 'A Nightingale Sang in Berkeley Square', 'Roses of Picardy' and 'It's a Long Way to Tipperary', together with 'When Irish Eyes Are Smiling' and a few Irish ones I knew from New York. A couple of guys with Irish tenor voices got up and sang 'Danny Boy' and 'I'll Take You Home Again, Kathleen'. Before we got too sad, a guy stood up and did a funny monologue in a Northern English accent, and even I was rolling about at the words, and at his face too.

When folks started drifting off home, Iris saw me out. On the way, her parents shook my hand and invited me back soon.

Her mother gave me a hug. "Pete, call me Ma. Come and see us again real soon. Come on a Sunday and have roast lamb with us."

As we walked out the back way, I saw a large room off the veranda, where the kids were squashed into a few beds. It made me think of Buzz and Luella and me in Louisiana. Some guys went in and picked up their kids to carry home.

Most folks had walked or come by bus. There were precious few cars parked out front. I offered lifts and got a carful.

When I farewelled Iris, we talked about going dancing at the Palais de Danse at St Kilda Beach.

I was desperate for a chance to see Faye but it would have to wait because, the next day, I was flying north.

Sydney, Queensland, New Guinea

Sydney was my first stop. It was noisier and pokier than Melbourne. The harbor was huge and beautiful, but much of downtown was as dirty, run down and crowded as parts of New York. There were grand houses, but not the overall sense of big money and a secure, exclusive upper class that hit you in the face in Melbourne. Sydney folk were harder to place on the pecking order, and many of them seemed tougher. So did some of the girls, the ones that were mighty keen to meet Yanks.

Right close to downtown Sydney, there was a distinct low-life area, around King's Cross, where crime and vice were visible, much more than in Melbourne's St Kilda, which still had some old-world European charm and the veneer of a fun fair. Our air force was training in Bankstown, a poorer suburb out of the city. The guys were having a good time, mostly via the officers' clubs, where respectable Sydney girls welcomed them. I spent a night or two at these clubs. Plenty of good-looking girls flounced in, none of them a patch on Faye. Or Iris, for that matter.

I flew on to Charters Towers in Queensland where we were setting up a training camp. I liked the old buildings, with pubs everywhere you looked, but the place was hot as hell and stuck in the middle of nowhere. A train track ran between Brisbane and Townsville. I didn't envy the troops who would take the long, hot trip through hundreds of miles of land that looked all the same – unless you were walking through it, I guessed.

I didn't stay more than a night at the Towers because I was bound for New Guinea. What a place. Despite what I'd heard, I wasn't prepared for how wild it was, like something out of a boy's storybook about jungles. Miles and miles of thick green hills where no white man had ever gone. The Aussie survey guys said the vegetation was so thick it was hard to hack a path through. The inclines were so steep that supplying was a major job. Clearing for airstrips took more men and time than anywhere else.

The Japs had just invaded and had the only other decent airstrip, on the north of the island. When I looked at the maps and then flew over our area, the Japs felt mighty close to Australia – to Charters Towers anyway. Thank the Lord, not so close to Melbourne.

I couldn't say I liked the look of where I'd be fighting, or living. Apart from the main white settlement at Port Moresby, run by the Aussies, the place looked straight out of *King Kong*. The few natives we saw looked like a time machine had zoomed them out of some ancient era. They were amiable, apparently, but so wild and unreadable that I found them kind of creepy. I was the last person to dislike black skin, after my years with Momma and Buzz but, for the first time, I had an inkling of how the slaves had mystified and scared white folks back in the South.

13. Shady Grove, My Sweet Love

Peter:

Melbourne, March 1942

When I got back to Melbourne, a week later, I didn't go see Iris. She wasn't the one I kept thinking of every night. I felt like a heel to be dropping her, but I'd be a bigger one if I kept stringing her along. I went to the Windsor the first afternoon and just hung around my billet that night.

The next day I wandered over to St Anthony's to take some fruit and candy to the kids. The other time I had turned up there, I'd asked Mother Agatha if she needed anything done or wood chopped. This time I brought along some tools from my billet to mend a fence. After I finished, the kids taught me more about cricket.

*

That weekend, General Maddox and his family were to visit Major General Beauregard and his wife, Lady Lillian, at their country house for afternoon tea, and Maddox's Press Officer let me know that I was wanted there, along with the Movietone crew. The other two newsreels had shown me practically at Maddox's elbow and the commentary made me squirm. This time, I was more than willing to play along because I figured there was a good chance of seeing Faye.

The party was at Mount Macedon, a posh hillside region a little out of Melbourne, with lush private gardens every way you looked. I drove up with the press guys and told myself to be like an English gent around Faye's folks, to behave like Hube as much as I could.

For as long as I could remember, when I was bored and couldn't leave, I used to sing in my head. The glimpses of these gardens brought back an old country tune I learned as a kid on the Murrays' farm:

> Peaches in the summertime
> Apples in the fall
> If I can't have the gal I love
> Won't have no gal at all
> Shady grove, my true love
> Shady grove, my darlin'…

When I walked into the garden of tall, bending ferns, there she was, sitting by Lady Lillian and her mother in a big cane chair. She sent me a nervous but warm smile. She looked fresh and graceful, like Ingrid Bergman, in a pale dress and a wide-brimmed white hat that dipped over her forehead. The garden was shady with heavy overhanging trees, soft ferns and low plants with huge flowers. The trees were greener and thicker than gums, yet there was something Australian about the ferns and some of the flowers. And beyond the shade, you could always see that deep blue sky and piercing bright light.

Apart from short greetings, I couldn't get near Faye for some time because the press guys were lining up angles and using me for focus and all. Then Maddox and his wife and their little boy were lined up, often with me or General Beauregard.

With more friendliness than I expected, General B chatted about New Guinea, which he seemed to know better than other Aussies I'd met. Sir Henry joined us. He joked about when the press officers had jumped with fright to see a snake near their car. The general assured me only the brown ones were poisonous. I knew that Mrs Maddox had made enquiries and was careful lest her son should get bitten; fair enough, I thought. Sir Henry boasted about the many snakes he and the general had killed on their property, even as kids. I listened politely. What would he say if he knew I had a knife in my boot? I always carried one, force of habit since I was a kid. I had needed a knife and a gun on streets where the threats were human.

When he asked if I rode horses, I almost laughed out loud. I could show you old guys a thing or two, I thought. He talked about horses at his country station and his time in the cavalry and then asked where I did my riding. I spoke of my seasons on the ranch in Texas, even though my horse-breaking job sounded pretty low-class compared to his times on thoroughbreds. But I was glad I'd told him. He had some idea of what it took to break wild ones because his eyes showed a new respect for me. General B looked pleased and left us.

It didn't surprise me that Sir Henry then interrogated me for a good half-hour. He asked about London, the damage, the restrictions, and the black-outs. Then he moved onto me. "Your mother and father must be very proud of you."

I couldn't pretend; or talk about Momma, who sure was proud of me. I told him the truth: my father died in the first war, and my mother when I was small.

"How old were you?" His eyes were sympathetic and concerned. Was he sorry for me or worried that I could hardly be whole? "Who took you in when your mother died?"

It riled me that guys like him thought they had a right to know everything about guys like me. I didn't mention the boys' home. I just told him about the Murrays, who adopted me after those first months at the home that had seemed like years. As I expected, he liked the sound of church-going farmers. When he asked about my schooling, I didn't say a word about my first school at the home. Those stories would have made his eyes pop but would also put me at the bottom of the heap, out of line for his daughter. I mentioned my next school that I had left too soon, the one when I lived with the Murrays, but I couldn't bring myself to talk about the lady teacher there, the only good, kind teacher I ever had. He pressed on – where had I attended college? Fat chance I ever had of getting into college, I almost said; instead, I told him how I had graduated from the Empire Air Training Scheme in Canada, the only pilot school open to nobodies like me.

It made me edgy talking to him. I was too thin-skinned, I know. It had been a while since someone had shown such curiosity about my past, but his air of a guy who could see through anyone irritated the hell out of me. Who had he ever had to stand up to? Guys in politics, I guessed, but they just fought about ideas and money, not for their goddamn lives. And who would be good enough for him? Such a privileged, powerful, protected man would find my past despicable. The ignorance of men in authority staggered me. Most of them knew nothing about the lives of the poor and unprotected. If they had a clue, they didn't care; they blamed folks who had no choice.

I looked over at Faye, so secure and happy. Would she go against her father for me? Some girls were eager for a showdown with their folks, but she looked mighty comfortable with hers. Once again, she and Edward were talking nineteen to the dozen. He had influence with her. Obviously, he got around more than his oh-so-important brothers. Right now, he was charmed by the Pirate Pete war stories, but who knew what he'd think of me later. He was the smart one you would always want on your side.

Faye came over and joined her father and me. She led the talk around to what parts of the country I should try to visit. I got a glimpse of their family holidays, which sounded swell.

They hadn't been to Darwin; I had hoped they could describe it to me. I didn't mention the Jap air raid and the losses of Aussie planes and people, and some Yanks. The news reports had understated the damage and fatalities almost ludicrously. But with censorship and the distances involved, I guessed no-one would be any the wiser in Melbourne. The true story would have been disastrous for morale, so early in the piece, when folks were already well aware of how easily the Japs could sweep down by air to attack the top of Australia, or any part of it. It had stunned me to learn how small our defences were, how huge the coastline was, how vast the lands were in the north and west, and how sparsely populated they were by whites or blacks.

The local papers had daily headlines about a possible Jap invasion. Prime Minister Curtin spoke as if it could happen any time, and you couldn't blame him, especially after the collapse of the British in Singapore. I heard around Maddox's office that when Curtin had insisted on the return of some Aussie troops from Europe, he had faced opposition from Churchill. Curtin made it plain in his punchy speeches how much he wanted help from the US and how glad he was that Maddox had come to Australia to lead the war effort. I could only guess what Australians felt like, waiting to see if any Japs appeared, feeling more nervous after the bombs in Darwin, wondering if Sydney was next or even Melbourne. Downtown in Melbourne, I sometimes caught the feeling "it couldn't happen here," but at night, folks blacked out their windows, and I heard very few complaints about the limited street lighting, the darkened trains and trams, and the return of horse-drawn cabs to supplement taxis and to save petrol. Sometimes, I caught a whiff of panic in the movie theatres during the newsreels. No wonder they were treating Maddox like a messiah.

Faye's sister, Edith, and her cousin, Nigel, joined us. I barely remembered Nigel from the ball, where he had hardly got a word in. He was the business type and struck me as clever that way. Unlike most Australians I met, he seemed aware of how the US was supplanting England as the world's commercial leader. Surprisingly, he didn't imply it was a bad thing, or a reason to dislike me.

His mother, Mrs Minsky, Faye's Aunt Isobel, came over to meet me. I almost fell in love with her, too. She had eyes so like Faye's. In manner, she was the opposite of her brother, Sir Henry. Edward wandered over to join us, and Sir Henry went to sit with his wife and the Maddoxs. Nigel and Edith joined the General and Lady Lillian and some officers. Then Isobel asked me about jazz in New York, and soon we were deep in one of the best conversations I'd had in Melbourne. It turned out that Isobel and her late husband had spent a lot of time in New York, going to places in Harlem as well as Broadway. So had Edward, who broadened the talk to the South as well: Savannah, Charleston, and New Orleans. I didn't want to talk about New Orleans; I hadn't had much chance to enjoy the music there.

Edward said, "I'll never forget seeing Billie Holiday."

I looked at him in surprise. "Me neither."

He smiled.

Faye confessed she hadn't gotten used to Billie's raspy, breathy style.

I told her to get hold of Billie's 'Night and Day' and said I thought she'd love it. "Fred Astaire sings it like a dance tune, all dramatic and exciting. He's great when you're dancing. But Billie sings it like the blues."

"Exactly," said Edward. "She shows us the loneliness in the song. And the despair."

"She's the goddess of hopeless love." I had thought that for years but had never said it.

He nodded and his eyes went dark.

I said, "Do you like her singing 'Careless Love'?"

He smiled. "Ah yes. I thought it was a trite country ditty before I heard her – and the great Bessie Smith, of course."

"You know how Bessie sings it, Faye?" I asked.

"No, I've heard an American Country singer. I don't recall his name."

"It's not a country song… well, not a white song," I said. "It's blues."

"Certainly is," Edward said.

"It's more a woman's song," I said. "Bessie sure makes you think so." I heard it again in my head, and recited it softly:

> If I was a tiny bird,
> I would fly from tree to tree.
> I'd build my nest so high up in the air
> That the bad boys couldn't worry me.

The words gave me a jumpy, blue feeling; they took me back to music that used to seep out of the queer bar in Bourbon Street.

Edward's smile turned sad and sardonic. I wondered what bad boys he was recalling.

I looked at Faye. "But now, Billie, she calls it 'Loveless Love.' She sings different words:

> If I had some strong wings,
> Like an aeroplane,
> I would fly away forever,
> Never to come again."

The words that had always felt like they were made for me had an awkward ring about them when I said them to Faye.

The colour came to her cheeks. "I'd love to hear her sing that, Captain."

When was she going to call me Peter? I had barely noticed myself slipping into using her first name – how could I talk the blues to her and call her Miss Beauregard? We would sound like some sad old story from the South.

Edward grinned. "Faye, I'll lend you some Billie Holiday recordings on the condition that you won't play them to your parents. Billie wouldn't be to their taste, and I wouldn't want Henry to insult her."

I laughed, and then stopped because, although Isobel smiled and rolled her eyes at Edward, Faye didn't seem to share the joke.

Edward said, "I noticed Henry quizzing you, Peter. His inquisitions are the terror of the State."

He gave a droll look, and I laughed. Faye looked a little alarmed.

"He wants to understand you better, Captain," she said quickly.

"I'm not sure I passed muster." I said it like a joke, but I was eager to hear their reactions. Talking in Billie's language a minute ago made it hard to go back to my usual lies. "He asked who I had as stand-ins for my parents. Kinda tough to answer. I didn't have folks sometimes."

"Of course," Edward said, with that smile of his that made you feel completely understood and okay. "That situation might not occur to Henry. It's Moira and other good ladies who worry about orphans. Did you live in an orphanage, Peter?"

I swallowed. "Yeah, well, not for as long as heaps of kids, I guess."

"I'm glad. I expect that Henry would have been looking for an upright gentleman in your background, someone who taught you right from wrong, preferably a relative or a clergyman."

"I guess I mentioned someone like that." I tried not to sound irritated. And not to think of Father O'Malley, with his deathly, droning sermons and his hellhole of a room. What I did call to mind was the hullabaloo in Momma's church, the piano pumping and everyone dancing and the fat preacher singing. That made me smile. But I wouldn't mention a Black preacher to these people, or to anyone. I went on, "Mr Murray was the closest thing I had to a father. The Murrays adopted me when I was six going on seven."

"Well, that's lucky," said Edward, grinning. "Henry would approve. One of the few things he agrees with Moira's Catholics about is the Jesuit maxim that a child is formed by early influences, and the magical cut-off point, they claim, is seven.

So, you were lucky to be at the orphanage only for a short time."

I swallowed and stared at their sympathetic faces. No point lying to these three. And like I had with Hube, I wanted Faye to know. I pushed away the memory of the grey stone steps up to St Joe's front door, Father O'Malley looming so tall on the top step, with his sarcastic, satisfied smirk. "Well, Mrs Murray died, and he sold up the farm and moved on. I went back to St Joe's. Did a second stretch."

Faye leant in a little closer, with a look of concern.

"That was hard luck." Edward glanced at me. "I get the feeling the place was no fun – like something out of Dickens?"

I smiled. I wished I could have managed a laugh. Thanks to Hollywood and Hube's books, I had some idea of what he meant. "Yep. The real motto of the joint was beat 'em, scold 'em, and starve 'em. No idea what the Latin above the door said. I left before that lesson. Got out and found some kind folks."

I tried not to choke, thinking of the gang I had pushed my way into as soon as I could because anything was better than living on the streets of New Orleans, even filthy rooms, and undressed sad-looking gals lolling about, and gunfights, and Hogshead Harris tormenting me. But it was Momma I meant, of course, she was the only one who helped me later on. Goddamn it, I should have shut up. It made me all wound up talking of it again. I hoped to hell Edward would change the subject.

He must have heard the tension in my tone and said in his relaxed, warm way, "Yes, you found folks of your own. And you no doubt met heaps of people in England. We're not exactly like them here, of course. I wonder if you notice any differences?"

"I like that you all are less formal."

He smiled. "True, with a few exceptions."

I wondered if he meant the judge.

I wondered, too, not for the first time, how much Faye had discussed me with Edward. And what he said. His attitude seemed so approving. He didn't just think she might as well have a fling; he thought I was okay. It was mighty relaxing to be with him, especially because despite what I had said about Australians, the afternoon had felt formal to me, and I had felt pressured every second as they all scrutinised and dismissed me, except for Edward, Isobel, and Faye.

When I drove home with the press guys, the numbing heat of the city hit us. I missed the fresh, cool air of the hills.

14. A War Party

Peter:

Melbourne, March 1942

The next day, I had a meeting at HQ downtown. Driving beside the Yarra along looping, curving Alexandra Avenue, I eyed the large homes on the hills of Toorak. What did they cost? The Beauregards probably thought I was the next thing to a beggar. But money was one of my talents. My air force pay amounted to quite a stack now because I was good at spending almost nothing. I could make a packet in this little town. Air transport would be enormous after the war.

Faye had mentioned yesterday, with zero embarrassment or sympathy, that men on the dole had built this lovely avenue during the Depression. Poor devils must have looked up at the mansions and apartments on the hill. After the war, would any of them get up there?

With a small detour, I could drive past her house. I had seen a letter addressed to her mother at Maddox's Press Office. Her street was a just a left off the Avenue, so I took it. The house was an old, two-storey place of brick and stone, big but not grand, to my relief. It had a small circular drive. Big blue Jacaranda trees. Plenty of flowers. I drove on and turned back to St Kilda Road.

I hadn't a hope of visiting Faye, but I had received an invitation from her Aunt Isobel. She was on a committee to welcome Yanks. Melbourne had started setting up a few reception places for servicemen, some run by the churches. They didn't attract me, but they provided somewhere for younger guys to find a cup of tea and a kind of small-town atmosphere.

Isobel did more than give cups of tea. That Friday night she threw a party for servicemen – Yanks as well as Aussies.

Her house was an old, redbrick, two-storey, turreted place with huge windows, surrounded by wonderful tall trees and masses of flowers, and right by the Yarra. You could get to it by boat, though Melburnians rarely did that anymore. I grabbed a Forces car and drove by myself. I had the dumb hope that I might end up driving Faye home; unlikely, but I would hate to miss the chance. I drove up the swirling drive to park alongside the Bentleys and Chevrolets.

Isobel welcomed me warmly. I felt jumpy scanning the crowd for Faye. Then she saw me, and we walked towards each other. Seeing her excitement made me feel so fine I lost my jitters. She twirled around the relatives, introducing me as if I was someone they should know. I couldn't wipe the grin off my face.

"Come and we'll find Nigel," she said. "He's at the pool." Her dimple played around her mouth. "Bring your swimming things with you."

I was dying to dive in. It was one of those warm, dry Melbourne nights where the air was still and oven-hot. I couldn't wait to throw off my clothes and plunge into chilly water.

My buckles and buttons took longer to dispose of than her summer dress, so she was already at the pool when I emerged from the men's bathroom. She was in a one-piece, and her legs were as well-shaped as in my imagination. I saw her eyeing me as I walked up to her and Nigel. She flushed as I reached them. She surveyed me as though I was a surprise out of uniform; did she expect I'd be weedy or flabby? I always had to remind myself that some girls weren't as prone to mentally undressing folks as guys were. But with Faye's eyes on me, I felt on top of the world.

We joined the group of Aussies and Yanks in the pool. Diving in was heaven, and I thanked Buzz for all those times in the water in Louisiana, where I learned to take care of myself and move fast. Faye was a good swimmer and a capable diver too; I forced myself not to stare at her supple little figure above and under the water.

You couldn't stay in too long. Getting out into the hot air felt great. When my clothes were back on, I still felt fresh and cool.

Faye waited for me to walk up to the house. She led me off the paved path onto a short-cut under a huge drooping fig tree. We lost everyone else. I was gearing up to hold her hand when we came around a high shrub and found ourselves creeping up on Faye's mother and another lady sitting together on a bench-seat. Trying not to laugh, I looked at Faye, wondering if we should walk past, or go back and find a different way.

Faye stood still and rigid. She stared at me with a look of concern before I took in what the woman was saying.

"These Yanks are leading our girls astray with their chocolates and cigarettes and stockings."

Faye pulled a face.

I shrugged. Would this dame have refused chocolates if she'd been pretty enough to score some?

She ranted on. "Any of the Yanks here tonight could be the monster who's killing our girls."

My skin started to crawl. Two girls had been raped and killed downtown this fortnight. The newspaper headlines kept screeching, Brownout Strangler, Killer Yank, despite Maddox hitting the roof. The clues pointed to a GI.

Lady B said, "Oh, Nell, I don't think so."

Faye moved forward, so I followed her. The ladies looked up. Lady B had the decency to look embarrassed.

She didn't meet my eye. With a polite, impersonal smile, she introduced me to her sister-in-law, Mrs O'Brien, who Faye called Aunt Nell. Lady B gave me my due, mentioning the Battle of Britain and my position in Maddox's office. The women stood up, and all four of us walked towards the house.

From the veranda, Isobel was staring at us. She led us into another room to hear some music.

Faye said softly, "Not dance music, unfortunately. Isobel said the committee thought it might lead to a little too much mingling." She gave a quiet laugh. "I wish we could dance."

"Me, too." I grinned.

But I was glad not to be facing anyone, even her. We sat side by side. I could feel her warmth to me. It was the only thing keeping me in the room.

The music was too fancy for most of the American guys there, though it was familiar to me from occasions in England with Hube; I couldn't have told you who wrote it.

In the pause, Faye said softly, "I hope that wasn't boring for you, Peter? Do you like string quartets?"

"Yes, but not as much as opera."

She looked pleased and surprised. "Oh. Did you go to the opera in America?"

"I saw a couple in London. I want to see more. Well, maybe not Wagner, he's Hitler's favourite, but I want to see the Italian and French ones."

She smiled. "What have you seen so far?"

"*Carmen* and *Madame Butterfly*. At the end of *Butterfly*, I could hardly stand up, it was such a knockout."

Thank God I was with Hube; he waved his other friends away and sat with me till I calmed down.

When I apologised, he said, "Shut up, Pirate. You and I know more about last goodbyes than this whole fucking country."

Her eyes were bright, thrilled. "I love those operas too. They're so heart-rending and romantic."

I nodded. "I used to think the blues said everything about love, but opera cuts your heart open. You feel like you're flying and like life is a wonder."

She smiled. There was a new thread between us.

A pianist and female singer arrived, and the tempo relaxed into some American show tunes.

When we went to the front room for supper, Faye's sister and other girls clustered around her. Lady B appeared and shepherded me onto the veranda. She knew how to corral a guy. Straightway, I was on my guard.

"Captain, I wanted to ask you about one of the trees. It's a magnolia, and they are the trees of your homeland, aren't they? It's just along here." She took my arm and led me across to the edge of the garden. It was so like the sort of thing Hube's mother did that my prickles went up. I waited for the insult.

"Captain, you are going to meet a lot of our young ladies here. All of Melbourne is desperate to meet you."

I tried to smile and hoped my face didn't show what I thought of her lie.

"You have probably heard that Faye is engaged to be married." She paused and forced me to nod. "I wanted to make sure that you understand her position. She is not able to go out with young men. She is such a dear, friendly girl. I don't want you to misunderstand her situation."

"I understand, Lady Beauregard. I know I can only be her friend."

"Thank you so much, Captain, I felt sure that I could count on you. Melbourne is full of social gossips, and the press takes friendly meetings out of context. I am sure you would be horrified if Faye's reputation were harmed, or if she were upset by talk. One must be so careful."

"Sure. I don't want to cause problems."

"Of course, you don't. And I probably didn't need to give this word of warning. Please don't feel offended, Captain. I know that you are adept at handling the press, and no doubt you have heard many mothers fussing about their daughters' reputations. Perhaps you have a young lady back home?"

I almost laughed. "No. I'm not looking to settle down – anyway, not till the war is over."

Her eyes were sympathetic, but did she really hope I wouldn't make it? My death could be her answer.

She went on about the damned tree, and I half-listened as we went back inside the house. Faye appeared and walked me over to Nigel and some others.

On the veranda, Faye's Aunt Nell was with a group of older folks. There was a shaking of heads going on. She probably thought we couldn't hear, or did she?

"Even that Stephens bloke could be the killer. How do we know? His manners are rough and ready even for a Yank. He's not like the usual officer, is he? He's no gentleman. I bet he's looking for a rich wife while he's here."

Nigel looked away, embarrassed. Behind him, Faye stepped quickly to the open French window and glared at her aunt.

"Excuse me, Aunt Nell, you seem to be under a false impression. Captain Stephens is our family's guest tonight, and a friend."

Lady B moved forward, her face alarmed.

My voice rang out. "Don't worry about me. I'm just here to die for your country."

That shut them up. I rushed past, grabbed my cap and left. I marched down the path and didn't look back. Then I felt Faye beside me.

I heard Edward saying, "He's our guest, Nell. Imagine how he feels now."

Nell's sharp tone carried. "You always like strangers, Eddie, don't you?"

I shuddered.

Isobel hurried after us, calling, "Captain, pay it no mind."

"Thanks, ma'am." I swung around. "Thanks for the party."

"It was a privilege to host you, Captain. I'll see you again."

She smiled and turned back.

Faye and I walked to my car.

She said, "I would leave with you, if it wouldn't make things worse. I don't care what people say about me, but I don't want to cause more talk about you."

I felt a rush of heat. She leaned against my car. I needed to get the hell outa there, but there'd never be a better time to get close to her.

"Your mom was sore about what you said."

She laughed. "I don't care."

"Thanks for speaking up for me. I'm sorry Eddie got his head chopped off."

"Nell was so rude."

Again, I wondered how much Faye understood about him. And if Lady B or Isobel knew. I figured they did, Isobel anyway.

Despite the look on Faye's face, I felt cold with fear; not about the gold digger charge, she wouldn't buy that, but because she might see soon enough that the other criticisms from her aunt were true.

Faye trusted me, so much more than I deserved. She wanted to see more of me. The thought sent panic charging through me, and the bluest feeling, except when we locked glances.

I looked away into the shadow of the dark trees. I was tense as wire. I wanted to hold her, but anyone peering from the front windows, let alone the veranda, would see us. We couldn't disappear into the garden.

"Can I see you again?" I had planned to lead up to it, but now I asked point blank.

She smiled, like we were about to kiss.

"Tomorrow night? Somewhere your lot won't be watching?" I sounded like a rude jerk, but I couldn't calm down and control my words, and I knew that for once it didn't matter.

"St Kilda Town Hall," she said. "It's a public dance with a good band. I'll meet you in the foyer at eight."

I took her hand for a moment. She gave me her million-dollar smile and turned back to the house.

15. Shame

Peter:

Melbourne, March 1942

I jumped into my car and roared round Alexandra Avenue like it was a racetrack. In the brown-out, my car lights on low beam were the brightest spots. Then, back at my billet, all my energy vanished. The blues slouched back. Like the arrogant, tough old foe that you hoped you had killed. My muscles stiffened; my nerves jangled. I trudged upstairs and grabbed my mouth organ. The place was deserted, a lone guy manning the phone and door. I crept around the side veranda and slunk onto the tiled floor. With my back against the cold stone wall, I wailed every freight train and blues song I knew.

Why hadn't I joined the navy? I could have spent my leave in Hawaii, where Buzz was stationed, and we would have met up, however tricky it was. It was so long since I'd seen him.

My anger was nearly played out, like my repertoire. A sadness shrouded me, as familiar as my shadow. The night had cooled, but sweat was running down my chest and back. I'd never be free of people thinking I was scum.

What the hell! What a sucker! Like I learned God knows when, I made myself breathe slow and even, till I could be somewhere else, and now I was up in the air, on the way back from shooting everything that got in my way. My body went loose; my skin cooled. The only crazy sap alive who remembered missions to make himself feel better. Another thing I could never tell a soul. Buzz would be revolted; maybe even Hube would despise me. What a nerve I had, thinking that Faye could be my girl till her real guy came back. Just as well the Nips would succeed where the Nazis had failed. My don't-care-if-I-die lucky charm had to run out soon.

The aunt with the harsh voice had said it, but they all thought it. A nobody. A gold digger. Trash.

I pushed my clenched fist into my thigh. I was too angry to laugh, but what a joke: I could show them how to make money out of air.

They had never been alone in the world without a cent.

Could they even see how much their money had given them? Or what the lack of money stripped from guys like me?

Faye must have thought I was weak, the way I yelled and ran away. How could she understand what it felt like to be talked about like that? Iris would have – though none of her family would have insulted me. They got a kick out of having a famous Ace at their parties.

I went up to bed, stretched out, and covered my face. Thank Christ I had kept my mouth shut. Almost. I learned a long time ago the less you said, the better.

But the way she looked at me – a shiver shot up my spine. She cared for me. A girl like that. I basked in the warmth for I don't know how many minutes, but it was no surprise when the spell wore off. She had fallen for me, and I wanted her, but how could it work? Could I swing it? Could I be that guy she thought she was seeing? I listed my shortcomings and tried to tell myself I could fix them. One minute, I was grinning and sure of it, but next minute I knew that loving her now would leave me in a hell of blues in the end.

What the heck was I doing? I had a bunch of reasons for sticking to good-time gals and never getting involved with serious types. Why was I chasing this one? It made no sense. I wished I could have talked to Buzz. No, to Hube. He knew how it felt when love and fear, longing and hate, were all mixed up inside you.

Later, when the guys rolled in, I still couldn't sleep. I silently counted the horses I broke in, years ago. I pictured the head trainer, Mac, standing against the rails of the roping yard, a smile creasing his lined face, his eyes gentle as he gave me some of the best advice I ever heard. "Kid, the difference between a happy guy and a miserable one is thinkin' about the good times."

I promised to keep that in mind, and I did. Often, it was as hard as hell. I tried to focus on how great it was that Faye liked me, but how long would she think I was what she was looking for? How long could I be that guy? How long till the Nips would solve it for me?

*

In the morning, I went running early in the park near my billet. A little bird, fast, black and cheeky, sashayed around, twitching its tail and darting out of my path. Larger grey-pink birds, fat and slow, waddled near me. White cockatoos screeched and zoomed about, far above. Now and then, bright, coloured parrots, blue-green with flashes of yellow or red, flitted past me in pairs.

After breakfast, I read the newspapers with Chris.

"How was the big party?" He grinned.

I shrugged. "I'm not one of them, never will be."

Chris nodded sympathetically. He was dating one of Iris's friends, whose family thought he was tops. "Well," he said, "ten to one they'll learn to like you."

"Her aunt accused me of being a fortune hunter."

"So much for the famous good manners of Melburnians."

"The aunt who made the crack didn't seem as classy as the others." I shot him a glance.

"An in-law?"

"Yep."

"Maybe she knows about fortune hunting."

109

"She's not a Beauregard. She married into the other side, Lady Moira's. But maybe you're right. Turns out they aren't so poor, a dairy farm or two and grocers' shops." I managed a smile.

I took out a cigarette and strolled over to watch the chess champs. Hube had started teaching me, but I was still a beginner. The players soothed me with their confident, calm determination to win.

Tonight, I would dance with her.

16. No Promises

Peter:

Melbourne, March 1942

> Heaven, I'm in heaven,
> And my heart beats so that I can hardly speak
> And I seem to find the happiness I seek
> When we're out together dancing
> Cheek to cheek.

I didn't need to wonder if she was feeling the same way – she was glowing.

The dancehall had a fast floor, high ceilings and fancy lights. The band was swell. She said she didn't think her friends would be there. I figured it was too far across town and too expensive for Iris, so we both felt like we were in our own new city. We cut up the floor, and I lifted her higher than I had dared at the Governor's Ball. I taught her some new dance moves, and she caught on fast.

She had arrived in her father's car, driven by the chauffeur, but had sent him back. When I asked if I could drive her home, she looked pleased. The gardens around the town hall were filling up with couples, but I figured she wouldn't go for that. We walked straight to my car. I felt like a movie star handing her in and closing the door.

Almost straightaway she said, "Tell me about yourself, Peter. I haven't heard much about your family and where you grew up."

I never wanted to talk about that, let alone then. I never talked about Mom or about Momma Johnson and Buzz and Luella, though I thought about them often enough – especially

Luella when she was little, how I used to hold her while she shifted her tiny feet forward like a doll and crowed with joy.

Faye looked at me as I drove on, mute.

Finally, I said, "I never knew any family except my mother."

"Did you father die when you were little?"

"I never knew him."

She stared.

"The Great War." I glanced at her soft eyes.

"I'm so sorry," she said. "That's very sad."

I choked back a bitter laugh. Wait till we got to my mother. But she was right. The real tragedy had been my father not coming back. If he had, my mom would have lived longer. And easier.

"You lost your mother when you were a young child, Dad told me. Was she ill for a long time?"

"No." I looked away. I hadn't talked about that time to many people. Not since Momma asked me, years ago. I shouldn't have been surprised at how much it still hurt.

Faye was staring at me. "Peter, I don't want to make you sad. Don't talk about her if you don't want to."

I glanced at her warm eyes. "It's okay. I have good memories. I'm lucky that way. Not like kids who are dumped, or who never felt their moms touch them, or who can't remember."

She asked what I remembered about my mother. I didn't mention the washing Mom took in, or the babies of various colours that I helped her look after. I said I often recalled walking with her, or sitting together on our back porch and in the little garden. I didn't say it was just a boarding house.

"Did her relatives look after you when she died?"

"They wouldn't speak to me." I saw again the white columns, the tall door, the sad voice of the black man in fancy clothes who avoided my eyes.

She looked disgusted and shocked. "How could anyone turn

away a child, especially one of their own blood?"

How did she think places like St Anthony's filled up?

"Guess I was a ragamuffin."

Wouldn't Faye recoil in horror from a child as dirty and poor as I was then? I could still feel how the stones of that long driveway had hurt through my worn shoes.

"The servants gave me some food."

"They had servants? They were well off?" She tensed with anger. "Oh, that makes it even worse."

"Lots of folks had coloured servants. But I'm pretty sure my mom never got a cent from her family, once she ran off with my dad."

She said, "That's dreadful. I forget how lucky I am to have parents like mine. All my family are such dears. Except Aunt Nell."

I smiled. She had relaxed. Her legs were crossed, and her hands were loose by her side instead of clasped demurely in her lap.

"Peter, were you taken to the home straight after your mother died?"

"Uh-huh."

"I'm sorry, especially since it was an awful place."

"There's always pain in those places," I said.

She gave me a quick look. Maybe it was news to her. She touched my arm, and I put my hand on hers and held it there. The warmth in her voice and the soft pressure of her hand drove the blues away. I breathed in deep, like I hadn't since we danced.

She said gently. "Were you badly treated in the orphanage? I thought that you were half joking about beatings when you first mentioned the place."

I took a breath. "Let's just say, the guy who ran it was nothing like Mother Agatha at St Anthony's."

I hadn't thought of it in ages: the narrow white room, Father O'Malley and me; the cane cutting my bare ass; the clattering as he threw the stick down; him ramming and ripping me near apart; my fingers pulling my trousers up over the pain; the black cross on the white wall.

My hand was gripping hers. She was looking at me with concern. My worst memories might be the key to catching her. But I couldn't do it. I couldn't tell her even if I wanted to.

I relaxed my hand.

She said quietly, "Did they beat you at school, too?"

"I didn't go to school much," I said, and then wished I hadn't been so frank.

"That's surprising. You must have educated yourself. You seem like someone who has read a bit, and thought about things."

I glanced at her. "Yeah? Guess I picked up some clues along the way. I would have liked to finish school, and college too, but there was no chance of that."

Her questions felt different from her father's. She wanted to get the picture because she seemed to care for me. I hoped like hell it wasn't just pity.

She said, "What were your adopted family like? Did they treat you well?"

I felt rattled. For a moment, I couldn't recall if I had mentioned Momma and Becky that day at Mount Macedon, but, of course, I hadn't, only the Murrays. "No complaints. Except for old man Murray dumping me back at the Home, but I understand that now; lots of kids had it hard then."

"You had it harder than most, I think, Peter. I'm starting to see that you can't help feeling angry. It makes me sad to think of how you must have felt when you were sent back to the orphanage."

I pushed away a close-up: the pitted stone steps of the Home that I stared down at, rather than up at Father O'Malley as his big hands took hold of me again. I forced myself to speak. "It wasn't Mr Murray's fault. He couldn't look after me once Mrs

Murray died. He worked hard but he couldn't keep his farm. Times were getting hard."

Her eyes were full of sympathy. "The Depression?"

"Yep. I guess you had bad times here, too."

"Oh yes." She checked herself. "Well, I didn't really myself. But I knew that people were nearly starving, just down the hill, across the river from us. Nearly every day, men used to come to the gate and ask for work. Mummy always gave them food, even if there was no work, and she insisted they were fed first before they did a tap. She said they looked weak enough to drop down dead. She gave them extra food to take home. I'll never forget their faces. So lined and worn. And embarrassed. I humiliated one of them by giving him money; of course, he gave it back. After that, I used to hide it in the food packet they took away."

I could see her, as a curly-headed kid. I smiled.

"Unfortunately, Mummy found out. One of the men thanked her when he came back again. At first, she thought it was Mrs Mac, our cook, so I had to own up."

"Where did you get the money?" I couldn't picture her snitching it from her mom, and still less from her dad's desk or pockets.

She looked surprised. "Oh, I used my birthday and Christmas money. My grandparents often gave me money at other times too. But Mummy was taken aback when she found out."

"Why should the down-and-outs get her kid's presents? I can see her side of it."

"But I had plenty of food and a lovely warm house, and my father had a job," she said, her eyes wide. "I was shocked when my parents disapproved. They didn't punish me, but they didn't let me give away any more money. My uncles had the opposite reaction. They shook my hand. Mo said, 'We're all mates in this world, we ought to look after each other,' and Eddie said, 'I like to see a girl who shares her wealth; most females just wear it'."

"Ha! Sounds like him. Why do you call the Major-General 'Mo'?"

She laughed. "When I was little, I couldn't say Maurice, so I called him Uncle Mo. He wanted me to keep calling him Mo because it's the name of his favourite comedian."

I laughed. The funny little guy in baggy trousers at the Tiv, the one the General had roared at. "Oh yeah, Mo McCackie. He's an original, isn't he?" I paused. "Have you seen him?"

"No." She didn't comment on her uncle's low-class taste, or mine. I could imagine how much her mom hated the Tiv. "I've heard him on the wireless. He's too old-fashioned for me, but I like the way he shouts, 'strike me lucky' when some ridiculous or difficult thing happens to him." She paused. "Did you go into the air force from the orphanage?"

I laughed for a second. Then it struck me that her father hadn't told her my career history. He wouldn't say anything that might encourage her interest in me. "I would have never got there from the boys' home. I kind of got myself there. One thing the war has done for mugs like me." I realised that other girls had never asked these kinds of questions.

She asked where I learned to fly, so I told her about barging into carnival shows, hanging around helping the grease monkeys, doing risky stunts on planes till I pushed my way into flying the dodgy crates myself, and then going to Canada to the Empire Training School and being selected to fly fighters. She smiled and nodded. Not many folks caught onto why guys like me were desperate to zoom up to the sky. I hadn't told many folks how I had wangled it, only Hube and a few other flyers. I liked telling that story: it brought back the excitement and fear of those days, and the hope I had. Then she asked me about the RAF and Hube, and, when I changed gears, she moved her hand.

"Ah, do you have to? Faye, there's so much I want to ask about you. Can we walk a while? Is there some place we can sit and talk?"

She flushed, and her breath caught. "Yes, if you drive up a little further, and take the road down to the Yarra River, we'll be quite close to my street. The gardens alongside the river should be quiet. There's a rotunda where we can sit."

My eyes were on her. It was hard to look back at the road. I laughed softly. "Faye, I sure would love to sit in a rotunda with you."

She gave a tinkling laugh and explained what it was, as if we might not have them in America.

I parked and we walked under great, draping trees on the soft grass above the glimmering river.

"It's still so warm," she said.

I loved the way her voice could go from crystal to velvet. I could listen to either tone all night but the velvet one near drove me crazy. I stroked her bare arm lightly.

She flushed. "You grew up in a hot climate, didn't you?"

"Yep, at first. Steamy in Louisiana, hot and dry in Texas. I love heat. Hate the cold. I froze half to death when I moved to New York. In Canada, it was colder, of course, but I had better clothes." Someone like her would never have given a thought to how much easier it was for poor folks where it was warm.

We walked inside the rotunda and sat on the wooden bench. She looked up at me. I stroked her face, and she touched my cheek, light and sweet. We kissed, gentle at first till it grew, like a song. She gazed at me, excited yet still, and it drove me near crazy but made me kind of calm too, like everything would always be okay between us.

"When did you know how you felt?" I heard myself ask. I never went in for that kind of talk. She turned me into someone else.

She smiled. "At the ball." She looked shy for a second. "The way you looked at me. And when we were dancing, when you said you were crazy about me." Her cheeks flushed red.

I kissed her face and the hollow above her breasts. I knew I'd never get enough of the feel and smell and sound of her. "You're the loveliest girl I ever met. You're different from everybody else – I never felt this way with anyone. I can't find the words."

She snuggled into me. "I think I'm falling in love with you, too, Peter. It's all new to me and quite astonishing."

It seemed like a movie. Maybe I was saying what most Yanks would say. I didn't give a thought to how crazy it was for me to talk like the average guy. She made me feel I was telling the truth.

She curled up on my lap, her face against mine, as a tram whirred and clattered down St Kilda Road.

"That's the last tram." She laughed softly.

"Do you have to go?"

"Not really."

"I wish we could stay like this forever," I said, surprising myself again. I hadn't seen anyone so happy since Buzz. I had forgotten how free and loose a happy person made you feel. I lived life all wound up, ready to spring; she made me stop watching and waiting to pounce. "Faye, you don't have a sad thought in your head, baby, or a mean one." She looked surprised, and I hugged her tighter. "You make me feel like life's ok, like it's always gonna be fine between us, you know?"

She held my face and kissed me. We stayed entwined and still. There were barely any sounds except our breathing and our heartbeats.

At last, I said, "Faye, should I take you home? I'm happy to sit here the whole night through, but your folks are gonna hate me."

She uncurled out of my lap and stretched, and we drove back to Anderson Street and walked up to her house. I held her against me as we walked in step.

At the house next to hers, I lifted her up and whispered, "Do

I go back to pretending I don't know you?"

Her face fell. "No, no. But it's awkward for me to hug you in front of anyone, for the present, anyway."

She hugged me hard as if to make up for it. I didn't dare give her engagement a thought.

I said, "Where can we go tomorrow night? The movies maybe?"

"I can't, but on Monday night let's meet at the Metro Theatre in Bourke Street just before eight. I'm unlikely to see someone I know there."

She walked up to her front door and gave me a look before she disappeared. I kept remembering her tinkling laugh as I ran down the hill to my car.

*

Monday night, we snuck into a back row after the lights had gone down, so any folks she knew wouldn't see her. Maddox, the top brass and I flashed up on the screen in the newsreel and her eyes shone. The feature was *Sergeant York* with Cooper. I was interested to catch it. I was more interested in my companion, but I figured she wouldn't be ready for anything, especially not in public. When the movie started, she whispered that I looked like Gary Cooper, and I laughed out loud. Some old folks turned around to shush us but then grinned at me, and I held her hand.

We strolled along the river back to her house. The movie had churned me up. Not the war scenes really, but the whole business about York being a hero, being shown around by generals and politicians like a prize bull and making money from folks who would never go near a war. Making money for them, too. Then settling down like it all never happened, like he was as gentle as a babe, like he was a normal guy still, and he *was* normal, he was a good guy with a family, a Bible, and a clean name. Out of the shadows, blues started itching. Why the hell had I been turned into a poster boy to advertise the war effort! – I wasn't a heroic, famous leader like Sergeant York. Was I doing much good for my fellow servicemen? I couldn't wait to get back into combat; thank God it would happen soon. But when the war was over, I wouldn't snap back and fit in like York. When did I ever fit in? Only when fighting – and killing.

How could I be with a girl like Faye? Not because she was rich, but because she was so decent. I felt like I couldn't make another move on her. She thought I was a nice guy, a hero. I could never live up to it. I shouldn't hurt her with this pretending. I should come clean.

She said, "Peter, did the film upset you? I'm sorry, it was thoughtless of me to choose a war film."

"No, it's ok. I wanted to see it. The war scenes didn't get to me."

"But something about it distressed you."

"York was so decent. He didn't want to kill a soul. Me and some of the guys I fought with, we couldn't wait to kill. I mean, to win." Take it easy, I told myself. She would think I was crazy. She would see what I was.

But her gaze was gentle. "You don't have to feel bad for wanting to win. I suppose all soldiers do, or almost all. York did, surely. He couldn't have bossed all those Germans around if he hadn't wanted to win. He grabbed his chance to shoot and imprison lots of them."

I met her eyes. "But he was a peaceful, decent guy at home beforehand."

She smiled. "Probably. But don't you think the film makers, and perhaps the army, have knocked the rough edges off his story to make him seem more heroic? And Cooper's acting and his face make York seem noble and gentle. The real Sergeant York was heroic, but he couldn't have been perfect."

Her face was lit by the moon. I was glad mine was in shadow.

She gave me her sweetest look, and I couldn't lie.

"York was a real hero. I'm not like that. Not like your uncle Maurice or your father. What your aunt said about me, she hit on the truth. It's a fluke that I'm an officer. I don't deserve the praise folks are heaping on me, the admiration from kids and guys like Edward, and girls like you. What I've done, it's not like in books. Not like in the war movies when guys fly straight at the enemy. Fighters like me, we kill by stalking. It's like hunting."

Like shooting a guy in the back. We picked out the most defenceless enemy, then the next and the next. We hardly saw the pilots. Just the planes. But we were shooting men – kids, really.

My voice came out rough. "I'm not some great hero, better than the rest. I handle planes well, but so do lots of guys. I'm not braver than the others." My voice dropped to a mutter, "I'm more used to killing."

I saw again what I'd always see: dark silhouettes dropping on the sidewalk, across from me, the gunshots of my gang nearly deafening me as I ran beside them, struggling to keep up, scarcely taller than Harris's waist and the Boss's fob pocket. Then, on the country trail, the pool of dark blood spreading out. The hole in the forehead. My first close kill.

I glanced back at her. She was staring at me intently, and, thank God, still with sympathy in her eyes, though worry as well.

I'd said so much I might as well say it all – what I had never told anyone, even Hube, though maybe he knew and felt the same. Her kind eyes made me go on speaking. "I can kill someone and feel nothing. No pity. Later, I feel sorry for some of the pilots, but I feel fine when I shoot. I shouldn't be like that."

What I couldn't say was how I loved it, how exhilarating each kill felt. I turned my face away. Of all the goddamn moments to make a good confession.

She touched my hand. "You have trained yourself to do this work. You're following orders."

"Like the Nazis?" That was starting to bother me, but she seemed okay with it, like everyone else. "Yeah, and we're trained to hate the Nazis and now the Japs – but I hardly needed that."

She said, "You mentioned the shooting you did before the war. I don't understand. Do you mean hunting?"

I couldn't tell her. Let her think I went from the boys' home to the ranch, not to a gang. I shrugged and stared into her shining eyes. I almost wanted to tell her, to make her understand how the poorest folk ended up fighting each other, how they didn't have jobs or homes, so the gang was like their work and their family, how gang wars were crazy but they just went on and on because the other guys would kill you if you stopped, and there was no way out because there were not enough jobs, and no way to get money except for crime and fighting.

There were gangs here in Melbourne; I had seen them mentioned in the local newspapers. She wouldn't know about that, about those parts of her town. Maybe her father would know, but only from his courtroom. He wouldn't go to the dirty and violent parts of town, none of her family would, not even Edward. She and her kind would never understand that not all kids in those street gangs were criminals, not at first, anyway. They were runaways, orphans, kids with no money, no shelter, and no food.

She was looking sad. "I can't imagine how life was for you, but I can see that it was hard. It must have been hard for anyone without a family and some money behind them in those years. But when you became a pilot, you left hunting behind, didn't you?"

"Yep." There was no need to figure how to answer, no need to hide things, because it was true. I had escaped into the sky. At first, it had felt like a win, but soon it was another sort of killing, even if it was for a better reason, even if it felt better, most of the time.

She said quickly, "The war made you fight again. It isn't what you are, or what you wanted all along."

I took a deep breath. "You're right. I started off harmless enough. I've done good things for people sometimes."

"I'm sure you have."

I looked away. My sort of good deed was nothing like what she imagined. Killing a guy to protect Momma was good, but would Faye think so? Maybe not. Her Dad would lock me up. And he might query my motives – sure, I wanted to protect baby Luella and stop that monster from raping her Momma and leaving her for dead, that was what made me grab my gun, but it wasn't my only reason. I had been hoping someone would plug Harris. It riled me how he never took a hit in shootouts.

My other best deed was a medley of crimes: buying a fake birth certificate for Rita to get her into a white hospital when she missed the curse, convincing her that no-one would pick her as coloured, and getting us fake marriage papers so she wouldn't be treated like trash. Faye would be horrified, but it probably saved Rita's life – and her chance to have more kids. And it saved a kid from a sad life, because I was sixteen and couldn't hang around, and Rita wasn't ready yet to be a mother.

I stared at the soft light shimmering over the river, and then back at Faye. "Maybe the war makes guys like me worse, but what can I do? You gotta defend your country and your people."

"And other countries and their people – you *are* a hero, Peter, you went into the front line for England. You didn't have to."

"Some folks in the States couldn't understand why I did," I said softly.

"I understand, and my father does, too." Her eyes shone. "I'm grateful for the sake of England and France."

I still felt churned up, though thank the Lord, not as shaky. "I loved London straightaway. But maybe I was just itching for a fight."

She said gently, "The fighting is bound to leave you feeling sad. I've heard Mo and Dad talk about it. Aunt Lillian says Mo has times of horror thinking of the men he's had to send to their deaths. But that doesn't make him bad, and the fighting you've done hasn't made you bad, either."

I shrugged. I wasn't so sure. I was bad long before the war. Had the war made me worse?

I wondered what she knew about American gangs from the movies. If she knew my gang story, she wouldn't be walking close by me now, with that look in her eyes.

She sighed. "I wish you didn't have to head off to fight again and again." Her eyes darkened.

"Hey, I'll be okay. Don't worry about me." I wasn't sure if she hated me fighting or feared I would die.

After a moment, we reached the rotunda. We sat on the bench and she wove around me, till I was half-crazy wanting her, but somehow near peace, too. I held her and drank in that calm strong happiness she had, and knew I would hang on to this girl for as long as I could.

*

I was to go to Sydney two days later, and I wanted to see her again before I flew out. She suggested we meet on the Flinders Street Station steps. I laughed. That was where nearly every serviceman in the city met girls of varying degrees of respectability. I suggested the river, near her place.

We met at the rotunda. I watched her swinging along the sidewalk, her curls shining copper on her shoulders, her walk jaunty and loose. We sat on the seat, holding each other, talking a little. A few people passed. You could hear the birds twitter and the clang and whine of the tram across in St Kilda Road. I wanted to stay there all day.

After a time, she said, "Are you going back to live in New York after the war?"

What did she daydream about?

"No, I'll go visit folks, but I don't want to live there. I used to think I could live in London for a while, but I'm getting to like Melbourne." I smiled.

"Really? You don't find it too quiet?"

"I like the quiet. I love the space. I like how it's kind of English but more relaxed, with no airs. It's more peaceful than the States. Folks mostly get on, don't they?"

"Yes, I think so."

I knew she wouldn't have a clue about the folks at the bottom of the heap, who no doubt had the kind of struggles I knew plenty about, but at least here I had no connections with any folks I'd rather forget. "You expect to live here all your life, don't you?" I smiled. "You're the kinda girl who has her whole life planned out. I bet you'll live it just as you planned."

She looked anxious. "I'm not determined to follow a particular plan. Except that I would like to have children one day."

I grinned. I could just see her cradling a child that looked like her, with soft hair and glowing eyes. What a picture, like an old painting in Hube's big art books.

She was saying, "Don't you look forward to having children?"

I felt my grin vanish. "Jesus!" I saw her try not to react and cussed myself for an idiot, using that word to her. "Sorry. I can't imagine being a father, being responsible for kids and showing them how to behave. I wouldn't be any good at that."

She smiled and shook her head at me.

I looked at the river quietly flowing. "I'd love to have kids. But I never think I really will. Faye, you plan out everything and you know you can do it all. I never plan anything – not long term. Once or twice, I chose to leave and go someplace better."

She smiled. "You chose to learn to fly, to go to England, to join the RAF, and then your own forces out here. You're a very decisive person, Peter. And a very effective one."

I couldn't help feeling pleased. "I guess I decided some things, and yep, mostly they've been ok." I drove away thoughts of my kills; most of those guys had it coming; Harris sure did. "Do you know, baby, you're the first person to make me think of my life that way." Before, I would have called it being on the run, hiding, grabbing, fighting.

She held my face in her soft, small hands for a moment and stroked my brow.

My shoulders felt heavy. "But like I tried to tell you, your Aunt Nell wasn't far off the mark. I'm a long way off being a gentleman. I've slept with too many girls I didn't care about. You don't want to get mixed up with a guy like me."

She looked almost frightened, maybe by my face as well. "Peter, I know about your kindness to the children at St Anthony's. I know how gently you treat me. Being a gentleman doesn't come from birth and wealth. I don't want to know about girls you've spent the night with. That's the past. It's your business. It doesn't have anything to do with us."

I smiled. "You're right." She saw the good, sunny side of the world. I felt great for a moment but then troubled again. She must have thought I changed my moods by the minute. "I just don't want to deceive you, is all."

She smiled and took my hands. "You just confessed to a lurid past! Don't tell me the details; I'll be intimidated. I get the idea."

"Baby, you have no idea." My voice sounded too sarcastic.

"Don't be so patronising!" She laughed but seemed unsure of herself for a moment. "I may be inexperienced, but I do have an imagination and a good knowledge of classical and French literature."

I laughed gently. "You mean you read a lot about love?"

"Books are very educational, don't you think?" She smiled and flushed.

"I do. I learnt a lot from the ones I borrowed from Hube. But there's a limit to what books can tell you. Can they compare with the real thing?"

We collapsed into laughter and kisses. Some passers-by on the sidewalk made critical remarks, and we shook with giggles. I whispered, "You better not show your face. These people might know you!"

"You do have a deceitful streak. I see you were honest about that," she teased.

I groaned to think how much I hadn't been honest about with her.

A loud family came and sat opposite us, their baby wailing. We straightened up and disentangled ourselves. We walked out into the gardens and down to the river.

"I'll miss you tomorrow," I said.

"Let's see if I can match those British heroines, farewelling their handsome heroes without a tear," she said, smiling.

I loved the laughing way she said it.

"It's not combat yet, but when it is, I'll come back. I always come back."

"I know. They don't call you Pirate for nothing."

"Does your fiancé get back sometime soon?"

She shook her head. Her eyes looked troubled, and I felt a heel. Why did I ask, when I wasn't going to challenge him?

She looked up at me with those clear, truthful eyes. "I don't miss him. I realised a while ago that I don't love him. I'm going to tell him and break my engagement."

I couldn't breathe. I stared at her, and she blushed. I drew her close. "Don't do that for me. I can't offer you anything. He owns half the state, doesn't he? Look, I don't want to wreck your life."

She smiled and touched my face. "You won't. You've done the opposite. I'm not expecting you to do anything, Peter. We are only starting to know each other. What I'm saying is that now I know I don't love him. I never did. I was lulled into thinking the match Mummy and most people thought was perfect was what I wanted. But it isn't. I made a great mistake. I should have stuck to my guns. I knew I wanted to love someone till it made everything else disappear."

What could I do but kiss her? I felt ashamed that I had nothing to match her words.

"I never asked a girl to wait." I stared at the grey, slow river and then turned back to her. "You're the greatest girl I've ever met. I used to say I don't fall in love, but that's not true anymore. I want you all the time. But when you get to know me, you'll get over me fast." When she started to protest, I put my finger on her lips. "I'm trying to say I'm not the kind of guy who makes plans. But when I'm away, I'll miss you every instant."

Her voice was unusually hesitant. "Peter, can I ask you something? You don't have to answer. Do you have someone waiting for you in the States, or in England? A girl, I mean?"

My chest and stomach felt tight. "No." That wasn't my problem, but she couldn't see it.

She smiled and her shoulders relaxed. We kissed, but I knew she wanted more from me – words, not action.

"You're the only one I care about, Faye. I'll think about you, baby, all the time. I'll be dreaming about you. It's crazy: I can chase a swarm of enemy planes, but asking the sweetest girl to wait for me scares me stupid. If something happens to me – and it won't – just remember I love you."

She was holding back tears as she smiled and kissed me. "I'll remember. I love you, Peter, whatever you've done, whatever you must do in this war. You remember that."

I felt my body go loose. "Don't get engaged to anyone else, okay?"

17. The Wrong One

Peter:

Melbourne, March 1942

I took a bus back to my billet. Two girls were standing outside the gate, Iris and her sister.

Iris walked forward, jittery on her high heels. "Pete, I had to say goodbye. I hope you don't mind." She held out her hand.

When I didn't take it immediately, she rested it on my arm.

"Okay, Iris. I don't know what to say. It's really hit me, with Faye. So I thought it was best not to see you." I examined her face. How much she cared for me was a mystery.

"She's fallen for you," she said flatly. "When I saw her at that ball, I knew. The way she dolled herself up for your flying demo, she was out to get you. And when you vanished a while back, I knew she bloody well had. I suppose we're finished. For now, anyway." She took a deep breath and looked away.

"Iris, you'll find a guy who's better for you."

"Aw, don't, Pete. I'll never find anyone I like better. But I might find someone who likes me more than you do." Her smile tensed.

"I mean you'll find a better guy." I looked past her at the long front garden. "If you really got to know me, well, you'd end up despising me."

Her laugh sounded bitter, older. "Aw, Pete, that's rubbish. What a helluva goodbye routine! The point is, whatever I might end up thinking about you, at least I would've had a choice." She looked away, too, up the tree-lined street.

"I'm sorry, Iris. You're a swell girl."

She broke down and put her face in her hands. I held her shoulders gently. I was aware of her little sister lowering her gaze; I guessed I had upset her, too, but maybe taught her a lesson.

"Pete, I'll always be your friend," Iris sobbed.

I was sorry, but I couldn't afford to say too much. "Sure, Iris, me too. But I can't see you anymore."

"I hope she appreciates you, Pete." Her eyes scanned my face. "Her lot are snobs about Yanks. And you know she's engaged, I s'pose."

"Yeah, to a serviceman, of course. I don't feel too good about that."

Her smile was both sympathetic and hostile. "She'll probably go back to him. Those society girls always marry the rich squatters. When she throws you over, you don't need to explain anything, Pete. Just come and talk to me anyway, if things get rough."

It made me kind of queasy to hear that. I'd been happy to be the back-door man sometimes – wasn't that what I was for Faye? I'd never heard a woman apply for the job.

"Thanks, Iris," I smiled. "She'll tire of me sooner or later. I'm not the sort of guy she'd marry."

"You're the sort *I'd* marry," Iris grinned and put her arms around me.

I had to go before things got worse. "Iris, try to forget—" I stopped, aghast at her expression. "Sorry. I'll always be fond of you, honey. I loved our times together. You're a beautiful, wonderful girl. Take care of yourself."

"Pete, you're the one that needs to be careful, for heaven's sake. I'll miss you so much – my whole family will miss you."

I tried not to show surprise. I should have expected as much.

"Will you get home ok?"

"We'll get the bus." She dropped her hands from me and stepped back. "I'll pray for you, Pete."

It struck me that Faye hadn't said that. Maybe she was too embarrassed to say it. Praying was just a habit, anyhow. It didn't mean Iris loved me more than Faye did. And who wanted prayers? I'd rather have Faye think hot stuff about me.

On my way to Essendon airport, I couldn't stop thinking of Faye. I wanted to feel her against my body. Her hair brushing my face. Her hands gripping my arms. Her eyes bright with love. I kept biting the side of my mouth, remembering the softness of hers. Things she said kept ringing in my head. If we had lived in some ancient time, my fighting could have made me worthy of her.

*

Three days later, I returned from Sydney by train. The trip took a whole day, and I enjoyed looking out at the countryside. Faye was going to St Kilda Town Hall with a girlfriend she trusted that night, and we would meet there as if by chance.

At Spencer Street Station, I sent my bag on to my billet with the other officers and took a cab to St Kilda Town Hall. Outside, I saw her chauffeur sitting on the running board of a car, presumably one Sir Henry used when he didn't want to waste his Rolls. In case her girlfriend had pulled out, and Faye was waiting in the car, I strolled up. Her chauffeur stood and gave me his lopsided grin. The car was empty.

"She's inside the dance hall?" I asked.

"That's right, Captain." He spoke with a thick Irish accent, and not a Northern one like servicemen I'd met in London. I guessed he was a Southern Irishman, not a British subject. Maybe he and his family were neutral or against the war. "Glad to see you back."

Was he waiting in case I hadn't shown up? For whatever reason.

He said, "I will be here, Captain, if there's any place you want to go later on. Or if the young lady's friend needs a lift home earlier."

I wondered what kind of hint this was. I shrugged. Maybe he assumed I would take Faye home, or maybe that I shouldn't take her anywhere, let alone home. He had a tough, scarred face and his arms were thick and muscled under his jacket. I felt an odd wariness about him, and maybe he felt the same about me. Knowing he worked for the judge and was countryman to Lady B was enough to put me off him.

Inside, the place was packed. I could see over most of the heads, apart from a few big Aussie blokes. I spotted her sitting at a table with a plump girl.

It was hard to rein myself in while she did the intro. Her friend Peggy was a bit snooty, but she blushed when I smiled at her. An old school friend, she was an office worker for the Aussie navy and had been there since before the war, so I gathered she wasn't as rich as the Beauregards.

Finally, she was asked to dance by some GI, and I whizzed Faye onto the dance floor. I steered into the crowd, away from the friend's prying eyes.

"I started to worry that I'd only dreamed you up, Faye," I said. "It's great to see you again, baby."

She laughed and squeezed my arm.

Pretty soon, we had to rejoin Peggy, who didn't seem to want to dance more than a bracket with a GI. She seemed happy to count me as a bit of an exception, on account of Faye's vouching for me. So, I asked her to dance and got her talking about Faye. She seemed a good friend because she didn't mind the focus of attention being almost entirely on another girl. Since she wasn't much of a dancer, I toned down my pace. She got all pink and delighted anyway.

I couldn't pass up the chance to ask about the fiancé.

Peggy didn't need much prompting. "The Wilsons are among the most successful graziers in Australia." Her upper-class tone had a hooting sound I'd heard before in England. "Of course, the Beauregards have more eminence in Melbourne, but Faye and Clive are an ideal match. Sir Henry and Mr Wilson must be pleased about the stations being joined up in the future."

I noted how Lady B didn't rate a mention; I pictured her battling her life away with dull women like this one.

"Faye will have marvellous houses. Clive has a sister, but she's marrying an English nobleman, and Clive will inherit almost everything. He has been devoted to Faye since they were children."

Peggy wasn't a jazz or swing fan, so the music was lost on her. She talked through the best songs. The main thing the three of us seemed to have in common was the movies. They said *Gone With The Wind* had been a tremendous hit in Melbourne; I held my tongue about what Buzz and his crowd made of it, and how it shocked Momma. Peggy claimed that Leslie Howard had the best speaking voice in pictures, but Faye shrugged and said it was a pity he looked so willowy. I had to laugh; girls like her used such polite words for insults. I asked if they had seen *It's Love I'm After*, where Bette Davis had him on toast. They laughed and said it was coming to Melbourne soon, and they were dying to see it.

Before the band had finished, Faye told me they had to go. I walked out the front with her and lost Peggy for a moment so we could manage a kiss of sorts. Then I escorted them to the chauffeur, who gave me a quick glance.

She threw me a warm look as they left and said softly, "Isobel is throwing a house party next weekend for American servicemen at our family house at the beach. You should come. Edith and I are going. See you at Portsea."

I walked up the road a way and snaffled a cab before it went into the queue at the Town Hall. The guy looked ecstatic when he learned I was going so far.

An invitation from Isobel and her committee was waiting for me at my billet. I grinned and then felt a stab of worry. At a weekend house party, it might be more torture than pleasure to be a few rooms away from Faye all night. Should I make a move? Would that be fair to her? It wasn't what she wanted. Or was it?

18. Sand and Heat

Peter:

Portsea, April 1942

As I drove down to Portsea with Chris and some other officers, I thought about how Faye never seemed to worry about what might happen, how to her it must seem simple. I knew the score with rich, respectable girls. They loved the necking and spooning, but cross a line, and they'd call the dogs on you, accompanied by fathers or brothers. Unlike fast rich girls, the well-behaved rich ones went all the way only with guys they might marry. I could see that, for Faye, it would be only with the guy she married, and probably after the ceremony.

But I loved every second with her, and she treated me as if I was the kind of guy she might marry. The problem was that no-one else in Melbourne thought I had the faintest claim to a girl like her, and neither did I. Being a Yank and a poor Joe was the least of it; not being the marrying type was less of a problem than I had thought. What really ruled me out was being the blue type with a head full of horror movies, the fierce type that's good for nothing but flying and killing.

The coastline we drove along was pretty and mostly deserted. There were only a couple of towns, and very few houses in between them. The water of the bay was calm and still; the sand was golden and wide in great sweeping arcs. There were scrubby trees beside the beaches for much of the way, but the sun, blue sky and sea more than made up for the lack of pretty gardens. A town called Sorrento near the end of the peninsula was striking, with pine trees and a grand hotel on a hill overlooking the water.

Even there, the houses were mostly small and modest, so I was unprepared for the grand houses of Portsea. Isobel's was like an enormous Spanish castle of pale stone, high on a hill, not on the bay side of the peninsula, but with its own private path to the ocean beach. Faye told me her grandfather had built the place, and she had stayed there often as a child.

Isobel had invited Edith and Nigel as well as some other young Australians to mingle with us Americans. Faye's parents were probably grinding their teeth, but at least the weekend looked like their daughters were helping their aunt in her charitable work with the lonely Yanks. Maybe Lady B thought her womenfolk were civilising us. I said as much to Faye as we were having welcome drinks on the long terrace that overlooked sand dunes and the blue ocean.

She laughed. "Mummy deserves that. It has astounded me how critical she is of American servicemen. I think it has surprised Dad, too."

"She's the model Melbourne lady, isn't she?" I tried not to laugh, thinking of how Hube had scoffed at Englishwomen of her type.

Faye turned serious. "She has to try harder than everyone else, being Catholic, not to mention Irish. The people she mixes with think she is ignorant. It's absurd, given how well educated she was. But it's only my generation that are being accepted a little."

I said, "You feel Irish? Folks call you that?"

"No, I feel Catholic, not Irish. We don't call ourselves Irish the way you Americans call yourself Irish Americans or Italian Americans. We do label everyone according to their religion, though. I was speaking as a Catholic, who went to a convent school – though I went to one in Toorak, so Dad's friends accept it, to an extent." She laughed. "What I meant was that in my generation, more Catholics are going to university, and some Catholic boys are accepted in the legal and medical fields."

"That's good to hear," I said. "Melbourne folk are like the English, aren't they, using where they went to school as a kind of pecking order."

Nigel laughed and turned to me. "That's right. It's probably more important than what your father does. My father was a refugee from Europe and not even British, so you can imagine the jokes I used to put up with. But Mum is unflappable, and Dad had a thick skin, so it never mattered, and of course, I did go to Grammar, so I have the right answer to the big Melbourne question. I hope Melbourne moves into the modern world once the war is over. We can thank you Americans for pushing us along a bit."

I said, "The US carries on about every American having freedom and opportunity, but there's an iron-clad pecking order there, too. Blacks are at the bottom, of course, but there's plenty of anti-Catholic and anti-Irish feeling, too. I noticed it here in your newspapers, but I guess I wouldn't see it round about."

"It's around," Faye said. "Isn't it, Edith?"

Her sister nodded. "Yes. Not in our family, of course, and not really among Dad's friends."

Faye said, "Not his friends, but among associates or acquaintances. Everyone is polite to Mummy in front of him. But then a few will sneer at her accent or her family's grocers' shops when Dad's not in earshot. So, I do find it puzzling that she's snobbish about Yanks."

"It's the fear of them grabbing her daughters," I joked, and Nigel gave a guffaw.

He said, "I must admit that Aunt Moira did say to my mother, 'It's all very well for you, Bel, you only have a son'."

I felt uneasy and snuck a glance at Edith. She didn't look perturbed. I wondered what Faye had told her about me.

Nigel offered me a good English cigarette, as we walked along the terrace and onto the wide lawn. "What line of work do you see yourself in after the war, Peter?"

I took a drag of the cigarette and examined his interested face. It was hard to imagine being a guy like him, sitting out the war, getting richer from his father's stores, and being the heir to Isabel's real estate. Maybe he found war talk a bore and couldn't wait till the conflict was over.

I said, "Guess I hope I can fly in some capacity. With an airline, or maybe test pilot work."

"In the States, or are you likely to settle here, or in England?"

I stared at the lush garden on the edge of the neat lawns. I doubted his mother, or Faye's, had put him up to asking such a question. Anyhow, I couldn't see the harm in being honest. "Not necessarily in the States. I used to think I'd go back to London, but you've got a great little town here."

He looked pleased. "Melbourne is wide open for development of aviation. So is the rest of Australia. I'm quite interested in investing in airlines and transport in general. If you're ever starting a business, charter flying or an airline, we should talk. Your war record would be an asset in getting established and in advertising."

"I'll keep that in mind."

Nigel looked young for such big talk, but his father had been a business whiz and must have made a heap. Friends of Hube's talked like that, as if they could create vast enterprises. Faye had said that all Nigel enjoyed was business, and that he had stopped being such a pal of hers once he grew up. But that sort of determined guy was the kind I got on well with, and backing like his was just what I would need.

I wished I could ask him about Faye's fiancé, and what dumping him would mean for her.

When I walked back to the terrace, Isobel drew me to a chair near her.

"Peter, I'm so sorry about what Nell said at my party. It was absurd and rude. Unfortunately, she's ignorant and has seen little of the world. Rest assured that no one took any notice of what she said. Henry demolished her just after you left – I wish you could have heard him praising you and your American colleagues."

I stared at her earnest dark eyes, so like Faye's. "Thanks, Mrs Minsky, that's kind of you, but I want to apologise for walking out of your house. You threw a great party. I enjoyed the swimming and the music."

Her eyes were soft. "You mustn't apologise, Peter. It was Nell's fault and I didn't blame you for walking away. Often that is the only retort to rudeness. My late husband, Alex often just walked away from insults and prejudice. It was strong of you to refuse to be a target of Nell's malice."

I found myself beaming at her. "Your late husband sounds quite a guy. Had he been in Melbourne long when you met him?"

"A few years. He had started a jewellery business with a partner. I met him in his shop and somehow whenever I visited it, he appeared and gave me special attention." She laughed. "I thought the attraction was restyling the Beauregard diamond rings, but then he asked me to dinner, and that was that."

I smiled. "He was a smart guy – must have been a confident one too."

"A strong personality, a strong character. He had survived horrors in Russia and managed to get himself to Australia, so I suppose winning over the Beauregards was not as big a challenge as one might think."

I figured she liked frank talk and to tell her love story. "I guess your parents had a certain kind of husband in mind for you?"

She laughed. "Oh, yes. But once I met Alex, that was it. English and Australian landowners and so on were such bores in comparison. Alex was interested in beauty and art and having fun – enjoying life. He built up a huge business, but he always made time for living and for people."

"I wish I could have met him," I said.

"You would have liked each other." She leaned toward me. "He used to say that Melbourne was a country town at heart, so he treated it as one."

"I'll remember that," I said.

When the Americans started to enthuse about Melbourne's social life, Isobel and I turned to listen.

Faye said, "There were lots more parties and balls before the war. Bigger and better ones."

Her sister agreed, but Isobel said, "Yes, it's different now but it's rather an opportunity, isn't it, to meet new people. We have been so English here and rather staid. America and Australia are young, and both finding new ways of thinking and living. It's wonderful to make new friends. War speeds that up, doesn't it? Young people like you are the right age to find the compensations of wartime – one meets interesting people one would never catch a glimpse of otherwise."

I met Faye's eyes. We couldn't help but smile. Were Isobel's words a stamp of approval for me?

I kept thinking about that long into the night as I failed to sleep in the luxurious sheets, down the corridor from Edith and Faye. I didn't try any lurking and prying, or mock innocent knocking on her door as I had sometimes done in big houses. Her calm face as she said goodnight told me she didn't expect any games.

*

The next morning, a strong wind was blowing, and the air was warm. Faye said a hot early April day could dry you out like a shoe left in the sun. Nigel ruled out the beach and suggested indoor games or swimming in the pool. But I was dying to get into the big waves Faye had told me about.

She laughed at my disappointment and said, "I'll go to the beach with you, Peter. It will be great in the water. It's just a pain walking down there on days like this. But you've only got today, haven't you, so you can't be as choosy as Nigel. Anyone else coming? Edith?"

Chris was the only other taker. My blood quickened, for he would be discreet. The three of us walked over the lawns and down the path over the sand dunes, out of sight of the house. The wind whipped up the sand in stinging whirls. No doubt that was what Nigel had been determined to avoid. I tied my handkerchief over my mouth and joked about cowboys. Biting the dust was exactly what you did when you fell breaking a horse, but only for a moment, if you were lucky. She tied a pretty scarf over her face and took my hand. We walked close. I couldn't wait to get out of the flying sand so I could kiss her.

The beach was long, and we had it to ourselves. We ran down to where the sand was damp and still. We stripped to our swimsuits and ran into the water. The chill hit me with a sting. The high waves churned fast. We swam out to where the water was up to her chest. After Chris swam off, I held her close, our legs wound around each other. We dove down and stared at each other underwater. As we surfaced, we kissed. The way she looked at me – no-one else had shown that much excitement and love, not even Rita.

It wasn't just because Rita was my first that I always remembered her. I hadn't a clue about making love that first night with her, and I was nervous and half wanting to run, yet it turned out better than in the movies for us. She told me how sweet I was, but it was her, all her.

I shouldn't have been surprised at how well Faye caught the waves. Her lithe body flexed and rode wave after wave into the foamy shallows. I started to get the hang of it and caught a wave or two, though not for as far as she did. It felt a bit like flying.

When we headed for the shore, Chris was sunbaking in a wind break behind some high rocks. He refused my insincere invitation to join us for a stroll.

Faye and I walked along the edge of the water, our skin cool from our swim. There were little rock pools and sandy hollows under overhanging rocks. I led her into one, and she sank onto the warm sand. I stretched out on top of her, and we kissed. When I rolled beside her and stared at her, I thought she would do anything, but she was scared, too. How ever much I wanted to, I knew we couldn't. I had a sudden flash of her mother's relieved face when I promised to keep my distance. But what did Faye want? I wouldn't hurt her, but why shouldn't she fly a little? There was a fever in her. I touched her and saw her start of surprise and excitement. She was getting there fast, but then she hesitated.

I paused. "Do you want me to stop? Nothing's going to happen that you don't want. I only want to please you."

Her eyes caught alight again, and she smiled. I didn't need to hear the amazement in her cry to know that she hadn't got there before. "Alone or with others," as the creepy priests used to ask in the dark confessional box. It staggered me how she was so innocent. Maybe the Catholic thing: the worship of virginity, the fear of hell? It hadn't had much effect at the boys' home, but I guessed life was different for happy little girls.

I had expected to be cool-headed, the one in charge, like with most girls. There was no chance of going all the way or of stripping off. Yet she swept me into a state I wasn't sure I had ever felt, maybe only at times with Rita, but with Faye there was frenzy and heaven and no embarrassment at all. No thought either, except to slide off her onto the sand before it was too late. I managed to stop myself hollering, for once. It was like I forgot who I was as I stared into her dazed eyes. Other people had felt like this with me, I realised, but I hadn't ever reached this sky-high joy with them.

She was hugging me fiercely and grinning like she had won a million dollars. We kissed and traced the lines of our faces and bodies with our hands. I thought of Buzz and his girl walking out of a dingy room in Harlem looking like they'd been to Shangri-La. I daydreamed about taking Faye somewhere beautiful for a year or two.

As she lost all heat, she looked at me, a little nervous. "Heavens. Peter, I had no idea one could feel so… so marvellous. I hope I let you feel that way, too. You did, didn't you?"

She didn't put on an act or think only of herself like some dames, the types that set the tempo and made me feel like a piano player.

I said softly, "It was more exciting with you than with anyone else, baby. I love how you get wild, and the next second touch me like I'm not a rough lug but like I might break. No-one ever touched me soft like that, like you were learning the shape of me to remember. I've been making a map of you, too. Hey, you're staring at me like I'm a work of art."

"You are," she laughed gently.

My words had taken the nervous look off her face, but she was the type who went over things. I liked that. I admired the way she could talk about whatever was on her mind. I hadn't spent time with anyone honest and confident like that since Buzz.

She said, "I've always been told men don't respect women who – I don't even know if Americans use the same words."

"That's all wrong about respect, with me at any rate. It's not like you do this with crowds of guys."

We laughed. Maybe now she felt it had been wrong? I was terrified that she might regret it. "Are you okay, baby? Is it gonna make you feel blue?"

"No, darling. I'm glad. It's the happiest day of my life."

"Mine, too," I said. She had me feeling like the hero in a movie again.

She smiled deliriously but then sighed. "I do love you so. But it's hard to forget all the things I've had drummed into me. You know, what my church says. That what we just did is very bad."

I grinned. "Churches are crazy. Did it feel bad?"

Her eyes grew startled, but they still shone. "It felt wonderful. I didn't know I could feel like that." She burst out laughing. "But you have no idea what the nuns and priests say about men and their ungovernable desires."

I refused to think about priests. "I don't know if men's desires are that much stronger than women's. Lots of men think they have the right to grab whatever they want. I hate that. I'm not a bully who can't control himself. Like I said, nothin's gonna happen that you don't want."

She snuggled into me for more kisses. I carried her into the rock pool, and we washed the sand off and walked back to Chris.

*

That afternoon I was to drive with the other officers back to Melbourne. I wished I could stay a week. Straight after lunch, Faye invited me upstairs to Isobel's private balcony. I saw Edith watching as we climbed the stairs.

Isobel joined us as we settled into large cane chairs in front of the view out to sea and, to my surprise, Faye said, "Bel, I haven't told anyone except Peter, but I want you to know that I'm breaking my engagement."

My face felt hot. I was glad neither of them was looking at me.

Isobel smiled and leaned toward Faye. "My dear girl, I'm glad. If marrying Clive was what you really wanted, I would never have uttered a word of criticism, but if it isn't, then I have to say, I'm relieved."

Faye looked surprised and thrilled. Maybe this was better than she had hoped for. She sounded breathless. "I don't love him, and now I realise I never did. Getting engaged to him seemed to be the logical step, but it wasn't." She laughed, and her aunt smiled and nodded.

My face still burned. What did these charmers expect me to say?

Faye said, "Peter isn't to blame," and grabbed my hand. Our eyes met and we laughed, and she said to me, "Well, you did hurry me up. I might have taken a lot longer to come to my senses and see how impossible Clive is, if I hadn't got to know you."

Isobel beamed and turned to me. "Peter, may I say you have done Faye a favour; in fact, you've done us all a favour."

"Yeah? I thought he was the number one guy all the girls wanted, the heir to half the state."

Isobel smiled. "His family has land and so on, but Faye means far too much to me to see her sold off. It's not as if she's poor and needs a wealthy husband."

I concentrated on not flushing again. It was a problem I'd never noticed before.

Faye said, "And I certainly don't need a husband who doesn't care about me. Bel, I hadn't realised you were so critical of Clive."

Isobel's smile reminded me for a moment of Sir Henry's. "I don't know Clive very well, but he seems just like his father." She turned to me. "The Wilson men are a stolid lot. Their land is number one to them; people come a poor second, especially women, I fear. To them, women are probably a third priority, after children, or perhaps a fourth, after livestock!" She gave Faye a serious look. "If Clive didn't impress you with his ardour while he was pursuing you, Faye, I don't imagine there would have been more of it later."

I wondered if the Wilsons had snubbed her husband.

Faye said, "Do you mind my asking you something, Bel? Did you ever go out with Mr Wilson?"

She laughed. "No, but he kept asking me for years. I was never interested in him romantically. I saw him at parties and in the country, of course. But he gave Eddie a very bad beating once when they were quite old. I didn't accept him even as a friend after that. Eddie would never speak about it."

"Do you mean they had a fist fight?" Faye looked astounded. "What on earth for?"

"I couldn't find out. Geoff went on far too long, and poor Eddie was really hurt. He should have given up, but then Geoff should have stopped. He was far bigger and years older. I never got any of them to tell me the reason for it. Even your father clammed up for once."

"Didn't he help Eddie, or take his side?"

"Well, they're so different, Hal and Eddie. Hal thought Eddie was being a bit of a sissy, I think, though he's never been as friendly with Geoff since then. Hal is a chap of the old school, like Maurice: you fight your own battles and take it on the chin. Eddie hasn't quite forgiven Hal for not cutting off the Wilsons – and I suppose Hal hasn't quite forgiven Eddie for letting the side down, the family reputation, as he sees it."

I presumed she meant more than just that fistfight. I liked the way she didn't share Henry's, and probably Maurice's, disgust at Edward.

As Faye stared, uncomprehending, Isobel smiled, "Anyway, it will be a relief to a few of us if you don't marry into the Wilsons."

Faye laughed. "Eddie made jokes about Clive. It was stupid of me not to ask him what he really thought. Of course, I couldn't ask Daddy." She put her hand on mine. "I had to learn for myself. Books can't teach you everything."

I smiled but felt that heat in my neck again and stood up

like a shot when Isobel suggested we stroll around the garden to get some air.

"Being in Australia makes me feel like a kid again," I told them as we roamed amid looming trees and unfamiliar scents. "All your strange plants and your animals and birds with their new sounds and songs."

Isobel guided us around her prized exotic and native plants. At the huge African gardenia tree, we breathed in its sweet fragrance. Bel gave me a perfect round white flower for my buttonhole and Faye picked one and put it in her hair.

It was so peaceful in Bel's perfumed, well-loved garden. I felt fine and sure as I left.

19. Shocking Peggy Again

Faye:

Melbourne, April 1942

I turned off the entrance lights and crept upstairs. There was a momentary stir in my parents' room but no light showing under their closed door. Would Mummy appear? I was too excited to report on the weekend at Portsea, or the version of it I could tell my mother. Those moments on the beach, I still felt them in my bones, on my skin – I couldn't bear to lose them yet. Thank Heavens Edith had gone straight to a shift at the hospital. I wanted to be alone. My room was dark with the blackout curtains. I turned on one small lamp and whirled around, my arms outstretched. I relived each second in the water and on the sand. It was a new world. He was my lover, or he would be. Could I dare? Hadn't I already begun? I couldn't stop now.

There were so many places I wanted to show him. Eddie was right: it was childish to worry about being seen with an American. Some of my school and university friends were going out with Americans now and were having a good time. Peter was fun. So unusual for a man. Apart from Eddie, and occasionally Mo, you didn't have fun with the men I knew. You had to be a lady, do all the right things, and make a good impression. But Peter seemed happy with whatever I did or said. He didn't find me unladylike when I let him go a bit far. Clive would have. Not that I would have had the nerve to be like that with Clive. And he would never have laughed with joy in my arms the way Peter did. Peter saw me as I was and loved me.

He had risked death and seen friends die. He couldn't waste time fussing about what didn't matter. Clive would never become like that, whatever his war experiences. He would always be a Wilson, always tell people what to do, and always see me as a Beauregard, and a lady who should behave exactly as his mother did. Well, now I had a man who wanted me, my heart, my soul and my body.

"Few of us get it," Eddie had said. I knew I was lucky. Peter was the love of my life – or if by some stroke of fate, he wasn't, then he was my first lover. I would love him for as long as he lived – no, as long as *I* lived.

I took off my clothes and stood for an instant staring at myself in the mirror. I looked different. My body didn't embarrass me. Perhaps I would paint it one day. Shivering a little, I slipped my nightgown on and threw myself onto the bed. Every physical movement seemed different. Oh, if only he were here.

But if he died? I had never taken the war seriously until now. It could ruin my life.

I had never loved Clive. It had been a game, just good manners, not this fire and ache.

I leapt up, turned off the lamp and ran to my balcony. In the dark sky, there were a few bright stars. God *must* bring him back each time he flew up there. Why should God kill him? Was God even there? Did he actually listen? The teachings of my whole life seemed mad and unreal. And yet, not believing in God would feel like being tone deaf.

I went inside, repositioned the blackout, and turned on my desk light. I took out a sketchpad and pencil: Peter's face in greys and dark shadows appeared beneath my touch. I loved the shape of his features. But I couldn't create his eyes, and certainly not in black pencil.

I knew a good photographer; we would get our portraits done.

That next week he had work commitments, and we could not meet till the Saturday night. Peggy and I often met for a film and a bite to eat after she finished work on a Thursday or Friday, so that week, I arranged to meet her on the Thursday night.

In the crowded picture theatre, Peggy and I watched the newsreel. How truthful was it? The cheerful servicemen seemed stagey, and everything looked too clean. Nothing seemed as bad as I suspected it must be, from the little Peter said. People talked about the newsreel and newspaper coverage as if it showed Australians exactly how the fighting was going. But any fool could see that it had been edited and didn't show the worst violence or suffering. On the screen came scenes of planes swooping over the Pacific. They were described as Allied bombers, and I struggled to separate the American from the Australian ones. Then a scene of fighter planes, some American. What would Peter be flying? I should have asked him.

General Maddox appeared on screen with the prime minister, and the commentary became even more fervent. This was at least the third time I had seen the general and Mr. Curtin together in a newsreel. How did Maddox have time to run the War Office? Perhaps he had done enough hobnobbing with Canberra now. The next item featured women in the forces. Another film of girls in ugly uniforms endlessly repeating some boring tasks. I looked out of the corner of my eye at Peggy. Probably she didn't share my reaction; she liked being at the navy office, doing clerical work.

The first feature was a comedy and the film we had come to see; it was the one Peter had mentioned to us at the dance, and it had some hilarious moments when Bette Davis fought with Leslie Howard. I didn't share Peggy's crush on languid, arrogant Howard, but I loved headstrong, stylish Bette. It was delightful to see her in a comedy; for once, she didn't have to die or double-cross someone.

Afterwards, we went for a light meal to Russell Collins, a restaurant close by that catered for ladies and families and respectable couples; I didn't feel like going to the Windsor.

"Well, Faye, it is nice to be noticed when you're not entertaining troops," Peggy teased as we sat at our table. "Tell me everything you've been doing… well, perhaps not everything. How is the photogenic Captain Stephens?"

I smiled. If I didn't talk about him, I'd burst.

"Peg, he's such fun. The way our school friends are, you know. He can laugh and be silly but he's serious as well. He's different from everyone I've met. Perhaps it's partly because he's faced such danger."

"Yes, it's amazing that he has survived so much. It's almost as though he looks for trouble." She broke off as she looked at me. "Not really, I'm sure. I didn't mean to upset you. He'll be fine, of course. He's one of those men who survive, isn't he?"

I sipped my tea. "Yes, you're right. But he will be going into combat soon in New Guinea, and then how can I not worry every second? Goodness, I hate this war."

Peggy nodded vigorously. "It's a pity General Maddox won't be keeping Captain Stephens here at Headquarters permanently, but he probably won't be put in harm's way, since he's so well known."

I sighed. "I don't think wars work like that. Anyway, he loves to fly. And to fight."

The way he had talked of his kills disturbed me more as I recalled it than it had when he first told me. But he worried about it, too. He wasn't a cold-hearted killer, whatever he said.

Peggy smiled sympathetically. "Have you heard from Clive lately?"

"Um, yes. I got a letter a couple of days ago."

I hadn't really read it. All his letters were much the same. I picked at my salad – it wasn't a patch on the version that Russell Collins used to serve before the war.

"Is he all right?"

"Perfectly, I gather. He doesn't have leave for a while yet." I manoeuvred the focus back to Peter. "Thank goodness I can go out dancing. I'd be quite miserable sitting at home all the time."

Peggy buttered her bread roll. "The Yanks make super dancing partners, don't they? Captain Stephens is a real Fred Astaire."

"He is. And rather better looking."

Peggy grinned. "Meg said the two of you looked marvellous dancing at the Governor's Ball. You looked super at St Kilda Town Hall the night I was there, too."

"We've been out dancing a couple of times," I said.

"Really?" Peggy looked surprised.

I couldn't curb my joy. "He's a wonderful dancer, and swimmer. He's so exciting, Peg."

Peggy flushed. "I'm sure he is but… he's *American*."

"He's different from most of them. And anyway, as Eddie says, it's horrid to discriminate against Americans, quite racist, in fact."

Peggy was practically open-mouthed. "Racist? Goodness."

"And fascist," I added.

Peg looked pensive and a little embarrassed.

"Peter and I aren't like those couples in the park and the street. He doesn't give me stockings." I laughed.

"Of course not," said Peggy quickly. "He's an officer and a friend of your family. He knows you're not available as a girlfriend. He knows you won't contemplate marrying him."

I broke into laughter.

"Oh, my goodness, Faye, you won't, will you?"

"Probably," I said. "I hope so." It was so good to say it aloud. The shock on Peg's face! Then I faltered. "If he survives." I felt tears welling up and forced them to stop.

"He will, Faye. Well, I hope so, I really do. With his

experience and skill, it does seem likely. But you're serious, aren't you?" Peggy lowered her voice. "What about Clive?"

I spoke softly, too; the tables were rather close together. "I'm breaking the engagement. I don't love him, Peg. I never did. He doesn't care deeply for me, either."

"But of course he does, Faye. He always liked you. He has probably always planned on marrying you. You haven't seen him for so long, perhaps it's hard to feel exactly the same as you did when he was here. These times are so unsettled. So many people seem to be changing how they behave and how they think. Shouldn't you wait and see how you feel after the war? It's not sensible to give up Clive Wilson."

I shrugged. She seemed to have no idea of what I had discovered with Peter. Was she aware of what I had tried to tell her?

Peg looked away. "I bet Clive isn't expecting this. He'd never expect a girl to reject what he can offer."

I nodded, then paused. "I'm sorry about it. I didn't set out to hurt him. Please, Peg, don't tell a soul till I have had a chance to tell him."

"I won't. But when will you write?"

"I think I should explain this face to face. It seems cowardly and mean just to write a letter, don't you think?"

"I suppose so." Peggy looked unsure, overwhelmed. "I'm not the best person to ask for advice on that, Faye. Shouldn't you talk about this first with your mother?"

"Mummy would just try to talk me out of it. Dad won't be upset."

"Really?"

"Definitely. I found out some past history. Not mine to tell, I'm afraid."

After a moment, Peggy said, "Faye, thanks for telling me. I would tell you if I had anything big to tell. But I have to say I'm worried. It's such an important step. Haven't you talked about it with anyone else? What about with your father?"

"He would tell Mummy. I wouldn't like to ask him to keep something from her."

"I suppose not."

"I've talked to Isobel. She thinks I'm making the right decision."

"She does?" Peg's eyes widened. "I see. Well, of course, she made an unusual choice of husband, a Jew, and not even one who grew up in Melbourne."

"She followed her heart."

Peg looked abashed. "Mm, yes."

"And she was happy."

"Of course, her husband became rich rather quickly," Peggy said. "I'm sure that made things easier. It might not be as easy for you, marrying an American without a fortune. I assume the stories about Captain Stephens coming from a humble background are true. If he keeps flying, he may become quite well off, I suppose, but he will never be in the same league as your family, Faye, financially or socially."

I hid my impatience. "Peg, don't you see how things are changing? Things will never be the way they were before the war. The Americans are going to be part of Australia's future. I don't just mean those couples who marry, but at the political and military levels, too."

"Faye, will you have to go and live in America?"

I smiled. "The lovely thing is that Peter wants to live here after the war."

"Oh, that's good," said Peg, beaming. "Your mother won't be as upset. And I would miss you so much. Melbourne wouldn't be the same without you."

We started on the so-called dessert, more syrup than fruit.

The chocolates I had taken to the picture theatre had been more of a treat than this. I wished we could have more tea, but the new war restrictions didn't allow for more than one cup; I missed the traditional teapots.

Peg sighed, "But throwing away a future with Clive Wilson! I can't get over it, Faye. Shouldn't you give yourself more time to think? How long have you known Peter? What do you really know about him?"

I wriggled impatiently. "You can get to know people quickly if they let you. The whole world knows a lot about him."

"Faye, we know some things he has done in wartime in the air. That doesn't reveal anything about his personal life."

I tossed my head, banishing a vision of the tall pretty girl beside Peter at the ball and the air show. Of course, that affair was over now.

Peggy said, "What would your life with him be like?"

"We think love and joy and kindness are the most important things. We love opera and travel and children. We'll find a good life together."

Peggy's eyebrows shot up. "Opera, good heavens!"

I laughed. "Yes, he's full of surprises."

Peg shook her head. "It just takes my breath away that you would throw the Wilson heir over for, well, a nobody."

"But Clive doesn't love me."

Peggy took a breath. "He's never taken notice of any girl but you."

"I wonder why. I hope it wasn't the Beauregard land."

Peggy flushed. "Surely not, though I suppose it would have been in his father's mind and perhaps his mother's. They may have influenced him."

"He's quite keen himself on land and wealth and being top dog, I think."

"He has been brought up to that, hasn't he? Goodness, Faye, it's quite a surprise to find you so cynical and so aware of money!"

"I don't care about it," I said quickly.

"Of course not, and you will always have some money of your own. You and Edith will inherit a great deal, eventually." She paused. "You don't think this is an infatuation that you might get over? I'm sure lots of wives aren't madly in love with their husbands, but they are still happy."

"They're the unlucky ones. It's not an infatuation, Peg. I can't pretend about my deepest feelings." I stared at her, wondering if she would ever understand.

Peggy looked away, her face embarrassed and a little excited. "All I know is that you were going to marry the most eligible man in Melbourne."

I laughed softly. "So now I'll marry the most eligible American in Melbourne."

Peggy didn't laugh. "Perhaps you will. It's no surprise that Peter has fallen in love with you, but it is surprising that he has taken so little time to propose." She looked sharply at me. "Faye, if he hasn't yet, that's good. It gives you more time to think about it."

"He has almost proposed. He's made it clear he doesn't want me to marry anyone else."

"I'm sure he doesn't," Peg said earnestly. "But his lack of a formal proposal means that you don't need to tell your parents or Clive."

I sighed. "I'm not looking forward to telling them, I admit." I gave her a cheeky glance. "Peg, you should write to Clive. As a friend, not about me. You really like him and perhaps you could catch him on the rebound."

Peggy blushed. "That's kind of you, Faye. But with Clive's high standards in female beauty, not to mention breeding, I'm not in the race. It's sweet of you to think I am. Thanks for wanting me to be rich and to win the prize husband."

I held my breath for a moment, anxious and ashamed. How could I have been so thoughtless? Had I hurt her? I was relieved to see that her face was calm. She was a generous, unpretentious soul. I took a deep breath. Visions of Peter came into my head and the warm, dizzying feeling that seemed part of me now came rushing back. I couldn't help teasing. "All right. But you have always been interested in him, haven't you?"

"Every unmarried woman in Australia is *interested* in him." Peggy laughed. "No other woman in the country would give him up."

"That's how I feel about Peter."

"There probably aren't as many girls wanting to marry him as there are in line for Clive," Peggy said dryly.

"Oh, I don't know." I looked away. "There's one very attractive girl who's interested in him."

"The one at the flying demonstration?" Peggy said at once. "It might be wise to find out what went on with her. It would be awful if she had some claim on him. I'm sorry, but she did look a little cheap."

"She's unimportant," I said. "It's over."

I sat back. I didn't feel like hearing any more on the topic from Peggy.

After a moment, Peg said, "I was wondering if you'd like to see *Ball of Fire* with Coop and Barbara Stanwyck next week? It's starting on Thursday at the Metro Collins Street."

"Peg, you know who Coop reminds me of, don't you?"

"Who? Oh, good heavens, not Captain Stephens!"

I smiled.

Peg became enthused. "There *is* a resemblance. But the captain looks more like Coop a few years back."

I nodded. "Exactly. In *Morocco* with Marlene Dietrich." When Cooper's face was as young and soft as Peter's.

Peggy smiled in agreement but then she looked serious. "I'm sorry, Faye, if it will upset you to see Coop, don't worry."

I laughed. "What a fate that would be – too upset to see Gary Cooper! I can hardly wait till Thursday to see him again and be reminded of Peter. Like in our English Literature essays, we can compare and contrast!"

We gathered our gloves and handbags and went outside to find Michael already parked, waiting to drive us home.

20. Once a Victim

Peter:

Melbourne, April 1942

At my billet, I kept to myself after I got back from Portsea. I was full of the excitement of her and missing her like hell. My duties and her family commitments meant that we couldn't see each other that week till Saturday. On Friday night, after most guys hit the sack, I was standing up in the mansion's high tower, leaning out of the archway, and staring over the treetops to where her house stood in the distance. In the moonlight, I could easily make out the gleaming line of the river and the dark shadows of the Botanic Gardens opposite her place. Melbourne looked serene and still.

When the duty officer came up to tell me a girl was on the phone, I felt surprised. Why would Faye be calling?

It was Iris. "Pete, I've had some trouble. I was attacked in the lane near the Tiv tonight. It'll hit the papers tomorrow, and I wanted…" her voice broke.

I swallowed hard, trying to ignore the churning in my gut. "Are you okay? What happened?"

"It was probably the same guy who got those other girls. He grabbed me. Did what he wanted. I was lucky to get away."

My heart raced. Sweat poured off me. Iris pinned down on stones in an alleyway, squashed, with his breath on her, in pain as he forced his way in. Now she knew the unique desolate loneliness and numb fear that wouldn't vanish. I gripped the phone. My hand shook. The duty guy stared at me wide-eyed.

I turned away, fell into a chair and tried to talk calmly. "Thank God you were strong enough to get away, Iris." I passed a weary hand over my eyes. Thrown to the ground. Struggling. Kicking. Being punched. Flattened. Pierced. I tried to stay on track and hear what she was saying.

"I would have liked to tell you face to face. But I didn't want you to read it in the paper or hear from your officers."

"Shouldn't you be in hospital or seeing a doctor?"

"I'll be all right." But there were tears in her voice. "I'm not looking forward to the stuff in the papers."

"Yeah, it's terrible so many people have to know. But our military cops or the Aussies will get the guy. You don't have anything to feel ashamed about, Iris. It's not your fault, honey. Have you seen a doctor?"

"Yes. There's nothing much …" she started to cry.

"Iris, do you want me to come to see you?"

"Oh, yes, Pete. Would you?" Her voice was still muffled.

"Is it too late? I could come first thing in the morning."

"Come over now, Pete. I won't get much sleep tonight anyway. Tomorrow I have to see the cops, answer all their questions."

"Okay, honey, I'll come right over."

I stood up and felt an odd dizziness. The floor had swerved. It was on a slant, like on a ship. Pirate Pete, comforter of the raped. I walked quickly to a car.

She must have been attacked leaving the Tiv after a show, taking the short cut along the lanes. He'd probably been watching her.

At the corner of her street, I felt like turning right around. But I would damned well go on and comfort her.

I went to the front door, unlike the other times. The brass doorstep shone in the moonlight, and the scent of flowers wafted from the garden. I rapped the brass knocker once and hoped it didn't wake Iris's little sister. I felt awkward returning after dumping Iris without a word.

Mr Kelly opened the door. He looked beaten. I couldn't bring myself to call him Jack; he barely noticed when I said Mr Kelly. He managed a civil greeting and led me down the narrow passageway to the breakfast room, where Iris and her mother and sister were sitting at the table. The room looked unusually messy. It was sad to recall how happy it had been the last time I'd been there.

Iris gave a cry and stood up. I greeted her mother, who looked shocked, red-eyed and exhausted. She grabbed my hand hard for a second. I hugged her shoulders for a moment, then held out my arms to Iris.

"Iris, honey. You're so brave."

She sobbed, collapsing onto me. Her mother motioned her sister away.

"There's tea in the pot, Pete, brandy on the table, beer in the ice chest. Just sing out if you need me, Iris love."

The others left the room. Iris's face, arms and neck were bruised. Was she paid per show? I would try to persuade her to accept some money from me.

I said, "Would you be more comfortable on a soft chair in the other room?"

She shook her head, and we sat on the wooden chairs, side by side. I saw the bruising on her legs.

"Jesus, honey."

"No ankle sprains, thank God. The doctor said there's no broken bones."

"No, and I can see there's no swelling." I reached for my cigarettes, lit two and passed one to her. I'd made a habit of doing that after we laughed at it in *Now Voyager* with Paul Henreid and Bette Davis.

She gripped my hand like a lifeline, took a long drag and looked at me calmly for the first time. "At least I got away." Her smile was bitter.

161

"Yep."

I hoped she would be ok. Her damn church didn't permit abortion, but I figured she wouldn't be fooled by that. I was trying not to see two sets of pictures in my mind. Like two horror movies, one above another. I concentrated on her oval face and her red-gold hair. This attack would take her ages to forget; it would ruin her brothers' next leave.

She took a pull on her cigarette, her hand shaking. "When he grabbed me, I tried to push him off, but he was too strong, and I fell. It was all I could do to stop him breaking my leg. Once I'd hit the ground, he was all over me. God, it hurt." She stared past me.

She was seeing her attacker, hearing and feeling it all. I stopped the movies starting up in my head. "Iris, we don't have to talk about it if you don't want to."

"I feel better talking about it to you, Pete. You and I had such gorgeous nights together. This bloke tonight isn't gunna break me. Nothing could ever spoil the times you and I had."

"That's about the nicest thing anyone's ever said to me, Iris." I stroked her hand.

"It's true, Pete. Didn't we have good nights?" She met my eyes.

"Yep, absolutely, honey, we did. Great nights." I smiled. It wasn't her fault that they hadn't meant as much to me.

"I'll be damned if I'll let that bugger make me feel bad about us, or about sleeping with anyone else," she said fiercely. "Why should I feel different? I won't!"

"That's right, honey. You keep on sayin' that." My jaw clenched. I stopped myself blurting out that I knew just how she felt. Thank Christ she wouldn't have it happen over and over. I held her hand tight and stared into her eyes. "You have to hang on to the good times and wipe out the bad. You're gonna get through this."

"I will. I know I will. I just… God, Pete, I couldn't believe how much it hurt. Not just him being so rough but my back pressing into the stones on the ground and his weight crushing my chest and his hands squeezing me like I was a piece of paper, and all the time I'm thinking I've got to get up from under him when he comes because that'll be my only chance or else he'll kill me, and when he finished hammering into me and came, he stopped gripping so hard and he reared his head and chest, and I kneed him in the crown jewels and ran for my life, and God, when I staggered into Collins Street I was never so glad to see drunken soldiers bailed up by a cop in all my life."

"Jesus, Iris. You kept your head. You were smart and brave. Thank God you can run fast. If there hadn't been a cop, someone would have helped you. Even drunk soldiers." We clung together, crying.

"Oh, Pete. Will they catch him? I have to describe him to a police artist tomorrow. That should help, shouldn't it?"

"Yep. It'll make catching him a helluva lot easier."

"He had an accent, American."

"Like anyone in the movies?"

"Not that I remember."

"Did you get a look at him?"

"Not really, I was struggling so much. He was only about my height." Her eyes clouded. "He had hairy fingers, a wide mouth. Strong, large hands."

I poured us a brandy and tossed mine down. Its fire preoccupied me.

"You're tired, Iris. I should let you get some sleep."

She sipped the brandy and then put it down with a shudder. "I'm too exhausted for that. And I'm sore all over. Will you wait for me while I go to the lavatory?"

I helped her down the steps of the back porch and along the brick path to the toilet. "I'll be right here, honey."

163

I remembered the fear. Unlikely as it was that someone might be prowling, it was possible. The fear of the rape could make it seem likely to happen again at any instant, and most likely as soon as you had pulled down your pants. Was it only the once that I stood in the grey orphanage urinal, shaking too much to unbutton my trousers, and peeing all over myself and the concrete floor?

"Thanks, Pete. It makes me feel safe to have you standing there. Gawd, what a baby I am."

"No, you're not. Hey, there are two possums in the gum tree near the fence. Little varmints, cheeky as can be. Cute curly tails."

"They'll be thundering over the roof soon," she said. "Then they're not so cute."

I heard the lavatory chug and flush. She unlatched the door, and I helped her down the step. I turned on the light for her to wash her hands and face in the laundry room next door that they called the washhouse.

We walked slowly at her pace up to the back door.

"Do you want me to clear away the cups and things?"

"Nuh, leave it. Mum won't mind."

"Do you want me to call your Mom to help you undress?"

She shook her head and leant her weight on me. I held her with one arm as I turned off the lights, except for the one in the passage. We reached her room. I sat her on the chair and turned down the bed. Her little sister was sleeping quietly across the room.

She felt limp as I gently helped her undress.

I whispered, "Am I upsetting you?"

"No, you couldn't ever," she murmured.

I took her nightie, as she called it, from under her pillow. She put up her arms like a child to let me put it on her. She left her underpants on and reached out for me to lift her onto the bed.

I covered her and tucked her in lightly; those sore legs didn't want tight bedclothes. I bent and kissed her cheek as she smiled wearily.

"Thanks, Pete. G'night."

"I'll call you tomorrow, honey. If you want, I'll go to the police with you."

She nodded hazily. I touched her cheek and tiptoed out, turning off the light. As I was opening the front door, her mother appeared in a dressing gown, alert and strained.

"Pete, how is she? Do you think she'll sleep?"

"Yes, she's exhausted. Falling asleep as I left. She's dealing with it mighty well. You know how strong she is, Ma. But she'll need to take it easy for a while. She won't be able to stop thinking about it."

She nodded, her eyes moist. "I know. Thanks for coming so quickly, Pete. She's fond of you." Ma's face pinched, and then she smiled sadly at me.

"She's a great girl, Ma. She's gonna be fine. If you all want, I can go to the police with her tomorrow. I'll call, I mean, I'll ring you in the morning."

"Thanks, Pete. I'll check on her before I go back to bed."

I let the brake off and rolled away from the house. Only when I reached the intersection did I turn on the dimmed headlights and engage the engine. Probably it wouldn't have woken her up, or her father, if the poor guy was getting any sleep.

As I drove through the deserted, silent streets, faint light was edging up in the east. I whizzed over the old iron bridge with the soft weeping willows flapping around it, past the valleys and parks. Then I stopped suddenly and jumped out. I threw up the brandy and whatever else until there was nothing. Still, my stomach heaved and caved. I rolled over on the grass, my head in my hands.

The two movies I had been pushing out of sight flashed up. I was in them. The first: the sound of the cane whizzing through air to cut me. The grey shadow of the stick on the white wall. Watching it. Waiting for it. The burning as it whipped. The whack of the cane hitting the floor. Father O'Malley's thin hands grabbing me. His blurry shadow moving to its own rhythm on the wall. Pain like fire inside. The second movie: Harris looking down at me. Grimace of a smile. Pointing the knife straight at my throat. Pushing till it touched. Bled. Unbuttoning his trousers.

I rolled and rolled along the grass. I couldn't see a thing at first. Just darkness as though my eyes were shut. I stopped on my back. The stars were still out. The sharp, bright stars of this strange hemisphere. Another country. Forget. Faye lived by the slow river, near the fragrant gardens. We had slept a few rooms apart in that high stone house by the dark roaring sea.

Back in my room, I stood at the door and listened to my roommates' breathing. The gardenia from Isobel's was on my bedside table. I sniffed its sharp sweetness like a drug. I held the perfect flower in front of my face. Gleaming white and beautiful, it stood strong on its stem, but soon it would brown, wilt and rot. I'd never sleep. I couldn't conjure up how Faye felt in my arms. It was like she'd turned into a painting on the wall.

21. Need and Desire

Faye:
Melbourne, April 1942

I slept a little later than usual on Saturday morning and ran downstairs to find that my parents and Edith had finished breakfast. I took mine out to the courtyard. My father had left the newspaper on the table. The front page had the usual war stories and pictures, but a woman's face looked up at me from the side column. Something seemed familiar about her, but how could it? She was a showgirl. Even before I read the story, my breath quickened. This was the girl with Peter at the flying demonstration, the one at the ball.

Tiv Girl Attacked was the headline. Tivoli dancer said the caption under the photo. I wrinkled my nose. The Tivoli! Girls there were hardly dancers! Striptease and so-called 'nudes' were the style there. Someone at university had said that girls in Tiv shows were permitted to be naked if they didn't move, so they formed tableaux, and everyone gawped. No *lady* would step inside the Tivoli. Eddie went to see comedians and singers there. My parents didn't. I remembered the fuss when Mo, Bel and Eddie had wanted to see someone famous at the Tivoli and my mother had refused to go.

In the photo, the girl's costume was skimpy. She had super legs.

I took in the point suddenly. This girl was another victim of the rapist-murderer. What had happened to the poor thing? Was she dead? No, the headline said, just ATTACKED.

I read the details and felt sick. Not that the paper said everything, but I could imagine. Thank God she had got away, even if she hadn't been able to fend him off at the start. Who could? He was probably crazy and full of grog. MINOR INJURIES, said the report. What did that really mean? Wouldn't the attack ruin the girl's life? Not forever if she was strong, but even so.

The report said that Miss Kelly was assisting the police with a description of the criminal. As in previous reports, a US GI uniform was mentioned.

I thought of Peggy's gloomy predictions about this girl. Ridiculous. Peter wanted *me*, not this poor Iris. I drank my tea and looked at the photo again. How would Peter react? Would he go to see Iris? Would she contact him? I hadn't asked him anything about Iris, and that had been the right thing to do, but now I wished I knew more about their affair, and when they had stopped seeing each other. Peggy's words, "some claim on him" echoed in my head. Perhaps he might feel he should be helpful, and that would be kind and proper. But he didn't want Iris, he wanted *me*. He loved *me*.

Just then my mother appeared and saw me with the front page. "Oh, my goodness, isn't it dreadful? That poor girl. Thank goodness she got away. How sad that she was walking down that lane late at night. Whatever is in these girls' heads? Why don't their families or their employers escort them to the station? That's not to be expected of *Tivoli* people, I suppose. You know, dear, it sounds absurd, but there's something familiar about that girl. Don't you think so?"

I stiffened. "Oh, I'm not sure. Perhaps we have seen her somewhere at a dance or a war party."

"A dance?" My mother gave me a quick look. "I don't go to dances. She wouldn't have been at the Governor's Ball. Ah, now I remember, she was at the flying demonstration for the War Appeal; we saw her with Captain Stephens when he said hello.

Surely you remember, Faye?"

I hoped I wasn't blushing. "Oh, yes, you're right."

My mother smiled. "I wonder if the Captain is still her boyfriend. I don't think the Maddoxs will be impressed, except by her looks. She is a very attractive girl. Irish skin, of course."

I pushed my half-eaten eggs aside and pretended to eat my toast. Mummy wafted back inside the house.

The telephone rang. Ellen announced that Peggy was on the phone. Peg's tone of consternation and sympathy was irritating; she kept on about whether Captain Stephens was still involved with the girl, and whether that might be difficult for me when I told my parents about breaking my engagement. She advised delay in that matter. I ended the conversation swiftly.

I was halfway up the stairs when the phone rang again. It was Peter. He was taking Iris to the police. The Kellys didn't have a car. He had an emergency meeting in the afternoon at General Maddox's office. He couldn't say when he'd be free.

I was very understanding. Of course, he should do as much as he could to help. Perhaps he could phone later?

I put down the telephone and fled to my room, feeling flat and unsettled. He sounded upset. What had the girl meant to him? Had they slept together? Of course. A girl like that. And a man like him. I must not fool myself. I felt such a child, powerless and mystified. What did Iris know about Peter, and about how to love a man, that I didn't? Peter liked my inexperience, didn't he? Or did men really want what Iris and her kind knew? I would have to raid Eddie's books. But that wouldn't be enough. I pressed my hands over my eyes. He loved *me*, not Iris.

The phone rang again. I went to the landing and heard my mother speaking excitedly to Eddie. Then Eddie asked to speak to me.

"Awful story," he said, "but marvellous that Miss Kelly escaped. So much for Nell's spiteful accusations about Peter."

"Absolutely."

"Moira seems to think that Miss Kelly is a friend of Peter's, or was? Perhaps that's old news to you?"

"Yes. But they haven't seen each other for ages." I felt another stab of doubt.

He sounded relieved and then invited me to visit Meredith and Neil later in the day.

"I'd love to, but by dinnertime Peter may be free."

"Would you like to ask him to meet us there?"

"Will Meredith mind?"

"Mind? She's dying to set eyes on him."

I dressed, feeling more cheerful. I phoned Peter's billet house and left Meredith's address for him; he had already left – to support Iris Kelly, no doubt.

I was keen to visit Meredith and Neil and to see their art collection – and to be with people who weren't stuffy. I was curious to hear their reaction to the story of Iris Kelly. Most of Melbourne would see the attack as at least partly the girl's fault.

Eddie picked me up after lunch. I was relieved that he had a ration ticket for petrol.

"I haven't used the car lately," he said. "Easier to walk to most places in town."

I relaxed a little as we left the crowded suburbs. Meredith and Neil Black's property was in hilly bush land, the only building for miles. The home was pretty, a wooden double-fronted farmhouse painted in a pale pink like houses in the south of France. The woodwork on the facade and windows was elaborate. Flowers framed the front door. There were trees, shrubs, herbs and blooms everywhere you looked. I smiled, recalling my mother's scorn; she couldn't deny the beauty of this place surely, though she would think it a come-down from the Toorak mansions of Meredith's family.

Meredith welcomed me warmly. "When is your pilot joining

us? Eddie speaks of no-one else. I must congratulate you, Faye, on snaffling him from a Tiv dancer. Not many of us could beat a Tivoli girl."

I laughed, blushing. Thank goodness Mummy wasn't there! It was refreshing to talk of what was really happening. I noticed Meredith's loose-limbed walk and her sleek, comfortable blouse and trousers. Presumably, she knew a lot about love. I found her old, but apparently men did not. Thanks to her pedigree and wealth, and her loyal husband, she weathered rumours of affairs with artists. It was unthinkable for me to ask her anything about love or men, but I hoped, rather pathetically, that she might let something helpful drop. Reputedly, people said outlandish things in her house. I would notice everything.

It was afternoon tea-time, and Eddie had not exaggerated: it was a lavish feast of cakes and scones, with jams and fruits from the property. We sat around a long wooden table in the kitchen with three artists, a young man scarcely older than me and two older men.

"We have simple lunches," Meredith said, "Cheese and bread or soup, so by arvo tea, we are starving. It's my favourite meal."

The talk was not what one heard at afternoon teas in town. Little about the war and lots about art. Hardly any gossip about people in Melbourne. The Blacks didn't care who was doing or buying what. Or who was loving whom. It had taken me rather too long to realise that when people spoke of the Blacks' free living, they were using a Melbourne euphemism for free love.

When Iris Kelly was mentioned, I was not surprised to find a new attitude to the story.

"How do the well-off imagine a girl from the theatre gets home?" Neil said scornfully. "They probably think she can afford taxis."

I felt ashamed. I hadn't thought about what Iris earned or how she travelled home. Even my mother had been more aware.

I had spent half the day imagining Peter and Iris in bed or trying not to. It was selfish, and shallow, but I couldn't help it.

"Awful to think of that lovely girl mistreated," said the young artist called Herb. "Iris is an absolute peach. Bright red hair. Legs as long as a doorway. I wanted to paint her, remember, Neil?"

Neil looked blank. His demeanour did not stray from that of the devoted husband who never noticed other beautiful women. I wondered about him, but he had not flirted with me.

"Good God!" said Meredith. "Has she been here?"

"Once. I tried to sketch her, but she refused. She seemed terrified that I would paint her nude or in some embarrassing pose."

I couldn't help feeling impressed by Iris's surprising caution. "But doesn't she appear practically naked at the Tivoli?" I asked, trying to sound off-hand. I just had to know what Iris wore, or didn't, in those shows.

"She's not one of the pretend statues. She wears short costumes or ballet tutus. I really wanted her to sit for me." He shot a look at Meredith who fluttered her lashes and gazed out the window.

Neil sucked sympathetically on his pipe; I had to hide a shudder.

"A prim Tivoli girl," drawled Meredith. "How fascinating." Her smile to the men was shocking in its camaraderie.

"Does she do tap dancing?" I asked.

Herb nodded. "And a bastardised version of ballet. She's a star of the tap routines, such strength and speed."

Meredith passed me an exquisite old plate piled with plums. "I wish I had seen her. Or have I?"

Her carelessness made me hide a smile.

Eddie grinned. "You were with us at the Tiv on Cup Eve

last year, darling. We all saw Miss Kelly dancing on gold coins."

"Ah yes, that song from *Forty-Second Street*," said Neil, nodding.

"I can't pretend to remember much of that show," said Meredith.

"It was a very big night, buckets of champagne," Eddie reminded her.

"I'm glad she got away," Meredith said. "Good old Tiv girls. Long may they dance and kick."

Just before dinnertime, Peter arrived. I felt a rush of love to see him. Meredith grabbed his arm straightaway. I stiffened at the heat in the older woman's eyes, but immediately felt pleased by how adroitly he responded. He didn't turn off his charm and warmth, yet his posture created a distance. I wanted to hug him. My jealousy surprised me. How could I feel such rage not just at Iris, but at this dried-up older woman? Gazing at Peter, I really couldn't blame poor Meredith.

"May we call you Peter?" Meredith smiled up at him and slipped her arm under his. "Do come and look at the garden and the paddocks before the light goes. After dinner, we'll look at paintings."

We all strolled down a valley to the river among gardens that were nothing like the symmetrical showplaces of Toorak or Macedon. The trees were mostly native gums, and despite the kitchen garden and the fruit trees higher up on the hill near the house, the place had a free, wild feeling that I liked. The atmosphere of woods and park merged into bushland away from the house. The fragrance in the air was unfamiliar at times, and now and then like in the bush around my grandmother's station. There was nothing planned or grandiose or English.

"How *is* Miss Kelly, Peter?" Eddie asked gently as we sat down at the table in the kitchen.

Everyone looked relieved when he told us how quickly she had escaped and how well she was coping.

Eddie said, "Peter, we saw Miss Kelly in the *Forty-Second Street* numbers. Terrific dancer. Picturing her getting away from that cad is very cheering."

"Yes, lots of girls wouldn't have the nerve to fight back," I said.

Peter squeezed my hand.

Meredith raised her beer. "A toast to Iris. Eddie, give us something witty, darling."

He stood. "To Iris and the girls of the Tiv: may they never have to do a thing they don't want."

The older men laughed. I saw Peter's face darken.

Meredith and Eddie showed Peter and me the art in the house and studio. One of the older artists had arrived from Europe just before the war; his work was full of the suffering in his homeland in Eastern Europe. Peter stared at the paintings for a long time; I saw how deeply he was moved.

The other older artist was Australian. I was startled by his work: Melbourne scenes, but so stark and unpleasant. The effect of the war, as he saw it. Peter seemed to recognise the mood in these pictures. I was shocked at the bleak depiction of frenzied, drunken encounters between leering men in uniform and women who looked garish and uninhibited. Were these scenes real or from the artist's morose mind? I saw so little of my town.

I noticed Peter warding off waves of exhaustion and suggested we should leave. Eddie was staying, as he often did, apparently.

Nestling in Peter's car, I said, "I can't get used to driving into Melbourne and not seeing lights bright in the distance."

After a moment, he said, "Art is what you really care about, isn't it? What kind of things do you paint?"

"Mostly portraits." I snuggled into his shoulder. "I'd like to paint you, though I doubt I'm good enough to catch your moods."

He stared at me for a second, looking surprised and a touch embarrassed. I stroked his neck.

"You control your moods very well. I can see how deep your feelings run. Sometimes your face shows such a mixture of emotions I can't work them out."

"You don't want to know, baby." His grin was wry, almost bitter. "Have you sold many paintings?"

"None. I just dabble."

"Won't you have an exhibition?"

"I don't expect so."

"But you enjoy it, that's great." His face softened.

"We all need to do something we love."

His face turned dark and serious. I wondered if he was remembering before the war.

We reached dimly lit, ordered streets.

I said, "We're very close to a lovely park alongside the river. If you're not too tired, we could see it."

He insisted that he wasn't tired. He drove down the winding narrow road to the water and parked near a footbridge. We walked under huge gum trees and sat on a bench by the river. No one was there. All around us were tall gum trees on hills flanking the river. The only sound was the rustling of the leaves and the soft ripple of the water.

"You wouldn't know that downtown was a few miles away." He sounded sombre and weary.

I said, "It must have been awful for you going through all that horror with Iris and the police."

With no warning, he collapsed onto me like a drowning man. His racked sobs echoed in the moonlit park. For a second, I felt close to panic, but I held him fast.

It was frightening, the way he stayed silent. As though he were far away. As though despair had him by the throat. As though it left no breath for desire.

"I know you can't talk about it, darling," I whispered. "I wish I could help you more."

He didn't move a muscle or say a word. I stroked his back and held him close.

After a long time, I said, "Are you all right, darling? Let's go to your billet and I can call a cab from there. I can drive if you like. Or do you want to stay out? I couldn't bear it if you were sad and alone."

He sat up but did not meet my eyes. "I'll drive you home. I'm okay now."

We hardly spoke on the way. When he stopped the car a few houses down from mine, he said quietly, "I'm sorry you had to see me like that."

I protested, but he said, "Talk about weak. Some hero, huh?"

"Peter, it isn't weak to feel sad about cruel things. The way you reacted shows me what a good man you are. I already knew you were a hero. I'm glad I was here."

"I don't know what I would have done if you weren't. I couldn't sleep last night. The only thing that got me through the night was thinking of you in Isobel's garden with that white flower in your hair."

22. Finding Fault

Peter:

Melbourne, April 1942

The next free night I had, I took Iris out. I didn't tell Faye. I was feeling bad about Iris, and close yet not close to Faye. I took Iris to the American Officers' Club to cheer her up, but made sure a girlfriend of hers came too, so she didn't get the wrong idea.

She joked to her friend, "Pete's taking a night off from the toffs."

I laughed and squirmed.

Iris said, "I told Mollie about your rich girlfriend."

"She's not my girlfriend. She's gonna drop me sooner or later. Her family won't have a bar of me."

"And she's engaged. Not that she seems to worry about that." She grinned at Mollie. "Guess who she's engaged to – Clive Wilson."

Mollie's eyes darkened. "Then I feel sorry for her. Yeah, Iris, I know you hate her guts, but I feel sorry for any girl mixed up with Wilson."

I leaned forward. "How come?"

Mollie flushed. "Aw, I can't tell you."

I tried to catch her eye. She never seemed to look at anyone, like she was unused to staring at folks. I said, "I don't wanna pry into your personal business."

"Nah, I never went with him. I knew better, thank God. I seen what he was like."

Iris touched her arm. "Gee, Mollie, I wouldn't blame anyone giving it a burl with a squatter. But I'm glad you didn't if he's a bully. Lots of those rich blokes are."

"Yeah, he's like the rest."

I said, "I don't stand a chance with Faye in the long run, but she's a sweet girl, and she doesn't have much of a clue about guys who push gals around. I wouldn't like her to get hurt. She's thinking of giving him the brush, anyway."

"Tell her to get away from him." Mollie spoke softly, her eyes down.

"I will. She's gonna think I'm just jealous. But like I say, she was thinking of dropping him anyway."

Iris gave me a dirty look and downed her drink. Then she asked, "Mollie, did you hear about him in the country?"

Mollie nodded. "He owns all the land where we come from. We aren't supposed to even go there anymore but the old people do."

I felt the hairs standing up on the back of my neck. I recognized that story of being told where to live, where not to walk. "I hear what you're sayin' Mollie, and I'm sorry."

She met my eyes for a second. "Thanks, Pete. Iris, you have to promise, if I say any more, that you won't tell anyone at the Tiv."

I tensed up. "Mollie, I don't wanna cause trouble for you."

Mollie turned to Iris. "I reckon I can trust you, can't I?"

Iris nodded. "I won't tell a soul, love, promise."

"The Tiv woulda never given me the job if the boss saw my family, even photos of 'em – or met my auntie."

Iris said softly, "Geez, are you saying you're a—" She stopped.

"Yeah, I'm one of them."

Iris gaped. "Cripes, they mightn't keep you on at the Tiv if they knew. I had no idea. I didn't know Abos could be pretty and so good at dancing."

I felt myself reddening. My foot started tapping an angry

rhythm.

Iris saw me glaring at her and said, "But it makes no difference, Mollie, we're mates."

"Yeah, you've been a good mate, Iris. I wouldn't have got through me first weeks in the show without you. The blokes took notice when you shooed them away."

Iris said quickly, "Well, you're just a kid. I know you said you were eighteen, but I picked you for a bit less, love."

I grinned. "I've done that heaps of times. You have to, don't you?"

Mollie relaxed a little. "Yeah. I couldn't keep stayin' at Auntie's for free, I had to get some work."

Iris was still wide-eyed. "But you're only a quarter caste or something anyway, aren't you?"

I said quickly, "Hey, I hate those labels."

Mollie glanced at me, with a half-smile. "My parents had white dads, some of my brothers did too. Blokes like your girl's fiancé."

I felt my skin prickling. "Yeah?"

"Two cousins in my family, they have kids of Clive Wilson's. One of them has two of his."

Iris had a malicious glint in her eye that I wished I wasn't seeing. Did she hate Faye or just resent her?

She said, "Bloody hell!"

I said, "I hope he at least gave your cousins some money or housing."

Mollie shook her head. "The kids are gone. Taken. In a State or Church home, because they are half white and Wilson didn't want to know about them, though my cousin told him. None of us are allowed to know where they are." She grabbed her drink.

I felt a surge of rage at Wilson and all of them. And I worried that I had brought down the blues on this girl again. But I had to know more. "How old are the kids?"

She said, "There's a boy about four, a two-year-old girl and a one-year-old boy."

"And your cousins were grabbed by Wilson on his land? Were they working for him?"

"No, they live with our family in the closed settlement, but sometimes everyone goes to the special places with the old people, the places where we belong. That's how come they were there when Wilson was looking for girls. Bad luck, ay, because he isn't there all the time."

She looked down and I thanked her again. I felt a wave of rage. Did guys like Wilson know which times of year to find the black girls? Even if it was haphazard, it was so cruel I couldn't speak.

Iris moved the talk onto something else, and I tried to keep up my side of things. Then I went to get drinks and food. When I came back, Mollie seemed to have relaxed a little and Iris, bless her, was hugging her arm.

*

When I asked some of the posher Aussie pilots about restaurants downtown, preferably Italian, they said that Italian was a bit on the nose now and lots of Italians were in work camps, but some old Melbourne places were open because there was such a demand. One of the best was Florentino's in Bourke Street. So, the next night we could meet, I took Faye to dinner there. It was a relief when she said she had been there before the war with her family, rather than her fiancé. I liked the place straightaway. The wood-panelled walls were lined with paintings of famous places in Italy. On the tables were bowls of gleaming black olives, and lamps that gave a soft flush to the room.

We sat upstairs, overlooking the big trees along the street, but I asked for a table at the back. Faye was nervous someone might see her and tell her folks. The place was full of couples and almost all the guys were in US uniforms, so she said she felt safe. I stuck my neck out and asked if she expected to see gals in her circle with Yanks soon; she said one or two had already taken the plunge. I smiled to see that it didn't worry her.

I waited till we finished dessert. "Faye, I found out something about your fiancé."

She looked at me. "I'm going to break it off with him next month. He's been re-assigned to an Australian post. He's not injured, just coming home because of his family connections and their sourcing of the war effort. So, I'm going to tell him."

"Maybe you should write him," I said. "Don't feel you have to treat him gently."

She stared.

"I'm sorry if it makes you feel bad, but you ought to know this. When I took Iris and a friend out for drinks the other night to cheer her up, it turns out that the friend has relatives in the country, and to get to the point, Clive has had two women up there, and they have three children."

She froze, troubled, unsure. "How do you know?"

"The friend found it hard to tell me because the women are her cousins, and she was sad, almost ashamed about it. So I'm sure it's true."

Her eyes were furious. "How could he? How dare he treat me like that? When did he start with the first one?"

"Over four years ago."

"Before he asked me to marry him? Well, I suppose that's something. But what about the second girl?"

"That was later and probably went on till he left to fight overseas. Her kids are aged two and one."

Her eyes widened with shock and anger. "He kept on even after we were engaged? That is unforgivable."

"Give him the brush-off at your house. When your dad's home." I pictured the judge ordering Clive out of the joint.

She frowned. "Of course, I'll tell him at home. Wild horses wouldn't get me out with him, or even inside his parents' place."

I squeezed her hand. "I'm sorry to make you blue. But the guy's worse than you thought."

She drained her wine glass. I wondered if I should wait to refill it, but I poured us both another glass anyway.

"Faye, I can't understand how he could two-time you, of all girls." I felt a stab of guilt: hadn't I done just that?

Though her mouth smiled for a moment at my compliment, her eyes glanced off me. She said in a new, harsh tone, "I wouldn't go to a hotel room with him. He knew he couldn't even ask me."

I stroked her hand. "It's not just that. He didn't love you."

"But men think they have a right, don't they, practically all of them, to have what they want, not to wait." She stopped and half-sobbed.

I wished we were in a booth, so I could hold her.

She said quietly, "Even you, Peter. Even when you acted as if you were in love with me, you waltzed off to Iris."

I felt myself flush. "Yep. I'm not the kinda guy to do the right thing all the time. But I didn't go back to her after we really started seeing each other." I looked away from her scrutinising gaze. Who was I kidding? And how about the way I treated Iris? I was like most guys, looking out for my main chance.

I bent over and kissed her fingers. "I'm sorry. I didn't aim to hurt you. You're damned right. Men are heels most of the time. But I care about you, Faye. Don't let this news get you down. He's not worth a second of your pain." I smiled, gazing at those eyes of hers that I could swim into forever. "Pity the story hasn't got around a bit more," I said softly.

She stared past me. "Yes, if only we could tell my mother! That would put her off him."

I grinned at the gloating tone in her voice. "So why not tell her?"

She grimaced. "It's not the sort of thing we talk about. I couldn't explain how I found out. Perhaps I could ask Eddie to tell her." She gave a feeble laugh. "She would refuse to believe it anyway. Vera's son with bastards."

I felt a stab in my guts.

Faye wasn't looking at me. "Were the women married? Did they pass off the babies as their husband's children? If Mummy could be convinced of this, it would be marvellous."

"There's more that might turn her off." I was dying to get to it.

Her eyes had a new glitter. "What?"

"The thing is, the girls were Aboriginal. So he felt he could do what he liked."

I waited for her look of surprise, and it was there, but so was humiliation. That hurt me. Her shock looked close to shame – because he had slept with black women.

She sat silent for a long time.

At last, she met my eyes. "I don't believe this. It must be gossip spread by people who don't like the Wilsons."

I breathed out in disappointment. "That's unlikely. People hear about these things. Even rich guys can't hide a few children from everyone, especially from the Aboriginal relatives. And it doesn't sound as if naming a white guy as the father gets a damned thing for these Aboriginal girls, doesn't even let them keep their kids. They wouldn't say it if it wasn't true."

Her eyes were cold. She slid her hand from mine and clasped hers tightly together. "I don't believe it. Why would he? He can get any girl."

I stared at her. "Iris's friend says he thinks he owns everything and everyone."

Her eyes met mine, fearful.

"She said he doesn't help the mothers with money or anything." I couldn't be bothered keeping the hard note out of my voice.

"But the children may not be his. They could be anyone's. How many men would those women sleep with?"

I felt my leg hammering out a rhythm under the table. There was no point arguing against her insult to the women, but I felt it. "Don't white guys sometimes set up a house for their black woman and kids?"

"I have no idea," she said coldly, looking at her hands in her lap.

"They let their kids get rounded up, do they? Dumped in the church homes." Now my hands started drumming on the table. I stilled them. "Do the fathers see the kids or send them money?"

She shrugged. "I've never heard of that happening. The Aborigines don't live the way we do, anyway."

Her cold air of distaste annoyed the hell out of me. I wanted to ask if she'd accept those kids as her stepchildren if they were white.

She said, "Peter, I've never come across any Aborigines on our land. I can't recall seeing any on Clive's property for years either."

I took a big swallow of what passed for coffee. "Sure. They keep out of the way of your horses when you ride."

"But most of the Aborigines around here died out a long time ago, Peter."

"Not the girl who told me. Not those girls in the country or their kids."

She didn't look abashed. "They are half or quarter caste, or less, the remnants. The real blacks died out a long time ago. Before my grandfather's time."

I said, "I bet the grandfather of Clive's kids remembers how his father or grandfather got shot down."

She looked affronted. "They died mainly of diseases, Peter, admittedly ones introduced by my British forebears. But people must explore and settle new lands. It's progress, civilisation."

She showed no hint of uncertainty. "If you look back through history, Peter," she said dismissively, with a calm that turned my stomach, "it is always the stronger, more developed race or group that takes over. That's progress. Look at Britain."

I stifled a groan. I tapped my fingers on the arms of my chair. It hadn't occurred to her that Americans had had a bone to pick with the British, but that wasn't what was riling me. "You didn't like it some time back when I argued there would always be wars, but now it doesn't seem to bother you."

She eyed me as if I was impolite, but she would overlook it. Apparently, she didn't see the conflict in her country as war, however many natives had died. I felt a wave of tiredness. I thought of Buzz and all the dangerous, heavy-lifting jobs he did and would do till he was too old or injured. If he survived the war. I thought of Becky working in the field with us, her huge belly getting in her way, or her new baby strapped on her. I wondered what shit job Luella did now.

What was I doing here with this woman?

I paid the bill, and we walked downstairs. Outside, we walked to my car in silence. She didn't sit close like before, and that was fine with me.

I pulled out from the kerb. "Aren't there Aborigines in the Aussie army?" I glanced at her blank face. "You don't know or care, do you? But you can just bet there are. Fighting and dying for you and the Wilsons. While their sisters get raped by your men."

"Oh, Peter, that's an awful thing to say. For heaven's sake, if such things still happen, they are certainly not commonplace. You're over-reacting to what is mere gossip. Sad things happened in the past, but what have they got to do with you or me?"

"Sad and bad things like that are none of my business, huh, so I shouldn't care about them? Well, I'm not from this country. I don't know your fiancé. But I care about those black kids of his because I know what happens to black kids back home."

Her face barely changed. I wished I was smart enough to describe Becky's flimsy little Louisiana house and Buzz's crowded Harlem rat hole, but I couldn't draw them so she would care; she'd just be mystified, or disgusted.

She said, "Were there black labourers on the ranch where you worked?"

"Sure, but the ones I knew best were folks I worked with, ate with, went to church with, and lived with."

She looked surprised. "Oh." Her detached tone made my spine tense up even more.

"I helped them work the farm they leased," I said. "They're like family."

She looked startled and uncertain.

"Buzz is the best friend I ever had. Closer than a brother. His mom, Bernice, I call her Momma. She's been like a mom to me – she scolds me about manners, and she sees how I'm feelin.' Her daughter, Luella is like my little sister. I practically taught her to walk. Momma's sister, Becky and her man, Paul and their kids are like family too."

Her face was tense with surprise. "Did they adopt you?"

I laughed. "Couldn't happen in the South, ma'am."

She flushed. "I mean, are they your… relatives?"

"Don't worry, I don't have darkie blood, ma'am, as far as I know."

She shook her head as if she hadn't thought I was a half-breed for a moment, and said, "I just thought it was unusual for a young white man to be living with a Negro family."

"It's unheard of. You don't cross the colour line in the South. I've never told anyone before. Anyone white. All I'm gonna say is that when I was a kid, Momma and Becky gave me a home."

What I wasn't going to say – to her or anyone – was how it happened, how Momma and I looked down at that sadist's stiffening carcass, my perfect bullet hole in his forehead, watching the blood spread out around his head, and she said, "You don't have no place to go, do you, child?"

You could say she and her folks owed me, but they didn't have to take me in.

I said, "I had no place to go, no work, nothing."

Fear was all I had back then.

I turned to her. "They didn't have to let me stay as long as I wanted. They didn't have to love me, and not for always."

Faye nodded; she looked surprised and thoughtful.

What I didn't dare tell her was that they hid me in their part of the country when I was going to be rubbed out and no-one would have missed me. My life was at risk every day for years in gang fights, but once I killed a white gang member to save a black woman, my punishment would have been torture, then a drawn-out, dirty death.

We drove in silence and crossed the river. I felt tense as hell. If she had a clue about how violent my life had been before Momma – I stopped myself remembering and focused on the road. I realised I had avoided the route past the rotunda. We crossed on an old narrow bridge of ornate iron. I parked alongside the river, at the bottom of her street. It was dark with the brown-out, a great spot for cuddling, but I didn't feel like it.

She said, "Peter, I feel I've disappointed you. I know you understand more than anyone how children suffer without a mother. I can't accept that what you told me is true, that it concerns Clive, let alone me, but you have made me feel sorry for those Aboriginal mothers and children."

I jumped out and held the door for her. We stood opposite each other. I couldn't wait to get out of there.

She looked up at me. "Don't be angry with me, Peter. We must try to see things through each other's eyes and that's hard sometimes."

Without touching her, I muttered goodbye, ran round the front of the car and jumped in. She looked upset but smiled and started walking up the hill. Usually, I walked with her. What if she was attacked, what if some guy leapt out of the dark shadows of the Botanic Gardens? I wrenched the car around, drove level with her and swung open the door.

"I'll drive you up to the house."

"Thank you." Her voice was quiet, with no resentment. She climbed in, her face uncertain. I stopped at the house next to hers, and she said, "Peter, half an hour ago, you were telling me you love me. Now it feels as if you want to say goodbye."

"Do you?" I couldn't help saying it roughly.

She took in a breath. "No, I couldn't bear it. Peter, there are bound to be times when I don't understand how you see things. That doesn't change how I feel about you. You told me an awful story tonight, and then suddenly you stopped caring about how I feel. You started acting as though I were upsetting you. I see that I did upset you and I'm sorry, but I was trying to speak honestly."

I could barely look at her. She didn't have a clue about how she had made me feel, or about what I had tried to tell her. "We just don't fit, do we?"

"You mean because of this difference of opinion – well, of experience, really – this difference of attitude towards black people? That isn't all important, is it, Peter? What does it have to do with you and me? You said your black friends are like family to you, and they must be good people, but we're going to live here, aren't we?"

So, you'll never have to meet them, I thought. If you ever did, you'd look down on them and never talk to them like people, only like servants.

She tried to catch my eye. "Peter, I'm not the sort of person who looks down on blacks."

No, only on your own Aborigines – my Negroes woo you with song and dance.

My voice came out cutting and sarcastic. "All men are created equal, huh?"

"That's what I've always believed," she said. "I admire you for having friends among black and white."

"I'm not looking for admiration." How would she feel if she knew about Rita and the coloured showgirls I had slept with? She couldn't believe Clive would stoop to black women; could she suspect it of me? But dammit, I didn't care, because they suited me fine and I didn't meet many white girls who made me feel as great as they did. Except this one, sometimes, but she was worlds away from me and we would never make it. She gave me the blues the way she was so sure of her place in the world, above folks like Buzz and Luella and me.

Her clear, clever eyes were honest, but too calm for this topic and this moment.

She said, "Peter darling, there's not much more I can say. I haven't met any Aborigines. I've led a rather narrow life, really."

I stared. Heaps of girls would never have admitted that. Why did I expect more of her? Iris didn't know Mollie's Aboriginal relatives; would never want to meet them; she wouldn't understand why I was interested in their fate. I had thought Faye was twice the girl Iris was. Fury rose in me. I had to get out of there.

"I'd better get some sleep – see you," I said, though right at that moment I had no intention of ever seeing her again.

She climbed out and turned to gaze at me and say goodnight. I stared straight ahead. I drove off fast and didn't look back. What a mistake to think this could work. I'd never end up with a girl like her.

23. Face to Face

Faye:

Melbourne, Late April 1942

I waited the next day, and the one after, but Peter didn't ring. On the last day of his leave, I wondered if I should go to see him. By the late afternoon, I had persuaded myself to do it. So, I telephoned his billet – was he really not in? My message would surely be given to him, and then, wouldn't he reply? I sat at home, gazing at my book or out my window, thinking about what I should have said, and not said, in our last conversation. How could he expect me to welcome such news about the man I had agreed to marry? What could he expect me to do about those children, whoever their fathers were?

He did not phone, and the next day he was gone.

I hoped each day for a letter from New Guinea. None came. Terrified, I wrote, waited, and wrote again, aghast to think that we might turn into strangers. Perhaps he wasn't a letter writer, perhaps there was no time to write now he was in combat. He hadn't decided to stop seeing me – I couldn't bear to think that he might feel so differently about me now, that he might find me so lacking, that he might give up on me.

I felt a chill remembering his face that night after our dinner at Florentino's. But when we saw each other again, we would get back to where we had been, or to a new closeness.

Two weeks later, Clive was back from Europe.

The day before he arrived in Melbourne, I asked my sister to come for a walk in the Botanic Gardens opposite our house. She was rostered at the hospital the following day and wouldn't be back for two days. If I didn't tell her now, she would hear after everyone else.

We sat under huge spreading oak trees that were shedding their leaves.

I said, "I didn't tell you this before because I didn't want to make things hard for you with Mummy or Dad, but I've decided to break my engagement. I realised a while ago that I don't love Clive, and I suspect he doesn't feel much for me. I'm going to tell him tomorrow. I haven't told anyone else apart from Bel and Peggy. Bel thinks I have made the right decision."

Edith's smile was reassuring. "Good for you, Faye. I don't think Clive appreciates you. He doesn't value the things you care about, and he doesn't understand the things that are unique about you. I'm glad that Bel agrees. What you're doing is sensible and courageous."

I hugged her and cried with relief. Why had I kept her at such a distance? But I couldn't tell her about Peter, not yet. What could I say: I love him, but he won't talk to me? Why make Edith hide that from Mummy?

Telling Clive had seemed almost a joy when I presumed it would take me a step closer to a life with Peter. Now, though I refused to believe that Peter had dropped me, I had lost my confidence. Not in him, but in my idea of us as a couple. Had I been fooling myself? – Had he ever loved me? Did I have any influence on him? Was he the sort of man who couldn't settle down? He had been loving, yet when the future was mentioned – and wasn't it always by me? – he had never talked as if we would spend our lives together.

The night before Clive's visit, I paced about my room, pressed my hands together and told myself that pilots at war didn't have the luxury of long-term planning. So I would simply love him and wait for him. If all he wanted was evenings out dancing, then I would remember them all my life. The only thing I couldn't bear to think about was that he might not come back. If he returned and didn't want to see me, I would endure that, somehow. If he went back to Iris, I would be heartbroken, but I would hope it brought him happiness, for I would go on loving him always.

Half of my anxiety was for Mummy, not Clive. It would be such a shock. I wished I could have prepared her somehow, but Clive had to be told first. That seemed only fair. And then Mummy couldn't exasperate us both by trying to change my mind.

If only I could tell Mummy what I'd heard about Clive. She would be horrified and would have something to hang onto, a reason to be glad about my decision. But she would find it dreadfully shocking, perhaps incomprehensible. What would make her believe such things of Vera's son? And what if wasn't true?

I felt more nervous about my father's reaction. Would he see me as flighty, immature and irresponsible, having leapt into a relationship without sufficient knowledge, and without sufficient consideration for everyone involved? He despised impulsive people.

*

After dinner, I stood in the front parlour, waiting for Clive. The bay window's blackout curtains were so gloomy. If only I could see the trees and the river. I wasn't looking forward to telling him, but it would be such a relief once it was over.

I heard Clive's cab. He rang the bell. Ellen announced him. I stood stiff and straight, my chin high, hoping rather unconfidently that my posture might give him a hint of how I had changed. He rushed up and kissed me hard on the mouth, squashing me and ruffling my hair. I took a step back and enquired about his time at the front.

"Don't waste time talking about that." He grinned. "I'm out of it. The old man has bagged me a desk job in Western Australia. About time. I've got too much to lose to risk my life, eh? With the properties and all."

I stared, affronted: no mention of losing or distressing me. "Clive, I have something I need to tell you."

"Let's sit down, where I can get at you," he said, flopping onto the couch. He seemed more confident than when he'd shipped out.

"I think I'd better stand. Clive, I'm breaking our engagement. I'm afraid I don't feel the way I thought I did, the way I thought I would. I made a mistake. I'm terribly sorry, but it's better to break it off now than to make a worse mistake. I'm giving you back the ring." I indicated the tiny box on the table next to him.

He gave a stunned laugh. "What are you talking about?"

I looked at him gravely. He needed time to take it in. His eyes grew dark and angry as he stared at me and then at the little box. He swiped it to the floor and stood up.

"How dare you?" he yelled. "What on earth has happened? Who's been talking to you? You can't do this, Faye. I won't have it."

"I know it's awful, but I can't pretend to feel things."

He lunged at me. His skin had gone red and blotchy; his eyes looked bloodshot. He yelled, "You can show a bit of loyalty and do your duty."

"Duty?" I was shocked by the word and at what he meant. "I think my duty is to be true to my feelings, and to be honest with you, not to stick to a promise I can't fulfil."

"You can talk as grandly as you like, but your parents are going to make you eat those words, my girl."

I gasped. "I'm sure they will not. I think it would be best if you went home now, Clive. I'm sorry it's been such a shock, but I felt I had to tell you face to face. It didn't seem fair to just write."

"Fair?" He exploded. "Don't you dare use that word. Who are you seeing? Who is it? Some bloody pen pusher? One of those smart-aleck Mahoneys? What kind of bloody double-crosser steals a fighting man's girl?"

"Oh, Clive, it isn't like that." I started to feel shaky. If only he would go.

"It's not one of those bloody Yanks, is it? My God, Faye—"

I didn't blush, but my eyes must have changed.

He grabbed me by the shoulders and shook me. "How could you be such a whore?"

I wrenched myself out of his grasp. "There's no need to talk like that."

I held my head high. Half of me felt frightened; the other half felt overwhelmed with relief. I moved to the door. He rushed to the servant's bell near the mantelpiece and tugged it. We stood glaring at each other in silence. I opened the door, but he did not go.

A moment later, Ellen appeared.

"Ellen," said Clive, "tell Sir Henry and Lady Moira that I want to speak to them."

"Ellen," I said, "that won't be necessary."

The old servant looked from me to him, confused and uncomfortable. "Yes, miss, sir."

"Now, Ellen," he said in his bossiest tone.

I shook my head at Ellen, and she scurried out.

"Clive, there's no need to involve my parents. It will only embarrass and distress them."

"Ha! It'll embarrass *you*. Your parents know this is the best marriage you could possibly make. You're lucky I still want you."

"Clive, there won't be a wedding." My blood was rising. I turned to the blacked-out window, my head throbbing.

I couldn't wait to flee to my room. But my mother glided in, followed by my father.

"Clive dear, how lovely to see you home and looking so well." My mother gave him a warm smile and then turned to me with mild puzzlement. "Faye, darling, whatever did you say to poor Ellen?"

"Sir Henry, Lady Moira," Clive shouted, "Faye is talking nonsense about breaking our engagement."

Mummy went pale. "Faye, have you lost your senses?"

Clive smirked.

Dad turned to me and said gravely, "Faye?"

I faced him. "I've just told Clive that I can't marry him. I'm not in love with him. So it's better to end it now than to make a terrible mistake."

My father nodded. I would always remember his acceptance.

My mother said sharply, "How could it be a mistake? Faye, stop this at once."

I stared, astonished. She had never spoken to me like that.

Dad looked dismayed. "Moira, calm yourself." He turned to Clive. "This is painful, but my daughter has spoken honestly. There's no more to say."

My mother's voice shook. "What are you doing, Henry? How can she do this to Clive, to Vera – to me?"

"It is the twentieth century," said Dad. "My daughter may marry whomsoever she chooses, and she is at liberty to change her mind."

I wanted to hug him.

Mummy kept her voice low but looked even tenser. "Henry, your daughter needs your guidance."

"Moira, please, I think the less said now, the better," Dad said quietly.

"No! There are things that must be said. Why, Faye, just tell me why?"

"Moira, this won't solve anything," Dad said firmly.

Clive stared exultantly at me. "Yes, Lady Moira, I want to know why, too. I understand she's been seeing an American."

Dad looked surprised.

Mummy's tone turned even sharper. "Faye, what have you done?"

I said, "Clive is jumping to conclusions. There's nothing to tell."

When I saw my father's relief, guilt stung me; how would he feel when he learned the truth?

Clive turned to my mother. "She's seeing some Yank. She's guilty as sin. Sneaking behind your back."

My mother opened her mouth, but I cut her off. "I have not set out to deceive or betray anyone." I stared stonily at Clive. How I longed to ask him about his affairs.

My father opened the door. "Clive, our man will drive your home."

"I'm going to the club. I'll walk, thanks, sir." He swung around mid-stride and pointed his finger at me. "Don't think I'll forgive you. You'll be begging me to take you back, but you won't have a hope. There are heaps of girls dying to take your place, girls who know how to treat a man like me. You never did—"

I turned away.

My father said severely, "There's no need for talk like that, young man," and showed him out the front door.

My mother wept noiselessly, drooping over the side of the chair, not looking at me. I longed to run up to my room.

The instant Dad re-appeared, my mother wailed, "How could you put us through that, Faye? Why didn't you talk it over with me?"

I collapsed into a chair. "I intended to tell you as soon as Clive left. If he had behaved like a gentleman, instead of rudely summoning you—"

She snapped, "Why shouldn't the boy speak to us when you were making no sense at all?"

"He should have let me speak for myself. And he should have accepted my right to my own feelings."

"Your feelings should be love and loyalty to your fiancé."

"But I don't love him. And I don't think he loves me either. Look at how he spoke to me."

"He was upset. You had insulted him."

"I did him the courtesy of telling him face to face."

"But why change your mind? What has he done?"

"He has done things I would be ashamed to talk about."

My father looked sharply at me.

My mother stared as if I were speaking Greek.

"Don't be silly, Faye. Who has been telling you this nonsense – that Captain?"

"He doesn't talk nonsense." I felt desperately tired.

"Faye, if you throw away the best match in Australia for a Yank from nowhere, you're a fool, and I don't know you at all."

At that moment, I felt exactly the same about her.

My father said quietly, "Faye, do you have anything else to tell us?"

"No."

"Then we should not talk any more this evening."

I nodded, but my mother cut in. "You're going to run off with that Captain, aren't you? You'll have some horrid, quick wedding, like the cheap girls we see in the newsreels. You had the match of the country all sewn up. The heir to the land next to yours, the only wealthy family who don't care that you are Catholic. It was perfect. Hal, you know it was. Oh, this awful war is turning everything upside down."

I had never seen Dad look so disappointed in her.

I said quickly, "I don't intend to run off with Peter. I like him very much, and I think he's fond of me. Perhaps we will marry, but I have no wish to rush into anything, and I certainly don't want to talk about him to anyone outside the family."

My mother wailed, "What am I to say to people?"

My father snapped, "That is of no importance, Moira."

It shocked me to hear him use that tone to her.

Mummy stared resentfully at him. "It's all very well for you, Henry. Your half-dead old judges aren't going to laugh at you for letting your daughter throw away the wealthiest man in Melbourne for a penniless Yank."

Dad gave her one of his courtroom glares.

As he turned away, she cried and tugged at his arm. "Hal, don't blame me. You know that hurts me even more than Faye's mistake. Especially when I am right, when I am the only one acting in our daughter's and our family's best interests. Both of you are behaving like fools, and yet, in your eyes, I can never right this wrong step."

I stood aghast. I had an impulse to apologise to them, though it wasn't my fault. Surely Mummy was being over-dramatic? Would Dad always think less of her, over this? Yet I thought less of her now, so why wouldn't he? I gazed at them, my mother drooping again over the back of the armchair, her eyes fixed on Dad while he stared stonily past her. So estranged, angry and sad, this pair who had been my definition of love.

My father turned to me. "Faye, you have shown good sense in disentangling yourself from a most unpleasant man. Now you should have an early night, my dear. I must finish some work for tomorrow."

I gave him a subdued smile, and he nodded, leaving the room without a glance at his wife.

I said quickly. "I am tired. I'm going up now."

My mother's fierce glare was like a punch in the face. "How could you be so stupid? So disloyal to me, to your whole family? You know how much we lost in the Depression. You could have built us up again. Nigel will do his bit. But you could have got more land and houses than the Beauregards ever had. I thought you understood. I never had hopes for Edith. She'll marry some lecturer or lawyer. But you could marry anyone, and the best person asked you. I didn't think you were like Isobel, a slave to your passions." She hesitated, changing to a wheedling tone. "You're not really like that, dear. It isn't too late: call Clive back. Go to him and say that you don't know what came over you, that you had prewedding nerves, ask him to forgive you. He doesn't want to be humiliated. He'll take you back. Won't you do that, Faye, for all our sakes?"

I walked slowly past, ignoring my mother's sobs. I would never forget them. It took so long to get out of the room, through the hall and up the stairs.

I shut my bedroom door and leaned against it. I closed my eyes. After a moment I went to my cupboard and took out my photograph of Peter from its hiding place under my chemises. I placed it on the bedside table. I put my head on my pillow and stared into his eyes. After a long time, I put away the photograph, found paper and pencil and sketched his face from memory.

24. Fear

Faye:

Melbourne, Late April–May 1942

I came downstairs too late to see my father, not really on purpose; he left so early. I ate breakfast by myself, glad that Mummy had not appeared. I wanted to talk with someone, though not Peggy or anyone who approved of Clive. So, I phoned Eddie. Mummy had a telephone upstairs but surely she wouldn't listen – anyway, what would it matter? To my relief, Eddie answered straight away and invited me to lunch.

"Thanks so much," I said. "I was hoping I could come around. I'm in a spot of trouble here, and there's something I must tell you."

"Good heavens," he said. "Come at once. Have morning tea *and* lunch. Meredith and Herb are coming, so, if you come now, you can tell me whatever it is before they arrive."

"I've hardly slept, so I might not stay for lunch," I confessed. "But I'll come straight over."

I set off on foot, leaving a note for Mummy, aware of how much my running straight to Eddie would irk her. It was a fine, crisp morning. The river was grey-brown and high up on its banks. Eddie's house was in the opposite direction from the rotunda and gardens where Peter and I had walked; just as well: being near those memories might have made me weep. I walked fast, and the exercise lifted my spirits.

When I told Eddie, he said, "Oh dear, I'm sorry that Moira has taken it badly."

"I'm frightened she won't get over it. The way she looked at me after I told them. She hates me." I shuddered and sat down on the hearthrug in front of the unlit fire.

He smiled bitterly. "It hurts when someone hates you because of what you feel, because of what you can't help feeling."

I wondered again how estranged he had been from his father, who had wanted him to have a career like Dad's or Maurice's, and from Gran, who adored him but only recently complained she'd given up waiting for him to marry. Had Grandfather died without reconciling with him? The role of confirmed bachelor was respectable enough, but his rejection of religion and military service were not. And the family despised his bohemian friends.

He touched my shoulder, and the hardness left his face. "You're a strong person, Faye. And your mother will get over her disappointment and forgive you. It's not as if you won't be a successful wife and mother no matter who you marry, so she'll get most of what she wants. She's proud of you."

"I'm not sure she is anymore. Last night, it was as though she gave up on me, as though she felt I had challenged her and won. I wasn't trying to attack her – it isn't about her."

"No, it isn't. It's your heart, your life, your future."

I was touched by the tension and sadness in his face. Was it pity for me that made him look so wistful or was he thinking of someone he loved?

"But Dad accepted my decision."

Eddie looked pleased. "The old softie, and ever the judge, getting Clive's measure straight away. He'll help bring Moira around. But how did Clive react? Was he frightful?"

"Yes, rude and insulting. He accused me of being led astray by an American!"

Eddie gave me a mischievous grin. "Ha! Fellows like Clive should be daunted by the dashing Americans."

"It was awful when he said that. Mummy assumed it was Peter."

Eddie looked concerned. "Oh, and you didn't want to talk about him, not then, especially. I don't think Moira can stop meddling – she may try, God only knows how, to discourage Peter." He gave a sarcastic smile. "Sorry, it isn't funny, really, but she'll find herself quite out of her depth there. He's even more of a fighter than she is, isn't he? Faye, you poor dear, it must have been dreary standing up to her."

"I'm not going along with her plans anymore. She wants me to apologise to Clive and say I was just having nerves. She's sure he'll take me back!"

"Good grief! Well, she's right. He probably would take you back, if only so that no-one would know you had rejected him. He must be very miffed. His father, too. But who cares!"

"Exactly." I took a deep breath. Thank goodness for Eddie's clear, independent thinking. Perhaps he was right that Dad would bring my mother around. I drank my tea. "Eddie, you have to prepare for your luncheon. Can I help?"

"Thanks, Faye. Would you like to get started on the fruit for dessert? I have a cake baking, and the fruit will go with it. I'll make the salad dressing while you arrange the fruit on this platter."

I cut some pears and spread the slices around one of Eddie's beautiful dishes. "I don't want to give anyone the idea that Peter caused the break-up. I'm in love with him, and he's fond of me, but that's not the only reason I'm breaking off with Clive. Whatever happens with Peter, I can't marry Clive." Goodness, did I sound like a foolish girl in a wireless serial?

Eddie nodded. "You're well out of it, Faye. You've had a lucky escape."

"That's virtually what Dad said."

"Did he?" Eddie looked intrigued and pleased. "Good old Hal. You see, I was right. He wasn't happy about it, but he didn't want to challenge what you and Moira seemed so thrilled about."

Then I told him what Peter had said about Clive and the Aboriginal women.

Eddie's face darkened. "Appalling. Those poor girls. They'd have no hope of reporting him to the police, not the Wilson heir. They wouldn't be believed. They probably wouldn't accuse any white man; his word would always win over theirs. Oh, Faye, how ghastly of him to betray you and treat you like that."

I said, feeling less confident than I sounded, that I couldn't believe it for a moment.

He said quietly, "I don't go up to the country much, as you know, but I think many white men there still think that Aboriginal women are pretty much theirs for the taking. The Aborigines don't stay put all the time on the new settlements. They need to move about and congregate for their own ceremonies. When I was young, it was well known that men from the bosses down made regular visits to the blacks' camp. Geoff was involved. It wouldn't occur to him to stop his son."

I was cold with horror. And angry that no-one had thought of telling me. How could they believe that young women were better off discovering it later? "Would Vera have been aware of it?"

He sighed. "I don't know. I presume so. I asked my mother about it when I was about fourteen. She was embarrassed but at least she answered me. She said nothing was going to stop the men from using Aboriginal women. My father never took part, she swore. She had asked him to speak to Maurice and Hal about it, warning them not to get involved." He looked at me. "Hal wouldn't have, even if she hadn't warned him. Not just because he's decent, but because he has a gentle streak buried away behind all that punishing and finger pointing. Mother said everyone ignored the goings on with Aboriginal women. She tried to help them with their babies until the infants were taken to church orphanages. Later, when I was older, I heard that some of the babies were the result of long relationships, and others from one-night stands, some of which were probably rapes. Mother remembered cruelties to the Aborigines in her childhood, but she didn't say much about it. She told me she had seen them driven off or dying; the poisoned flour was in her parents' time."

He made another pot of tea as I stared at him in horror. Surely, he was exaggerating? Such misdeeds hadn't been mentioned in my history books at school, yet listening to him, I felt unsure now about my denials to Peter. It was chilling that Eddie had only vouched for Dad, not for Mo. Could Lillian be aware of this, too?

I said slowly, "You think it's true, then, about Clive?"

Eddie asked for the source of the information and, after I replied, said gravely, "It sounds convincing. But I suppose you feel it's worse because the girls are Aboriginal."

He started washing vegetables for the salad.

I stared at the river outside. "Peter was horrified about the children being taken away. He thinks it's unjust and cruel."

Eddie said quietly, "He's right, isn't he?"

I couldn't answer for a moment. Then I said, "But why should the children have to suffer the ignorance and disease and alcoholism of their people? They need to go to school."

He spoke more urgently. "I'm sure there is some exaggeration in the accounts we hear of drinking among Aboriginals. Splitting up families is the last thing to cure alcoholism, surely? And wouldn't it be better to have Aboriginal children in proper schools with everyone else? How else do children learn to accept different races? We certainly didn't in our church schools, did we?"

I shook my head, surprised at such views, even from Eddie.

He smiled. "Peter seems to be a good friend for you."

"Yes. He's sensitive and soft-hearted."

He nodded. "I can see that. An amazing description for a man with that war record, that face and that manner but, wonderfully, it's true. As they say in America, Faye, he's quite a guy."

"I don't know if anything will come of our friendship – whether we will marry, I mean."

"Of course. He will give you so much, whether he stays around or not." He looked at me gently. "Just enjoy the present, Faye, and half your luck. He may not be the marrying kind, hmm?"

As he said it, my heart froze. Did he understand Peter better than I could? Was I expecting too much?

*

That autumn, once or twice a week, I went horse-riding around the tan with Bel, who still kept horses in town. One sunny May morning, I ran in from my ride and, to my surprise, found Dad in the hall, apparently back very early from work, talking to my mother. They looked stiff together, but they mostly did now. What alarmed me was Dad's sombre face, which didn't light up when I greeted him. As I took off my boots, I worried that something had happened to one of my cousins.

When Dad began to tell me, a chill went right through me, and I knew. But Peter couldn't be dead; he would come back.

"I am so sorry, my dear. I came to tell you as soon as Maurice phoned me. I couldn't bear to think of you finding out from the wireless or the paper. Maurice and Lillian were concerned for you; they had the impression that he was a friend."

I winced at my mother's look of hostility tinged with revenge. How could she be glad? How could she wish him dead?

Dad said, "There is only sketchy information. Captain Stephens may have swum to an island or been picked up by a navy vessel. Maurice will tell us the instant anything comes in."

"If the plane was on fire, Peter would have parachuted out,"
I said.

"Very likely. He's a survivor, experienced, strong and fit."

When he left, I could not stay near my mother. I ran upstairs
and held Peter's photo to me.

> In the silence
> Of my lonely room
> I think of you
> Night and Day.

I began to draw his face again. I covered page after page.

> A voice within me
> keeps repeating,
> You, you, you,
> Night and Day.

25. Faith

Faye:

Melbourne and Sydney, May 1942

S t Francis was the Catholic church in the middle of town. Unlike St Patrick's Cathedral, which stood astride the eastern entrance of Melbourne like a tall Gothic bluestone statement of Irish defiance and dignity, St Francis was a pale, low building right next to the shops. It was the church that people dropped into when they only had a moment, a place where people came anonymously for prayer, forgiveness or solace.

I hurried in there one wet afternoon after a gallery visit with Eddie. I didn't tell him where I was going. It had become my habit to say a prayer, or hear a Mass, for Peter. I wished I had arrived for the Mass, but it was finishing. I walked up to Our Lady's side chapel and knelt behind a huddle of lumpy ladies in drab coats. Some of them were saying the rosary in urgent whispers. Along the pew, a sad, thin man mumbled and shook, whether in prayer or aftermath of war, I couldn't tell. I bent my head and prayed. Then I walked up the aisle, lit some candles for Peter's safety and put my donation into the coin box near the candelabra. As a child, I had loved doing this, but now it had a nightmarish feeling.

I opened the heavy door and stood in the dark porch to open my umbrella for the walk out to the taxi rank.

A woman's voice spoke from behind. "Excuse me, Miss Beauregard, can I ask if you've heard anything?"

I turned. The person moved forward into the light. It was Iris Kelly.

"Miss Kelly, I'm afraid there's no news."

We stared at each other. Iris wore a tweed coat, a plain hat and no make-up. Her skin was pale and fine.

She said, "I thought you might have heard something, being related to the general."

"He has no more information, nothing new," I replied. "We have to hope that Peter got to an island or will be picked up by the navy."

"Did he crash?" Iris's eyes darkened. "All I've heard is that he's missing. I was scared he was captured."

"Oh, goodness." My stomach lurched, and I shut my eyes for an instant. "I don't know that he hasn't been. He sent a message as his plane was going down over the sea, that's all I've been told."

"Over the sea? In enemy territory?"

I shook my head and couldn't speak. My eyes were filling with tears.

Iris smiled wanly, her eyes moist. "You don't know? You do really love him. I s'pose I'm glad. I never had much chance with him. He's wild about you."

"Thanks," I smiled. Most girls would never have said that.

"I realised you were serious when I read that you'd dumped Clive Wilson. He must have been ropable," As she grinned, I could see that her teeth were crooked and slightly grey.

"Did the paper say I *dumped* him?"

"No, that's my word."

I found myself laughing. "He seemed to see it that way."

"Those types think they can buy you. I don't mean to be rude, but you've made a smart move dropping him."

I nodded. Did she know Clive – and Peter – better than I did? I said, "My uncle says the crash probably happened somewhere up north near the islands. I don't know what's happening to Peter. I don't understand the war up there."

"Doesn't it make you mad? Do you watch those bloody newsreels and feel none the wiser?"

"Yes, I do. Miss Kelly, I could telephone you if there's any news." I took out a pencil and notebook from my handbag.

Iris smiled eagerly. "Thanks. I'll give you my number at home and at the Tiv. Lately, I've been in the evening shows."

As Iris wrote, I blurted out, "He would have jumped out. I know he's alive."

"Yeah, I know he is, too. He's a tough guy, Pete."

I felt a surge of gratitude that someone shared my faith. "A survivor."

"Too right. We'll keep praying for him, eh? My whole family's praying for him."

Lucky Iris. Her family must have made a fuss over him.

"Are you quite recovered from that terrible attack? I admired the way you looked after yourself. You were very brave."

"Thanks. Yeah, I'm all right. He was a rat of a bloke. The cops'll get him soon."

We said goodbye, and Iris walked off quickly into the rain. I felt a little embarrassed that I hadn't moved to first names, and that Miss Kelly hadn't either, probably not seeing it as her place. How Peter would hate that; Eddie, too. I hailed a cab and wished I had offered Iris a ride, even though it would have looked odd if anyone had seen me dropping off a girl at the Tivoli.

*

The next day, I had morning tea at Bel's. It felt mournful, despite the sun streaming through the bay window. I kept remembering Peter there at the party, before he strode out.

Bel stared at me. "You're fading away, my girl. Your father said that to me the other day. You must keep going, darling. Don't withdraw into a dream world. I don't mean to be harsh. I know your pilot is a very attractive man, and he did seem to be in love with you. He looks like the sort of man who doesn't fall in love easily, though who knows if he would have gone back to America? There was a restlessness in him, wasn't there? I don't mean to hurt you, but even your sweetness and confidence might not have overcome his unsettled nature. Well, I don't even know if it was his nature; meeting someone during a war makes it hard to know them. Faye, you will get back to being your vibrant, happy self. You will find someone else. And thank goodness you were saved from Clive Wilson – no-one could go back to him after Peter."

I could have challenged her on a few points, but I was so tired, and why bother? He was coming back.

Bel said, "I know he was a wonderful boy, Faye, but if he doesn't come back, you must have a full life; it will be richer for having loved him. After a time, you'll be ready to turn to someone else."

I lifted my head with effort and forced myself to meet my aunt's eyes. "I still believe he's coming back."

"It pains me to criticise such loyalty and bravery. But don't hold your heart and soul in the balance. If he doesn't—"

"Has Mo told you something, or General Maddox?"

"No, of course not."

"Bel, I can't abandon him when I haven't been told he's dead. That would be obscene."

Did people think I could forget him in a month? The winter closing in felt eternal, but feathery leaves would sprout on the trees, the magnolias would flower, and after that the heat and the gardenias would come to bring back the feel and smell of him, and how could I bear it?

I caught sight of myself in the mirror over the fire. I saw what Bel meant. I had withered. At twenty-three, I felt that my life was waning. Girls of my age sometimes callously said of their mothers, in times of conflict over outings, dresses or men, "she's had her life." Perhaps now it was true of me.

Every night, I looked at photos of Peter and told myself he was still alive. There were women all over the country, all over the world, whose men had vanished. I wept for us all. So many men, and women too, had disappeared after the unimaginable fall of Singapore. Dad said that they would be imprisoned for the duration of the war. When I asked him how long he or Mo thought that would be, he hesitated and admitted, "A few years yet, probably. Oh, my dear, I'm sorry."

Bel was stroking my hand. "Faye, I'm going to Sydney for a while. Would you like to come with me? The weather is much warmer up there. We might do a spot of shopping. We can't sail, now that my yacht is part of the war effort, but we could swim in my pool and walk on the beach."

I smiled at the relief of escaping from under my mother's roof. Not having to see her was even more appealing than Bel's lovely house in Rose Bay.

As I packed, I put on the recording Eddie had lent me of Billie Holiday singing 'Night and Day.' Her cracked, abrupt voice was lonely, but her forcefulness such a comfort.

*

Sydney, which had always been a joy, seemed to wear me out in half an hour with its noisy crowds and narrow, cluttered streets. For the first time in my life, I didn't enjoy looking at the vast, sparkling harbour from Bel's balcony, or standing on the deck of a ferry swaying over to Manly. Shopping tired me. I couldn't get excited at Bel's couturier, among some good coats, so hard to find with the war shortages. I saw Bel's disappointment. I chose a coat, but for all the joy it gave me, I might as well have been buying school stockings.

Each day that passed – and now it was weeks – with no news of him brought me closer to a terrifying judgement: I had seen the best moments of my life; I was not destined to be happy; I was a weak person who couldn't cope with the sorrow of war.

After a few dinners with Bel's friends where I pretended to eat and to enjoy the conversation, I couldn't face more company. I begged to dine at home. I had spied *Pride and Prejudice* on Bel's bookshelves and declared that re-reading it would cheer me up. Bel said there was a good drama on the wireless.

It turned out that the drama was real and all around us. When I heard the warning signals and when the wireless stopped transmitting, the elderly butler and I looked at each other and quickly bundled everyone into the make-do shelter in the cellar. It felt like a British film. I wished we could have had some company, local families, people who knew each other, who could keep up a casual, normal atmosphere.

I didn't know Bel's staff well. They were quite old; any young ones had been swept up for war work. They kept deferring to me and asking questions I couldn't answer. Their unspoken assumption was that I was in charge; that I would know what to do.

I announced calmly, "We will be safe. The Japanese will attack big ships and military targets, not ordinary houses."

Bel's personal maid declared that she had a date with a dish of a Yank later, and she wasn't going to miss that. The other servants looked at her disapprovingly. I was surprised – she looked too old to be gadding about with Yanks. But good on her. I felt a rush of excitement at the thought of *my* American, and it was lovely to get that feeling back, rather than to go on mourning him before he was dead.

I suggested that we play cards to pass the time. At my hint, the butler produced supplies of sherry and wonderful fruitcake from Bel's emergency cupboard. While I tried to keep up a cheery atmosphere, my mind was full of 'what ifs'. Sydney might be under prolonged attack. Could I be the one missing, when Peter came back? One of us in danger had been more than enough. It was eerie and frightening to wonder if I were facing death. How much more terrifying it must be for men at the front – the booming din, the unpredictable attacks, the weapons and men rushing at you, the screams, pain, wounds and blood.

I *would* kiss Peter again in Melbourne in our rotunda. I pictured it as the hours ticked by.

*

Bel and I listened to the official statement about the submarine attack on the wireless the next afternoon. It explained that Japanese midget submarines had failed in an attack against Sydney and had been destroyed.

Bel frowned. "But the loss of one of our vessels – how many sailors died? I wish Mo could tell us more, but he probably can't. I put in a call to him early this morning. I hope he rings back soon. I think we should go home to Melbourne."

Half an hour later, Geoffrey, the butler, came in with the telephone on its long cord. It was Mo, but to our surprise, he was asking for me.

"Good news, Faye, Peter is safe."

Time stopped. My spirits leapt, but to my astonishment, I couldn't speak to ask the questions that had plagued me for so many days.

Perhaps Mo realised that I was frozen. Perhaps he was used to this happening when he gave such news. After a moment, he said, "He's on a carrier. A destroyer picked him up and took him there. He's well. General Maddox just told me. He and Mrs Maddox wanted you to know."

"Oh, thank you, Mo, and thank General and Mrs Maddox." I felt a new warmth for the couple I had dismissed as preening and pompous. "Peter isn't injured?"

"Nothing serious. Exhausted, no doubt. Maddox says there's no mental breakdown. Now, Peter won't get back to Australia for a while, and it's likely that he will have leave in Brisbane."

The black phone felt heavy at my wrist. "And then what?"

"Probably, he will go back on duty. Perhaps a leave in Melbourne after that. Sorry, Faye, I can't offer any certainty."

"Will he get my letters on the carrier?"

"Very soon. The Americans have excellent mail arrangements. He's been on the carrier a few days now so…"

"A few days!"

"Yes, dear, official debriefing had to take place before anyone else was notified."

"Sorry, I know I'm selfish. I don't have to put up with much compared to you and the servicemen."

"Faye, it's marvellous that he's safe."

"I believed he would come back safe, you know. I wasn't just pretending."

"Your faith is justified. I'm glad."

"Can you tell me anything about what happened to him?"

"We can't discuss that yet; I don't know much. Thank God he wasn't with his captors for very long. He didn't suffer burns in the crash. As the Yanks say, he's a tough guy."

"He is!" I surprised myself by laughing.

"Faye, you mightn't hear back from him in a hurry. His debriefing will take time, and after something like this, men often have a period of exhaustion and can't communicate well, even to the people they want to talk to. Such reactions are common and usually temporary. Now I trust that you and Bel are returning to Melbourne poste-haste?"

"Yes, the Japanese will never come there, will they?"

His two-second pause shot through me like the blast of that awful siren last night.

The silence wasn't caused by the telephone connection; it was Mo deciding how honest to be.

"Unlikely," he said. "Don't worry. Put Bel on – and Faye dear, I'm delighted about Peter."

Hanging up the phone, Bel said, "Let's have champagne." She hugged me. "How wonderful, darling. We'll drink to the captain's health, and then we'll phone Henry!"

I smiled. "I should make another call. Do you mind if I ring Iris Kelly?"

26. Melbourne Blues

Faye:

Melbourne, Early June 1942

Melbourne seemed surprisingly dull when I returned home. I wished I could have stayed another week in Sydney after the glorious news about Peter, to start enjoying the place and its warmer weather. Bel and I had driven south through the New South Wales outback, staying with one of her friends, then with another family friend near the Victorian border and after that at an hotel in Bendigo. Whenever people heard we had come from Sydney, they flooded us with questions. Everyone was stunned. There was a new jumpiness, despite the Allied successes in the Coral Sea a few weeks earlier, which had been hailed as saving the supply lines and stopping more Japanese attacks in New Guinea. The papers had been triumphant. But now there was a question: where would the Japs pop up next? In the sea or in the sky? It was comforting to hear General Maddox declare confidently that they were being stopped.

Coming home was painful for the first time in my life. My mother and I stared at each other like mere acquaintances, unwanted, unwelcome. Of course, it was lovely seeing Dad and Edith. They were thrilled to talk about Peter.

My mother merely said, "I'm glad your worrying is over."

The other three of us heard, and felt, the jarring note, but we had to pretend it wasn't there. Pretence didn't suit my family. We had always felt safe and joyful together.

I missed Bel's energy and light-heartedness. My parents seemed older and restrained. Edith was as dear as ever, but she lacked Bel's spontaneity and verve.

A few days after my return, the papers were full of the Allied victories at a place in the Pacific called Midway. Edith and I went to the pictures and watched the newsreels. They made me feel ill. The commentary declared that the victory had delivered safety for Australia. Maddox, other generals and admirals were on the screen, beaming at their success in destroying four Japanese carriers and halting the Japanese invasion in the South Pacific. I shrank in my seat at the sight of a burning aircraft carrier.

"It's Japanese," Edith whispered, squeezing my hand.

I would have been relieved except that the commentator was reeling off the American losses, including a carrier and many aircraft.

"Mo would have rung us," Edith whispered. "Peter must be all right."

A woman in front turned a furious face at us. It wasn't done to talk during the war footage. Everyone listened in silence as though they were in Church or at school Assembly. No one struck a match. Smokers seemed to delay puffing. Even the chorus of coughing stopped.

I tried to quell fear. What if Maddox didn't know Peter's fate yet or hadn't told Mo yet? What if Peter had gone back on active duty? He had a choice, after what he'd been through. *Stop being a hero! Just come to Melbourne.*

I was desperate to contact Mo. I couldn't phone him from home because my parents would disapprove. So, when Edith and I left the cinema and walked over to afternoon tea at George's, I headed for the telephone in the Ladies' Lounge.

Getting through to Mo was surprisingly fast.

"Was Peter at Midway?" I demanded. "Is he all right?"

"Yes, my dear. He was on the sidelines, on a carrier but not the one that got hit. I was going to ring you tonight. Peter has leave in Melbourne, probably from next week."

"Oh, thank goodness."

"I'll let you know exactly when."

"I'm so grateful, thank you, Mo. Sorry to interrupt your work."

"That's all right, Faye dear, cheerio now."

I raced back to Edith. "He's all right! He's coming to Melbourne soon!"

"Faye, I'm so glad. Thank goodness he got through that battle. It did look fierce on the newsreel – I'll admit that now."

I helped myself to some cake and felt my muscles relax for the first time for so long.

Edith smiled. "It will be wonderful to see him. Of course, he may be in a state of shock. I've noticed at the hospital that a significant number of men are quite withdrawn. Still, Peter's a seasoned warrior, isn't he? And he seems to love it in a way, well, the good side of it, I'm sure."

I frowned. I recalled Mo's warning that Peter might not be able to communicate. "I don't want him withdrawn or different. I know I sound selfish. But it's not fair that the generals could spoil my life – and Peter's – by their decisions. Oh, stop looking at me like that! I know we have to defeat the Japanese. Edith, if you don't mind my leaving you again for a few minutes, I should ring Iris Kelly. She'll have seen the newsreels, too, and she'll be worrying."

"That's nice of you, Faye, but are you sure you want to talk to her?"

I had not revealed much to Edith about the conversations I had already had with Iris. Only Bel knew about the call from Sydney.

"She's actually a nice person."

"Just as long as she's not intending to cause trouble with Peter," said Edith firmly.

I smiled; Edith's idea of a Tivoli showgirl was pure Hollywood, a plotting femme fatale. "She accepts his love for me. I don't think she expected anything permanent with him."

"Or with anyone, perhaps?" Edith said.

I didn't reply. How unsympathetic Edith could be. Recently, I had been to one of Iris's shows with Eddie and some of his artist friends. Of course, I hadn't mentioned this to Edith or our parents. Watching Iris kick and twirl had tested my determination to be friendly to her, but I just had to know what Peter had seen.

27. Revenge

Peter:

US Navy Carrier, Pacific Ocean, Early June 1942

I threw myself on the bunk. It tired me even to close my eyes. The Intelligence guys had gone on for so long I thought I'd fall asleep mid-question. They gave me the shits. The old guy who'd actually seen action wasn't so bad. He got the point: I had knocked out a post of Japs. But I wanted to throttle the other two. Their shocked eyes as I spilt the details. What had they expected, that I would sneak around like a boy scout and no-one would notice? One of them went pale when I had to spell it out: yes, I cut the throats of the islanders who were force marching me while they slept, I set fire to the whole damn place, and I made sure it spread to the Jap quarters.

"Christ, how do you think I got out?" I couldn't help snarling at the guy who'd turned white and sweaty, from horror or excitement, I wasn't sure which. I was trying like hell not to remember the moment just before I cut the first islander, and the moment when I did.

For Chrissake, hadn't these pen-pushers seen photos of the cities and civilians we bombed? Didn't they know that the navy – ours and the Aussies' – sometimes went in and shot up islands just in case? Why was anything I did worse? It was harder, that was all. Harder than with a gun. So much closer. You felt the instant of the kill, the give of the soft or solid matter of the body. Even if you didn't touch them except with your knife. You were passing a barrier. You could only do it if you had been stamped down into almost nothing, until all you had was the will to stop them killing you.

The next day we would have reached the Jap camp and that would have been it for me. Better to kill my guards than have my head sliced off by Japs or starve to death and, either way, vanish into letters on a monument.

Maddox wouldn't blame me.

I still couldn't sleep. I was so used to catnaps and waking at the least sound that even the calm rumble of the carrier engines couldn't set me off. There was no point taking the pills they'd given me; the medics didn't get it: I didn't have the usual post-mission regrets to drown. No pills would stop me seeing the line on those islanders' throats, black and wet in the dark. Pills would send me into a dead sleep, and I'd wake up spooked. I'd just wallow and break down.

I couldn't wait to fly again. The one good thing about being dumped in the sea and having to island hop for so long was that I'd got right off drink and smokes. Maybe I'd stay off the booze. Some guys in Britain and New Guinea flew half-tanked, they swilled so much, right up to the night before. It affected you for hours. Some guys' hands were shaky the day after; it could make the difference to their timing or their turns. I knew why it was never mentioned. Too many guys would never get into the cockpit or face another day without it. I almost felt sorry for those who got courage that way, but you had to resent their lack of precision, and lack of killer instinct. The navy had the right idea: no liquor on board. No wonder their top pilots were so good. I decided to keep off cigarettes, too. Just like times when I'd had none, or gone off them to save money, I felt better. Cleaner. Tobacco only made you cough your guts out in the end. Old smokers made me feel like throwing up, like the breath of the old guy on the debriefing team. Jesus, I was sick of rotten smells and bodies. My first shower on the carrier had been bliss, despite the cuts, scars and rashes all over me that stung like crazy.

I stared out the porthole. The letters I'd been given sat on the ledge under it. I wondered if I would ever feel like reading them. It didn't feel like they were for me.

The hard, narrow bed in this small cabin felt like heaven. Like when I arrived at the Murrays' house from the boys' home, everything was clean and neat; everyone behaved exactly as they were supposed to, every day the same, the ones in charge bossy but never angry. No need to watch my back. No need to hustle for food. No need to watch in shame while kids were bashed into weeping, drooping submission and my uppermost feeling was relief it wasn't me, and my next feeling was a wish to do something way worse to the bashers. No waiting for the unpredictable moment when Father O'Malley would pounce.

I rolled on my back and stretched out. It made me sick the way I kept seeing scenes from years ago. I shuddered: maybe I'd be remembering my time in the islands for the next twenty years. Maybe? Who was I kidding?

Soon, my two cabin mates would come in. I hadn't spoken to them. There was nothing to say. They were officers; they knew better than to chat. At least they didn't stare at me. At breakfast, the first couple of times, guys looked at me with awe and curiosity till I felt like throwing a giant lance through the lot of them, skewering them as they stood in line.

My mind had turned into a mad cartoon. I hadn't admitted it to the Intelligence guys or to the captain with his shrewd eyes, but I knew how far I was from normal. I was between life and death. The impulses that ran through me were still the ones I had summoned up on the islands. They were hard to shut off. I had found that before, when I left the gangs and lived with Buzz's family or with the carnival show. It took a long time till you stopped automatically figuring out the quickest way to kill everyone around you and get out. My hand felt for my knife. I wouldn't let that go, no matter what the rules were. It didn't matter that I wouldn't have to use it in any circumstance on this carrier. I needed to feel it hard against me all the time. In the shower, I placed it on the top of the wall, safe and unseen.

I wouldn't tell anyone what I saw in my head, what I felt in my skin and insides, all the time. Not just the blood, the sounds of people dying, the hiding and running, but being the target, the thing they kicked the guts out of.

The old guy might have had a clue but one of the young interrogators queried how I had avoided being murdered. I could have told him: kid, a captive stranger has to do things you've never dreamed of. He must take whatever's dished out. The interrogators' questions would never go anywhere near that stuff; the old guy wouldn't broach it. A long time ago, I learned how to tell which guys knew about pushing someone beyond the limits. The old guy knew. The moments I would rather wipe out of my mind were weirder than old times in Bourbon Street, and that was the truth. I wished I could have stayed on the first little island. The people were all over me. They treated me like a king, not a captive to overpower and humiliate. They were happy and sang and treated their kids kindly. But I would never have been picked up there. Not a plane or sea vessel came near.

If I even hinted at what I had gone through on the last island, the clear-skinned boys questioning me would puke. It was a long way from fraternity pranks or even West Point initiation. Boys from Easy Street, sticking to their desk jobs, never got it that unleashing the dogs of war meant putting someone like me in the way of guys just waiting for a stranger they could break. For an enemy that looked so different, they could do anything to him. And they had to treat him worse than their lowest misfits. They made the queers of Bourbon Street, preying on starving boys, look kind and sane. They near made mincemeat out of me to show their fighters what being a tough boss meant. Allied ships, Yankee planes and Jap soldiers had all attacked them; they were in the middle with no choice, cornered, fighting for their pride and their lives. Knowing that, I felt more afraid. I knew what it could let loose.

I could stand anything, I kept telling myself, as they shoved and kicked and beat me, just as long as they didn't burn me. Constant cuts, blows that made me cough blood: all that kind of stuff would heal. Burns or a broken neck wouldn't. I had to hold up, keep more or less on my feet, or all fours, more or less conscious, so they could get their kicks, so they could show that they had me cowering and suffering, but defiant, so they could still enjoy the game. If I rolled over and submitted, passed out or wept and pleaded, I would be a goner.

Who would have thought I had learned something useful from Father O'Malley and Hogs-head Harris? Visions of Harris flitted through my mind often during the sessions with my captors; I hadn't given him his due as a master of war. Recalling his routines with enemy gangs – or women or kids like me – was how I could guess what my guards might do next. It helped me stand aside from my bleeding, filthy carcass and watch them, and tell myself I'd kill them all and get out.

When would I have the strength to chuck away moments I thought I had left behind at twelve? I grabbed the letters, tossed the official one aside and stared at the others. Only Faye would write. I hardly dared think of her. I stopped myself picturing her face and all. There was no going back to a girl like that now. Or maybe any girl. She had probably gotten over me and found someone else. I knew I was kidding myself. But so what if she was a romantic sucker? There was nothing I could do about that. After the war, I'd just keep moving. Get flying jobs. Life would be what it always was for me: moving on. I put the letters down and closed my eyes. I concentrated on remembering the beach on the first island in exact detail.

*

The official letter was signed by Maddox. The captain had probably expressed some concern about me – not quite all there, not back to shipshape, a touch punch-drunk. The letter was a morale raiser. I was so valuable, blah, blah, blah. After the war, he might want me to appear with him in motorcades and rallies as he made his run for the Presidency. Sick as I was of being the boy for the men in love with power, I'd do it. I was lucky he needed me; I'd never get anywhere on my own.

The most recent letter from Faye was pretty and expensive looking. I put it to my face without thinking, as if it might somehow have her perfume, her real French stuff, sweet and strong. 'Joy' it was called – didn't that fit her to a 't'! I seemed to smell it. Was I crazy? I couldn't tell. It worried me that I couldn't gauge where my mind stopped and the real world started. Would the ability just come back one day, automatically, or would I have to learn it again? I was sitting on my bunk when the mess bell rang. I had stayed like that for three hours. Instead of putting the letter down, I found myself shoving it in my pocket.

At dinner, it poked out of my shirt pocket when I moved my arm and my jacket gaped. One of my cabin mates commented on the number of pretty envelopes arriving for me and I smiled politely, though I felt my teeth grit. I put the envelope in my jacket pocket where it wouldn't show. I felt like an orphan kid at a family picnic, like at the Murrays'. I was handling the table manners all right, but chitchat and appropriate jokes were beyond me. My powers of speech seemed disrupted after weeks of hearing only strange languages. Now, I was like a recent arrival in New York who understood the natives but couldn't frame answers, or who worried that his accent and grammar would be so wrong he'd better not speak. The only thing I took in was the astounding fact that in the last week, Jap submarines had made it into Sydney Harbour. Right into Rose Bay.

At first, I spent most of my time on my bunk except when I took exercise. I was getting fitter with the regular food and rest, though my insides still worked to some odd regimen of their own. I had a sore foot and leg, but I was used to ignoring them and didn't tell the doctor who gave me the once over. I avoided limping because I didn't want to be long off active service. When I got the chance, I went up to the flight deck to look at the planes. I couldn't wait to get the stick in my hand and feel the engines under my ass. As usual, I got on fine with the grease monkeys. I started to learn about the torpedo bombers and dive-bombers and asked the head pilots about going up with one of them. They grinned and asked if I needed a clearance from Maddox. I said I had his go-ahead. I knew he'd back that up if they asked him. He liked more famous people than me to do one-offs, people like film stars and Charles Lindberg.

One day, after I'd been up as an observer in a bomber, I dressed for dinner and felt the crackle of Faye's letter in my pocket as I slipped on my jacket. I looked at the other letters from her, still unopened. I picked them up and stared at the elegant, firm handwriting. It looked like a fancy label for luxury chocolates. After dinner, when I came down to my cabin before my companions as usual, I looked at the writing again.

I considered throwing the letters out of the porthole.

But I sat down and pulled the recent one from my pocket. I opened it slowly like an old man expecting bad news. What a wreck I'd become. I couldn't laugh at myself; I was too disgusted. But I would have to write something to her eventually, if only to say I couldn't see her anymore – that knowledge was like a stone in my chest.

When I was back in action, they might ask if I wanted leave in Brisbane or Melbourne. I'd say Brisbane.

She'd expect a letter once my return was official. General Beauregard would tell her immediately. What day was it? He would have told her already.

The paper felt smooth and waxy. I couldn't afford to begin thinking about how hellish it was that I had to give her up. There was no other possibility. I would never catch up to nice people, not anymore.

As I read her words, I could hear them in her sweet, musical voice with its warm, calm tone. I saw her little heart-shaped face, her swirls of copper-bright hair, her confident, happy eyes. My face was wet. I blinked my eyes clear and grabbed her other letters. I read them from first to last. In the later ones, as she got no answer, she would surely become less certain, less loving, less trusting. She didn't. She was more than in love with me. Like Hube, she found me fun. Like Buzz, she saw the best in me. Like Luella, she looked up to me. Like Momma, she refused to stop loving me. She believed so strongly in the guy she thought I was, the guy I had tried to be. But I couldn't be him now, however hard I tried. You don't know where I've been, Little Red Riding Hood. My head was pounding. I hadn't dreamed her. That thrilled me for a second, but then the force of her feelings made me so sad I forgot to breathe for a while and stared out to sea.

Why hadn't I let myself die? On impact, in the sea? It would have been better. Where was that fuckin' death wish I always thought I had? Jesus, I had fought every way possible to live. I didn't have a clue why, because my life was a flicker away from nightmare, except when I was flying. Was it for her? Because she loved me? I never cared about anyone the way she loved me. People always move on, I used to say. I'd always move on. The only one I'd always look out for was Buzz. I'd die for him any day. And for Luella. That seemed the only kind of love I could feel, long-term. Everyone I mixed with now, especially the naval officers on this carrier, would have been astounded and contemptuous if they knew that my only loyalty was to penniless Louisiana negroes. I was fond of Hube, and of Isobel and Edward too, but rich, kind people like them were just a moment's rest in my life. I had no place with them.

I felt a wave of nausea and stood up to get myself some water. Christ, I'd wreck Faye's life. Even more than I had already. She was the sweetest person I would ever know, but I could never see her again. Just the thought of her little body dancing against mine…

> Like the beat, beat, beat
> of the tom-tom
> when the jungle shadows fall;
> like the tick, tick, tock
> of the stately clock
> as it stands against the wall;
> like the drip, drip, drip
> of the raindrops
> when the summer shower's through,
> so a voice within me
> keeps repeating
> you, you, you
> Night and Day
> under the hide of me
> there's oh such a
> hungry yearning
> burning inside of me…

I heard the steps of my cabin mates and turned my face to the wall. I kicked off my shoes and pulled my blanket up over the letters and me.

*

After the mission, the guys who made it home were yelling, laughing and patting each other on the back. I felt great too. I knew what they had hit. I waited while they confirmed it. Command was mighty pleased. The atmosphere was different from in New Guinea, where the guys were relieved if they made it back, especially since a lot didn't; they couldn't handle the P-39s, which were unwieldy if you couldn't get the hang of their tricks; they weren't in the same class as the sublime Spitfire. The losses weren't bad at all on this mission. The navy pilots were disciplined but they exulted in the damage they did more than we had in the RAF. I used to feel a moment of sympathy sometimes after the thrill of the shot, when I saw the plane dive down in flames. Maybe the pilot was a committed Nazi or maybe just a German fighting with his countrymen, but either way, he was a good, trained flyer, and you could tell he loved to fly.

Even after Pearl Harbor, I secretly admired the Japs for a while. Hube had shown me a book about the Samurai, and I was impressed with their toughness, commitment and loyalty. But the word from the Brits and the Aussies was that Japs treated prisoners like scum. They were trained to choose death rather than be captured, so they despised captives. The glimpses I got of them on the last island raised my hackles. I would have done anything rather than end up in their hands. Hell, I *had* done it. So, I felt great watching our guys hanging in the sky, just waiting to rip into them. When we got a bullseye on the Jap carrier, and it spewed up dirty orange clouds, all I thought was you signed on to die for your emperor, so die, suckers!

28. Denial

Faye:

Melbourne, July 1942

I peered out of the back seat window as I arrived at Essendon Airport in my father's car. Michael, the chauffeur, consulted me about where to park, and we chose a spot facing where the men would come out. I was early. I pulled out the letter I had from Peter, the only one, sent from Brisbane. I read it again, though I knew it by heart. The tone was all wrong: stiff, morose, and with a goodbye sound. It could have been written as an exercise by a military cadet. Despite what Mo had said about after-effects on war prisoners, I was shaken to the core by Peter's tone; it was excruciatingly cold, distant, and depressed.

I covered my ears as the plane landed. The men walked down from the aircraft and across to the building. There he was, striding perfectly. Thank Goodness. I crossed myself and said a prayer. Eddie would roll his eyes. There was a wait while the official business went on inside. Soon, the men appeared.

There he was. He hadn't seen me. I opened the car door and climbed out. Several men turned to look at me. I slammed the door. He turned. A Gary Cooper troubled face. No smile. We stood twenty yards apart. Time slowed down. I took a deep breath and walked towards him. His face looked dark and hollow. What had happened to him? His arms were stiff by his sides. I felt a sob rising.

"Peter, darling."

His face muscles tensed. I moved close. When I hugged him, I could only reach the middle of his back. I nestled my face against his chest. After a pause that cut like the coldest wind, he put his arm on my back; it could have been a block of wood.

I looked up and touched his face. It felt cold and dry. He didn't meet my eyes.

I shivered. "Darling, come to the car."

He stepped back. "Faye, I'm sorry. I'm tired to death and I have meetings tomorrow. I'll go in the staff car."

I felt my smile stiffen.

He looked away. "I'm no company at the moment."

"What happened? Did a friend die?"

"I don't have time for friends, but yeah, a lot of guys died." His voice was different, sarcastic.

"I'm sorry," my words came out as a whisper. "But we don't have to talk. You can rest in the car."

He stared over my head. "No. You better go. Take care."

He walked me back to the car, opened the back door. I gazed at his ice blue eyes that wouldn't meet mine. He left without a word. I staggered in and fell onto the seat. He strode away swiftly.

Leaning forward to tell Michael to move, I realised that he had already started. Grateful for the curtains, I closed them on all sides.

The next half hour passed, silent and blank. I sat as though paralysed. Too sad to cry. The motion of the car felt like a nightmare out of my control.

Thank goodness I hadn't told anyone where I was going. Michael wouldn't tell. Even my father couldn't get him to talk. My parents were out that night, and Edith was on a shift at the hospital. Suddenly, tears ran down my face. When we reached Swanston Street, I peeked through the curtain up the Bourke Street hill and then the Collins Street one. The brownout had been eased in the city now, and there were more people out again, couples and servicemen. The car turned into Batman

Avenue and drove along the Yarra. I opened the other curtain to look at the water shining in the dusk.

*

In the morning, after hardly any sleep, I kept busy preparing some parcels for St Anthony's.

That night, the telephone stayed silent. After dinner, I listened to the wireless with my parents, and knitted socks for the Red Cross appeal. Later, in bed, I shook with sobs. After five hours, I got up and went to my writing table. Tears fell on the paper. Would he see them? Would he even read this?

I fell exhausted into bed and slept till the birds woke me.

After breakfast, I went back to my room and a few minutes later, Edith knocked on the door.

"What's wrong?" she asked gently.

"I went to meet Peter. He didn't want to see me. He was like a different person."

Edith said, "Perhaps he was just tired. He must have had a long journey to get here, and those boys often can't sleep."

"He didn't smile, didn't even take my hand."

"Perhaps he has battle fatigue."

"But he's been through battles before. Is it because he was a prisoner? We don't know what's happening to our men, do we? We need to know."

"Not everyone could cope with that, Faye."

"I'll go to see him if he doesn't contact me. I can't let things just stop."

Edith nodded and hugged me.

In the middle of the night, I wrote him another letter. Then I drew him as he was months ago. Perhaps one day I would be able to draw him as he was at the airport – but not yet. I was reading *Persuasion* again. Its sadness yet sureness fortified me. I read far into the night.

The next day, I coaxed the car-keys from Michael and drove to Peter's billet. My mother and grandmother's voices resounded in my head: a lady never contacts a gentleman; she waits. How many women went mad following those rules? I laughed. There's a war on. A gal's gotta do what a gal's gotta do!

At the gate of the billet, a sentry bent down to my window. "Do I have to say whom I'm visiting?" I asked.

"Yes ma'am." His American drawl made me suppress a smile.

Peter was in. My spirits rose. But what if he wouldn't see me? I parked and checked my face in the mirror. I jumped out, almost locking the keys in the car. Then I took a deep breath and calmed myself as much as I could.

The grand house had a lovely veranda and a huge front door. It must have been a beautiful home before the war. When I rang the bell, another guard with an impossible accent appeared. I gave my best commanding stare, nothing compared to Dad's, no doubt, but the soldier lowered his eyes and showed me to a sitting room. I perched on the edge of a hard leather chair. How fast the heart could beat. Let him walk in as my Peter, the Peter of old.

The door opened and I looked around with a smile. Peter entered, his face grave.

His tone was formal. "We can't talk here."

"Can we walk, Peter, or go for a drive?"

"Let's drive." He sounded weary.

When we reached the car, he held out his hand for the key and opened the passenger door. My legs trembled as I climbed in. He shoved the cushion away from the driver's seat; it sat between us. He drove quickly to the park near St. Anthony's. He stopped and turned off the engine. I hadn't taken my eyes off him the whole time. I hadn't a clue what he was feeling. He lowered his gaze, his hands still on the steering wheel.

I leant over and ran my fingers along his forearm. He tensed.

"Are you all right, darling?" I moved my hand up to the muscle in his arm and up to his shoulder. It was like touching a highly-strung horse. "It's so lovely to see you." My tone seemed to soothe the tension in his shoulder; his eyes lost fire. "Peter, everything's going to be all right."

He gave me a dejected look and turned away. He opened the car door. The cold air made me shiver. He sat with one arm on the open door. I tried to touch his face. He reared away suddenly, his eyes fierce.

"Faye, can't you see? – Everything's not gonna be all right. I'm nowhere near okay. I'm not the kind of guy who has a steady girl. The war just makes it worse."

I was fighting tears. "Darling, what you're going through in this war is more than anyone should have to bear. Don't decide anything now." My hand was in midair between us. I slowly rested it on his arm.

I stared at his jaw. Fear tingled up my body.

He said, "You should be with someone who's ready to look after you. I have enough trouble looking after myself – and the guys I fly with. I'm bad news. You're better off without me."

"Peter, that's not true. I love you."

"I don't know what that means. I can't say it back. I don't know what sort of person I'll be in a year's time, let alone after that." He ran a hand over his eyes. "You can't depend on me, baby. I was only play-acting before, trying to please you."

I sobbed. "I can't believe that. What you mean to me is real, Peter. It's the fighting that makes you feel different, but that will pass."

"Can't you hear what I'm saying? It's over. I should have left before. You'll get over me."

"I won't. Not ever. I've never loved anyone else." Another sob cut through my words.

He glanced at me – distant, but in some pain – how sorry I felt but how glad to see that it hurt him too, this conflict, this separateness that he was creating.

"You'll love another man." His jaw clenched. "Just pick a better one."

"I won't love anyone else. We can't just stop, Peter. We haven't even slept together."

"At least I did that much right."

"Are you saying you don't want me?"

"I *wanted* you – you know that. The only thing I've done right is to stop myself. But when you find a good man, he'll be glad he's the first."

"I want you, Peter, not any other man."

He stared out the window. "You'll get over me. Desire dries up like dead leaves."

"No," I said, reaching for his face.

He leaned away. "A moment's pleasure isn't worth a lifetime of pain."

I could hardly breathe. "You sound like a priest. From the crazy churches, you called them."

He stared at me "You've changed, too. Because of the war, I guess."

"Because of *you*, Peter. I love you, and I know you feel something for me. I didn't dream that. I wasn't pretending. You weren't either. Don't push me away."

"I'm only gonna bring you more pain if I keep seeing you. Just remember that." He turned away. "Are you okay to drive home? I can walk."

He sounded so cold and matter-of-fact that I had to stop myself from breaking into sobs.

"So, you'll drive me home, get out and never see me again?"

"Nothin' else I can do."

"Then I'll drive myself home."

As he got out, I slid across the seat and put the cushion back behind me so that I sat forward enough for my feet to reach the pedals. A scene from an American film flitted into my head – Barbara Stanwyck? Joan Crawford? The spurned woman setting off on her drive to death. But I wasn't crazy, and I would wait till he came to his senses.

"Peter, phone me soon. I want to stay at Eddie's with you." I tried to give him a pert look. He must remember me at my best.

His eyes melted for a second. His mouth twitched.

Got you! I ran my fingers through my hair and gave him my best smile. Drat, my eyes were filling up again. I blinked furiously and turned on the engine. He was still looking at me. I slipped the car into gear and slid off, blowing him a kiss. In the rear-view mirror, I saw his lips curve into a twisted smile I didn't recognise.

29. Truth Telling

Peter:

Melbourne, July 1942

The next Saturday night, Iris talked me into a double date. Her friend Jean was having a hard time getting over Chris's death. His loss hardly scratched me; I was practised at losing pilots. We went to the Officers' Club in Toorak. Some place with a decent band would have been my choice, but Iris thought the club was posh and modern.

Iris needed a good time, too. Her rapist had struck once more, it seemed, same story, same clues. Third woman murdered in Melbourne. The press went crazy with front page stories about 'the Brownout Strangler'. Iris had to view long line-ups of GIs. She admitted that she wasn't sure, couldn't really pick the guy. Then the American officials and the press crowed that he had been caught. His strangeness had been noticed by other GIs, and then he had confessed. But Iris wouldn't get her day in court, on the stand. Or even in the gallery. It was to be a court martial, run by the Army and American lawyers. Apart from the military, only the press were admitted. Iris would be stopped from watching the trial, like most of Melbourne.

She knocked back the cocktails fast and went over it again.

"What really made me mad," she said, "was how the day after the Yanks announced they'd got the bloke, reporters from *The Argus*, *The Age* and *The Herald* came to interview me, senior reporters, front-page men. They took up all morning talking to me, but didn't print what I said. Only *The Truth* put in a line about me, and their bloke spent just five minutes with me."

"That's how things are, honey. The guys in charge just decide what we get told. Happens most of the time, and now we're at war, all the time." My mouth went dry. Maddox would say the important thing was for folks to think the Forces had everything under control. I said, "Maddox's guys want to wipe it off everyone's mind."

She gripped my hand so hard her fingernails dug into my skin.

We hit the dance floor. She liked to jitterbug. She said it helped keep her in shape when she was between shows. We always seemed to dance fast now. Everything felt fast. It. wasn't from fear. The fear of invasion had evaporated. After the battle of the Coral Sea, everyone was reassured that Australia's supply lines were secure. The word around Maddox's office was that the Japs would not invade Australia, not after the destruction of their carriers at Midway. Maddox and Curtin conveyed confidence. Maddox was moving his office to Brisbane by August, and the mood in Melbourne had changed. Now, we just had to get the Japs out of New Guinea and the rest of the Pacific. The Aussies on the ground in New Guinea were doing it hard. My squadron and others were working non-stop, but we were not very effective yet, and I found that hard to bear.

Stately old Melbourne had sped up. Everyone was crazy for fun, booze and sex. Looking around the roomful of tanked-up kids, I felt old. Most of these rookies were straight out of school or college. I felt older, too, because I was off the booze. The leaves were so short there was no point taking it up again because I'd have to wean myself off it on the days before I flew. Being the only sober person, I noticed the frantic way people shouted and shrieked with laughter, and spilled liquor over everything, and threw up everywhere, and screwed each other in any corner they could find. Iris said she had never expected me to turn into a killjoy. I wasn't so sure it was me who had changed. It seemed to be most of Melbourne, and anyhow, it wasn't joy I was objecting to, it was something else. She told me to relax. I tried; I just couldn't tear my mind off the mess up north. The planes were still shit. Rookies crashed them like dodgems. We couldn't get enough wariness and aggressive, tactical skills into these kids.

Iris was the centre of attention. She had the men in the room drooling. Pity I wasn't in love with her. At least I'd always been honest about that. She didn't ask about my feelings or the future, she was so relieved I didn't turn her down when she called and asked to see me. How could I? Once I knew she was going through the rape and the police questions all over again, I couldn't be nice enough to her.

But I told her it didn't mean anything. She caught on. Like me, she knew how to forget about the future, how to have fun but not throw your heart away.

Not that I could have fun. I had lost all that. It was gone. Iris had a point about me. I had changed again that way, and this time it felt permanent. The military doc I had reported to in Brisbane said I would get myself back to how I was. I nearly punched him. Not really, of course, but I must have given him a look because his face turned scared, and he finished my session quick-smart. Before he let me go, he even apologised for suggesting that I wouldn't manage it with girls for a while. I just shrugged. But when I had gone with Iris to the Fed last week, I damned well nearly couldn't; even when I could, it was only, horridly, like firing a gun. I told her I couldn't sleep with her for a time; she just nodded. I tried to say I couldn't feel anything for any girl now, that it wasn't her fault. She took my hand. I couldn't say another word. When I drove her home, I felt like an old wreck.

One of these days I'd forget the look on Faye's face when she met me in the front room of the billet. And when she drove herself home.

But what was the point of starting over? I couldn't do it. At least I'd told her the truth.

Some tipsy couple careered into us, so we moved over to the other end of the floor. It was then we saw her. On some goon's knee, holding a drink and a cigarette – when did she start smoking? The guy began devouring her face. She even looked dainty in a clinch with an ape.

"She shouldn't be here like that," I muttered to Iris.

"She knows where she is, Pete."

"Maybe not. I'm gonna have to get her outa here."

"She can look after herself. You think it's her first time here?"

"You've seen her here before?" I stared straight at Iris; one thing about her, she couldn't lie, not to me anyway.

"No, but she's on the prowl. She knows what she's doing."

"I'm not so sure. I'll get her into a taxi."

Iris looked thunderous but retreated to find Jean. I approached Faye and the goon. I outranked him, and he should have known who I was, though lots of GIs didn't. He was good-looking, I had to admit, in a Midwest, boyish way. He looked barely twenty.

I gave him a glare. "Beat it." It took him a moment to get the picture and scram.

"Why, Peter," she looked up at me with a mischievous smile I didn't recognise, "that wasn't very polite."

"Let's go." I gently took her arm. What a mistake. I felt the current of her warmth and for a moment I could have taken her out back to the garden and joined the other desperate couples.

"I'd love to, wherever it is you're taking me." Her voice had a thrilling sharp sweetness even when it was blurred a touch by booze.

We went outside and I found a cab.

"Anderson Street, Toorak," I said, putting her in and shutting the door.

"Oh no, the Trocadero, please driver," she piped sweetly, with a laughing look up at me. "Home would be dreary. I can't spend another night writing letters you'll never read, darling."

I pushed in next to her. "Anderson Street, mate," I repeated, before the car pulled out.

She leaned her head on my shoulder. "I wish this was a hansom cab."

"Huh." I looked out the window and thanked god it wasn't. I might not have kept my distance in a dark, slow carriage.

"Are you all right, Peter, darling? You don't look it."

"You should talk. What are you doing, trying to drink those Yankee concoctions? You better lay off them. You're not used to booze."

"Oh, but I am, darling, it's my new best friend."

I stared quickly at her and saw her eyes cloud and her mouth tremble. I never would have picked her for a drunk. "Don't be crazy. There's no way out with booze. You just find yourself in a hole, and then you suffer while you dig yourself out."

I spoke more roughly than I meant to, and she collapsed on my chest. I felt her shaking with soundless sobs. "Hey, kid, c'mon, take it easy. You'll be okay." I looked out the window. In a few minutes, we'd be at her place, thank Christ.

"Peter, can we go somewhere, please," she whispered.

"No point. Nothing more to say." My words sounded brutal, even to me. Her tears started. Jesus, would we never get there? I said loudly to the driver, "Hey, step on it, buddy, will ya?"

She put her arms around my waist. They felt light and warm. She said softly, "Darling, it can't just end. I can't give up trying, Peter."

I was going to miss the way she said my name. I felt myself committing it to memory like the line of a song.

We were at the Gardens' corner at last, her street. "I warned you. You don't wanna get involved."

Her eyes flashed with anger. "Can't you see how involved I am? You're part of me now. I don't pretend. I don't put a time limit on my love."

"Well, I guess I do."

We arrived. I got out and opened her door. She climbed out slowly, shakier than I'd ever seen her, clutching the car as she stood up. I stayed out of her reach. I heard a door open at the side of the garage.

The chauffeur surveyed us. "Good evening to you, Miss Faye. Evening, Captain, sure it's grand you're back." He nodded at me in a friendly way but then took in Faye's tear-stained face and glared at me like I was Jack the Ripper. "Is there anything I can do for you now, Miss?" he asked, as she kept gripping the car.

I glared back at him. He was itching to throw me out. You couldn't get near me, I thought, though I noted again how tough his face was. I looked at him hard for the first time and recognised a fighter, and not one to write off.

"It's all right, thank you, Michael," she smiled. "I'm going inside."

He retreated into his doorway but kept watching me.

She went to the door, turned the key, then looked back at me. "Do telephone me tomorrow, Peter. We must talk."

I mumbled a non-committal goodnight, silently cursed the watching Irishman, and got back into the taxi. I felt too churned up to go back to Iris. At my billet, I gave the driver a big tip. Even so, he looked at me like I was scum. I sat out in the cold air for a while on the dark veranda. What the hell was I doing? I didn't know any more. I went and got my mouth organ and played some blues softly. Most guys were still out, but there were a few in bed already. When the kids started pouring in, tanked to their eyeballs, I went to bed but stayed awake till first light. Had the chauffeur seen Faye coming home with drunken GIs? I rolled over and faced the wall.

Later that morning, I ran in the local park. The waddling pink and grey birds and the sashaying wagtails didn't cheer me up. After lunch, I sat up in the tower and finally answered a letter from Hube. I wished I could talk to him about Faye, about whether her love was a blessing or a curse. What scared me was the thought that maybe love was often both – or always would be both for me. I'd be a curse to her.

The rest of that leave, I couldn't be bothered going out with any of the guys. I didn't have the energy to take Iris out, but at the start of the last week, I called her.

When she heard my voice, hers turned harsh. "So, how's the posh end of town?"

"I wouldn't have a clue."

"Ha! Don't make me laugh."

"I'm not seeing Faye. It's over."

The line crackled; she was silent.

"Iris, how are you, anyway?"

"I'm not stupid. You're still keen on her."

"Ah c'mon, I – why do you think that?"

"Because of the look on your face when she's within fifty feet. She's got you, and she's not gunna let go."

"Nah, she'll tire of me."

"I've spoken with her, Pete, and she's serious. She's not giving up."

"You spoke to her? When?"

"A few times, first when you went missing—"

"Where?"

"At a church, St Francis-"

"You and she go to the same church? You're kidding!"

"Well, no, it's not her church, or mine, it's the one in town, on Lonsdale St."

"How come you both were there? Was it Sunday Mass?"

"No, I go there sometimes and apparently so does she. It was just a coincidence that I saw her there, and I thought she might know something about what had happened to you."

"Who was she with? Her mom?"

"No, she was alone. She was praying and she lit a candle."

I paused for a second. "Huh. And what were you doing there? Praying too? What the hell!"

"Yeah, praying for you, you dope."

Were they both praying for me? I felt a thrill of pleasure at the vision of Faye lighting a candle, I let myself think it was to keep me safe. "So, you bowled up and asked her for information?"

"Yes, and then she rang me a couple of times." Her voice sounded pleased, teasing.

"What the hell for?"

Her laugh was bitter. "To tell me you were alive."

I took a breath. "Jesus."

"Before you go thinking she's an angel, let me tell you she thinks she's got you, and I'm just the ex-girlfriend."

"She said that?"

"No, of course not, she's a smooth talker, like all those posh girls."

"Well, I won't be seeing her."

"Sooner or later, you will, or she'll find a way to see you."

"No."

"All right then, how about meeting me after my show for a drink, or we could go on to the Fed?"

I paused, not wanting to see her and not knowing how to get out of it.

Her voice clanged hard on my ear. "Yeah, I didn't think so. Well, just take your time, Pete, and you can bloody well leave me alone till you've got over her!"

30. Fighters

Peter:

Melbourne, July 1942

On my last night of leave, I ate early with the few guys who hadn't gone out yet and then wandered outside. I squatted against the wall, took out my mouth organ and wailed the blues, song after song. When I heard footsteps crunch up the gravel path, I had my eyes closed.

The chauffeur, Michael, was in his driver's uniform, but without the jaunty cap. He held an envelope in his hand.

"Nothing like a harmonica, is there?" he said. "Unless it's the pipes. I've got this for you, from the young lady."

He held out a letter.

For a second, I wanted to turn away, but I took it and stared at the chocolate box writing. Would her perfume be on it? It was all I could do not to hold it to my face. I ripped it open roughly. I could barely read in the dim light of the veranda, but her rich indigo ink was strong enough. A declaration and a plea. Not unkind. Not desperate.

I felt a vice on my chest. I folded the paper and shoved it in my pocket. The Irishman stood patiently, looking out at the large front garden. I couldn't speak.

Eventually, he said, "Have you walked in this garden? It's a beauty, isn't it? The young lady is at a dinner in a big house nearby. Lovely gardens there, too. Water fountains and all."

I recalled Faye telling me he had taken over their garden after the regular man joined up. He caught my eye. Surprisingly, he wasn't hostile.

"If you feel like writing a reply, Captain, I'll take it and be on my way."

I caught my breath and shook my head.

"Ah, sure. She'll be disappointed, but maybe you're not one for letter writing. Me neither."

I grabbed a cigarette and lit up. Further movement wasn't an option yet. I leaned back on the wall. Michael stood motionless, at ease, still staring at the garden. Was he waiting till I told him to go? Surely, he knew he didn't have to act like a servant around me. I figured he sensed there were questions I wanted to ask him. So, I held out my cigarettes, and he took one with a nod of thanks.

"Cup of tea, beer, whiskey?" I asked, the hoarseness of my voice embarrassing me.

"A small one, good on you, Captain."

I motioned him inside to the bar and poured him a drink and me some water. Two older Aussies were playing cards, so I led Michael to the chairs on the veranda.

As usual, there was nothing to glean from his expression.

I asked, "Have GIs been bringing Faye home?"

He cleared his throat. "Sure, there's been a procession of them, Captain."

"She's been going out with them?"

"I'm not after sayin' that. She asks me to drop her off at the dance halls. The first night I waited and drove her home, but other nights she told me to go, and she arrived home in cabs or American army cars. With one chap, like, well, except one night, when there were two or three – I'm not sayin' there was anything goin' on; she's a real lady, Captain; I know that, and you know that."

"Yep," I said quickly. "But some ape might not realise it."

"That's right," he said, puffing clouds of smoke. "That's why I'm doing me best to keep an eye on her. I mean, I'll always be on the lookout for her, as long as I'm on me feet. She's a grand girl, the best of the family, though lately she's been givin' me nerves a goin' over with her gallivantin.'"

"Where does she go?"

He stared straight ahead. "Only place to worry about is that wild dump by the river under Princes Bridge; used to be called the Green Mill. What d'they call it now, the Trocadero? It's no place for her, Captain, unless she's with you. One night, she walked in by herself. Can you imagine that? And, to tell you the truth, she'd a drop taken."

My heart chilled. "You could see?"

"She holds it well for a little woman, but fellas might pick it, all right."

"Can you tell Eddie or Nigel?" I turned to him.

He blinked dismissively. "Mr Edward would do his best to help her, but he couldn't look after himself in a place like that. Neither could young Nigel, and he'd never keep his mouth shut. The young lady is doin' a fine job of keepin' her shenanigans away from himself and her ladyship."

I grinned.

He gave me a quick glance of comradeship.

I said, "Where else does she go?"

"The Officers' Club and the St Kilda Town Hall." He spat it out, but his look was concerned, not critical. "Captain, the young lady has been out a lot lately. She's got the miseries; I reckon she was hoping to go dancing with you again. But I know how it is when you're back on leave; you can't gad about with the carefree types who never saw a speck of blood. The fightin' is with you even when you try to forget it for a night. It keeps on; it wears you down."

I slumped in my seat. "It feels like it's never gonna stop."

He nodded, took a large gulp and looked down at his glass. "You live down a dark hole, kill anything that moves. All you have is your gun and your comrades, but they keep dying."

The cool breeze buffeted my face. "It's like only the killings are real. I don't care about anything else."

He nodded and cleared his throat. He gave me a quick look then spoke more quietly. "You see a man's head split like a log, runnin' with blood, and you walk past. You blow up a house full of people without your heart skippin' a beat."

He turned to me, his eyes dark and tense, complicit. I nodded and breathed out slowly. For the first time, someone was talking about what really happened.

I said, "But you gotta keep fighting. It's not like you have a choice."

He drained his glass. "You tell yourself, day after day, that you have no choice, that the war is more important than everyone, more important than your brothers, even more important than her, but it isn't." He took a breath. "We say it's for freedom – and it mostly is – that's the sad part, freedom is what we're looking for, but all we find is blood. We walk on dead bodies like they're paving stones. We chase our own death."

I wondered how many brothers and friends he had lost. Had his war been longer and more vicious than mine? Had it finished when he walked away? Had that taken courage, or been forced upon him?

I said, "Dying starts to look like a relief."

He nodded. "Folks think fellas like me and you were born for war, but it's just that we've seen worse things than they have. We've learned to do what no-one should have to think about."

I looked away. "Yep. They call you a hero when you know you're nothin' but a hunter, a slaughterman, a killer."

"Aye. Few see that. Fewer admit it."

He met my eyes for a second.

I wondered if he had chased death as I did, with such excitement.

I said, "You were fighting for your own family, your own people, your own land."

He nodded, his face sombre.

I looked away. "I've been fighting half my life, but just to stay alive. And now, it's like you said, except it's not only that I have to fight – I want to."

He shrugged. "I would have said the same thing, back then. And maybe I was right. But then there's a cost, to everyone, not just us."

We sat in silence for a while.

He smiled at me; it took years off his face. "I reckon you were a hero, doin' the dirty work before they asked you. And I reckon you can stop running in first to the fray. Don't waste your youth courtin' death. You should be payin' your attentions to the young lady. You won't find another like her when you're used up and spat out by your old generals." His mouth turned down, the lines beside it etched deeper. "I'll tell you something, lad, the minute the fightin' stops, no-one wants to remember a thing about it; they don't want to know the ones who saved them; they blame us, like we caused all the trouble, like we were the bloodthirsty ones. They forget how glad they were to leave it up to us. When you get back in one piece, you find some other fella talkin' sweet to your girl, and she thinks you're cold because you don't love her, not because you're half dead."

The misery on his face. A war without glory. A girl, a home and a country lost. I wanted to commiserate, but he would probably squirm at that. In a few years, I'd look like him. I'd never love another woman, either.

I put my hand over my eyes. "Yeah, but she deserves the best – I don't wanna wreck her life."

"It's what's been happenin' lately that's rooin' it, if I can be frank with you."

I stared at the tall gum trees, dark against the sky. And I remembered the feel of her hands on me, the exact weight of her softness, the fragrance and warmth of her.

So maybe I shouldn't push her away. Maybe I wouldn't. But maybe I was incapable of that much kindness.

Anyway, wouldn't she end up marrying one of her crowd?

He gave his wry sad grin and refused another drink.

"You look after yourself now, Captain. I appreciate having a word."

I nodded. "Yep. Same here, Mike. Tell her—" I paused. "I'm going away for a while."

He stood silent for a moment.

"But you'll be back in Melbourne some time?"

"Sure," I said, though who knew.

"And you'll not be tellin' her not to write."

I shrugged. He gave the sad grin again and started off down the path. I watched him get to the gate, turn and wave. I waved back and then re-read her letter. It made me smile and it brought me near despair. I took it upstairs to keep with all the others. Her words rang in my mind half the night. Should I try to answer? One moment I'd think what's the point of dragging it out, and the next moment I'd see her face as she opened my letter. But what could I say? Best to say nothing.

31. Home Front Blues

Faye:

Melbourne, July 1942

A bus pulled into the Essendon airport car park, and I spotted Iris getting out. She looked at my car as she walked with the other girls to the fence. My chest felt tight. Had Peter kept seeing her all of this leave? No doubt she had asked him to comfort her about the strangler case. Had they written to each other all these months?

Staff cars arrived, and there he was, getting out with the other officers. His gaze didn't linger a second on my car, but I knew how quickly he observed everything. Iris was running up to him. He held out his arms to her but then seemed to stiffen. Well, that was something. I put my hand over my mouth to stifle the sobs. My hands were shaking. A sick taste welled up in my mouth. They were embracing, and then he kissed her. I blinked away tears. I couldn't miss a second of this agony.

As he turned to leave, his face was hard, with a bitter smile. I wound my window down, and he glanced over – was it the sound or a change in light he noticed? His face tightened again, tension wiping away the harsh smile. I brushed away a curl from my eye and waved to him, summoning a smile for him that seemed to carve out my flesh. His mouth softened, he nodded, and then that haunted look I remembered came back. Now I was the reason for it. He wheeled round and strode into the airport.

Iris waited till he was out of sight then walked quickly to a taxi. I tapped on the front divider glass and wound up my window as the car rolled off. Near the exit, I passed Iris in her taxi. For an instant our eyes met. I felt a rush of fury. If there had been anything at hand, I would have thrown it. She had her family and friends to support her through the strangler trial publicity – she didn't need to grab Peter again. What sort of female snatched a man back when she knew he loved another girl?

As my car sped through the dark, drab suburbs, I leaned back and poured a half glass of sherry from the flask. Iris didn't make him smile, let alone twinkle or laugh. I would win him back, however long it took.

I couldn't bear to peer out at the people in the city streets or at the shining river. When we reached home, Michael got out and opened the door for me. I had told him that was never necessary. Climbing out, I composed my face, but Michael looked more mournful than ever. He gave a sort of bow. Dear, funny old thing.

Eddie was visiting, and for once it was an effort to face him. Apparently, he had come to see *me*. He got me out of the house, thank goodness, ostensibly to go out for dinner, but, when he offered to take me to his place instead, I thankfully agreed. Exhausted, I sank down with a sherry in front of his fire and stared into my glass.

"Does your artist friend still like Iris?"

"I suppose so." He looked quickly at me.

"Can you reintroduce them?" My voice sounded raspy.

He came and sat next to me. "Oh, Faye, I'm sorry."

"Yes. I'll never speak to her again. But don't worry! I'm not giving up." A sob broke out. "Sorry. I'm almost past crying. Anyway, he doesn't love her. I saw them saying goodbye. She doesn't make him feel better, let alone happy. With her, he doesn't have a twinkle in his eye." And no sultry smoulder.

"I see." He squeezed my hand. "Well, he looked happy with you. But you know, Faye, there's a lot happening to him. He's probably reeling from it all."

"You're right. Love is not the main thing in soldiers' lives at the moment. And Mo explained to me that the fighting can lead to emotional withdrawal. Edith says lots of the men she sees in the wards can't respond to anyone."

"It's a mad time. You can't tell what things may be like later, when all this is over. And yet, my dear, perhaps you need to prepare yourself to accept that he may not be ready to have a long relationship."

He had made a comment like that before. I had to ask, "Has he said anything to make you think that?"

"No, of course not. But he doesn't seem the most conventional of men, does he?"

"He certainly has some outlandish views – on religion and Aborigines, at any rate." I tried not to think about our argument that night at Florentino's.

"He's a bit of a lone wolf, I suspect." Eddie took out a cigarette. "And a rebel. That sort of person doesn't fit into the usual romantic scenario. Or perhaps they don't settle down till they're much older."

I gazed at the fire. "But he loves me. He needs me. Perhaps I want him more strongly, but he does want me."

He said quietly, "Wanting someone is not always enough, I fear. Some people don't follow their feelings. Or the cost is too high for them."

"What cost? I don't understand."

"Well, if you find it hard to commit yourself to anyone, then you may just avoid seeing the person who wants you most, or whom you want most."

"Yes, but I don't understand why people find it so hard to make a commitment." I turned to him and studied his face.

He looked tense. "It's difficult for someone like you to understand."

"Like me? What am I like?" I couldn't help sounding hostile.

"You're so sure of yourself, of who you are, what you want and your right to have everything you want. You can't imagine feeling guilty or unworthy, or as though your desires aren't worth fulfilling." He looked away. "I'm sorry, my dear, perhaps I'm talking nonsense that has nothing to do with the case."

"No." I put a hand on his arm. "It reminds me of something Peter said, that he was bad for me. He said, 'I'm bad news.'"

Eddie looked sad. "Perhaps he meant to be kind, my dear. He may have been speaking honestly."

"But he's wrong. How can he be bad news for me?"

"Well, he has made you cry lately, Faye," Eddie said gently.

"Only because of his mad idea that he's not good enough for me." I paused. "He and Iris would have slept together right from the start, wouldn't they?"

"Probably," Eddie said.

"He told me that the one thing he's done right was *not* sleeping with me, leaving me a virgin for my husband. That's so awful, Eddie, it's not what he believes, or what I believe."

"No, but it is what the men who'll want to marry you may believe. It's clever and kind of him in a way, unselfish."

"No, it's selfish." I took a breath. "I see what you're saying, but Peter took me out of a life with old fashioned, narrow-minded people. How could he turn into a guard, protecting my virginity for men like Clive?"

Alarm flooded over his face. "You won't go back to Clive, Faye, will you?"

"Of course not, but Peter is giving me up so that men like Clive will still want me. He expects that I'll marry one of them. He should know me better than that. If I can't have him, I certainly won't want some bossy, moralistic man."

Eddie looked concerned. "What have we done to you, Peter and I? Now I feel guilty, too. In the end, you will want a marriage and children."

"Yes, with Peter."

"Ah. Isn't that where we came in? If he won't, or can't, be a husband and father, then you may have to accept his decision." We sat silent for a moment.

Eddie said, "He's trying to leave you the freedom and choice to marry someone else, someone who might not settle for, well, what's labelled by that hateful phrase, damaged goods."

"The last thing I'd be is damaged."

"I admire you for saying that. It's probably true."

"I'll be *damaged* by his rejection, Eddie. Why can't he see that?

"He might think that it would cause you more pain to start an affair and then have to end it."

"Why end it? – Oh, all right, his fear of a permanent relationship."

"And Faye, I think he realises, as most young men wouldn't, that it might be too hard for you to have an affair when it came to the real decision."

"I've thought about that. It would be difficult, but I'd be prepared to do it, even if there was no promise of a marriage."

"Ah. Does he know that?"

"No. He hasn't given me a chance to say it. Eddie, perhaps you should be my go between," It was mischievous of me, but I wasn't serious.

My poor uncle looked alarmed. "That's a dangerous role. I'm not sure I could, or should, assume it."

"Relax. I'm only kidding, as the Americans say."

Eddie looked at me rather anxiously. "Faye, to have an affair with him would be a very major decision emotionally, even if you don't give a hang about what anyone thinks or says. Imagine how hard it would be to give him up, to have him say goodbye and go back to America."

"But isn't that what you expected me to do right at the start?" I heard my tone cut the air. "At the Governor's Ball, when you encouraged me to consider him, didn't you imagine I'd have a temporary fling?"

He winced. "Yes, but I was heartless and foolish, I see now. You're the sort of person who loves completely and absolutely. There are so few of you around, my dear. Forgive me, I have been such a flippant advisor. He's a strange person. I don't feel I have the least idea of what he's been going through in the war."

Unaccountably, he looked close to tears, so I patted his hand. "I'll write all this to him. Oh, I hope he reads my letters. He used to." I took in a sharp breath. "You know, Eddie, I think, despite my letters, that he had decided not to see me, when he came here this time."

Eddie squeezed my hand. "Come over to the table. Let's have some soup and talk of other things. Though I must say this: I've always believed it's better to have loved and lost than never to have loved. I still believe it, but I never wanted you to be hurt. I'm desperately sorry about the way this is turning out."

"It's not over, Eddie, darling!" I laughed, hugging his arm. "What's that line from the movies? Was it Al Jolson or Jimmy Durante? – 'You ain't seen nothin' yet!'"

32. At Risk

Faye:

Melbourne, Late July 1942

Washing my hair, late in the morning, I found tiny twigs in my curls. I felt cold at the thought of the man I had gone outside with the night before at the Trocadero. Not a detail of his appearance came back to me. The memory of him handling me made my stomach churn. Of course, I had been desperately sad and a bit crazy from drinking, but what a risk – what if he had been less drunk and had actually managed what he intended? What if he was diseased? I remembered raving about going back into the dancehall, but it struck me now that I had been almost passing out. Who else would have grabbed me if I had staggered back to the bar? I had got out of the place by the skin of my teeth. By instinct. Somehow, I had got through the park to Princes Bridge.

I felt again the violent force of my legs kicking out and hitting the drunken soldier with my thick high heels as he tried to follow me into the taxi. The taxi driver had leant over and slammed the door and given me a look, half-approving, half-disgusted, before he sped me away home. It was like a nightmare that couldn't have happened. Now I understood how women found themselves pregnant to people they hardly knew. I could have ended up an unmarried mother, hiding away for almost a year and then giving up my child, like the girls at Wilsons' station. Who would have married me then? A girl could throw away privilege, overnight. But luck was mine. My mother believed in guardian angels. Some Catholics believed God was always watching over them. Both ideas seemed medieval. Who had watched over those women killed in Melbourne this year? Iris Kelly had saved herself.

When the taxi got me home at heaven knows what time, Michael had appeared from the garage. He and the taxi driver rolled their eyes at each other and kind of saluted. I shoved a large tip into the driver's hand.

"Thanks so much," I mumbled. "You're a good man."

"Got a daughter meself, love. Don't you go to that dump again by yourself."

Michael steadied me up the path. He was so quiet opening the front door that my parents hadn't stirred, thank goodness. He waited at the foot of the stairs till I got to my bedroom door and then let himself out silently.

Once my hair was towel-dry, I ran down to the kitchen, and Mrs. Mac made me tea and toast. She told me that Lady Beauregarde was out and that Sir Henry was coming home for lunch. I took a tray into the breakfast room and sat looking out at the courtyard. It was a cool morning, but the sun was coming out.

I phoned Aunt Lillian and arranged to see Mo the next morning.

I went to his office in St Kilda Road. I felt privileged to be admitted to the building – such a hive of activity. I felt guilty taking his time and using my connections, but I would be brief.

"Mo, there must be something useful that I can do. Not just giving cups of tea to soldiers, as Bel does, something a bit harder and more time consuming. I'd be hopeless as a nurse's aide. I'm too squeamish and impatient. I thought you might have something in an office, or driving, or in a factory."

Mo grinned. "I don't think your parents would thank me if I sent you to a factory, my dear. But there is actually something that you would be excellent at, if you don't mind travelling to a rather unglamorous office a little out of the city."

"No, of course not."

"You'd have to go by train; petrol rations wouldn't stretch that far."

"What sort of work is it?"

"We need women with quick brains and preferably with education in a foreign language and mathematics—"

"I've been studying French and Latin at the University. And I did rather well at maths at school."

"You would miss lectures and might be too tired to go to evening ones."

"There's a war on." I smiled. "I can finish my course later. If I don't do anything for the war, I'm going to feel quite ashamed. Besides, I'm bored and missing Peter. If I were doing a job that mattered, I'd feel better, Mo."

"Oh, this job matters all right You won't be able to tell anyone – not even your parents – exactly what you're doing. Your father may guess, of course, but you won't be able to say anything about it."

"Is it translating? I don't know Japanese or Polynesian languages."

"Of course not. You will be trained enough to be useful."

So, I was interviewed by a couple of old army chaps. The training sergeant seemed a little fazed by my surname and possibly by my accent. The other girls looked hard at my clothes the first day, before my uniform was issued. Although they were mostly Protestants from grammar schools, they were quite accepting of me. Working for the war effort was bringing people together. No doubt my colleagues realised who my uncle was, but I hoped they would like me for myself before long. The unit was part of an American office. The accents and casual movements of the American officers were comforting.

The job was wonderful. Being sworn to secrecy was exciting, too. When outsiders asked, I said I did office work, people believed me, and that was that.

Only Dad hinted at the truth. "You process printed material, darling, do you? Well, of course you can't say. I hope it's not dreary, once it ceases to be a novelty."

My mother looked sour. "Why on earth would you want to go all that way to work in an office?"

"It's where the need is, for educated girls who can read fast."

"That's ridiculous. You can't type. And you won't be able to finish your subjects at the university. You'll be wasting a year – or more."

"I'll find it easier when I go back, if I do," I replied.

That silenced my mother. Was she wondering if I intended to marry instead of returning to university?

Having a job was fun, even though the hours were long, and the work wasn't easy. Mostly, we had no idea what our little pieces of work meant, and I gathered that we would continue to be kept in the dark, but it was marvellous to be a part of things. We worked in shifts of several days and had to sleep at the unit. The dormitory accommodation was ridiculously Spartan, rather an adventure. The food was terrible, but the Americans gave us chocolate, ice cream and coca cola. The first week, I felt embarrassed accepting these extras, but I took the chocolate home to share with my family or with Peggy.

Most of the girls had boyfriends or fiancés in the Australian forces. One girl was becoming rather friendly with an American staff officer at the unit. I watched their flirting with sympathy. His appeal was obvious, though he wasn't in the same league as Peter. No one commented or criticised. Friendships with Americans were commonplace now, and engagements were announced often in the paper between Melbourne girls and American servicemen. The cinema newsreels featured deliriously smiling couples, the guys flashing white smiles, the girls flourishing bright rings.

33. Wounds

Peter:

August 1942, Brisbane to Melbourne

I hauled my bad leg up the steps and shoved my way along the crowded platform. The train door was open, so I climbed in okay. I threw the crutches up in the luggage rack with my bag and took off my coat. I would need it when we headed south into the night.

It surprised me how much I was looking forward to Melbourne, the familiar old buildings and the cool mornings. I wouldn't see anyone. I wouldn't even have to think about it; I'd be hospitalised. When I got out, I'd see the kids at St Anthony's or send something to them.

The carriage filled up with officers. Two boozed-up guys fell onto the seat opposite me. I opened the window to its maximum. A jerking, wild-eyed kid I'd have to watch sat near the door. The platform seethed with girls in light dresses. Some blew me kisses, and I made myself smile and wave. The corridors filled up and the engine started. The train wasn't fast, but the city was soon behind us. Brisbane wasn't far-flung like Melbourne.

We were in paddocks quickly and then passing plantations of pineapples and bananas. I loved the country. Maybe after the war, it would be the place to come. Further north, the sugar cane plantations needed men. Maybe Buzz would come here. Coloured guys in the north worked alongside whites, more or less. Maybe we could get a piece of land together, and no-one would run us off it at gunpoint like they would in the States. I knew he was in Hawaii and surviving, so far at least. If he died, it would really hit me. I leaned out of the window into the fresh air.

The Melbourne docs had better know what to do about my leg. It was swollen and hurt like hell all the time, not just where bones were broken in the ankle and foot. I had shrugged off crash injuries since I was a kid in the carnivals, but this felt way worse. It would be weird if after the war, I was a cripple and Buzz was whole.

The kid in the corner started mumbling. I waved at him. "It's okay, pal, everything's okay. You're gonna be fine."

Another guy offered him a smoke, and he quieted a little. The dusk drew in and birds were flocking around great trees as we whizzed past. The coast came into view. Marvellous beaches. I wished I was in the air to see it all properly. One day, I'd fly all over this country. Fear gripped me again – what if I they couldn't fix my fucking leg? I'd still be keen to fly whether the leg was live or dead, but no-one would hire me.

I shared my water and fruit with the twitchy kid who had no food with him. There was a café-mess car but neither of us could get to it. The darkness fell quickly, and the wind was much cooler. I closed the window almost shut. The sozzled guys facing me were chain smoking as well as guzzling from bottles, so I needed some air. When they headed off for the bar, I stretched out and reached in my pocket for my harmonica. The guys next to me grinned, but the nervous kid didn't see it. I blew a fast train blues or two and then some old favourites. The words ricocheted through my head with the rivulets of chords:
Motherless children have a hard time when the mother is gone... Oh sinner man, where you gonna run to... You better live a Christian, for you gonna die... Don't know the minute nor the hour... Don't a man feel bad when his baby's on the coolin' board, don't a man feel weary when that hearse rolls up to his door.

A life with Faye was never going to happen. She might as well be dead. I would never love her. As some old guy said, probably in New Orleans, "I sing the blues to make me feel better." Even the poor nervy kid seemed to have relaxed some. I leaned back on the leather seat and shut my eyes for a stretch.

Some god-awful time in the morning, the train stopped for a spell at Sydney. After the corridors had emptied, I grabbed my crutches, limped down out of the carriage and headed to the men's room; the ones on board were awash, and it was awkward with crutches pushing through the packed corridors. There were women on the platform – keen to make a fortune in ten minutes – and respectable girls smiling and offering tea under the hawk-eyed supervision of older men and women. Some of the girls gave me the eye, to my surprise, and I looked away.

When we started off again, I slept a little and woke when the sun was up. An officer came to check on the twitchy kid, but he had been asleep since we started again. It was sad that he had no pal but not surprising; he'd gone right away from everyone. I guessed he'd be heading to the hospital, too, the psychiatric section.

If the Melbourne docs said I'd be a cripple, I'd put a bullet through my skull. Sorry, Hube. Sorry, Buzz. Or would they understand? I couldn't bear thinking about the one who would really mourn me – and mightn't be able to stop. The one who seriously thought she could have me as her own forever, when I could never love anyone enough, or long enough, let alone a girl like her. The one who dreamed of a wedding and a home and babies and growing old with me – all that lovely stuff I couldn't understand, couldn't promise.

We stopped again at Albury and then it seemed not long till we were passing through the outskirts of Melbourne, with its straggly small farms, pretty orchards and wooded hills. Soon we chuffed past sprawling houses with faded red rooves and then grey factories and terrace houses, some dilapidated, with their iron rooves half askew. A horse-drawn cart meandered up a street. In back yards, roosters and chickens crowed and clucked. A few workers strolled towards the train line; others cycled along main roads. Further on, a tram clanged past, city bound. As we neared Spencer Street Station, our destination, guys were waving and leaning out, yelling and whooping. The platform would be packed with girls, lots of them probably not waiting for a particular guy or a special one. The desperation of this public desire made me tired as hell. I looked at the twitchy kid and gave him a smile. He was waking up and the horrors hadn't reared up to grip him again yet. He gave me a childish, open grin. I tried not to wince. No wonder he had been broken. The officer came back to shepherd him off the train and nodded at me.

I waited till the carriage was empty before attempting to get out. In the corner of my eye, I saw a girl moving along the platform. She reminded me of Faye, the same small stature, graceful, easy walk, and long curly hair. Fuck it, if I was going to see her everywhere, I would go even crazier. As if she would be at Spencer Street in this kind of crowd. I got myself down onto the platform. Then I heard her sweet voice call my name. I never had my knees go weak, but I swear my good one almost did then. She was holding her arms out to me, and I knew I would never forget the look on her face.

34. Fighting the Crowd

Faye:

Melbourne, August 1942

"I'll see you soon, Michael."

"Good luck, Miss Faye. Take care in that mob. Don't let them jostle you off your feet, now. I should be walking in with you, but I don't dare leave the car unmanned in a place like this."

"I'll be quite all right. I'm used to platforms now, you know."

I stepped down from the car. Streams of people were rushing to the platform, so I didn't need to ask which one.

I pushed my way forward, ignoring furious glares from both elegant and blowsy-looking women. When they saw my Yank, they'd understand! The day was cold, but the crowd insulated me. When I ducked under someone and reached the front, the wind nearly blew my hat off.

The noise from the crowd welled up before you could even see the train. I was afraid to move any further forward and stayed locked in the line. You could get pushed onto the tracks if you weren't careful. Was it always like this when the boys came into Spencer Street? It was thrilling. I hadn't heard a crowd roar so loud since the last Football Grand Final. My ears were ringing. Women near me were jumping and waving. The train chuffed in, and men were leaning out, throwing little packets – good heavens! Girls near me threw flowers on the tracks. The driver was grinning and the black faced stoker too. Here were the first-class carriages. There he was! I took a deep breath and struggled to hold my ground as the crowd swelled forward. Men were jumping off and shouting girls' names. The woman next to me, forty at least, was screaming, "Max, Maxie!" I laughed.

Tears were cold on my cheeks, despite the heat of the crowd. Why wasn't he coming out? I stood impatiently. He was standing at the back of the carriage while others got down – a poor twitching boy and some older officers. How I wished he would look for me.

He slowly climbed down onto the platform. His face was strained; the jaw and mouth looked different. He seemed to focus on me, but he did not speak.

"Peter!"

A faint smile. I watched his slow progress with the crutches and the dragging leg. Some yards from me, he stopped. He wiped his eyes with his sleeve. Like a child.

I ran up and hugged his chest. I looked up at him, blinking away tears. I reached for his face and neck. His eyes were soft as forget-me-nots at dusk.

"Faye, I didn't expect you here."

"Darling, your leg. Is it painful?"

"I'm fine. You look so beautiful. I'm not fit to be seen. That train ride was some marathon."

"Yes, it must have felt unending. I've got my car outside."

"I have to go straight to the hospital. That was the deal with the docs; they let me come in an ordinary carriage, and I promised to go straight to the hospital. I have to report there and get my leg checked out pronto."

I stroked his face. "Of course, darling, but I'll drive you there. Michael's waiting outside. We can relax and talk, and I don't care if you think you're a grub, I still want one private hug in the car."

His expression softened then tensed. He looked around restlessly. "Yeah. Let's get outa here. It's like a zoo. You'll have to put up with me walking slow."

"Don't be silly, I don't mind. What have the doctors said?"

"They're not much use – the ones in Brisbane, anyway. I'm pinning my hopes on the hotshots here. Or the guys with more experience. It's gonna take a lot of work to get the movement back, that's all. I can't go dancing with you. I'm sorry." His smile looked a little twisted.

"You are cruel to a girl!" I flashed a cheeky smile at him, in case he took it the wrong way. "But you will dance soon, darling," I said gently.

"Yep, I sure will."

I looked up expecting to see his earnest Gary Cooper face. Instead, the morning sun was bleaching his features and fading his eyes glassy pale and sharp. He moved off slowly on his crutches out to the car. When we climbed in and the crutches were out of sight, he seemed to relax a little. He turned to me and touched the sleeve of my coat.

"You must have got up mighty early to get there this morning and to be in the front row too."

"Rather early. But don't feel bad. I didn't get there at dawn. I pushed my way to the front."

He burst into laughter. "Faye Beauregard pushed? I wish I'd seen that."

"Well, I'm short. I couldn't see at the back. And I had to meet a hero." I stroked his face and ran my fingers down his chest. He pulled me to him and put his face against my cheek, then into my hair.

"Ouch! Whatever is this?" I reached into his chest pocket and pulled out a harmonica. "Oh, do you play it?"

"Yep."

"What fun. Did you play it on the train?"

"Uh-huh."

"I'd love to hear it one day."

"Sure."

I leant up and kissed him. He seemed restrained; perhaps he was worried that his breath might offend me. I stroked his shoulder and his side. Oh yes, the smouldering look was back. But when would I see the twinkle as well?

"Tell me how you really are, Peter. You don't have to shield me from things. I'm not a China doll."

He grinned. "Ha! You are, baby." He touched my cheek. "Priceless porcelain."

"Is your leg hurting very much?"

He shrugged. There was fear in his look.

I caressed his face. "Don't worry. I'm sure the doctors will find an effective treatment."

He gripped me. "That's what I've been telling myself. It's gotta get better."

"Darling, just as long as the pain goes or can be managed," I said softly. "That's the first step."

His face tensed. "I'm not the kinda guy who could take being a cripple—" he broke off and turned away.

"You'll never be a cripple, Peter."

"If this goddam leg doesn't get its movement back, that's exactly what I'll be. I remember old guys hobbling round after the last war. I tell you, Faye, I won't be one of them."

There were many men like that in Melbourne. And so many of them had lost limbs – was that his fear? And that he wouldn't fly fighter planes? "You'll never be like those old men, never. The doctors now are much better; medical knowledge has advanced so much."

"Yeah, at least I haven't any gangrene."

I tried not to shudder. "Don't worry until you know all the facts. I've read of cases of war injuries coming good on their own. There was one of temporary blindness the other day. Something about the nerves and their connections to the brain."

"I'm hoping the nerves in my leg aren't caput."

"Just wait and see, Peter."

Terror seized me. He would never want to be any less than a top fighter pilot. If he couldn't go on flying, how would he bear it? Would I be able to comfort him? Was I strong enough to carry us both through such disappointment, depression and pain? How would we raise children? What would be left for him – a job training pilots, in America? How much of the Peter I loved would survive?

He spoke fast. "I figure I'll keep exercising, and then the muscles and nerves will have more chance of recovering." He sounded overwrought. "The kids I knew who had polio or broken legs recovered faster if they kept up exercise."

I stroked his forehead. He was getting lines there and deeper ones beside his mouth. "Yes, I'm sure exercise is tremendously useful."

"Baby, I didn't want to burden you with this."

"Peter, I'm not just a pretty face," I grinned.

"I'm starting to see that. I didn't expect you to be at the station, but I'm glad you brought Michael and the car." He paused. "You mustn't travel on trains with the returning troops. It's no place for a lady like you."

"Of course I had to come here. How else would I give you a proper welcome home kiss?"

He folded me into him and despite the whisky and peppermints I could taste, it was the best thing in the world to feel his lips again. Did he guess how often I had imagined this? In the cinema, in my bath, in my bed?

The car was pulling to a stop outside the hospital drive.

"We don't have to go straight in, do we?" I murmured.

"No," he said softly. "They'll expect me to take a bit longer because of the queue for staff cars and taxis."

I tapped on the glass partition. Michael lowered it a little.

"Would you drive around the park for another quarter hour, Michael, thank you. We're a little early."

"Right you are, Miss Faye." He raised the partition. In a minute, he parked near a copse of trees, got out, and walked off, lighting a cigarette.

I closed the curtains across the glass. We sank back together on the smooth leather. Peter traced the shape of my face with his hand.

I slipped out of my coat and moved closer to kiss him. He lifted me quickly onto his lap. I could feel his hands almost trembling as they moved over my shoulders and breasts. He had never trembled before. It disturbed me the way his face kept shifting between joy and sadness. I hugged him as we kissed. He sighed then smiled the way I remembered. He wriggled me across him and the twinkling, smouldering look that would make me do anything flashed across his face. I took a long breath to keep control.

"Darling, when you're out of hospital we could stay at Portsea for a while. I can let my parents think I'm at work. Or, if you can't get away, Eddie has said we can use his house when he's at the Blacks' place."

He stared at me. His eyes were still soft and warm, his cheeks were flushed, but he shook his head. "Oh, Lord, baby. That's what I fantasised about when I was stuck on that island and way before that, at the rotunda, the first time I held you. I wanted to drive off with you." He took a deep breath. "But you can't, can you? Your mom? Your reputation?"

"I don't care about all that. How could I bear it if you didn't come back? I believe you will come back. I know you will." I held him tighter.

He passed his hand over his eyes.

I slid off his lap, worried that I might be hurting his leg or his hip, or distressing him with my talk. He looked so tired.

"Peter, don't worry about anything now. You just concentrate on getting well again. I'll come and visit you every day I can."

"I don't deserve a girl like you, Faye." His eyes were grey with tears.

"Perhaps not, my Pirate, but you've got me." I kissed his face and stroked his hair that was stiff with oil and sweat.

35. Reflections

Peter:

Melbourne, August 1942

When we came up for air, I leaned into the firm leather of the back seat and stared at her. "How did you know I was on that train?"

"General Maddox told Mo, asked him if the Beauregards could keep an eye on you."

I grunted. Maddox or Mrs Maddox? Because they thought I was cracking up, or because they thought Faye was a possibility for me? Surely not even their American confidence could expect her family to offer more than polite wishes while I was convalescing? But I was impressed that one or both of them were giving Faye a free pass.

Michael moseyed back to the car, finishing a smoke, staring at the trees in the park.

*

I stood at the entrance of the hospital, watching Faye's car circle away. Her happy face was at the back window, blowing a kiss. I waved and grinned like a kid at a circus. She could warm me right to the bone. And soothe me like no-one had for a long time. I had forgotten how good it felt with her. I hadn't wanted anyone so much for as long as I could remember, except her, from the first time I saw her walking into the Windsor, trying like hell to ignore me.

But, as her car disappeared, I couldn't help feeling it was still hopeless, and I could no more deny that than forget how I had become a starving, whipped dog of a prisoner, scavenging for garbage. Despite what Michael had said, and what she thought, I'd ruin her life and hurt her more than I had hurt Iris and all the others.

It was unbearable thinking I might never dance with her again, let alone never wake up with her. And yet, as I approached the front desk, I couldn't stop picturing her visiting me.

*

The next day, she waltzed down the ward in a knock-out of a dress, with that walk of hers, half lady, half movie star. The whole ward was crazy about her from the first. She swept the curtains shut around my bed and moved in for a long kiss. The prissy matron poked her nose in, and Faye, quick as a flash, turned into the Toorak grand lady. I laughed silently as the nurse backed off.

On her second visit, she showed me a painting she had done of me. She had made me look like a film star, and a hero. The way she saw me – even Hube mightn't live up to that. Then she handed over a sheaf of sketches of me, and I didn't know whether to laugh or cry. These guys weren't heroes. They were more Humphrey Bogart than Gary Cooper. She caught me with a kind of crafty look and a blue one. I felt as uncomfortable as in a debriefing, or at a cop station, and I had almost always steered clear of those.

"These are like photos, from the scene of the crime," I said.

She squeezed my arm. "I hope they don't upset you. I wanted to study your different faces, your various moods."

Could she love a guy who looked like this? "You're mighty good. You caught me red-handed."

She stroked my face. "What goes on in your head is still a bit of a mystery. You're so different from everyone."

"That's what fascinates you as an artist?"

"And as a woman," she said back, quick as a whip.

273

My spine caught fire. She looked down and flushed for a second.

"When did I look like this?" I held up the crafty one.

"Once when you were talking to Dad." She smiled.

"Okay, and this?" It was the blue one.

"Lots of times. When we were saying goodbye, or when you talked about your childhood," she said softly.

I suppressed a shudder. Her pencil was a goddam lie-detector. The sadness, hurt and hate that I thought I hid so well were there for all to see. I got to the end of the pile and there I was with a ridiculously cocky grin. She smiled lovingly at it. I shook my head.

She held my gaze. Funny thing, eye contact: in the boys' home, it meant fear, shaming and submission; in the gang, never step out of line; in Fighter Command, it was about knowing your place, too, though they gave you more respect. But Buzz could give a long stare and say half a book. Momma, too. You knew where you were with them; they wanted you around and wanted you to feel fine. Hube, to my astonishment, was the only other person who really looked at me. After bad losses, we could comfort each other with a silent stare, reassure each other that we had done the best that could be done, or if for once we'd made a mistake, it was one in a hundred and no sane pilot could blame us.

He said I made him able to bear his nasty family because of my fuck-them-all look. Apparently, I wore it at all times in their company. I hadn't had a clue what look he was talking about. But she had drawn it. I didn't think much of it. I had imagined more dignity than anger in that look. But it was like Jimmy Cagney at his darkest. Folks who hadn't seen his early gangster flicks couldn't imagine how fierce he looked, how mean his smile was. Close to crazy. But she seemed to get a kick out of that look of mine, like Hube did.

Hube and I were full of anger; we raced against time to spend it all.

How angry I had been when Faye and I had argued about Clive and his abandoned children. I had lost any right to accuse him, or her ancestors. I started to sweat. The still bodies of the three natives, their heads back, their bodies coiled and slack; I'd always see them. Lately, it terrified me to think of looking Buzz in the eye.

She took my hand, and I thought of our walks by the river. She wasn't scared of the fierceness in me. I started to breathe in her peacefulness and her love of life, that rare kind of love I hadn't seen since Buzz. She still lived to the tempo of pre-war; she hadn't turned hectic and frantic, despite her times with drink.

"You could draw for the cops or the spies," I said.

She flushed. I wondered if her war work might be more than mere translating. I asked her about the location of her job and whether Yanks worked there. When she told me, I grinned. In that location it could be military intelligence work, but I knew she wouldn't be permitted to speak about it.

I said, "Do you draw the Yanks you see at your work?"

She laughed. "They're not in your league, darling, for looks or charm – or brains, in most cases."

"Brains! I'm not smart."

"Pilots like you need to be more than smart, with the sorts of decisions you need to make and the speed at which you have to make them. It's not only the amount you've learnt, but the way you can use it, the way you can adapt and think in the face of danger and unpredictability. Just as well that you're so good at it, for you and for everyone. It's a rare gift, though these days, droves of men are expected to show it."

I pulled her close; the matron wasn't in sight.

*

The doctors decided against hacking my infected limb off. One of the old doctors said the nerve pain in the leg might just go away by itself; he'd seen it happen. They said the smashed bone in the foot from the last crash landing would come good soon, if I kept off it, and the new whizz-bang pills would probably defeat the infection. They found signs of an earlier ankle fracture; I knew it was from an old flying carnival injury that had healed badly. The old doc said I should try to wind right down, shouldn't see any more action. I didn't think much of that. He noticed, and asked what I was hoping for.

"To shoot more damn Zeros out of the sky, of course."

He said, "Most people would think you have done your bit, son. You've seen more action than most. Don't you deserve to look after yourself?"

"I'm no coward. I can shoot planes down better than I can do anything else, so I damn well can't stop till the Japs give in."

"You don't mind the fighting?"

"I can do it, that's what I'm saying, doc. If you saw how bad some of the rookies are, you'd want guys like me showing them how to get themselves and their planes back in one piece."

He smiled. "Some bastards don't know when to stop."

I worked out every day in the rehabilitation wing. Sometimes Faye wangled her way in and we would scamper into the small storage room to cuddle and all. They were my best moments. We couldn't stretch out or even sit, but it didn't matter. I got to know more of her than ever, and it would never be enough.

Back in the exercise room, the many amputees and half-paralysed men horrified me. There was no point staying alive like that.

*

I expected a quick, cheery visit from General Beauregard, but then Faye's father came in to see me, which was a surprise. His friendliness was, too. He was more like her than I expected. I could see why his confidence in his own judgement annoyed Eddie, but there was more to him as well.

I wondered what he was hoping – that I would ask Faye to marry me when I got out of rehab? He was such an interesting storyteller that I forgot to be wary.

"A most extraordinary chap appeared in the dock today," he said. "Blind as a bat, but a thief! The whole court became quite pally as he explained how he managed his last job. We almost sympathised with him for getting caught. A cheery fellow. Completely beyond the control of his counsel. The only politeness he showed was to me, so, of course, I was quite well disposed to him. Had to give him the minimum, and anyway, what's the point? He will never stop and will usually be caught."

I chuckled and felt cheered. It reminded me of when Hube had read me scenes from Dickens.

But how the judge would loathe me if he knew half my history. Guys like him, guys with power, couldn't get it through their heads that some folks never have a chance unless they grab it and shoot everything in their way.

*

Eddie often called in. If Faye was there, he left early and gave us time together. Talking to him was relaxing. He didn't talk about the war. He stuck to his anti-war attitude. I liked that strength. I liked even more the way he never gave me the sort of look I didn't want. He didn't bother guys for his own amusement. I guessed he had accepted his love of men when he was a kid; he was at ease with everyone. He didn't accept that there was anything wrong or inferior about him, and I didn't either.

On his first visit, he said, "Don't feel bad about Clive. The Wilsons are quite happy for everyone else's sons to be slaughtered protecting Wilson land and wealth. At least Henry and Maurice are honest patriots, wrong though they are about war."

I nodded. It made me mad to think of cynics who skulked through this war, hanging on to everything they had. Though I'd never be enthusiastic about war again, this one still had to be fought.

He stared out at the garden. "You do know that Faye was in Sydney during that business with the Japanese submarines?"

That sat me up straight. "She didn't tell me."

"She was at Isobel's house in Rose Bay."

My throat went tight. "Jesus!"

His eyes were tense. "Nineteen sailors died. And a ferry sank. Not the one Bel took back from Manly, thank God."

"You must despise this war more than any of us."

He nodded and looked away. "I couldn't bear to lose Faye or Bel, and now I couldn't stand it if you vanish again or even if you can't bloody well walk properly."

He poured us tea but looked like he could have used something stronger. "Henry was glad she called it off with Wilson. And Moira will come around – after all, you're a wounded hero. Sympathy for fighters is in her blood!" He grinned.

I wriggled. "Maybe they expect me to pop the question?" I hoped I didn't look scared or worried.

He gave one of his dry looks. "To be frank, Peter, I'm sure Moira would rather you didn't. Her nightmare is that you and Faye will elope, flouting her tiresome Roman Catholic rules and robbing her of a huge wedding. Faye denies any such intention, by the way."

I felt a flash of relief.

Eddie's eyes danced. "Whether Moira would mind so much if you were to take things slowly and have the big wedding after all, who knows? Hal only wants what Faye wants. He thinks you should see out the war and then consider your situation."

"Thanks, it's a relief to have the cards on the table," I said. "I guess you get to hear all sides."

"Usually not so much of Hal's, but he came to see me after Faye dropped Clive, and when you disappeared. He spoke to her, too, but he finds that strangely difficult, whereas he can say anything to me."

I hadn't expected that Faye's action would bring the two brothers closer. I hoped she knew.

"Moira came to see me too, separately, partly seeking sympathy and partly dying to yell at me." He laughed. "Whenever Faye shows the slightest deviation from her mother's views, I get an interrogation from Moira: 'Whatever have you been telling her now, Edward?'"

I laughed, then looked away. "I'm not much of a bet, you know. When Faye knows me better, she might figure that out."

Great talker that he was, he knew when to say nothing. He lit a cigarette and gave me his wonderful accepting smile.

*

Isobel and Eddie covered Faye's absences. Isobel brought a whole afternoon tea with her and engineered a private corner for us on the veranda. On the first occasion, I told her how lucky I felt.

"We feel lucky to know you, Peter. I'm tremendously glad for Faye. You've made her so happy. She has grown up since she met you."

"Haven't I split up the family? She and her mother were so close."

"Faye is entitled to marry the man she loves, not the one her mother picks," Isobel said.

"Sir Henry approved of Clive, didn't he?"

"He was deferring to Moira. I suppose she takes property and position so seriously because she grew up without much of either. But Faye needs independence and her own interests. I would hate to see her stuck with a selfish, uncultured husband. You saved her, my dear."

I nearly laughed – she was calling me cultured! Thanks to Hube, I had a few clues, yet wasn't I still set for a rambling life, worlds apart from this elegant, generous woman? "That's kind of you. I'm glad if I've done anything for her. But her parents don't want me to take Clive's place."

"Moira needs time, but, when you were missing, Henry told Faye and me that he would do all he could to help her marry you. He was devastated to see her suffer, unlike her hard-hearted mother."

"I'm only acceptable to Sir Henry because she's crazy for me." I said, sounding too bitter.

"That's fair enough, isn't it? He can see that you will make her happy."

Wasn't he just hoping like hell, the same as last time with Clive? Somehow Henry and Isobel thought I was as loving as they were, when for me it was a first even to recognise the real thing in Faye's eyes.

"I'm not in her class," I said. "Even if I was the type who settles down."

"It's your decision whether you do or not," she said softly. "But don't worry about class differences or things like that. None of that matters when people love each other."

I thought of her choosing her refugee over graziers and tycoons and English guys with titles. But her Alex would have been decent and sure of himself. I said, "That's true if you're the kind of person who can stick around – the marrying kind."

She smiled. "A lot of men discover that marrying isn't such a strange thing to do at all. It has always struck me that it's the woman who has the most to lose in marriage, especially if she has wealth and independence. Marriage doesn't change things much for most men."

I stared. There was some truth in that. But I couldn't fulfil the basic requirements. "Trouble is, Bel, I can't get the hang of how love feels, or I get it then I don't. I mean I change from time to time." I stopped myself. Why was I saying this to her? It was Eddie who would have caught on to what I meant.

She looked worried. "Peter, perhaps you shouldn't think about this now. Get well and see how things look from then on."

I looked into those eyes so like Faye's and said, "Bel, I'm scared I'll wreck her life. I couldn't stand hurting her. Maybe I'll get shot down, but, if not, I'd just better go away."

"Peter, she loves you with all her heart and soul. That would break her heart."

"I might break it more by staying."

"That's not true at all. She would rather try to make a go of it and fail, than not try. Wouldn't you, Peter?"

I met her eyes, then looked away. She touched my hand, and I grasped hers for a moment. She poured more tea and talked of her plan to turn her house at Portsea into a rehabilitation home for servicemen, both Australian and American.

36. Dancing and Saying Goodbye

Faye:

Melbourne, September 1942

I scanned the crowd in the Australia Hotel lounge as I walked in with Peter. It was the place where most American officers took their girls for drinks, dinner or dancing, even though some of the senior officers lived at the Windsor now – to my mother's consternation. The Americans had established the Australia Hotel as their stamping ground, where they would be in the majority and accepted, for they were not welcomed warmly everywhere anymore. Melbourne's earlier enthusiasm for the Yanks as saviours had cooled. Now, Americans were often resented, mostly for foolish and mean reasons, such as the good manners they usually showed, though I had come to understand that the money the Yanks had in their pockets contrasted starkly with what most of my fellow citizens had to spend, especially on outings.

But arriving in this crowd on Peter's arm was fun. How I loved watching the reaction he got – stares, waves and raised glasses sometimes, too. In an alcove, my old schoolfriend, Joan was sitting close to her American fiancé. The room was dotted with such couples. Because the Yanks were all officers, there were no snide glances at the Australian girls accompanying them; among the Australian patrons, there seemed to be a respect for rank and an expectation of some genteel standards of decorum. The room was humming with quiet laughter, though some embraces led to tears from the women, many of whom were in farewell scenes. I felt for them – and for myself.

Peter and I finished what passed for afternoon tea these days and then the orchestra struck up in the smaller ballroom nearby. He stood and held his hand out to me, and we walked towards the music. The crowd was growing, but there was room for him to swing and lift me a few times, and for us to move around the whole floor. Thank goodness his leg had healed. The doctors were delighted with the success of the new medicine. As we danced, I couldn't stop smiling, it was so good to be moving as one. After relishing some slow ballads where I melted into him, I yearned for a few numbers where we could move fast. At last, the band played 'In the Mood,' and we got up to speed.

I took his arm when we left, and he carried my work bag as we walked up Collins Street and into Swanston Street. At the corner with Flinders Street, we were faced by dozens of staggering men weaving their way through the crowd.

"Still can't believe that pubs shut at six here," he muttered.

"Yes, some of the workers try to fit in too many drinks after work," I admitted.

"Some? More like half the male population of Melbourne, baby. Inside the bars, it's absolute hell. You haven't seen that, of course. Guess that's why they don't let women in. Guys act like pigs, totally out of control."

Just then, one of them vomited in a gutter, not far from us.

"You mean like that?" I grimaced.

"And worse." He shuddered. "Just as well some of the restaurants have liquor, or all the servicemen would be just as bad. But these guys making asses of themselves in the street, half of them probably go home and beat up their wives and kids."

Shocked, I couldn't think of an answer. Of course, nice men didn't do that. None of the men I knew. Melbourne wasn't depraved; it was known as the most civilised city in Australia. Didn't working class men get drunk after work everywhere?

Well, not in the main streets of Rome or Florence or the Riviera, I had to admit.

We went into Flinders Street Station, dodging a line of smelly older men in working clothes or shabby suits and hats – more of the pub clientele. I led the way to a waiting room where there was enough room for us both to sit down, though no privacy, of course. People were kissing, eating, changing shoes or outer clothing, and reading newspapers.

I smiled at Peter. "You don't have to stay, darling. I'll be quite all right."

He shook his head. "No, I'll wave you off."

"What will you do tonight?"

"Go back to the barracks and sleep," he laughed. "You have so much energy. Isn't your job tiring?"

"Not really. I love the pressure, and the way everyone is so purposeful and concentrated."

"Your dad is mighty proud of you."

I nodded. "Mummy's not thrilled. She doesn't understand why I need to work – or the usefulness of it."

"I thought she might not get it. Is she happy with you seeing me now?"

"Oh, she's thawing." I would not distress him with Mummy's vehement opposition. As Isobel said, she would probably come around. I took a breath and pushed away memories of Mummy's coldness. "It's just as well you're so charming; you'll win her over when you see her again. Dad's on our side. Mummy can't hold out against him, you know. The old folks will be okay, as you Yanks would say! Have you noticed that I've caught some American expressions from work?"

"Well, yeah. I hope the guys there aren't fresh towards you."

"Oh, you're worried, are you?" I laughed.

He flashed a quick smile. "I'm just saying they should have

good manners when they're in the company of a lady."

"Very gallant of you, Captain. It's all quite proper, though I'm certainly meeting all sorts. The girls in my unit are interesting, and I would never have got to know them outside of work."

He nodded. "Yep. There are heaps of people I've been lucky to meet, too. They face danger and loss and loneliness and then start again as though nothing had happened. Like Maddox: he has so much confidence, ambition and force, it takes your breath away. And the pilots, ready to risk it all. And you, brave enough to take a chance on a strange pirate like me."

I hugged his arm. "I think about it all the time, how we might never have met."

He gave me a look that sent me tingling and shivering, and then he kissed my hand. I wouldn't have minded a real kiss, despite the crowds.

"I think about that, too," he whispered. "And how I could never have felt like this about anyone else."

I smiled up at him. "Oh darling, I do feel a little guilty that the war has made my life so wonderful when it's brought so much suffering to other people. We must cherish our joy."

His eyes were soft and dark blue in the evening light. "I love how you say things like that," he said, his voice low. "You're right. We have to grab the good out of the bad. Strange how love just turns up."

"Yes. We can be happy. We owe it to the people who have suffered." When his eyes suddenly went misty, I put my arm around him and rested my head on his shoulder.

Soon, I felt his body relax. I wanted to leave him on a lighter note. I said, "It's marvellous for me to have the work. I love being part of the show, instead of being sheltered away from everyone else's struggle. I know that, like most women, I'm protected from the terrors and horrors that the fighting men endure, but at least I'm doing something."

"Yep." He gave me a *Sergeant York* country boy smile. "Funny thing, isn't it, how war is sheer hell, but those moments when we work together and achieve results are so damned good."

"They are." I hugged his waist. "We will always remember these days."

The train was pulling in, and we hurried to find me a window seat. Once my belongings were in the luggage rack and my seat secured with my coat and book, he caught me up off guard for a kiss.

Oh, again, please – did I say that aloud? He kissed me once more and then went back onto the platform before passengers rushed onto the train.

I leaned out of the window as he came up to it. Another kiss, but how I wanted a whole-body hug.

The train started. It seemed so odd that I was the one leaving and he the one waiting. We grabbed one last kiss, before I watched him become small, further and further away.

37. Death and Dancing

Peter:

Melbourne, Early November 1942

I came back into Melbourne on a transport plane a few days before the Brownout strangler was to be hanged.

I felt more tired than I could remember and kept to myself once I got there, except for seeing the kids at St Anthony's. It gave me the creeps to see them now, however much they enjoyed the chocolates I handed over. The place and the kids brought back memories of a darker place and sadder kids. I didn't want to think about what the St Anthony kids would face.

It was a short leave, and I had come mainly to support Iris. I didn't have the energy to think about Faye, about what I would say to her. She had written of course, and I hadn't answered. I still didn't know what the hell to say. I hadn't told her I was coming. I guessed I would call her when the Iris business was done.

When I was with Faye, we were in a dream, a mirage. But to marry her felt impossible.

Yet if I survived, could I just walk away? I wasn't sure I had the strength anymore.

*

Iris was bluer and more jittery than ever. The convicted Brownout killer was to be hanged at the main jail. The day before the execution, I went to see the joint; its looming dark bluestone walls made me shudder.

The day of the hanging, I took Iris out; tried to find a pretty, quiet spot on a beach past St Kilda; drove past one called Black Rock, too dismal a name; found a pub on the beach further on, with a good sea view. Iris said little. I feared she knew I was there out of duty and pity. She socked down the drinks. I tried not to, which felt harder than I expected. There was no-one on the beach, it being a weekday. The sea and sand were lovely but mournful, despite the blue sky and dazzling sun.

The Brownout murderer was a creep, and the word was that he was deranged, yet I kept thinking of how he must have felt that morning, when he woke up – if he had slept – when he was offered food or a last cigarette, when he climbed the stairs to the noose, when he spoke his last words, words that no-one would report, or believe, when he felt the dark hood over his head, the heaviness of the rope. When he fell.

It was nearly my twenty-fifth birthday. That don't-care-if-I-die feeling was strong in me again. I couldn't throw it off. The rookies I trained and then mourned kept reminding me of the parade of orphans I'd marched with years ago, witless and luckless, powerless and used. Hardly any of us knew each other, not really. The couple of pals I had up north weren't close like Hube or even Chris; they were more like gang colleagues. We were all part of a grotesque death machine, and we didn't have the worst of it. There were men – and women and kids – marching, slaving or starving all over Asia and Europe.

The more information I heard, the worse it was. The public didn't know the half of it. Australians had no idea how many had died at Darwin in February, or in New Guinea since May. In our part of the action, far too many rookies died, crashing on take-off. New planes, the P-38 Lightnings, had arrived and were heaps better than the old Airacobras. They could whip the Zeros, but there were only a handful of them so far. No word about whether we'd ever get enough of them. But we were close to getting the upper hand on the Japs. It was just a matter of time before our air power and the Aussies on the ground would kick them out of New Guinea. Maddox wasn't bluffing about that. He booted out generals, both American and Australian, who he said weren't getting results fast enough.

Maybe I had battle fatigue. I could barely stand going back there. The smell of mildew was everywhere; you had to polish your boots and pistol constantly to stop them going green. The malaria pills made you feel weird. I wished I was in the Navy on a carrier.

What really made me jumpy and sick of it all was that everyone in the know, the Navy as well as Maddox, and the Aussies too, agreed that Japan would be beaten sooner or later. Since we had destroyed so many of its planes and carriers, it had to run out of men and equipment before we did. But we were in a nightmare, like a new version of the Great War, because no-one was putting a limit on how far we would take this contest. I kept recalling newsreels and movies I'd seen of the trenches on the Western Front – guys going over the top again and again for no gain. The Americans were rolling out ships and planes and ammo now like you wouldn't believe, but it would take a lot longer to finish the show. The desk jockeys in cities probably hadn't a clue why we couldn't wrap it up by Christmas. How many millions had died so far, here and in God-forsaken Europe? What in hell would be the final total? The generals talked of two or three years more of fighting as if it was only a matter of time, not corpses.

Iris and I went for a walk along the sand.

"So, has Faye caught up with you?" She stared bleakly at me.

"No, haven't seen her."

"I thought she would've rung you,"

"No."

"Hey, have you told her you're here?" She stared at me. "Bloody hell, you haven't. Why not? You're still keen on her, I can tell."

I looked away and said nothing. She wasn't wrong. But I sure couldn't talk it over with her.

She said angrily, "You know how I said months ago that when she gets sick of you, if she does, you can come back to me? Well, there's a boy in our parish who's really keen on me and you just might be too late."

I said gently, "If you like him, you should be with him, Iris. You can't rely on me for anything. You're a great girl and I'm fond of you but we don't have deep feelings for each other, really, do we? It's been fun and I'd do anything for you."

She turned away and ran fast to the end of the beach. I walked behind. She stopped and bent over. By the time I reached her, she was leaning back, her head high and her face calm.

"You're a bugger, Pete."

"Honey, you knew I was never gonna get serious, I told you how it is. I always move on."

"Yeah? I reckon there's more chance of me seeing you and her in wedding photos on the social pages than news of you going back to America."

I stared at her in shock. "Don't you see – I can't ask her even if I do love her. I'm no good. Not long term, not as a husband."

"Oh yeah? Why the hell not? I reckon I've seen enough good husband behaviour from you, here and there. What a line. It lets you right off the hook when the romance wears off!"

I shook my head. She couldn't see when I was dead serious, telling her my deepest doubts about myself. Her anger made me wonder if her feelings were deeper than I had realised, and I thought again of what she had said about our nights together. Was she mad because I preferred Faye, or did it hurt her now to be with me? I could understand how that felt.

I thought of Faye holding me when I broke down and cried that night, I thought of her letters. She caught on to my feelings, like Hube and Momma did, tried to make me feel better. I remembered that day with her on the beach, that exciting, loving hour with her. As soon as I got some sleep and felt half ok, I would call her. I had to see her again, I longed to, even just for one more time.

I stared at the sea.

Iris leant against me as we stood side by side and said softly, "Aw, Pete. Don't look sad. Jeez, I'm gunna miss you."

I gave her a hug and she stroked my face.

"Bloody ladykiller, that's what you are," she gave a twisted grin.

I shuddered and shook my head. "You slay them in the aisles yourself. I know you can take your pick."

She shrugged but looked back in control. She didn't want to swim, so we drove home. She stared out her window and we didn't talk much. At her place, I got out and opened her door, for once. She looked touched, but then looked close to tears.

"No hugs, cheerio, Pete."

She ran down to her back door and I drove off. I felt a fool for thinking we could have stayed friends.

*

The next night was a Saturday, and I was the only off-duty guy in the billet. Everyone had roared off into the city to dances, brothels or the streets. I sat outside for a while after dinner with my mouth organ and played some blues. I went in to listen to the late news in the radio room.

In the hallway, I saw myself in the mirror. Hollow-eyed. Almost stooped. I rubbed my hands through my hair. I was turning into an old wreck. Sitting around on my own was making me bluer and maybe crazier. I wished I had called Faye. I would call her soon.

Just then, the phone rang and made me jump. Odd time for a call. The duty kid came to get me. I picked up the black receiver. My heart turned over and my mouth went dry. That sweet, crisp voice.

There were no recriminations, no questions.

"Oh, Peter, you *are* there, darling. I'm so glad. I was afraid the children at St A's had started seeing visions!"

How could I say "no" to those dear tones? She was in a phone booth at a movie-house downtown, and now she wanted to meet me at the Trocadero. I would like their band, she told me. I did, but I couldn't say I'd been there with Iris. She laughed her tinkly laugh when I tried to talk her out of it; it was rough, too crowded on a Saturday, not her kind of place.

"For now, it's *our* kind of place, darling. I'll walk around there and wait for you. Of course I'll be all right; it's only a few blocks, and the streets are full of people, not to mention the police and military police."

I leapt into a jeep. All the way in, I told myself I was going nuts; why couldn't I quit this fooling with a girl you couldn't fool around with? It was cruel to her. And made me blue. This could be, should be, the last time. Yet heat shimmied up my spine.

When I reached the river, I remembered what Michael had said, but he didn't know the bunch of reasons that made what Faye wanted, and I wanted, hopeless. Still, tonight at least, I would not be ruining her life; she wouldn't have to battle the Troc solo and take her chances. She wouldn't have to drink away her sorrows. Unless that's what she had been doing and why she had called. I replayed her words and recalled her voice. Had she been tight? Maybe a little. She never seemed to slur the way some girls did, though I'd never seen her really plastered. I checked my pocket. Stupid! I'd never need them, never use them, but the little packet of rubbers eased my mind. In the city, I wound around the river and parked as close to Princes Bridge as I could.

Inside the dim nightclub, it was airless and deafening. Even wide open, the windows couldn't cope with such crowds. Guys lurched and girls tottered about. Couples tumbled everywhere. Clinches on the dancefloor were like dirty postcards. Only patches of the room were lit, and dimly.

I scanned all the tables. Jesus, where was she? It was so crowded she wouldn't be able to see me. I hoped like hell she hadn't gone outside; even regular cop raids couldn't clean things up there. It was the closest thing I'd seen to my New Orleans gang house in a long time. As I wandered out into the wrecked garden at the back, I half expected gunshots. Fistfights were starting up behind the outhouses. Was she in the bathroom? Out cold? A woman left the Ladies' and the door hung open. Empty. Under the door of the Men's were two pairs of shoes. Plants were trodden and mashed, bottles everywhere, putrid smelly patches of liquids and slimy mush in the undergrowth.

The slick band sound was pulsing out of the Troc, tight, disciplined and sassy. 'Stompin' at the Savoy'. Swell band for such a seedy joint. I walked along the river a way to where shadow couples writhed wordlessly. I peered at them in the moonlight. Not Faye, thank Christ. A mostly undressed couple didn't flinch as I nearly fell on them. Further on, some guy cussed me.

I turned back and covered the rest of the area. No trace of Faye, thank the Lord. Dumb of me to suspect her of coming outside; I must have missed her in there. The wide, curving river felt familiar to me now. Shimmers of moonlight sliced its darkness into jagged lines. I bent down and scooped a handful of water to cool my face.

Once inside, when I pushed my way to the bar, I saw Faye dancing. She swung her hips fast, dancing on the spot, with no room to move, flushed, happy. The guy held her so close I wanted to punch his lights out. Suddenly, she saw me and waved but kept dancing. I joined the guys propping up the bar and paid through the nose for a laced tea, one of the Troc's specialties and more than you could snaffle at most Melbourne joints after six. As the song ended, she came pushing through the crowd, with the junior officer still in tow. She seemed to know him. Another tidy Midwest farm boy with round eyes, he looked back with dumb respect when I glared at him. He couldn't help standing to attention and doing an embarrassed social version of a salute.

She laughed. "Tom, see you at work, all right?"

He grabbed her hand and said a goodbye that grated on me. Like he was putting down a claim, and he'd be back with her as soon as I was out of the road. Goddam nerve, and what did he have to offer her?

Her eyes were bright, and her cheeks flushed, but she didn't look plastered. Her dress was green with a touch of gold twisted through and tight-fitting till the hips. I shoved our way through a wall of people and found a chair. I sat her on my knee, and she wound around me, like one of those graceful '20s sculptures. She held her face close for a kiss. What the hell, in a joint like this, half the people in the dark corners were doing more than kissing. Once I felt her, I knew I'd have to pace myself and the liquor too, or I'd make a great mistake for both of us, and whatever she said, it would be a disaster, despite how she'd changed. We kissed till we were breathless.

Listening to the band, I felt my whole spine start to go loose. Since I last saw her, I had been all wound-up *jus' like a ball o' twine*, as the blues men sang. She took a small bottle of whiskey out of her elegant purse, and I fought my way through and extorted some glasses from the blank-eyed barman. I held her close and enjoyed the best jazz I'd heard for a while. We got up to dance, but it was so crowded that we could only sway on the spot.

"We could dance outside," she said.

Her face looked as innocent as usual, but I wondered if she was thinking of other things that people did outside. I tried to stop thinking of them because it was torture. Even the feel of her bare arms drove me crazy, but it wasn't going to happen.

The Troc grew hotter and stuffier the later it got, so you couldn't stay long. We squeezed our way through the smelly push of bodies out into the night, down to the river away from everyone, to sit against a great tree. She leaned into me while I stroked her hair. More kissing was far too risky, the way I was feeling. When she turned around to sit on my lap, facing me, my heart raced. It was like she'd turned into Iris, not that I minded, but it was a thrill with a bitter twist, because it had all been easier when she was the quiet, good type.

I rejoiced again that she wasn't. I felt happier than I had in a long time, but I said, "Hey baby, let's take it easy."

"Peter, shall we drive somewhere? I've got a key to Eddie's. He's at Meredith's." She looked excited, but a touch afraid.

"No, baby, for you it's gotta be like tap dancing or the tango, not dark and desperate." I tried to stop grinning. I wanted to dance her along Princes Bridge like Fred Astaire with Ginger: she'd asked Eddie – for me. I got a grip on myself and said, "Nothing's changed."

"But it has. You're slipping away. I know it's the war, but it's hard to bear, Peter."

"Doing something wild isn't gonna fix it," I muttered.

I couldn't meet her eyes. It felt bad to reject her, right though it was, as I told myself again. I was weakening, feeling myself taking her side, rationalising the inevitability of our sleeping together and sizing up the different places we might go.

She ran her fingers along my eyebrows, down my temple to my jawline, and moved in to kiss me. We had to get out of there.

"Come on. Let's find my car."

We fell into the jeep and onto each other. It was urgent and sad at first, but soon we were panting and sighing, like we were the only creatures on earth. Still, I didn't feel as elated as the other times at the beach or the hospital storeroom. I didn't want this kids' stuff. I was aching to take her to bed, to make love like a rocking-chair and every other way, to sleep entwined all night. But as strong as that desire was the sombre relief that I hadn't given in or made her go too far. No accidents.

Faye kept holding me close, like she knew as soon as she let me go, I'd be off. Her eyes were anxious. I hadn't said a thing to reassure her. I hadn't even said I love you, though she had said as much. She kept staring into my eyes till I felt like a criminal.

I said, "Baby, I love you more than I ever loved anyone. I wish I could make you happy. I keep trying to tell you."

"Then let me look after you," she said softly. "You do make me happy. Let's just live each day and night as if it's our last. We'll keep on feeling wonderful together. You don't need to think about the future."

I shook my head.

She stared for a time, and then said quietly, "Does seeing me make life harder for you? Does loving me make you feel sad?"

"No," I said. But as usual I was lying. Loving her gave me the blues for sure, maybe more than it made me feel great.

She held my face. She saw beyond my denials. "I love you so much. It shouldn't be like this."

I said quietly, "It's not your fault." That was the truest thing I'd said all night. If I was a regular guy, who knew how to be steady, we'd be fine. I guess she couldn't help believing that I could again be the guy I'd pretended to be at the start. It was dumb and made me blue, but it was so sweet it made me happy at the same time.

She let me go and sat back in her seat. She put her hands over her face. I started the car and roared off in a U-turn. We hadn't gone far when she said she felt sick. We walked around the gardens, and she took long gulps of water from the drinking fountain till her lipstick was smeared and smudged. Mascara was half-way down her cheeks, and her hair was tangled. She didn't seem to know or care. We sat on the running board and stared silently at the river. I'd run out of talk, not that it was the moment for talking. It felt like the end of the line, which sent me into a kind of dulled trance. She sat slumped, not like her at all, as though she was finally losing her nerve. It gave me the shudders. She was shaking a little, whether from the cool wind or what she was coming to realise about me. The white stone of our rotunda shone in the distance.

Her house was in darkness when we arrived. Michael poked his head out of his room near the garage. His face lit up in a grin, and he gave me a half salute before he disappeared.

I couldn't bring myself to leave till I saw her safe inside. I hoped Edith might be there, so Faye wouldn't be alone and blue. I went in with her. Silently, I watched her walk to the stairs. Above us, a door opened. We heard the judge's voice. With Lady Beauregard right behind him, he came down the staircase.

I stepped forward to face them, nearly at a loss for words. "I'm just bringing Faye home. I'm leaving now."

Lady Beauregard glared at Faye. "You stupid girl!" she yelled. "You're as unkempt as a girl from the gutter, and just as tipsy, I'll bet. I don't know you. You're not my daughter."

Sir Henry looked at her, astounded and distressed. "Moira, please."

She turned on him. "How far does she have to fall before you will tell her to behave? Do you think this is the first time she's got like this? Surely you don't think it will be the last? When girls slide like this, they make a habit of it. They turn to the drink and there's nothing to be done with them."

I wanted to hold Faye close. Yet I had to feel sorry for the old girl too, mean as her words were; clearly, she had suffered from drunks in her youth or feared them, and she knew what liquor did to drinkers. How much did she know of Faye's nightlife?

I said, "Lady Beauregard, this is my fault. Neither of us is drunk, ma'am. I made Faye feel blue tonight."

She scowled at Faye. "No decent woman, let alone a lady, would come home looking like that, no matter what her man had done."

To my surprise, Faye said, "I'm sorry. I hope it's the last time I upset everyone. I thought I was losing Peter, and I am, I suppose, aren't I, darling?"

How could she still look at me with such tenderness? Her lack of resentment made me ashamed; my throat hurt like years ago when Mrs Murray or Momma pointed out my shortcomings. Faye wasn't just great at forgiving; she didn't even take offence. While I spent half my life tensing up and hitting back, she kept reaching out; it wasn't just that she had scored a lucky start. How could I have been so hard to her – pretending, misleading, staying silent – while all the time she dreamed I was for real?

She looked at her mother. "You're right, Mummy. I *am* in danger of becoming the sort of woman who hangs around bars to find someone who looks like Peter, when no-one does."

It stabbed me like the guy from behind that you didn't see. I said softly, "Faye, I'll call you tomorrow."

She managed a smile though she was close to tears. "Goodnight, Peter, I'll look forward to that. I hope you don't disappear again."

I said softly, "Baby, I'm not goin' anyplace."

Sir Henry was looking at me more warmly.

"Sir, I'm sorry for this trouble," I said, and he waved my apology away. "Lady Beauregard, I'm sorry I brought Faye back so late and disturbed you."

I squeezed Faye's hand, then scrammed.

38. Avant-Garde

Peter:

Melbourne, Early November 1942

The next day, when I called Faye, we decided to go out dancing. I was surprised when she invited me to pick her up at her house, after eight. She apologised for not inviting me for dinner first, and I brushed that off. I wondered how Lady B would feel about seeing me back in her home.

Eddie was there, having eaten dinner with the family. Sir Henry offered us whiskey in the parlour. When Lady Beauregard swept in, she chatted easily enough but showed no warmth.

Then Faye came in. She looked stunning in a slinky black dress with the kind of straps that left her shoulders and her back bare. Her hair was swept up with a white flower in it, and her lipstick was deep red. She carried it off with her freshness and the joyful innocence she always had that made me hide my roughness. She took my hand and perched on the arm of my chair.

Lady B stood up, stiff and tense. She glared at Faye. "If you are trying to humiliate us by wearing that vulgar dress, you are succeeding."

Sir Henry looked like he'd been hit in the stomach.

Seeing his face, Lady B seemed less sure of herself. She snapped at Faye, "Why can't you dress like your sister? *She* knows how to dress like a lady."

Faye kept her poise. Eddie looked up for a fight but turned to his brother. Sir Henry scrutinised his wife as I guessed he would a minor crook in the dock.

Faye's eyes threw me a lifeline: *she's mad, don't worry.*

Her mother's neck pulsed with anger. "You're determined to make an exhibition of yourself in front of Captain Stephens!"

"Moira, please ..." Sir Henry began, then stalled.

Eddie stepped in, "Steady on, Moira, there's nothing to be embarrassed about."

"Not to you, Edward," Lady B said coldly. "I can't imagine what could ever embarrass you."

He gave a sardonic smile that only riled her more.

She turned to me. "Captain, *you* know that what a girl wears can give the wrong impression; you know how careful ladies must be in Melbourne now."

Before she finished, I had my guns aimed. "You're right, ma'am, about Melbourne, and I see what you mean about the dress. Most girls couldn't wear a new style like this. It's so French and modern. But Faye looks a lady whatever she wears. Both your daughters always look like ladies, ma'am. They have your elegance and class."

I was twinkling at her full blast, and thank the Lord, the tension slid off her shoulders.

"Captain, how kind of you."

"It's nothing but the truth, ma'am." I threw her my best smile, though I was dying to look back at Faye.

Sir Henry followed up his advantage. "Moira, as you well know, dear, I think you have brought up the two most impressive girls in Melbourne, even if I am a trifle biased. Perhaps the Captain is right about the dress being a new French style; it does look avant-garde."

Faye said smoothly, "It *is* French, made in Paris, though I bought it here, at Le Louvre in Collins Street."

I stopped myself from laughing. Melburnians could be cornier than Americans sometimes.

Sir Henry said quickly, "That's a good shop, isn't it, my dear? The woman who runs that is considered pretty much the thing?"

Lady B started talking about the shop-owner, Eddie picked up the ball, and the atmosphere calmed. Sir Henry and Eddie took turns telling amusing anecdotes, and Lady B turned her charm back on towards the men in the room, though she didn't look at Faye again.

When we left, Eddie followed us out onto the porch. "May the gods bless you, Peter, dear boy! Faye, my darling, someone at Meredith's must paint you in that marvellous dress."

"How long has your mom been like that with you?" I asked her, once we were in my car. "Since you dropped Clive? Why didn't you tell me?"

"No point, darling."

"You're quite a lady."

"So you said to Mummy," she laughed.

"You're tough, too. I know how hard it is to be that strong." Not to hit back, not to show when it hurt. The only way to survive was to ride the punches, then forgive and forget. Forget, anyway. Most of the time.

"I've had to face Mummy's worst side – I've realised recently how like her I am, how snobbish and unfeeling I can be. I could have ended up just like her: pushing people into being what she wants; lashing out at people who challenge or frighten her. Look at how she spoke to Eddie."

"Yep. Amazing how he stays so cool."

"Isn't he a gem?" she smiled.

At St Kilda Town Hall, we let our hair down. My dancing wasn't what it used to be because I was wary of overtaxing my leg. It was fine but had a bit of nerve pain still. Though I loved moving fast and spinning and lifting her, and feeling her cheek against mine, I didn't want to dance all night. I didn't tell her, but I was glad to sit down for supper, before a few last dances.

Afterwards, in the car, she said, "We could go to Eddie's. I have a key. He's going to the Blacks' tonight."

I sighed and put my fingers into the satin coils of her hair. "Baby, someone might see us; there'd be talk."

"I don't care."

"In the end, you would. Babe, you're still the girl in a white dress in a church." When she opened her mouth to protest, I kissed her. "I couldn't stand sneers and gossip about you. We can't do it – with your mom, the church rules and all."

"I don't care," she said again. "Anyway, none of that would matter if we were going to get married."

"That wouldn't make it all right."

"Now *you* sound like my mother – or a priest!" She laughed.

I felt abashed. Who was I to criticise her?

She said, "I know the Church doesn't think that marrying afterwards makes it all right, but the war has made their rules look unimportant. We love each other. The ceremony, whenever we have it, will simply bless our love, and help us celebrate it with our family and friends."

"If I'm killed, you'll care if the ceremony hasn't happened and people know you've slept with me. Folks will look down on you. The kind of guys you should marry won't want you. Even if I'm careful, we could be unlucky. I couldn't do that to you."

"I want our baby, Peter. Surely you know that."

It thrilled me but my throat went tight. "You'd be left alone; and the kid would be illegitimate."

"Was that your mother's story? And yours?" she said gently.

I nodded, glad that she had guessed because I could never have found the words to tell her.

"I think I understand how you feel, Peter. But never to sleep with you—" she shook her head.

The thought of never sleeping with her was one I had been taking for granted; now I saw its bleak sadness. Compared to her, I was a coward, an emotional half-wit. I said, "Yes, but I don't want to ruin your life, your reputation, your bond with your parents."

She smiled. "They're not just up to you, sweetheart. I can look after myself."

I shook my head. "Baby, what can I say?"

"I know you're a ruffian, darling, but I think we'll get along."

I couldn't help laughing. The words came out before I knew I was thinking them. "I love you. I never said 'I love you' to a woman and meant it before."

She snuggled into me. "We'll always remember these nights. You know, people may look back and envy us because we lived so intensely through times of terror and heroism – and excitement."

I held her closer. I loved her way of putting things.

She stroked my face. "If we had met at any other time, we would have loved each other just as much."

We stopped near the beach on the way home and cuddled on the car-seat. I kept myself in check, but she could fly a little. We steamed up the car, and we couldn't stay long. Besides, we didn't want to get back to her place too late.

At her front door, I said, "I love your dress, baby. It's my favourite. Get that painting done and I'll buy it."

Even as I said it, I didn't believe a word. Why did I get so carried away? Lying to her was hard to stop. As if I'd ever own a painting, or a home of my own, on either side of the world.

As I left, Michael was standing at the garage door.

He said, with his grin that came and went so fast, "Sure it's grand that you're dancing together and all. And that you're stepping inside the house yourself."

"For once," I said quietly. "No thanks to Lady Beauregard. She's never gonna give me another inch."

"Ah, I don't know about that."

I understood enough about how Irishmen spoke to realise he was giving me hope. He was on the level, no doubt, but I couldn't buy it; Lady B had melted for a second to me but not at all to Faye.

"I'm leaving soon. You'll take care of Faye, huh?"

"My word, I will."

I nodded and went to my car. To someone as pure and kind as Faye, life was full of good acts and exciting possibilities. It hit me how much I needed someone like her. The mad, wild side of me especially needed her.

Once I was up north in combat, would she again seem like a dream? Would I feel I could no more marry her than rewrite my past?

But there was no forgetting her now. Could I really move on?

For the first time in my life, it might be harder to go than to stay.

39. Travelling and Thinking

Faye:

Melbourne, Late November 1942

I stared out of the window at the empty platform as my train pulled out of Flinders Street. Now I was alone, for once, till I arrived at work. Time to think. The book and newspaper stayed in my bag. Peter's latest letter was in my pocket, and I loved every word. It sang straight from his heart.

> *Faye, baby, woke up this morning missing you, like every morning. But when I think of you, I stop feeling blue. There's a new patch of peace in my mind, and it's you. Your letter made me laugh and miss you and our times near the river. I'm sitting watching the light fade on the rim of the mountains and listening to the birds before they go silent. Hey, baby, did I tell you how I always like to watch birds fly? No surprise, huh? One day, I'll tell you about my favorites when I was a kid and the strange ones here. Last thing before I sleep, I think of you,*
> *Love,*
> *Peter.*

Two photos of him were in my purse. One was a small portrait from the first studio shots we had sat for last summer, and the other was a snap I had taken in the hospital grounds.

I remembered his face that day when I said, "I know you have to go back into action, and it's what you want to do. I'll be worrying every second, but I'm so proud." He looked embarrassed for a moment, and then gratified and content – the tension and anxiety left his face. I was glad I had said it. One could take so much for granted.

I wished I could picture his life up north. He had spoken of combat, with such guilt, and had denied being a hero, as though his successes were not deeds to be proud of but were shameful. I hadn't the faintest idea how it felt to kill, how you could make yourself do it, how you could do it over and over, how you would feel afterwards, how you would get over it. I hoped that I had reminded him that he was fighting unselfishly for me and for all of us.

It didn't matter that he still couldn't think far ahead. Everything felt strange and fast these days, so goodness knows how it was for him, with his two separate lives, here and at the front, and his old life in America. He never spoke about going home, even for a visit. He didn't seem to feel a need to see anyone back in the United States, not even the woman he called Momma. It surprised me that he felt so disconnected from her and her family; perhaps the differences between them had been exacerbated by the war and his years of absence. The only person he seemed to write to was Hube, his old flyer friend in England. I really hoped to meet *him* some day.

How well could you know someone? Feel what they felt? If I knew more of Peter's memories – if he could hand me a book of photos or tell me more stories… But even if he did, would I know how he saw things? He was harder to read than anyone I had ever known.

I feared there would be many times like this, feeling suddenly alone, wanting him by my side when he was so far away.

Time ran out so fast on his leave. We didn't waste our moments together on talk about the future. Although I didn't let on, I was disappointed. He couldn't plan his personal life; I understood that. Part of me was furious and wanted to shake him, but most of me wanted to hold him close and wait and hope. If he drifted off when the war was over, I would be angry and heartbroken, but beneath that, I would long for him and yearn to hear of him, what he was doing, who he spent time with, how he was. For now, I found a sort of patience. As long as we saw each other – as long as he was alive and whole.

Of course, it would have been fun to be able to tell everyone that we were engaged, but at least his indecision gave my mother time to come to terms with the idea of Peter and me as a couple, whatever sort of couple that meant. Sometimes, I joked to myself that I should have kept the booking at the Windsor, in case he changed his mind, though I couldn't feel at all sure that we would get around to marriage in the end. He called me the girl in the white dress at the church, but he never said he would stand there beside me. One day, would he leave? I didn't daydream about the future. I steeled myself to stay in the present.

40. The Flame Tree

Peter:

Melbourne, December 1942

Coming down to Melbourne from Brisbane on the rattling night train, I slept only a little. I had Faye on my mind. I went over and over our time together: how I had pursued her at first like I always chased girls, only more so; how I had thought that I needed her from time to time, but maybe it was all the time; how I was barely able to see what she was giving me; how I had walked away more than once but she wouldn't buy it; how she kept coming back; how she gathered me up in those slender arms and held me fast. What a fool I'd been, thinking it was a danger to love her, not just for her but for me. After those first delirious times, I was scared to go after her, yet when I was with her, I never felt safer. Had other girls loved me? Rita? Iris? Faye was the first to make me notice. And the one to love me the most – the most loyally, constantly, generously.

By the time light streaked the sky, I was wondering if I'd got it dead wrong all these years, never believing that a woman could love me for always. Apart from my three moms, that is. And two of them had died trying. Some score. The world was full of sad jokes like that, and there would be millions of them in this war.

Later that morning, I called her, and we met near the rotunda. The air was dry and warm. The trees along the river were bright with fresh leaves, gleaming in the sun.

I said, "Faye, I can't keep stringing you along, hurting you."

She stared at me as if I was a painting she loved and kept trying to interpret. "You're not hurting me, Peter. Is that what you're afraid of? Is that what happened with other people?"

"I never stay round long enough to know. I leave before everything gets blue."

She took my hand. Her eyes were warm yet sad. "So, I'll know you love me when you leave. I think I know why you stopped seeing me those times. It was kind, in a way, and it tells me that you care about me, but I'd rather have the blue times than miss out on the wonderful ones. Darling, you can tell me what you're feeling, what's worrying you. You can tell me anything."

That was just what I couldn't do. I couldn't decipher myself as I had been or as I was now. Whenever I tried, it made me feel mixed up, like I had been so many people.

She stroked my hand. "Peter, there's something I want to say now because I'm scared it might be my last chance. Darling, you'll never be the man you want to be if you keep running away; you'll never find the happiness you deserve if you keep thinking you have no right to be loved."

She would let me go, even though she thought it was the wrong decision for me. She didn't care that I wasn't good enough. She didn't see it.

We walked inside the rotunda and sat down beside each other. Instinctively, my arms closed round her. She traced the outline of my lips and kissed me – as always with her, it was like soaring in the sky with the sun behind you. She made me feel like I had a right to be with her, though that was still her sweet mistake.

She held my face in her small, soft hands. "Peter, I'll never stop wanting you. We can take things day by day, but, if you can't bear that, darling, if seeing me makes you sad, it's all right."

Something Mrs Murray used to say came into my head. Whenever I said "sorry" for not reaching the mark in some way I didn't really understand, she would say sadly, "Peter, the damage is done." It sent a chill up me, though she was kind and all. And though she hadn't given up on me, and never did till she died.

With Faye, was the damage done? Or could I prevent it? She'd never give up, either.

I stared into her dark eyes. "I'll want you till the day I die."

"Oh, dear God."

I held her tighter. "I'm gonna live through this war, I swear." I sounded crazier than ever, but if I didn't have a good chance, who did?

"I know you will. They don't call you Pirate for nothing. We'll have some bad times till the war ends, and perhaps even after it's over, but we can be happy."

She warmed my bones. She was giving me those looks again, like I was a guy worth all her trust and love. I remembered Bel saying how Faye would rather try and fail than not try.

I might fail her – but I could try.

"I won't run out on you again, baby. I couldn't bear it. You're always gonna be the girl in the white dress at the church, so if you want to marry me, well, you're crazy, but will you? Soon – not years off, I mean? I'm not so good at waiting."

She hugged me hard and laughed. "You're far too good at waiting. Yes, I will."

"I know we have to be engaged for a decent time, and long enough for you and your mom to organise the wedding you want. But everyone knows you're too good for me, and at first, they're gonna think you're making a fool of yourself. Can we announce a date soon for our marriage, so everyone knows I'm serious?"

And if I died before then, she and her folks could remember that I really loved her, that we would have married.

"Of course, that's kind, Peter. You care more about what people say than I do. Isn't it funny? And I have a white dress already – just as well, with the shortages now. I'll jazz it up a bit!" She laughed, and when we kissed, I felt no twinge of panic or sadness like before.

Afterwards, we walked to her house, and she told her parents that I'd be staying for lunch. Lady B seemed to take it calmly.

At the table, she leant towards me, smiling. "Peter, Mrs Maddox tells me you're a Catholic."

I heard the swish of her lasso, but I couldn't give a damn. I smiled back. It struck me that she saw the value of my connection to Maddox. She would be the last hostess to resent the Maddoxs being the new imperial couple in Australia. How she would gloat over dames who'd snubbed her. The fact that Maddox had moved to Brisbane helped my case, too. Lady B would love it if the Maddoxs attended her daughter's wedding, because they hardly came to Melbourne anymore.

I was so amused at the picture of Maddox using my wedding as a publicity opportunity assisted by an adoring Lady B that I almost missed the Judge's considerate comment about how religion seemed unimportant in a war, and people couldn't think about big questions while they were fighting. Faye nodded, and he touched her hand for a moment. Lady B gave me a friendly look. I figured she had drilled Nigel and knew I wanted to fly here after the war.

I said, "Sir Henry, Lady Beauregard, Faye and I have something to tell you."

Sir Henry beamed at us but I saw a shadow of worry on his face. He must be wondering if I'd survive the war. And whether it might be better if I ran out of luck so that Faye could have another chance, a safer choice. I couldn't blame him one bit.

"Peter, you and I are going to get on well, aren't we?" Lady B smiled mischievously. "I admit, we had a false start, but I think you'll be a great addition to the family."

Faye hugged her mom, who went all teary for a moment and then said, "Faye, you couldn't have found a more dashing fiancé. And he happens to be famous. Americans are becoming the new leaders everywhere. Peter, it will be grand."

Sir Henry smiled at me, and I grinned back.

He laughed. "Moira, if you'd only discovered a little earlier how much you like the Captain!"

She put her hand lightly on my shoulder. "I suppose I did, and he knew, didn't you, Peter?"

I shot her a look. "Oh yeah. You bet, Lady B."

It was funny how easy it was to be pals with her. She thought I'd fit in to this world. Could I? Then I thought of Hube saying, "Now you've got the hang of fish knives and cake forks, there's no stopping you, Pirate. Everyone is so mesmerised by your film star looks and your Wild West manners that they'll never notice what you get wrong; they'll think whatever you do is modern and American." I had laughed my head off, but he turned out to be right. I became a hit.

Lady B said more quietly, "I know it isn't easy for a fighting man. Especially a leader, a hero. The heroes are like martyrs, they sacrifice their own happiness and their wives and sweethearts."

I caught my breath. She was less dumb than I had thought and more big-hearted. I remembered Michael's words. I guessed she saw him as a hero. Maybe she knew as much of his story as he could reveal.

She said, "Michael says you're a good man, and he's never wrong."

Who had mentioned me first, I wondered.

Sir Henry chuckled.

She gave him a loving look. "Oh Hal, I know you thought so before Michael did." She turned to me again. "Peter, the whole family is fond of you."

Faye smiled. "They are. I'm so glad. I'm sorry I gave everyone such a hard time. Now you can all stop worrying about me."

I caught her father's eye. They would worry about her more now she was the fiancée of a flyer, one of the least likely to make it through.

I looked at Faye. "I'm the one who oughta say sorry."

She took my hand. "You've been fighting for us. It's marvellous that you have energy left over to think about me."

"Oh yes," Lady B said enthusiastically. "You fighting men endure so much."

As soon as we left, Faye said, "Sorry about Mummy and the Catholic thing. I know you're as irreligious as Eddie. You said a few times that I'm the sort of girl to marry in a church, but I won't be holding you to that."

I grinned. "Sure, you will. Or else I'll insist."

She laughed. "We don't have to decide right now. Mummy hopes that when we get to an altar, it will be a Catholic one, and the high altar. Because Daddy was an Anglican, they were married practically on the porch. Poor thing, she feels as though she's spent half her life huddling in the sidelines."

We walked across the road to the Botanic Gardens. I glanced at her striding happily in the sun and felt something new – pride, because I hadn't merely avoided causing her too much harm, I had managed to spur her to loosen the chains of the church, to sidestep the rules of her mother and to choose her own path. She was strong enough to be happy with my halting, crippled acceptance of her confident love. For a woman who could have everything, she was giving herself with no strings. Well, she should have whatever she wanted for the wedding, what difference did it make to me? I would be happy, and even happier on the wedding night and every night we shared.

"Bel wants you to come to dinner," she said. "She was sure I'd see you soon."

I grinned. "I bet. It'll be good to see her."

We came up to a huge bed of orange flowers, with no-one around. I lifted her up and she leant her head back for a kiss. I let myself imagine taking her upstairs at the Windsor.

When some people came along the path, we walked up the hill, past a grove of thick trees. She danced along, with no idea about my life, as it had been, and not much idea about my times in this war. She was better off not knowing my memories of fear, torture, and blood. The pain and guilt were mine.

I still couldn't imagine us living like a normal couple. One day, wouldn't she ask what she'd done to deserve a man with a mind like mine, a killer who couldn't tell her the truth?

Yet she would hold me fast for as long as I let her. As long as I could stay.

Remember this moment, I told myself, remember this wondrous park – not blood spurting from throats of native boys, not the hole in Harris's forehead from my perfect shot, not the blood around his head like a halo from hell; remember *her*, like soaring to the sky, like swooping past the birds, like climbing to the sun.

We walked for a while among the perfumes of the flowerbeds, with the sun warming us to the bone. There were some little hopping birds with scarlet breasts and green and blue wings. You didn't see them at first; they looked as green as the grass till you got up close and saw the jade, aqua and turquoise of their feathers. In pairs, they flew up, singing. I loved watching birds in the air: their precision, ease and delight. They perched in a bright orange tree silhouetted against the blue sky. I thought it was ablaze with red buds, but when we walked nearer, I saw they were tiny flowers like bells. So many had fallen. They splashed brightly over the green lawn. I spread my coat over them, and we sat in the dappled sunlight to watch the river gliding and to hear the birds sing.

In the evening, we ate at Florentino's, before we went

dancing. She wore the black dress her mother hated. I bought her a golden orchid, and she pinned it beside the neckline, its petals curving along her skin. Her hair was swept up, showing her shoulders. I couldn't take my eyes off her. She joked that the women in the restaurant spent a few seconds examining her dress and the rest of their time staring at me.

"It's the uniform," I said. "Or the newsreels."

She smiled and shook her head.

We held hands over coffee, hoping like hell we would have many dinners like this before the movies and opera and dancing.

Author's Note

The characters in this novel are imaginary, except for public figures.

The Allied Supreme Commander of the South West Pacific, General Douglas Macarthur, came to Australia with his wife, Jean and their young son, Arthur in March 1942, and were based first in Melbourne and from August 1942 in Brisbane. I have given them fictional names and have drawn characters to fit my narrative. Macarthur's headquarters in Melbourne were at 401 Collins Street. The Commander of Allied Land Forces, Australia's General Blamey, who was under Macarthur's command, had headquarters at Victoria Barracks, St Kilda Road.

The USA did not have a separate air force in 1942. Pilots were in either the army or the navy. Peter is in the United States Army Air Force. American officers in Melbourne were billeted in various private locations, and, later in 1942, this included the Windsor Hotel. The incident of Peter flying Hube back to England in a one-seater Fighter plane is based on a real event. Peter's flying demonstration in Melbourne is not based on a real event. Peter's experience as a prisoner of war is not based on a particular serviceman's record, but correlates with accounts of downed pilots from histories of action in New Guinea and the Pacific.

The dates of the Brownout Strangler killings have been changed in the novel to a month earlier than reality to keep a tight narrative timeline. No Tivoli dancer was killed by the strangler but three women in Melbourne were, and other women came forward with reports of being threatened by an American soldier; it has been argued that these threats were from the same serviceman. Line-ups were held and no one was identified. Private Edward Leonski confessed after other servicemen reported his behaviour as suspicious. American psychiatrists declared Leonski sane, though some historians argue that evidence of his disturbed thinking and behaviour was ignored. General Macarthur ensured that the trial and the execution took place in Melbourne. The trial was open to the press. The hanging took place at Pentridge gaol, Coburg, Melbourne, in November 1942.

The attitudes and atmosphere conveyed in the text are based on reading of documents, newspapers of the time and historians' accounts, and on interviews with Melburnians, and others, who were in Melbourne in 1942.

Acknowledgements

My thanks to Janey Runci for encouraging an early draft and for continued support and inspiration. Her guidance on technique and reading was invaluable.

Thanks to Peter Bishop, of the Varuna Writers' Centre, for sensitive, supportive reading of early excerpts, and for his enthusiastic encouragement of this novel.

Thanks to Lee Kofman, an inspiring mentor, for support, editing and advice on an early draft.

I am indebted to my late aunt, Commander Patricia Vines, former Director of the Royal Australian Naval Nursing Service, Royal Red Cross 1st Class, Queen's Nurse in Australia, Trustee and Life Governor of the Shrine of Remembrance, Melbourne, for her vivid recollections of Melbourne in World War II and for her support of this novel. Her accounts were crucial to my understanding of the atmosphere in 1939-45 and the experiences of women in wartime and after. This novel does not depict her experiences in any way.

Thanks to the judges of the Victorian Premier's Literary Award for an Unpublished Manuscript 2008 for their praise of an earlier, longer version of this story in their commendation.

Thanks to Andrew O'Sullivan, my son, for his enthusiastic response to an earlier draft and his helpful comments on character and storyline.

Thanks to Laura Vines, a writer and my daughter, for detailed, helpful comments on an earlier draft and for further helpful comments on characterisation and craft.

Thanks to my sister, historian Margaret Vines for support and positive comments on an early draft.

Thanks to Dr Richard O'Sullivan, my husband, who shares my fascination with flying aces and the 1930s and 1940s. His knowledge of military history and aviation, and his comments on a late draft were very helpful. His late uncle, Tom O'Sullivan gave illuminating recollections of 1940s war service in Australia and the Pacific, as did my late uncles, Captain Tom Connolly and Jack Vines.

Thanks to the Lyceum Club Melbourne Writers' Circle, particularly Tasma Wischer and Virginia Stretton, for their support. Recollections of World War II from the late Judith Harley, Pat Hocking, Elizabeth Marshall, Gwenda Schanzel and Connie Barber were wise and illuminating.

Thanks to Toni Jordan for helpful, detailed comments on an earlier draft and for useful discussions.

Thanks to Sydney Smith for lessons on craft and pivotal comments on excerpts of an earlier draft.

Thanks to Irina Dunn for her enthusiastic support and for her editorial assistance.

Thanks to Tess McCabe for her beautiful cover design. The photograph of the Windsor Hotel on the back cover is from the collection at the State Library of Victoria.

Thanks to Dr David Reiter for his astute editing and his meticulous preparation of this publication.

Bibliography

Beaumont, Joan, ed. *Australia's War 1939-45*. Allen & Unwin, 1996.

Berg, Norman E. *My Carrier War*. Hellgate Press, 2001.

Broughton, Irv. *Forever Remembered, The Fliers of WW II*. Eastern Washington University Press, 2001.

Campbell, David. *Strike*. Pandanus, Australian National University, 2006.

Claringbould, Michael and Peter Ingman. *South Pacific Air War*, Vols 1-5, Revised Edition. Avonmore Books, 2022.

Cooper, Anthony. *Kokoda Air Strikes, Allied Air Corpss in New Guinea, 1942*. New South, 2014.

Cusack, Dymphna and Florence James. *Come In Spinner*. Heineman 1951, and New Edition, Angus and Robertson, 1987.

Darian-Smith, Kate. *On the Home Front, Melbourne in Wartime: 1939-1945*. Melbourne University Press, 2009.

Forbes, Athol, Wing Commander, DFC, and Hubert Allen, Squadron Leader, DFC, eds. *Ten Fighter Boys*. HarperCollins, 2008.

Gailey, Harry. *MacArthur Strikes Back*. Presidio, 2000.

Gallagher, James P. *With the Fifth Army Air Corps*. The Johns Hopkins University Press, 2001.

Gallaway, Jack. *The Odd Couple, Blamey and MacArthur at War*. University of Queensland Press, 2000.

Green, William. *Famous Fighters*. Macdonald and Co., 1957.

Hammel, Eric. *Aces At War*. Pacifica Press, 1997.

Hayes, Mike. *Angry Skies*. ABC Books, 2003.

Johnson, J. E. ("Johnie"). *Full Circle, The Story of Air Fighting*. Cassell, 1964.

Jordan, Toni. *Nine Days*. Text, 2012.

Lewis, Tom. *A War at Home: : a comprehensive guide to the first Japanese attacks on Darwin.* Tall Stories, 2010.

Leinberger, Ralf. *Fighter.* Paragon, 1980.

Park, Ted. *Angels Twenty.* University of Queensland Press, 1994.

Mellinger George and John Stanaway. *P-39 Airacobra Aces of World War 2,* Osprey Publishing, 2008.

Veitch, Michael. *44 Days, 75 Squadron and the Fight for Australia.* Hachette, 2016.

Veitch, Michael. *Heroes of the Skies,* Penguin Viking, 2015.

Wurth, Bob. *1942, Australia's Greatest Peril.* Pan Macmillan Australia, 2008.

www.ingramcontent.com/pod-product-compliance
Lightning Source LLC
Chambersburg PA
CBHW060947030726
47503CB00003B/760